An evolutionary puzzle . . .

Marta had the images on the monitor now, and she looked back at the visiting scholar. "Sab Robinson?"

Robinson tore his eyes off the creature long enough to gape first at Yatzahl, then Marta, and then past her at the monitor. "Skeleton," he croaked. "Let me see that skeleton."

Trying not to smile too smugly, Marta opened the folder with the skeletal images. Robinson stumbled around the desk for a closer look, mouth slightly open, and manipulated the files himself, zeroing in on the foot, the pelvis, and finally the cranium.

"If this were a Terran animal," Yatzahl ventured, "I might say it was a bird without feathers."

But Robinson shook his head. "Not a bird," he said decisively. "The hip joint is wrong; the leg would bend the other way. No, if this were a Terran animal, I would call it a saurian," he informed Yatzahl, turning back to the specimen in its glass case. "A theropod, to be more precise. The shortened forelegs, the serpentine neck, the balancing tail— I'll be goddamned," he breathed, causing his hosts to flinch at the profanity, "if it doesn't look like a dinosaur!"

Catherine Wells

BEYOND THE GATES

A ROC BOOK

ROC
Published by New American Library, a division of
Penguin Putnam Inc., 375 Hudson Street,
New York, New York 10014, U.S.A.
Penguin Books Ltd, 27 Wrights Lane,
London W8 5TZ, England
Penguin Books Australia Ltd, Ringwood,
Victoria, Australia
Penguin Books Canada Ltd, 10 Alcorn Avenue,
Toronto, Ontario, Canada M4V 3B2
Penguin Books (N.Z.) Ltd, 182–190 Wairau Road,
Auckland 10, New Zealand

Penguin Books Ltd, Registered Offices:
Harmondsworth, Middlesex, England

First published by Roc, an imprint of New American Library,
a division of Penguin Putnam Inc.

First Printing, June 1999
10 9 8 7 6 5 4 3 2 1

 REGISTERED TRADEMARK—MARCA REGISTRADA

Printed in the United States of America

CHAPTER 1

The desert wind howled up from the bowl of Dhin M'Tarkhna and slashed stinging sand at Ari's face. He drew the edge of his headcloth tight across his nose as his father had shown him, tucking it in place to keep the grit out of his mouth. He hated this trip. Why, oh why, did his father make him come out here in the Western Desert to suffer? At home there was a house with sturdy walls, a cool sea breeze, and lots of friends to play with. Here there was only dust and wind and Mohat for company.

Hassan shot the last tent peg into the ground and glanced back to where his son Arimaddak, called Ari, sat huddled with his back to the pervasive wind. Self-reproach nipped at him, for he knew the boy had been left at home too long, coddled by his mother. He should have brought Ari on caravan two or three years ago, not waited until he was ten.

But here they were, Ari's first trip beyond the gates of Wasskesh, and there was much lost time to make up for. He laid aside the tent-peg gun and called his son over. "Where's your friend Mohat?" he asked.

Ari shrugged listlessly. "Well, find him," Hassan urged. "By the time we have the rest of the camp set up, Cook will have our Sabiss feast ready, and I want the two of you to have a good seat for the storytelling." They had stopped early to prepare for the Day of Rest; and because there would be no travel tomorrow, the meal would be a hot one and the entertainment lengthy.

Ari trudged off, not much encouraged. Storytelling! At home there were 3-D games and interactive programs and

*ice cream. Here there were just old men talking and sand
in all the food.*

*His mood improved a little when he got his bowl of
roasted kid and sweet potatoes and tart smook pudding.
By the time everyone had crowded into Hassan's tent, he
and Mohat were giggling and poking each other, and Ari
felt better. Then Ari got a surprise, for instead of asking
one of the other caravaners to tell tales, Hassan himself
began to speak.*

*"This is a story of our ancestors," Hassan began. "A
true story about a woman of Jinka, and how the All-
Merciful chose her from among all others to venture beyond the gates of her city, and to see wonders." Hassan
flashed a smile at the two boys seated almost at his feet.
"Long ago, when the Children of the Second Revelation
were new to this planet, the Most High spoke to a woman
named Marta. 'Go out into the Western Desert, to a place
that I shall tell you, and see what is to be seen. There I
will reveal to you a wondrous thing . . .'"*

It was always a challenge to get information out of
one of these nomads. Marta knew that to scratch out a
living here in the Western Desert of Innanta, one had
to be tough, tenacious and—frankly—a little daft. Or
maybe the sun simply scorched their brains. For whatever reason, the young woman knew it would be tricky
getting this man to answer her simple question about
sandslithers in Dhin M'Tarkhna.

"I killed a demon there this morning," he volunteered.
"It's been pestering my goats for weeks."

Marta and six other students of the College of Indigenous Life had trekked into the desert in search of sandslithers, one of the higher life-forms native to Dray's
Planet. Their plan was to tag the primitive vertebrates
and plot the range of their movements across the continent. She didn't think this statement about the demon
was useful, but it was hard to tell.

"What kind of demon was it?" she prodded, knowing
the word could refer to anything from a poisonous *lachet*
bush to a bloodsucking *maskoi* to a foul-smelling breeze.

"An ugly one," replied the nomad, ruling out the breeze. "It flapped around like a chicken with no feathers, screeching its demon-song, for half the morning after I struck it."

That truly puzzled Marta. Of the dozen or so native species known to inhabit the Western Desert, none could screech. A monkey, perhaps, escaped from some rich *kukhoosh*'s menagerie of exotic pets? Her dark eyebrows puckered in a frown. "Why didn't you stop its suffering?" she asked the goatherd severely, for it was forbidden to let an animal suffer cruelly when it was possible to give it a quick death.

The nomad was a full head taller than Marta, but like most of his kind he was intimidated by the dark-eyed young woman's air of authority. "Aii, if you saw its teeth, Sibna, you wouldn't ask that!" he defended.

Teeth! It must be a monkey, or some other Terran animal that had gotten loose and made a home for itself in the nearly unpopulated wasteland. Some Drayan marine species had cartilage protrusions which resembled teeth, but so far nothing like that had been found in a land animal. "Where did you kill the demon?" she asked the man, her curiosity roused.

He directed her over a rise and to a patch of thorny native shrubs, where she found the sun-warmed carcass of a creature she did not recognize. Its side had been bashed in by a sling stone, and the tracks of its dying agony were all over the sandy ground. Ugly as it was, Marta felt sorry for it. Its long, spindly neck was extended in the dirt, with one scrawny broken foreleg bent back at a painful angle and its muscular hind legs drawn up in a final convulsion. Picking up a stick from the desiccated vegetation that littered the ground, she turned the creature over. Dark fluid seeped from the wound and stained the earth beside the carcass.

"Fadnar, come here, look at this," Marta called to her companion. She tucked a strand of dark hair back under the flap of her headgear, resisting the temptation to wipe the perspiration from her neck. The droplets tickled, but they were meant to evaporate and cool her skin, not be brushed away.

Fadnar shouldered his pack with its precious water bottles and trotted over the rock-strewn ground toward her. Fadnar was twenty-one—younger than Marta by a couple of years—but he was fairly sure he knew everything there was worth knowing.

"What is it?" he asked as he peered at the creature over her shoulder.

"What does it look like?" she countered.

"Ugly," he replied. "Like a leather chicken."

Marta gave a short laugh. "It's one very nasty chicken," she commented. "Look at the teeth on it."

The goatherd had been right about that. This creature looked as though it could do serious damage to even a full-grown billy goat. It was only half a meter in length, but the single row of short, pointed teeth looked razor-sharp, and the spindly front legs boasted a wicked-looking set of claws for grasping and tearing. "A predator, no doubt about that," she murmured. "And a very efficient one, from the look of it."

Then Fadnar asked the obvious question. "But where did it come from?"

"Where, indeed?" Marta mused, her smooth olive skin furrowing as she puzzled. Since the Children of the Second Revelation had colonized Dray's Planet two centuries before, they had cataloged a variety of marine life, some of it fairly sophisticated; but nothing on land had yet demonstrated this degree of evolutionary development. Could it be some kind of bizarre cross between a native species and some Terran animal the colonists had brought with them? "Looks almost reptilian, doesn't it?" she observed.

"Can't be reptilian," Fadnar said decisively. "The only reptiles our forebears brought with them were a few tiny lizards. Nothing this big. Looks more like a bird, if you ask me. Without the feathers, of course."

"A *dinka-chak,* eh?" Marta suggested with a grin. In the local dialect, it meant "chicken-lizard."

Fadnar grunted. "A dinka-chak *p'trik nagg,*" he added—

a chicken-lizard with nasty teeth. "But it can't be indigenous," he insisted again. "We've cataloged every species on this continent, and there's nothing like it anywhere. Nothing even close to it. It must have come from offworld."

Marta shot him a sharp look. "Nothing comes from offworld," she said flatly. "You know that."

Fadnar shrugged, unimpressed. "It had to come from somewhere. Here. Let's put it in a specimen box and take it back with us."

Yes, it had to come from somewhere, Marta thought as she helped scoop the remains into a small crate. But where? The Children of the Second Revelation had no commerce with Unbelievers. There was exchange of information, conducted at a safe distance, but no exchange of goods or people. The dinka-chak *must* be native. Yet Fadnar was right—from an evolutionary standpoint, it couldn't be.

Three months later, back in the laboratory of the College of Indigenous Life, Marta still had no answers. The fierce little creature with its mottled skin and yellow eyes was now mounted in a glass display, every organ and joint digitized and stored in the College's electronic files. From its glandular system to its DNA, nothing resembled any known Terran species. It had to come from a separate evolutionary line.

"Then why is there nothing else like you on the continent of Innanta?" Marta puzzled aloud as she studied a series of images on her monitor. "Where are your ancestors, your cousins, your crazy uncles? Do you hide them in a cave, or in the treetops, or under the sand?"

She passed a finger through the 3-D replica of a pelvis formed by three separate elements. "Where, little one," she asked, "did you get these bones?"

Ari had read about the dinka-chak in one of his lesson books. He didn't think there were any left in Innanta. "Was it truly in this desert where she found it?" he asked when his father stopped for a drink of water.

"So it was," Hassan replied gravely. "Not fifteen kilometers from where we are camped right now."

Ari's eyes grew wide.

"Yes, down there in Dhin M'Tarkhna," Hassan went on, "where only the strong of spirit venture—that is where brave Marta found the dinka-chak. The sun is merciless there, and the wind incessant, but it did not stop her, for she was one of the Faithful. We Children of the Second Revelation, we are a special people, chosen by the All-Wise to bear up under every hardship."

Hassan looked meaningfully at his son. "We are as strong and as tough as this desert land; and though our life could be easier somewhere else, we choose to stay here, within the gates of Innanta, which the All-Giving provided for us. We prove to Unbelievers that we cannot be moved from our devotion to the All-Hallowed and the teachings of the Holy Ones. We prove that even under difficult circumstances, we remain true to the twofold quest that the Most High has given us: the quest for Knowledge and Beauty. It is what establishes us as Children of the Great Creator."

Hassan saw that his preaching did not hold Ari's attention, so he returned to the story. "Such an exemplar was Marta, patient in her research, passionate in her ardent pursuit of Knowledge. So passionate was she, and so wise, that even those who were her elders bowed to her wisdom . . ."

Marta had no patience for faculty meetings, and she was just as happy that, as a graduate student, she had been asked to leave after her presentation. Now they would wrangle for hours, each sure he or she had the obvious answer to the question of the dinka-chak. Sab Yatzahl had asked her opinion, at least, and she'd given it. She was fairly sure he agreed with her, too. But as Dean of the College, he'd have to sit and listen to everyone else before making a recommendation.

So Marta escaped gladly from the conference room on the third floor of the College's main building, trotting down the outside staircases to the courtyard below. A huge olive tree grew there in the sandy soil, and Marta sought its shade gratefully. Summer was due to break any day now, but until it did, the heat and humidity of the coast were formidable. Finding a spot where one of the breezeways channeled a breath of air her way, Marta plopped herself on one of the great tree's gnarled roots and sat with chin in hands.

"Oh, come now, it's not as discouraging as all that, is it?" called a merry voice. Marta's breeze died, and she looked up to see the enormous form of Kukhoosh Retneyabo blocking the breezeway across the courtyard from her. He did not stand for long, though, but crossed unhurriedly to join her in the shade.

Marta looked up at him from her low perch. Even if she'd been standing, she'd have had to look up at him, for Marta was scarcely a meter and a half tall, while the kukhoosh stood just short of two meters. His broad form was clothed in elegant flowing trousers and robe. With his covered head and curling black beard, he looked like something out of a fairy tale.

"They're having a faculty meeting," she explained with a little pout. "Still trying to decide what the dinka-chak is."

Retneyabo laughed roundly and dragged over a chair from the nearby patio so he could sit near her in the shade. "And you think all their talking is foolishness," he surmised, folding his beringed hands over a prosperous belly.

"I think the way to find out is to go back there," she said emphatically. "We need to know if there are more, or if this is a freak. Sab Yatzahl thinks it must be an egg-layer—it could have left a nest out there. We should have gone back first thing and searched for its nest."

"Patience, my little hawk," Retneyabo soothed. "No one goes into Dhin M'Tarkhna in the summer. Even an impetuous thing like you knows that."

Marta gave a great sigh and slumped back down, elbows on knees, chin on hands. That made the kukhoosh laugh again.

"You are like the great horned owl," he chuckled.

"Once it has fixed its eyes on its prey, nothing will distract it!"

Marta pushed at her long black curls, falling loose now that she was back at the University. They tumbled well down the back of her linen-colored tunic. She was not amused by the kukhoosh's observation, but she kept silent. She had too much respect for Retneyabo to flare up over such a trifle.

"Well, I have some news I think you will find pleasing," he went on placatingly. "They may argue all they like about the dinka-chak, but I have already decided what to do."

That got Marta's full attention. When Retneyabo decided something, it was as good as done. He was not only a shrewd and powerful merchant, he was also the sponsor of the College of Indigenous Life. Faculty, dean, even students—who were an opinionated lot—deferred to Kukhoosh Retneyabo. If he said the College would do thus-and-such, they would do thus-and-such. And if he said *he* would do thus-and-such—well, as the old saying went, "His promise is legal tender."

With a conspiratorial smile, the kukhoosh fished inside his great sleeve and produced a data sponge. In the absence of hard metals, the Innantans made extensive use of biological storage media. The specially grown organisms had each cell encoded with either a positive or negative charge, functioning much like the "on and off" switches first called bits. Retneyabo handed the data sponge to Marta, then leaned back in his chair again. "I have decided to bring in an impartial third party, an expert, to solve the question of the dinka-chak's classification," he told her with a twinkle in his eye. "On that sponge are three dossiers. Why don't you look at them and see which one you like?"

Curious, Marta took the data sponge and retreated into one of the study rooms which fronted on the courtyard. Loading the sponge into a workstation, she opened the first folder and gasped.

The man portrayed was an Unbeliever!

She opened the second, and the third. All Unbelievers.

Since the founding of the colony two centuries before, no more than a handful of Unbelievers had ever been allowed to set foot on Dray's Planet. Dray's had been granted to the persecuted Children of the Second Revelation as their homeworld, and they did not intend to see it corrupted. Communication with other worlds— mostly the exchange of scholarly information—was carefully monitored. Those few goods which were approved for purchase from offworld were sent down by drone shuttles, and the payment sent back the same way. The *mazhel,* the religious leaders who offered enlightenment to the Faithful, had taught them a genuine disdain of anything they did not produce themselves. If Dray's Planet didn't have it, her citizens neither needed nor wanted it. Thus spoke the mazhel.

But Retneyabo's thinking ran beyond that of ordinary men. If he thought an Unbeliever was necessary to solve the question of the dinka-chak, he would not for one moment be daunted by the fact that it was nearly impossible to get permission for one to come. He dealt on planes of thought and in political circles Marta did not try to comprehend. If he said he would bring in an Unbeliever, she would take him at his word.

After a careful review of all three files, Marta took the sponge back to the kukhoosh, who waited still in the shade of the old olive tree. "I like the blond one," she announced.

Retneyabo laughed heartily, the finely tooled beads on his chest shaking and catching the golden sun on their polished surfaces. "You would, my little predator!" he exclaimed mischievously.

"Oh, he is attractive, too," she admitted, giving her dark curls an arrogant toss, "in a foreign sort of way. But it says that he participates actively in the Interstellar League of Zoologists—even ran for an elected office. Lost, of course—too young. But he is ambitious; he wants to make a name for himself. Cecil Robinson will serve your purposes well."

"Very shrewd, my little falcon," Retñeyabo approved. "The blond one it is." With a great heave he pushed himself out of the chair. "Now I must stop dallying in the shade, for I have to see someone in the Provost's Office."

By that, Marta knew he had already chosen Robinson; asking her opinion was just one of his little games. Had she suggested someone else, he would have asked her subtle questions regarding the scientist's qualities until he led her to the same conclusion he had already reached. It was easy to understand how he had garnered such influence in Innanta—he was the most skillful manipulator she knew.

"May I keep a copy of Robinson's file?" Marta asked, as he tucked the data sponge away in his sleeve.

"I'll see that you get a copy," he agreed, nodding. "But keep it on your personal sponge, and keep it encrypted," he advised her. "Paun has been sniffing around."

Marta made a rude noise. "Kukhoosh Paun would sniff around a camel's behind if there were rumors of glory in the stable."

Again Retneyabo laughed, taking her face in his large hands and planting a kiss on her forehead. "If words were weapons, my dear, you could slay armies."

"Why would I need to, with you as my patron?" she asked in mock innocence.

Retneyabo's bushy beard parted in a broad smile as he chucked her under the chin. "The blond one, eh? I will see what I can do."

"And so the great Kukhoosh Retneyabo," Hassan said grandly, "appealed to the Holy Ones to bring an Unbeliever here to Dray's Planet. The Holy Ones in turn appealed to the Most High, who said to them, 'Bring among the Faithful this one man, and this one man only. Find the Unbeliever called Robinson, for there is much he can teach my Children.'"

Hassan was pleased to see Ari's mouth gaping a little as he listened raptly to the tale. Forbidding a smile to betray him, the father went on with his story. "And so the Holy Ones said, 'Let it be so.' And behold, a ship came from the stars, and who should be on board it but an Unbeliever named Robinson!"

It took the length of Innanta's hot, dry autumn for Kukhoosh Retneyabo to maneuver his proposal through the University bureaucracy; and after that he had to fight it around the Council of Kukhooshel and jolly it gently past the mazhel. By then the rainy coastal winter was nearly over, and faculty hurried to organize field expeditions for the coming spring. Marta waited, impatiently, for the arrival of the Unbeliever.

But it was to be a full year before Cecil Robinson arrived. Though the impetuous Unbeliever caught the first flight from his homeworld of Melius to Deca Portal, it was an eight-week journey. There he boarded a communications vessel which regularly took data back and forth between this gateway and others. Slipping through the nothingness of folded space, the ship arrived a thousand light-years further out the galactic arm almost instantaneously and deposited its lone passenger at the Emran Portal, which served the solar system of Dray's Planet.

But there the scholar sat for four long months, until a ship came through which would pass near enough to Dray's Planet to make a detour there economically feasible. Once aboard the ship—a freighter outbound for the GenOrg colonies—it was six months before they locked into orbit around the isolated world.

When the day finally came, Marta watched the landing on a monitor at the College, still pouting because she hadn't been invited to be in the receiving party. Frowning a little, she noted the bearers standing by in case the twenty-eight-year-old professor had to be carried from the drone shuttle to the waiting electric cart. Maintaining full-g for extended periods was still cost-prohibitive, for all the advances in technology, and so Robinson's yearlong voyage had been spent in low-g or zero-g environments. Chemical therapy could fool the human body into thinking its muscles were being taxed in a normal way, preventing the permanent loss of muscle tissue, and a rigorous program of exercise also helped, but he would still be affected by the sudden resumption of full gravity. According to Robinson's dossier, he was something of an outdoorsman, having hobbies such as rock climbing and sailing, so perhaps he wouldn't take *too* long to recover . . .

And there he was, stepping out of the shuttle under his own power and walking steadily, if gingerly, toward Sab Yatzahl. Oh, my. He certainly looked as though he'd kept up his exercises . . .

His face came into view. A small nose, but oh, those blue eyes! And look at that smile, forced out of a pale face which showed the strain of his landing, but a smile nonetheless.

"How do you feel, Sab Robinson?" she heard Sab Yatzahl ask him as the dean helped the Unbeliever into the open vehicle for the trip from the landing field to the control bunker. The camera which transmitted this scene was mounted on the side of the cart, so Marta could see nothing of Robinson now except his square shoulder and one trousered leg as he dragged that last appendage inside.

"Like there's a tiny weight hanging from each of my pores," he replied in a voice slightly breathless. "I was afraid to look behind me as I walked; I thought I might see my ass hanging six inches lower than it should."

Marta laughed at his outrageously honest reply. She couldn't wait to meet Cecil Robinson!

And she couldn't wait to see the look on his face when he finally saw the dinka-chak.

CHAPTER 2

"But why did it require an Unbeliever?" Ari wanted to know. *"I thought the scientists of the Faithful were smarter than any Unbelievers."*

"And so they are," Hassan agreed. *"But this Unbeliever came so that others beyond our gates might know the power of the Most High, and stand in awe."* He patted the boy's knee and went on.

"No one on our world had ever seen the like of this Unbeliever as he descended from his spacecraft and set his foot upon the blessed soil of Innanta. Robinson was his name, and he bore the aspect of an angel: a man of great stature, with hair like sunlight and eyes the color of the sea . . ."

"I hope you understand, patron," Robinson began carefully, using the proper form of address, "that pale is my normal color."

Retneyabo laughed roundly, his great belly shaking with the joyful sound. "Oh, yes, Robinson, we are not quite so ignorant as that!" he assured the zoologist. "We know that even our glorious sun will not turn your skin as brown as ours. Although the Children of the Second Revelation do not mix with Unbelievers, it does not mean we don't study them."

They were in the courtyard of the Infirmary, lounging in chairs of native *latsa* canes. Two weeks had passed since Robinson landed, and only now had the kukhoosh deigned to call on his guest.

"You, for instance," Retneyabo went on, "look to be of Nordic or Germanic descent with those smooth features and that broad forehead of yours—not that there's much difference anymore, the way the white races have slopped together." His dark eye sparkled as he surveyed the zoologist, who had begun dressing in native garb: bleached, baggy trousers, a long, flowing coat, and a colorful blouse. Robinson had even begun to grow a small mustache on his formerly clean-shaven face, in imitation of Innantan men.

"I only meant to say," the kukhoosh explained, returning to his original comment, "that on your voyage you had grown pale, even for one of your race. But you look healthier now than when you first arrived. Sunlight is a great gift, for which we thank the All-Giving. And by the Most High's grace, you will soon be well enough to begin your work here."

At that, Robinson leaned forward earnestly, his blue eyes sparking with interest. "Patron, I would be pleased to start my work just as soon as someone will tell me what it is."

Retneyabo feigned surprise. "I thought our invitation was quite clear," he said. "You are to be a guest professor at the University, attached to the College of Indigenous Life." The tradition of the visiting professor, like the exchange student, crossed cultures and was of long standing, and so had given the mazhel a graceful way to approve Retneyabo's request. He doubted, however, that it had fooled anyone—least of all Cecil Robinson.

Robinson's mouth twisted in a wry smile. "A professor's duties can be many and varied," he pointed out. "Lecture, research, writing . . . But it's rather obvious, patron, that you must have something unusual in mind for me. After all, yours is the College of *Indigenous* Life and, quite frankly, I know very little about the species native to this planet."

The kukhoosh permitted himself a sly smile. He liked this Robinson: sharp, succinct, and as easy to read as the glyphs on a public building. "But you are an evolutionary zoologist," he parried. "Dray's Planet is a relatively new world, and we are still studying the way native life evolved."

"I'm a taxonomist," Robinson qualified. "I group life-forms according to physical characteristics, trying to determine evolutionary patterns. I've seen the taxonomy your people have published on Drayan species—you don't need my help."

"We pride ourselves on the quality of our scholars," Retneyabo agreed. "Here on Innanta we cherish two things: Knowledge and Beauty. There is no higher calling than artist or scientist. That is part of the Second Revelation as given to the Holy Ones."

Robinson was not to be deflected from his quest by his host's subtle change of topic. "You have vertebrates in your ocean," he said flatly. "Of the thirty-odd settled worlds that have indigenous life, only three others have evolved vertebrates. Scholars have been applying to do research here for over a century; all have been turned down. Why did you ask me to come?"

This time Retneyabo's laugh was a chuckle. "Very well, Robinson. You are right. We do have a particular puzzle on which my faculty have been in disagreement for some time. It is my hope that someone with broader experience, such as yourself, can shed some light on it for us."

Robinson clasped his hands in an unconscious gesture of anticipation. "As long as I don't have to walk two or three kilometers to read the files," he said eagerly, "I'm ready to start work now."

But Retneyabo laughed and levered his great bulk from the chair. "Ah, but you must walk at least that far, Robinson," he told the younger man. "To see this specimen which puzzles us, you must come to the College, and that is a healthy distance from here. It is a sin, you understand, to ride in a conveyance inside the city unless you are on your way *to* the Infirmary."

Robinson's face fell, but he nodded grudgingly. "I understand," he said, although Retneyabo was sure he didn't. Unbelievers rarely understood the peculiarities of Innantan law, which was religious law. "Another week," he promised, "and Yatzahl will come for you. In the meantime, do look at the work our scholars have done on Drayan vertebrates. It may prove helpful to you in the coming months." With that, the kukhoosh took his leave and started for the door, where his bodyguard waited. At the last moment he turned back.

"You haven't done much fieldwork, have you, Robinson?" he called back to the zoologist.

"Taxonomy rarely takes one into the field," the scholar answered.

"Perhaps we will rectify that while you are here," the kukhoosh said. "Yes, I think we might have to rectify that."

The morning breeze swirled around Marta, stirring the folds of her garment and tickling the curve of her neck, but she hardly noticed. She was watching the Unbeliever toil up the hill beside Sab Yatzahl.

Marta stood on the roof of the main building of the College of Indigenous Life, an imposing structure three stories tall and a hundred meters long, constructed of sand-colored adobe brick. Abstract etchings adorned the central entrance, and a tile mosaic paved the way to handsome, heavy doors of polished wood. Like most of the buildings in the city of Jinka, it sported a modest parapet around its perimeter, turning the roof into additional space for working, dining, or simply lounging.

From this vantage point, Marta had been tracking the progress of the Unbeliever and his guide for half an hour. Though Robinson still suffered some from the effects of his spaceflight, she noted that he moved with a casual, athletic grace. Beside him, the lanky dean looked like a wooden puppet. Both men were dressed in the long coats and loose trousers appropriate to men of scholarly merit, but there was no doubt that Robinson cut the more striking figure. Being a head taller than Yatzahl helped.

Now they were almost here. In a matter of moments she would see him face-to-face . . . Marta had seen images of Caucasian men before, of course—in her textbooks and in the recordings of scientific conferences held on other worlds. But those were images. It was one thing to look at a man's image on a monitor, and quite another to stand in his presence. . . .

Turning abruptly from the parapet, Marta went back to the small table and chairs that provided a pleasant place to relax and catch the vagrant breezes of late summer. Retneyabo waited there, lounging on a cushioned chair and sipping at a glass of iced coffee. "What, not here yet?" he teased Marta, for she had paced back and forth from the parapet a dozen times to keep tabs on the approaching Unbeliever.

Marta pretended it was his impatience, and not hers. "They stopped a while to look out over the city," she told him. "I could see Sab Yatzahl pointing out the harbor and the bazaar and such."

"How inconsiderate of him," the kukhoosh bantered, "when my little falcon waits here so impatiently!"

"I had only hoped Robinson would be stronger by now," Marta grumbled, wrinkling her smooth features into a scowl at this nettling. "If he's to go into the Western Desert, he needs to be strong. The way he was panting when they stopped, I will be surprised if he has any breath left by the time he reaches the main hall."

"If he does, you will take it away," Retneyabo told her, admiring the gauzy white garment that flowed about her slender form, sometimes billowing up to conceal mysteries, other times hugging her close and leaving little to the imagination.

Marta only shrugged and did not answer, dropping herself carelessly into a chair. It felt odd to wear such finery here at University, but when one was invited to attend a meeting which included the kukhoosh, one had to dress the part. She stretched out a brown hand and studied the rough cuticles and blunt nails, wishing her hands looked half as elegant as her feet. Those had nails that were carefully painted a bright red, and toe rings that sparkled in the morning sunlight.

Now Retneyabo rose and carried his ponderous form to the parapet to look down. The two zoologists were passing into the main hall now, having paused to admire the tile mosaic and the etchings at the entrance. After a moment Retneyabo turned and came slowly back to the table, standing near Marta's chair. She raised suspicious eyes to his. What was the greatest schemer in all of Innanta up to now?

"As I think about it," Retneyabo said slyly, "I believe we should let you finish this little tour for our guest. Go downstairs and tell Yatzahl I want to speak with him here on the roof. We'll join you in time to show Robinson the dinka-chak."

Marta smiled broadly at the kukhoosh. "What is it you'd like me to find out?" she asked with a knowing glint in her eyes.

Retneyabo gave a short laugh. "Ah, my little predator! As usual, you are one jump ahead. A man will say and do many things with a beautiful woman that he will not reveal to other men. Feel free to toy with him as you like; then tell me afterward what your sharp mind and unparalleled instincts tell you."

"Your confidence honors me," Marta replied with a coy downward cast of her dark eyes. Then, turning away from him, she pinched her cheeks to bring up their color, adjusted the bands of green-blue shell on her bare arms, and started for the stairs.

The spacious, high-ceilinged main hall of the College, where Marta found the two scholars, served as a sort of museum. Here even the lowliest peasant on Innanta could come to see and to learn about the indigenous life-forms of his world, both zoological and botanical. Yatzahl and the Unbeliever were standing looking up at the great map of the continent of Innanta over the door when Marta slipped up behind them.

"Sab Yatzahl."

Both men turned in surprise, but whereas the dean only smiled pleasantly, Robinson's eyes widened, and his jaw sagged a little. Marta managed to suppress a smug smile. She knew very well the effect she had on men when she dressed like this, her arms and neck bare, her sandaled feet peeking out from beneath the flowing white gown.

"Forgive the intrusion," Marta continued, "but the

kukhoosh wishes to speak with you. He is waiting on
the roof." Now she let a coy smile slip onto her lips as
she turned to Robinson. "I will be happy to finish the
tour for Sab Robinson."

Yatzahl had not gotten the post as Dean of the College by being politically dense. He excused himself gra-
ciously but quickly and disappeared out the back of the
building, where the courtyard stairs would take him up
to the roof. He did not, Marta noticed, even bother to
introduce her.

"I'm Marta," she said, extending her hand to the Unbeliever in a custom not practiced on Innanta, but which
she had seen many times in recordings of scholarly proceedings elsewhere. "I am Sab Yatzahl's graduate
assistant."

Cecil Robinson took her hand, and his was warm,
strong, and gentle. His height of nearly two meters was
even more impressive when Marta stood this close to
him. "Cecil Robinson," he said as he gave her hand a
brief shake, then lingered over the contact. "Pleased to
meet you."

How striking blue eyes were when they gazed down
from such a height! Like pieces of a summer sky, bright
with a mild amazement. "Let me show you around,"
Marta offered. "We are very proud of our *simoorna-Ta-
pragal,* our displays-that-teach. They are the finest in the
entire University."

A slow smile spread across Robinson's features. "I am
sure people come from everywhere," he said slyly, his
eyes never leaving her face, "just to gaze upon the mar-
vels in this place."

Oho! A clever tongue on this one! Marta thought as
she retrieved her hand from his grasp. "We take scholarship very seriously on our world," she told him sincerely.
"The twin pillars of our aspiration are Knowledge
and—"

"Beauty," he finished, the smile still playing beneath
his bristling blond mustache as he spoke. "And what a
pleasure to find them both embodied here."

"You appreciate the architecture of our building,

then?" Marta asked with feigned naïveté. "I wasn't sure someone of your cosmopolitan background would be impressed with our sand-colored adobe and thick masonry construction. But we are a very simple and durable people; to us, strength *is* beauty." Then, before he could come up with another double entendre, she turned and led the way further into the hall.

Explaining the exhibits for her guest, Marta was surprised to discover he was as interested in their construction as their contents. In addition to paintings and photographs, there were actual specimens of more than fifty animals on display in the hall. Robinson, who was accustomed to computerized images and 3-D replicas, was taken aback to learn that these were the preserved remains of actual animals, and not artificial constructs. Marta could see the initial look of revulsion at that revelation. "Does it seem barbaric to you, Sab Robinson?" she asked him bluntly. He wouldn't last long in the desert if he minded squashing a few bugs.

Robinson shrugged. "I've spent enough time in bio labs dissecting actual creatures," he told her. "I'm not what you'd call squeamish about preserving dead flesh. It just seems a little—well, crude. Don't you people have animal-rights groups that get upset over this sort of thing?"

Marta bridled slightly. "The Manifest Revelations of the Holy Ones dictate that no animal shall be caused to suffer unnecessarily," she told him archly, "nor shall its suffering be prolonged when it can be expediently shortened. But animals are the servants of humans," she added decisively. "These animals serve us by teaching about their species."

"No criticism was meant," Robinson assured her with a mock bow. "You do things so differently here that I can't help commenting, but it's only a comment. I understand that you lack many of the resources we take for granted."

Indeed, the absence of not only hard metals but petroleum for plastics and carbon fiber made the manufacture of electronic equipment on Innanta minimal; using electronics for 3-D displays was unthinkable. What they had was used sparingly, for research and for communication with other worlds. For day-to-day living, Innantans must be content to manufacture from glass and wood, to load their produce on pack animals, and to sail in wind-powered vessels.

As they continued, Robinson showed polite interest at most of the displays, but it seemed to Marta he spent more time watching her than looking at the animals. "Do you have a wife, Sab Robinson?" she asked as they paused near a display which outlined the peculiar mating habits of the three-sexed *darpa*.

"No," he replied, obviously reading an invitation in that.

"You may wish to buy one while you're here," Marta suggested innocently, and reveled in the look of startlement that replaced the smoldering in his eyes. "On a short-term contract, of course," she added. "At the bazaar, you can find a very satisfactory wife who will accept a four-week or six-week marriage contract. A man of your means should not be without a woman to make his home and his life more comfortable."

The Unbeliever was actually blushing! "I appreciate your concern," he replied carefully. "But as I understand the . . . high value your people place on their religion, I doubt that any of your women would care to make a contract with an Unbeliever like myself."

Marta waved this concern aside. "It's not your soul they're contracting with. As long as your credit is good and your flesh is clean, it's all the same to them."

That made the color rise even higher from the collar of his blue-and-green blouse. "Admittedly, I know very little of your culture," he managed, "and I'm trying not to get myself in trouble. You'll forgive me if I wait just a little before I decide whether or not to . . . enter into a contract of that nature."

Marta's eyes sparkled wickedly as she moved on to the next exhibit.

By the time they reached the display on convergent evolution, Robinson had either recovered from his discomfiture, or the display was enough to force it from his mind. He was obviously fascinated by this comparison of several Drayan species to Terran life-forms, showing how species on the two planets had developed similar characteristics to cope with similar environments. "Amazing," he murmured, and Marta wasn't sure if he meant the similarities between species or the intricate detail of the charts, until he added, "A lot of very meticulous scholarship went into this."

"And most of it was Sab Yatzahl's," Marta replied with some pride. "You will find, however, that not all our faculty members agree with his assessment of parallel evolution."

Robinson shook his head firmly. "Those who disagree with him are wrong," he said bluntly. "Even with the little bit I could learn about Drayan animals before I came, it was clear that the principles of parallel evolution are very strong here." Suddenly he turned on his brilliant smile, which was all the more charming for its roguish touch. "If I were a less scrupulous man," he said, "I'd be tempted to steal his research and publish a paper on this topic when I get home. It would earn me an Ashdod Prize for sure."

Marta gave a throaty chuckle. She suspected that coveted prize was never very far from Cecil Robinson's mind. "The people of Innanta would take it very unkindly," she responded with a corresponding twinkle in her eye, "if you were to steal the glory which rightfully belongs to one of our scholars. Such glory is what a man lives for."

"Then your scholars should publish more," he came back. "I checked the Universal Library before I came to Dray's Planet; it lists only fourteen vertebrates for your planet, and all of them marine." He gestured at the nearby display of sandslithers. "There are at least seventy-eight listed in the files I was given upon arrival, with eight being land animals. I'd say your scholars are a bit behind in sharing their knowledge."

It struck Marta as amusing, standing there smiling benignly at the Unbeliever, that she had been sent down here to prod him a little, and here he was, trying to prod her. "That we have vertebrates is well-known," she replied easily. "The number is inconsequential."

Robinson, however, seemed to think it was very consequential. "Listen, Marta," he said in a tone which was far too familiar for their brief acquaintance. "Why don't you tell me what's going on here? I've pretty much got it figured out: you've got some kind of animal that doesn't fit into your careful, intricate taxonomy of indigenous life. So what? How do you think European zoologists felt when they first encountered the platypus of Australia? Laid eggs like a bird, nursed its young like a mammal. Nature plays tricks on us all the time. Why all the secrecy about this beast?"

Marta laughed at his insolence as much as his insight. "It would be inappropriate for me to speak to you on this subject," she said artfully. "Besides, this is a public place, and the knowledge is not yet public."

"Why is that?" he wanted to know. *Like a dog with a bone,* Marta thought with satisfaction. *Retneyabo will be most pleased.*

"There are those," she explained, "who would see the mystery as a defeat for our College and its patron. Still others would try to solve the mystery themselves and claim the glory which goes with it. We don't want either of those things to happen."

"And you think I can help you solve the mystery."

Voices sounded from the rear of the hall: Retneyabo's hearty laugh and Yatzahl's pleasant chuckle. Marta smiled up into Robinson's face. "We have a proverb, Sab Robinson: a fresh pair of eyes brings light. So we brought you to our project."

"We?" The seductive glint grew stronger. "Since you are Yatzahl's graduate assistant, will I have the pleasure of your assistance in this endeavor?"

Marta let her own eyes spark with the same mischief. "You will find me intimately involved," she baited. "But I guarantee there will be times you'll wish I were not."

"Never," he scoffed quietly as Yatzahl and the kukhoosh found them in the eastern wing of the exhibit hall.

"There you are, Robinson!" Retneyabo boomed. "My apologies for having kept you waiting. Ah, but I see you've had excellent company."

"Indeed, I have," Robinson agreed loudly, never taking his eyes from her face. "She has been instructing me in the appreciation of your twofold credo: Knowledge and Beauty."

"And who better personifies them both," Retneyabo exclaimed, taking Marta's tiny hand in his own large ones, "than my *sib-hinan*—my student-wife?"

"And there," Hassan told the gathered caravaners, gesturing broadly, "surrounded by the Knowledge and Beauty of the simoorna-Ta-pragal, Marta and the Unbeliever made a pact to search out the secrets of the dinka-chak and bring them back for the glory of the All-Hallowed and of the Children of the Second Revelation."

Then Hassan tilted his head back and gazed upward as though he could see through the roof of his great tent to the bold array of stars that bedizened the heavens outside. They were not as thick here as they were closer in along the galactic arm, yet there were enough of them to make the sky look like the folds of a black velvet gown across which white crystals have been strewn with the abandon of a wealthy kukhoosh. "You know the stars called the Shield of Knowledge," he said, referring to a well-known cluster of stars in the shape of a diamond. "Upon the Shield of Knowledge did they swear. And the Ever-Listening was pleased, because they held the pursuit of Knowledge above all else, and no other thought distracted them . . ."

Cecil Robinson was not a happy man as he started up the steps to Yatzahl's office. He couldn't help feeling that he'd been set up somehow with the girl. The kukhoosh's wife! My God, the man had to be twice her age! Or close to it, anyway. How was a fellow to know—and she'd been in on it, like as not. Flirting with him like that—he knew flirting when he saw it, and by God, she was flirting with him. She might have—

"Here we are," Yatzahl said, and Robinson's attention snapped back to the present. The slightly built Innantan had stopped in front of a wooden door on the second-floor balcony. He fumbled with a set of keys—actual keys cut from the thick shell of the *krazit,* a Drayan marine creature resembling a giant clam, and not the magnetic cards with which Robinson had grown up. "You must be tired, I know, Sab Robinson. You can sit down in here."

The four of them passed into a spacious office, paneled in richly grained native woods with a few works of art scattered tastefully about. Robinson spotted a sculpture of unique Drayan crystals which would have gone for a small fortune on Melius. Yatzahl used it as a doorstop.

Gratefully, Robinson eased himself into a chair. At least it took him half a day now before he felt as though his flesh were sagging off bones made of soft lead. He tilted his head back and felt the coolness of the room as a relief on his flushed cheeks, a relief matched only by Marta's disappearance into an adjoining room. She *was* beautiful, in a most exquisite, exotic way: dainty and dark, with high cheekbones and a sharp, bold nose, and hair so black and thick a man could lose himself in it . . . And she was *married,* damn it all!

"We thought it would be nice to have a reception for you, Sab Robinson," Yatzahl was saying. "Our faculty and students are most anxious to meet you. It is their first opportunity, ever, to converse with a colleague who did not attend our College. Electronic communication cannot substitute for face-to-face interaction. But I know you will be tired after today's visit, so I thought perhaps after Sabiss . . ."

He said more, but Robinson didn't hear it, for at that moment Marta returned with a wheeled cart on which there was a display case. Like those in the exhibit hall below, the cover was made of actual glass, not the lightweight, durable translucent plastic to which Robinson was accustomed. Neither case nor cart registered with Robinson, however. Even Marta herself did not draw his attention. All he saw was the creature inside. Why, it looked like—it might be—of course, it couldn't be, but—it *looked* like—

"And here is the reason we brought you all this way," Yatzahl said as he took the cart from Marta and presented it to Robinson. "Marta and some other students found it in the Western Desert over a year ago. We believe it's native, for the Martyrs brought nothing like this with them. But it is, as you can see, unique among the species we've found here. In fact, we don't know what class to assign it to, let alone what order or family."

Still all Robinson could do was stare.

"Here, let me pull up the 3-Ds on it," Marta offered, fishing a data sponge from a drawer in the display case and feeding it into the workstation on Sab Yatzahl's desk.

"As you know," Yatzahl continued while she operated the machine, "we have only two classes of vertebrates, and neither has legs. There is a protoreptilian group—legless air-breathers—and a piscine group which strains its air from the water with a mechanism very much like gills. This is obviously neither one. It has four legs, but walks—we think—on only two. We refer to this specimen as a female, since there were undeveloped eggs inside, but it is unclear if the creature is an egg-layer or a live bearer. It is unclear how the eggs are fertilized—inside or outside the mother's body—and we don't even know if they are fertilized by spermoids from a male creature, or if it is a three-sexed species like the *darpa*, or even a hermaphrodite."

Marta had the images on the monitor now, and she looked back at the visiting scholar. "Sab Robinson?"

Robinson tore his eyes off the creature long enough to gape at first Yatzahl, then Marta, and then past her at the monitor. "Skeleton," he croaked. "Let me see the skeleton."

Trying not to smile too smugly, Marta opened the folder with the skeletal images. Robinson stumbled around the desk for a closer look, mouth slightly open, and manipulated the files himself, zeroing in on the foot, the pelvis, and finally the cranium.

"If this were a Terran animal," Yatzahl ventured, "I might say it was a bird without feathers."

But Robinson shook his head. "Not a bird," he said decisively. "The hip joint is wrong; the leg would bend the other way. No, if this were a Terran animal," he informed Yatzahl, turning back to the specimen in its glass case, "I would call it a saurian. A theropod, to be more precise. The shortened forelegs, the serpentine neck, the balancing tail—I'll be goddamned," he breathed, causing his hosts to flinch at the profanity, "if it doesn't look like a dinosaur!"

CHAPTER 3

"Someday, I'm going to discover a new species, too," Ari whispered to Mohat.

The other boy elbowed him and put a finger to his lips imperiously. Then he turned his great dark eyes back to Hassan, and they glittered with interest as he listened to the tale.

"In those days, the Unbelievers possessed some knowledge that the Faithful did not. So it was that when this Unbeliever gazed upon the dinka-chak, he knew at a glance that Marta was right: the dinka-chak was the very image of the great giants which once roamed the land of Father Abraham. And he was amazed by her wisdom and praised her greatly, calling the Children of the Second Revelation both insightful and blessed, because they saw how like the Earth was Dray's Planet, and how like Earth's creatures were those native to Dray's . . ."

The kukhoosh had gone; Robinson sat in Yatzahl's office with the dean and his graduate assistant, firing one question after another at them. Where exactly had they found this thing? Had they seen any others? How long ago had this specimen been taken? What happened when they went to look for more? And—

"What do you mean, no one's gone back?" he demanded incredulously, forgetting how important it was to accept their ways, blend in with their culture. They were scientists: how obtuse could they be?

Yatzahl shrugged, toying with the *pidagon* shell he used for a paperweight. Its rough gray exterior looked like so much sand glued on a soap dish, but the interior was a lustrous black that glistened like polished jet. "Dhin M'Tarkhna is an inhospitable place," he told the visiting zoologist. "The caravans cross on its northern rim, skirting the Maknial Mountains, but people rarely go down into it. Certainly not in the summer." He steepled his fingers as he leaned back in his upholstered chair. "Besides, we were waiting for you to arrive."

To Robinson, a man of action, this was unbelievable. "Why?"

Marta snorted, in complete agreement with Robinson's implied disapproval. Yatzahl, however, stroked his chin and considered his words before speaking. "If this creature is not a freak," he said slowly, "but part of a colony—if it is, in fact, a new species—it will be an extraordinary honor for those who prove it."

"So why do you delay?" the Unbeliever persisted.

A small smile twitched Yatzahl's mouth. "Sab Robinson—are you the only zoologist who would like to present a paper on this new species?"

"Don't be foolish," Robinson fairly snarled. "Every zoologist with the drive of a gnat would . . ." His voice trailed off as he began to grasp what Yatzahl was driving at. "Do you have more than one university here?" he asked. He knew all too well the bitter competition among research institutions elsewhere. Funding always went hand in glove with reputation: no breakthroughs, no grants; no grants, no graduate students.

"No," Yatzahl replied, "but we have more than one kukhoosh."

Understanding dawned in Robinson's eyes.

"It is impossible to keep an expedition to the Western Desert quiet," Marta explained, although somewhat grudgingly. "Once we go, others will follow. We must be first, and we must be right; Kukhoosh Retneyabo wanted an unbiased expert to validate our hypothesis."

"An unbiased evolutionary zoologist," Yatzahl added, a mischievous glint in his dark eyes, "whose hobby is paleontology."

An ironic smile spread over Robinson's face as he realized that it hadn't been his brilliant scholarship

which garnered him the invitation, but his lifelong fascination with Earth's dinosaurs, his schoolboy projects on
the taxonomy of lizard-hipped saurischians. To seek out
an actual paleontologist would have tipped Retneyabo's
hand about the suspicions of his faculty; but a zoologist
whose *hobby* was paleontology . . . "Very shrewd," he
murmured, going back to flipping through the data files
on the dinka-chak. "Well, it's not a true dinosaur, of
course," he commented after a moment, "although the
adaptations are so similar it's spooky. But it's not any
cross between some native creature and a Terran rep-
tile, either."

"Then where did it come from?" Marta challenged.
"You have seen our taxonomy, the catalog of the various animals we have found on this planet. Where did
our dinka-chak come from?"

"I'll be—" Robinson caught himself just in time to
keep from using an offensive word. "—hanged if I know.
But I'll tell you one thing." He lifted piercing blue eyes
in a challenge of his own. "We'll never know till we find
more of them. We need to make that expedition to the
Western Desert, and we need to make it now."

Retneyabo watched the young zoologist pace back and
forth on the brick paving and marveled at the amount
of energy a man could expend going nowhere. The kukhoosh had learned long ago to make all his energies
carry him toward a goal. But Robinson was young, the
product of a culture which fretted and fumed as though
life were a race, and the one who bashed headlong into
death first was the winner. Children of the Second Revelation knew that life was a garden: if you nurtured the
living things around you and pulled out the weeds, you
could live in beauty and in plenty for a good long time.

"We'll need a trailer air-dropped in," Robinson was
saying, "for our base and field lab, and a couple of jeeps
to get around in. I can draw up a list, but one of your
people will have to price it for me—I just don't know
how things are valued in your economy."

"Apparently not," Retneyabo agreed. They were in a

small private courtyard of the University's guest housing, where Robinson had been given an apartment. "Robinson, we don't have aircraft. Nor do we have 'jeeps,' as you call them. Our only motorized vehicles are solar-powered electric carts and a couple of steamships."

Robinson stopped his pacing to stare slack-jawed at his host for a moment. Then, "Damn, I forgot," he muttered.

"I must ask you to refrain from the use of profanity," the kukhoosh reminded him, seated in a latsa chair in the shade of a lush pomegranate tree which dominated the small courtyard.

Robinson winced in apology. "Sorry," he said. Curbing his tongue was the most difficult part of adapting to this planet. The absence of alcohol was annoying, and the prohibition against work on their holy day made him chafe, but neither of those tripped him up the way his mouth did. "But your faculty and students have made trips to the Western Desert before. Obviously someone knows how to plan one properly."

"Obviously!" Retneyabo laughed. "In fact, I have the services of the best wilderness guide in Innanta at my disposal. The expedition will be well planned, I assure you."

"Great!" Robinson exclaimed. "When can we leave?"

"When you and my guide agree that all is ready," Retneyabo said firmly, like a master horseman reining in a spirited yearling. "I would like to keep a measure of secrecy in this as long as possible, so I will ask the two of you to meet at my house. Your visit will appear to be a simple courtesy call."

Unable to contain himself, Robinson leaped to shake Retneyabo's hand. "You won't be sorry, patron," he assured the kukhoosh. "I have a feeling in my gut about this. There's honor and glory for everyone in it!"

"No, I shan't be sorry," Retneyabo agreed mildly. "But you may be."

His words hauled the Unbeliever up short. "What do you mean?"

Retneyabo laughed roundly. "You've already been

warned about the rigors of Dhin M'Tarkhna. Your little camping and hiking excursions on Melius can hardly compare. But beyond that, there is the matter of Paun."

"Paun?" Robinson took a chair opposite the kukhoosh and waited to be instructed.

"Kukhoosh Paun," Retneyabo obliged, "is one of many kukhooshel who would love to have the same honor I covet, that of discovering this startling new species. I would be surprised if you were the only zoologist taking an expedition into the desert this season."

Robinson felt a tingling run through him. "You mean we'll have competition." His nostrils flared slightly.

"Secrets can only be kept for so long in Innanta."

"Then we have to get there first."

"You must be thorough," Retneyabo cautioned. "A sloppy job is worth nothing to me. But—" He smiled broadly at the vessel he was shaping with such craft. "I have every confidence that you will be successful, whereas other contenders will fail." And with that, the kukhoosh heaved himself up out of his chair.

"I'm flattered by your confidence," Robinson said, rising also.

"Oh, don't flatter yourself too much!" Retneyabo laughed as he brushed a stray leaf from his voluminous coat. "You were, in fact, my second choice; but my instincts told me that my first choice would be truculent and hard to deal with. So I have invited you instead."

Robinson bristled a little. "And who was your first choice?" he couldn't help asking.

"Soln Shipner, of course."

Robinson's eyes blazed. "That motherless son of a—" He stopped just in time. "Shipner's an ass," he snarled with more anger than Retneyabo had seen in him yet.

"Yes, but he's a brilliant ass," the kukhoosh replied. "Still and all, it is you I have chosen and upon whom my honor rests. Do not fail me." He turned and started for the breezeway, where his bodyguard waited. "Come to my house next Tuesday to meet with your guide," he called back to the Unbeliever. "I'll send a boat for you."

*   *   *

Retneyabo's bodyguard fell into step beside the kukhoosh as they left the apartment building. "Patron," he
said softly, "a message from Hashi: the spacecraft will
reach Dray's in five days."

Retneyabo nodded but said nothing. Five days! Paun
must have purchased the entire ship, and its cargo, in
order to divert it to Dray's on such short notice! Robinson wouldn't have much of a head start, then. Pray
the All-Hallowed it was enough.

Striding along briskly, Retneyabo ruminated again on
Paun's relentless pursuit of power. As the newest member of the unofficial Council of Kukhooshel, Paun was
as hungry as they came; and with no college to sponsor,
she had resources to implement all manner of rash plans.
Retneyabo hadn't been that surprised when one of his
graduate students was bought and turned up in the employ of his adversary, along with copies of the dinka-
chak files. But that Paun had been able to bring another
Unbeliever to Innanta—Which mazh had managed that?
The Holy Ones were beyond corruption, but . . .

Retneyabo suppressed a sigh. Never mind how Paun
had gotten the mazhel to agree, the fact was that this
ship was now bringing another Unbeliever to Innanta,
and that Unbeliever would lead a rival expedition to
Dhin M'Tarkhna in search of the dinka-chak. Robinson
and his entourage must succeed first.

There was far more at stake here than honor, though
Robinson need never know that. The politics of the unofficial Council of Kukhooshel were not the business of
an Unbeliever; decisions which could alter the future of
Innanta forever ought not to be discussed by a tongue
that profaned the Name. But there was need for absolute
unity among the kukhooshel if they were to sway the
Holy Ones . . .

And the Holy Ones must be swayed. How long could
they ignore the world beyond their gates? Could they
afford to let two more centuries pass during which the
Unbelievers increased their technology at an exponential
rate, while the Faithful declared that hard metals were
unnecessary, that petroleum could be replaced by sap

from rubber trees and oil rendered from animal fat? Preposterous! It was the duty of the Faithful to excel, and not to fall behind the Unbeliever! But for Dray's Planet, which was so much younger than the Earth it resembled, native petroleum was wishful thinking. And how would they ever locate deposits of hard metals without the proper equipment to detect its presence? The mazhel must be made to see, they must . . .

It was complicated, and very delicate—but no need to trouble Robinson with any of that. He merely had to know that there were competitors in the field, and that those competitors could be—well, rough. Yes, the kukhoosh had to see that Robinson was advised of the dangers.

Retneyabo wondered, though, how wise it would be to tell his Unbeliever that Paun also had brought in an evolutionary zoologist: Soln Shipner.

Retneyabo's estate sat atop low cliffs on the southern edge of this inlet, a veritable palace of white stone sprawling back down the gentle western slope. Three large windmills positioned on the eastern brink generated electricity for the compound. On the north, a steep staircase was cut into the cliff face for those hardy enough to use it as an approach, but there was also a cable car which ran from the terrace to the shore. *Will he take the stairs?* Marta wondered. *Or the cable car?*

Robinson stood in the bow of the small sailboat as it approached the dock far below, a man at ease with himself and the sea. Truly, she had seen other men stand so posed and not been moved like this. What was there about the Unbeliever?

Perhaps simply that he *was* an Unbeliever. Oh, it was not the wickedness of such a man—Marta had known plenty of wicked men, for the caravans were full of them, and she found them somewhat contemptible. No, it was the *foreignness* of him that intrigued her. He did not know the Manifest Revelations of the Holy Ones. The All-Hallowed was a stranger to him. He had never heard the stories nor sung the songs that she had known from birth. Instead, there were other stories and other songs that shaped him, other truths that charted the course of his life.

Watching him leap deftly to the pier, though, Marta had to admit that his blond hair and athletic physique didn't hurt. Would he try those stairs, and appear sweating and panting here above?

But the effects of the long space voyage were still with Robinson; he took the cable car. Marta retreated across the white stone terrace to lounge nonchalantly against a pillar and wait for him.

Moments later the old servant Nak helped Robinson disembark. The Unbeliever sauntered across the terrace toward Marta, stopping a good two meters away.

"Sibna," he greeted formally.

Marta laughed. "That address would be appropriate if I were mistress of this household, but I am not. Believe it or not, your status is greater than mine: I'm a graduate student, you're a professor. Call me Marta."

She was wearing the filmy white garment again, traditional house dress for wealthy young women. "You might have mentioned," Robinson chided, "that you were married to the patron of my College."

"I might have, but I didn't." With a coy downward sweep of her long lashes she added, with just a touch of reproach, "On Innanta, the women who attend the University are more likely to be married than not."

Robinson gave a mock bow. "My apologies. Your ways are still very foreign to me."

Marta straightened up and indicated a nearby table and chairs. "The kukhoosh is occupied within; but we can get started without him."

Robinson's eyebrows knit together in puzzlement. "Started?" Then he took half a step back as he realized what she meant. "Oh, no. Don't tell me *you're* my wilderness guide!"

Marta laughed again. "Of course, what did you expect? Some wizened old caravaner with one eye missing?" She led the way to the table. "That can be arranged, of course, but he wouldn't have any idea where to look for the dinka-chak."

Robinson hesitated a moment before taking a chair across from her. It was the second time Retneyabo had set him up; what else did the tricky old goat have up his sleeve? "Forgive my error," he said petulantly, "but in that dress, you don't look much like a wilderness guide."

Not only did Marta know that, but she loved to capitalize on it. There were few sports she enjoyed as much as baiting self-assured young men. So she gestured dismissively at her apparel. "This? An illusion. Created with clothes and jewels and hairstyle. But in here—" She tapped her forehead. "In here are my real tools.

"I've been crossing the Western Desert by camel since I was five," Marta boasted casually. "My father is a caravaner, and he used to take me with him back and forth to the fishing villages on the Western Coast. I know that desert like the beads at my throat, and I know how to survive in it. I have learned from the best."

"So what kind of place is this, uh, Din Met—whatever?" he wanted to know.

"Dhin M'Tarkhna," she corrected as she reached for a pitcher filled with a dark liquid and tinkling ice. "It means Valley of Desolation. We have kept our native tongue, you know, even though Standard is the language of scholarship and is spoken by nearly everyone." She poured a glass of the beverage and handed it across to him. "Dhin M'Tarkhna is an ancient lake bed scoured by hot, dry winds. Very little grows there."

Robinson took the glass and sipped at it gingerly. The liquid was thick and sweet, some kind of fruit juice. "If it's so barren, it should be easy to find the dinka-chak," he observed.

"You'd think so, wouldn't you?" Marta mused, pouring a glass for herself. "But in fact, caravans have been traveling that northern rim for more than a century, and nomads have grazed their flocks down into it longer than that; but this is the first report of such a creature in all that time."

"Maybe it came over from your other continent," he suggested.

Marta looked at him in surprise. "Dhrusil-matkhashi?" Her voice reflected her incredulity. "Dhrusil-matkhashi is a wasteland. Nothing lives there. No plants, nothing. The soil is sterile. Why do you suppose we stay on this continent?" She shook her head at the Unbeliever's stupidity. "But to go on about Dhin M'Tarkhna—there are no roads going in, not even a dirt track. Only in spring and autumn can it be braved, and fortunately, we are just coming into autumn. It will still be hot, but bearable. We'll take nonperishable food—dried or sealed—and sturdy tents against the wind; and of course, all the water we can carry."

"And you'll pack this in how?" Robinson asked, then added, "We don't have to ride camels, do we?"

"Camels are very practical for the caravan trails," Marta told him without a hint of mirth. "They have toes rather than hooves: two large, leathery toes which spread out under pressure to provide a firm footing for them on the loose sandy soil. But Dhin M'Tarkhna is another story. The ground there is hard and rocky, mostly sandstone and limestone, with loose stones and boulders for seasoning. We'll take donkeys; they're better suited to that kind of ground."

"Donkeys?" Robinson asked incredulously. "We're going to ride *donkeys* on this expedition?"

Marta laughed, and not too kindly. "Well, you may ride a donkey if you like," she told him, "but personally, I prefer one of the electric carts; they smell better."

Robinson didn't have a very high opinion of the electric carts; with their open-frame construction and a top speed of less than 70 kph, they struck him as slow and unstable. But they were better than donkeys, he had to admit that. "Do the donkeys haul the equipment, then?" he asked.

"Water and supplies, yes," she replied, without the edge this time. "They're very efficient: the ratio of load carried to supplies consumed. We won't need much actual equipment: some basic bio lab equipment, tents, of course—"

"What kind of recording devices can we get?" he interrupted. "I want pictures, preferably 3-Ds, of dinka-chaks in the wild. I'd like to set cameras up and record them for a couple of weeks, day and night. We can analyze the images later, but we need to get the raw data while we can. Then, of course, I want some live specimens to bring back with us. What kind of live catch traps do you use normally?"

Marta described a few for him, then said, "It would be better if I show you. Why don't you come with me to the bazaar tomorrow? I have to hire drovers and arrange for our supplies. I can show you some traps, see what you think." Eyeing the finely woven fabric of his colorful blouse, she suggested, "You should look for desert gear while we're there. I can make sure you get a fair deal—otherwise, they'll cheat you blind."

Robinson gave her a lopsided smile. "What? Good, religious people like Innantans are going to cheat me?"

"As Children of the Second Revelation, we are forbidden to take advantage of the poor," Marta replied. "But at the salary the College pays you, Sab Robinson, you hardly qualify." Then she waited until he had raised the glass of juice to his lips. "I can negotiate a temporary wife for you, too, if you want."

Robinson choked on the drink, coughing and sputtering indecorously.

"You are no doubt aware," Marta went on blithely, "that there is no prostitution in Innanta. But the Holy Ones teach us that it is not good for a man or woman to be without sexual fulfillment. A marriage contract of four weeks, or even two, is an acceptable solution for a man of your station. I can negotiate for you, if you want."

"Thank you, but—uh—" he stammered, "I think I'll forgo the, uh—" The word *pleasure* caught in his throat. "The opportunity. On my world we're not accustomed to taking wives so . . . economically."

"Ah." Marta nodded as though just now recalling.

"That's right, in your culture, men and women seldom formalize marriage contracts."

"Well, I wouldn't say *that*," Robinson protested. "But we do take marriage very seriously, so we are often reluctant to . . . to . . ."

"—make a formal contract," she finished for him. "That is because you imprudently recognize only one kind of marriage. Here we have at least twelve, and new ones can be approved by a mazh. A wife from the bazaar would be perfect for you, when you are not on expedition. I don't encourage bringing them along on expedition, they tend to complain a lot. But in the city, they're almost as good as a servant because most of them will cook and clean in addition to providing carnal pleasure. And they're less apt to steal from you than a servant is, because you pay them a bonus at the end of the contract if they have behaved satisfactorily."

The Unbeliever was as discomfited as Marta had hoped he would be. Like many of the cultures beyond the gates of Innanta, Robinson's connected marriage with lifelong commitment and, above all, romantic love. He would have no qualms about seducing a woman he cared little about, just for an evening's pleasure, or living with one informally for a length of time; but the idea of drawing up terms to make the arrangement legal was terrifying to him. He was still having trouble speaking, as though his tongue were suddenly too large for his mouth. "I think there is still a good deal I need to learn about your culture," he managed, "before I . . . participate . . . in such a contract."

Marta smiled to herself and sipped at her juice. Oh, this was much more fun than toying with the cow-eyed boys at the University. She must remember to thank Retneyabo for the opportunity.

Just then the kukhoosh finally made his entrance from the sprawling house. "Ah, Robinson! Forgive my tardiness in greeting you," he called as he approached, "but a messenger arrived just before you with very important news. I trust Marta has made you comfortable?"

"Yes, thank you," Robinson replied politely, although

comfortable was hardly the word to describe how Marta made him feel.

"Good, good." Retneyabo pulled up a chair and leaned his thick forearms on the table, hands clasped. "Now, tell me the plans you have made for this expedition."

Instantly Marta became all business, outlining their journey. The first leg would be to Ballabim in the nearby hill country, a motorized trek which would take only two days. At Ballabim was the last river they would see, and there they would fill all their water containers. Then they'd hire pack animals for the second leg into the Western Desert. The scientists might scoot ahead in one or two carts, depending on circumstances, and let the donkeys and drovers come along at their own pace; but they dared not venture down into Dhin M'Tarkhna itself until they had their entire entourage together. For one thing, the precipitous drop to the valley floor was beyond the capabilities of the electric carts; they must be left behind or lowered over the side of the rim on ropes. For another thing, it was extremely easy to get lost on the featureless floor of Dhin M'Tarkhna. Getting separated from the group at that point could mean wandering hopelessly in a hostile, forbidding landscape.

"I don't think you should leave your pack train behind at all," Retneyabo advised. "That is because of the news I just received. As I suspected, you will not be the only ones searching for the dinka-chak this season."

"Paun!" Marta spat with contempt. Robinson's ears pricked up.

"Indeed, Paun," Retneyabo agreed. "Once I had obtained permission to bring an Unbeliever here as a guest professor, Paun took advantage of the loophole to bring in another zoologist."

"Paun has no College to bring a guest *to*," Marta objected.

"A kukhoosh does not need a College to have a house scholar," Retneyabo reminded her. "My illustrious peer has simply chosen to have a zoologist for a house scholar."

"Fine, if he stays in the house," Marta snapped. "When will he arrive?"

"He is already here," the kukhoosh informed them. "He landed by drone shuttle not an hour ago. Apparently he reached the Portal station only a week after you left, Robinson, and within three weeks Paun had found him a transport. It will take him some time to recover from the effects of spaceflight, but his low-g time was about thirty percent less than yours, and my informant says he appears to be in excellent physical condition."

Marta noticed then that Robinson's face had grown dark and cold. "Who is it?" he asked through jaws so tense they barely parted to speak.

Retneyabo considered not answering. It was a sin to lie, but it was no sin to keep quiet. It was clear from Robinson's eyes, though, that he already suspected. Well, perhaps it would prove additional motivation for the man. "The description I was given confirms an earlier report," the kukhoosh responded. "It is Soln Shipner."

Robinson exploded from his chair with an oath, paced halfway across the terrace toward sea, and then turned back. "That arrogant, asinine megalomaniac!" he snarled. "If I didn't know better, I'd swear he did this just to thwart me!"

"Come, come, Robinson," Retneyabo cajoled, "I doubt it's personal."

"The man is my curse," Robinson insisted, striding back to the table. "He killed my paper four years ago and came near to killing me after that. Now he's come to take this away from me, too."

"Yours is not the only paper he has kept out of publication," the kukhoosh pointed out reasonably.

"The one you wrote for the ILZ conference on taxonomy?" Marta asked. She had seen a reference to that in the Unbeliever's file: while still a doctoral candidate, Robinson had been invited to submit a paper for the conference; but when the work was sent to a referee for review beforehand, it had been rejected out of hand.

"It was a brilliant paper!" Robinson defended. "It was well researched, well documented, and it proved absolutely that cladistics is a sham, that there are numerous instances where a species has mutated into three and even four new species from the same parent stock, not the ironclad dual split upon which all of cladistics is based. And this—this hack, this traditionalist, Shipner, tore it apart—called it an infamous piece of bad scholarship and worse writing."

Marta had studied evolutionary taxonomy, but in truth, many of the organizational details seemed superfluous to her. So what if a generation of spiny fish divided into three new species or only two? Who cared? But she cared very much about the kind of man who would be their competition. "I understand your distress at being excluded from the conference, Sab Robinson," she lied, "but what do you mean, he nearly killed you?"

Robinson sank into a chair and ran a hand across his flushed face. He took a moment before answering. "Oh, I guess I came as close to killing him as he did me," he admitted. There had been a paleontology exhibit, he explained, at a colony called Fiver a little over two years earlier. More than six hundred dinosaur skeletons had been replicated and put on display. Robinson made the journey to Fiver with friends, "just to stand in the presence of T-rex. I've seen plenty of 3-Ds, but there's nothing like the humbling experience of standing in the presence of the king."

Shipner, whose avocation was likewise paleontology, had come to the exhibit, too. Robinson ran into him at a bar one evening, where both of them had too much to drink. Robinson asserted that dinos were a class separate from reptiles because they were endothermic, warm-blooded; Shipner held that there was no conclusive evidence for what he termed a "pop theory from the twentieth century," and that as a subclass of reptiles, dinos were more likely ectothermic. The argument turned into a brawl, with Robinson and Shipner bouncing off tables and chairs in Fiver's .8 gravity. Fortunately, both were too drunk to inflict more damage than some cuts and bruises before their respective colleagues broke up the fight.

"He's a pompous, closed-minded blowhard," Robinson concluded. "And I'll be—" He cut himself off just short of a profanity. "—I'll be hanged if I'll let him take this one away from me!"

Marta looked at the kukhoosh and smiled. Robinson was definitely their man.

"Well, he won't be able to start on his expedition for at least three weeks," Retneyabo reminded the Unbeliever. "You'll have the advantage of a head start."

Robinson threw the kukhoosh a look. "Why three weeks?"

Retneyabo wondered if the Unbeliever had grown suddenly obtuse or was simply absentminded. "Because of his space voyage," the kukhoosh said pointedly. "It has taken you nearly four weeks to regain your strength and shed the effects of the drugs; even given Shipner's shorter time in low-g, it will take him at least three weeks to recuperate."

Robinson looked unconvinced. "You *do* know he's a Nechtanite."

The kukhoosh blinked. "Yes, that was in his file."

"What is a Nechtanite?" Marta asked.

"A warrior sect," Retneyabo explained. "Early settlers of the planet Valla. There's only a small community of them left anymore—so many of the men hire out as mercenaries that their mortality rate is extremely high and their birth rate extremely low. They espouse a rigorous lifestyle that cultivates body, mind, and spirit—what is the credo? 'Make the body a hammer, the mind a sword, and the spirit an arrow.' Very militaristic. But since Shipner has been on the faculty of Mal Surjan University for fifteen years, I assumed he was not a practicing Nechtanite."

"With respect, patron," Robinson replied, having calmed down enough to remember his manners again, "you assumed incorrectly. Their warriors are all scholars, and their scholars are all warriors. Half the faculty of Mal Surjan are Nechtanites. Shipner's as mean and ugly as any of them; and believe me, when it comes to a body like a hammer . . ." The Unbeliever fingered his jaw in painful memory.

"I spent a lot of time in the ship's exercise room on my way here," he told them. "Half from discipline and half from boredom. But you can bet Shipner has spent twice as much time—it's a religion with him. If it took me four weeks to bounce back, it will take him two or less. Furthermore, at fifty percent of his usual strength, he could probably run rings around your faculty." Robinson stopped and made a mocking bow toward Marta. "Present company excepted."

Marta ignored the jibe and looked to Retneyabo, but the kukhoosh did not appear the least bit worried by this report. "Then your head start will be shorter," he said with a shrug. "But not by much—he must still complete his inoculations, after all, no matter what his strength. And then he must find the dinka-chak, which is the real challenge." With a smile, Retneyabo took Marta's hand. "My guide is better than his," he maintained, and kissed Marta's fingers.

"You flatter me, patron," she responded, eyes glittering with the same seductive charm she had turned on Robinson at their first meeting. "But with your permission, I'll return to Jinka tonight. If I go to the bazaar first thing in the morning, I can have the entire expedition ready to leave just after Sabiss."

"As you wish," Retneyabo granted. "Dine with me, both of you, and then I will have Gadn return you to the city. May the All-Gracious smile upon your endeavor, and keep you in the palm of blessing."

"Do you think the Unbeliever knew that the All-Hallowed was using him?" thoughtful Ari inquired.

"No," Hassan answered unequivocally. *"The Unbeliever is never aware of the hand that guides him. Sometimes the Faithful are not aware either, but the Unbeliever—"* Hassan shook his head. *"Had he known what the All-Powerful had in store for him, he would have balked at every turn . . ."*

CHAPTER 4

"In those days," Hassan elaborated, "Jinka was the most beautiful city in the world. It was the city of the University, that Font of Knowledge; it was the city where dwelt the mazhel, the Holy Ones. In it were the most beautiful buildings and the most splendid harbor, a beach of white sand and lush vegetation. All was clean and bright. It was a city of polished stone and sun-drenched adobe, of flowers and green trees; and the purity of its sky reflected the hearts of the Children of the Second Revelation . . ."

The coastal city of Jinka boasted the largest bazaar on the continent, and Marta waded in with the confidence and determination of a channel swimmer. "Here is the heart of the city," she told Robinson. "People and goods flow in and out of it like blood through the heart, spreading out to every house and hovel in and around Jinka. Here, you cannot live unless you come to the bazaar."

They had walked from the University, a distance of five kilometers, to the crowded, noisy market. Marta had traded her finery for traditional student dress: loose trousers and a lap-front tunic cinched by a broad leather belt. The clothing was a nondescript light color such as any laborer might wear, but the belt was finely tooled and boasted an elaborate bone clasp, and the knife in her belt sheath was of rare and well-tempered steel. Her hair was tucked up under a cap which had both a bill to shade her face and a canvas veil on the back to protect her neck. Tough leather sandals with thick soles completed her rugged look.

Robinson lagged half a step behind his guide as they wound through the narrow aisles between stands and carts, booths and benches. The streets had originally been built wide enough to accommodate cart traffic passing over the brick surface, but eager merchants had soon constricted the passageways until pedestrians could hardly walk two abreast. A baker had set up a booth in front of an olive oil vendor's shop, and a cart parked in front of him to sell cheeses. Across the way a potter allowed a fruit merchant to set up before his house, and a string of donkeys for sale was tethered just beyond reach of the dried figs. The hum of flies and other imported insects was drowned out by the yapping of dogs and the drone of human voices hawking, mocking, bartering, bickering. It was the personification of confusion to Robinson.

And the smell! Mingled with the harbor smells of dead fish and rotting seaweed were the pungent aromas of freshly killed animals, spoiling fruit, and manure; and blending with it all was the pervasive odor of sweat. Sweat was an integral part of Innantan life. It trickled down foreheads and necks, staining the clothing of men and women alike. It lathered the sides of pack animals toiling along with their burdens. Summer or winter, midday or midnight, it seemed that every living creature in Jinka boasted a perpetual sheen of sweat.

Even Marta was sweating, an escaped strand of dark hair stuck to her face by moisture, but she seemed not to notice. "We'll go to Street of the Martyrs first," she told her companion. "That's where my father always got his drovers and laborers."

The Street of the Martyrs was one of the oldest in Innanta. Two hundred years ago, when the Children of the Second Revelation had first arrived on Dray's Planet as refugees from a larger religious sect, there had been no Portal to fold the distance between the world they left and the star system to which they came. Ten years had to be spent in a low-gravity environment; and by the time the voyagers arrived, their muscles had deteriorated so as to leave them invalids in their new home.

They were the Martyrs, sacrificing gladly so that their newly ordained faith could flourish in future generations on this secluded planet.

With the aid of intelligent tools and robots, they managed to survive and raise the first generation of native-born Innantans. Humbled by the sacrifice of their parents, these new citizens gave all honor and care to the Martyrs, and the street where so many of them lived was usually one of bustling activity. As the city grew and spread, however, this center of activity became a natural center of commerce. The bazaar sprang up nearby, and after two centuries it had engulfed the old district where once children came to pay homage to the elders in their elaborate wheelchairs and breathing suits.

Now the Street of the Martyrs was a winding, unpaved cart track fronted by crumbling adobe shops and inns. Day laborers loitered in the shade outside, plainly available, while the more skilled workers sat indoors or drank coffee in cramped courtyards, waiting for employers to seek them out. They stared openly at Robinson as he passed, for none had ever seen a pale-skinned man before, and few had even seen images of one. Some of them tore their eyes away from him long enough to leer at Marta as she strode past, and one even called something to her in the native dialect; but a sharp reply from her shut him up and caused his fellows to pull back, leaving a path for her to the front of a squat little building with an open door.

The proprietor recognized her at once, rushing to bow obsequiously before her. "Ah, Sibna!" he cried joyfully. "You are a candle in a dark room, water at midday! You are bread to a hungry man and nectar to the weary. Each time I see you I marvel that the child who stood as her father's shadow is now a woman and a sib-hinan. Your beauty is a flower, and your mind a marvel."

Marta was unfazed by this rhetoric. She glanced around the dim interior of the place, frowning slightly as she took in the dozen or so men lounging on soiled cushions. "I'm looking for Ibna. Is he in the courtyard?" she asked bluntly.

"Ah, you are seeking drovers for your father's caravan?" the shopkeeper asked, eyes alight. "A man would
be honored to water the camels of—"

"I'm taking a scientific expedition to Dhin M'Tarkhna," Marta interrupted in a voice unnecessarily loud.
"Only a man of Ibna's character would understand and
endure such a journey for the sake of Knowledge."

At the proprietor's greeting, all eyes in the shop had
turned on Marta; now they shifted away uncomfortably.
"Perhaps for Beauty," suggested a voice from the corner, "if I had a *sib-dhrusna* such as yourself."

There was a murmur of laughter, which died as Marta
threw a daggered look at the corner. "The only *sib-
dhrusna* you can get is a camel," she sneered. "If Ibna
is not here, I will look elsewhere."

"He may be in the courtyard, Sibna," the shopkeeper
answered quickly. "Let me send one of these worthless
fellows—"

"What wages do you offer?" piped up a rangy man
at a low table. He was drinking thick black coffee.

"The expedition is sponsored by Kukhoosh Retneyabo," Marta replied haughtily. "Your wage will be fair,
according to your conduct."

A teenager came forward into the square of light spilling in from the open doorway to the courtyard. "I will
go," he said boldly.

Marta turned away in disgust. "You are a boy."

"But I've been a donkey drover since I was a child,"
he replied with a touch of pride. "None better. And I
know the desert. I will go with you for Knowledge."
Then he added shyly. "And for Beauty."

The men broke into laughter at this confession, and
the boy shrank back a little as Marta turned slowly to
rake cold eyes over him. Robinson stood fascinated,
wondering if the tigress would lash out or merely toy
with the lad. "How old are you?" she demanded.

"Sixteen."

"Why aren't you in school?"

The boy shrugged. "I am *grib'gahner*," he told her.
"I'll get back to it."

"And how many years have you been *grib'gahner?*"

His answer was forestalled by the sudden darkening of the shop as a form filled the open door to the courtyard. A giant of a man stooped through the opening and stood blocking the light, his headcloth brushing the plastered ceiling. He was easily two meters tall, with square shoulders wider than the doorway and a barrel chest that failed to narrow at the waist. His face bore the lines of many years in the sun and wind, and a scar that crossed his large, crooked nose gave him a malevolent appearance. "Who wants Ibna?" he rasped.

"I do," Marta replied, facing him.

Instinctively Robinson moved closer to her shoulder, lending strength to her stance with his height. He couldn't help noticing that the blade depending from the giant's belt was fully twice as long as that he'd seen on anyone else since landing.

Ibna squinted his sun-blind eyes first at the Unbeliever, and then at Marta. He took two steps toward them. Then, "Sibna," he said humbly, bowing and touching both hands to his seamed forehead. "Wherever you go, I am there."

Robinson drew a breath of relief, but Marta gave a small, sober bow to the trusted caravaner who had stood at her father's shoulder for so many years. "I'm taking an expedition to Dhin M'Tarkhna," she told him. "I need six men to handle donkeys and supplies. We leave after Sabiss and won't return until the winter rains threaten."

Ibna frowned as he reflected on that. "There are only five men I can recommend for such an undertaking," he said after a moment. "I will need to search for a sixth."

Marta cast a glance over at the boy, who had faded back among his elder companions when Ibna entered. "Will you truly go for Knowledge?" she demanded.

"Wha—what do you mean?" the boy stammered.

"Instead of wages, the kukhoosh will sponsor you a year at a residential school. Will you do it?"

The boy's jaw worked a moment before he could get sound to croak out of his throat. "I will."

"Good," Marta said decisively, turning back to Ibna. "Now we have six. It's stuffy in here; let's go to Ashtamelika's to talk."

Ashtamelika ran a spice shop, but on the roof he kept a bistro for use by select customers. Here Marta, Robinson, and Ibna sat at a small table sipping spiced coffee while the boy Tookh squatted nearby. They discussed quantities of supplies, the number and breed of donkeys they would need, and whether or not it was advisable to take a motorized transport down into Dhin M'Tarkhna. Finally Ibna went off to locate his men, and Marta scratched out a note on a sheet of paper. "Take this to Hetz the olive oil dealer in Alley of Shadows," she told Tookh. "Then meet me at the fountain by the wife market."

"With all haste, Sibna," the boy exclaimed, jumping up.

"With very little haste," Marta said drily. "I intend to finish my coffee before I go anywhere."

Tookh flashed a toothy grin and disappeared down the stairs. "It seems you have a devoted servant," Robinson commented.

"I should," she replied, leaning back in her chair. "A year's residency is generous for three months' labor." Pray the All-Merciful they would be through in just three months.

"What was the phrase he used?" Robinson asked. "Girb-something?"

"Grib'gahner," she said. "Literally, it means 'restless' or 'agitated.' We use it to describe that period in a young person's life when he or she has difficulty concentrating on studies." Although the Innantans prized education highly, she explained, they recognized that adolescence was sometimes better spent in other pursuits. Then when the child had matured, learned some of the lessons that could not be found in books, he or she was likely to benefit more from scholastic learning.

"And do they actually go back to school?" the zoologist wanted to know.

"Some yes, some no," Marta admitted. "There is a danger in it. The poor, especially, have difficulty going back. That is why I offered this boy such an extravagant reward." But she insisted that nearly all the middle- and upper-class children returned to their studies. "Take the kukhoosh, for example. He was grib'gahner for six years, and built quite a little business for himself during that time. But he reached a point where he knew that if he wanted to be really successful, he needed the knowledge of his ancestors, as well as the knowledge of the streets. So he went back to school. It wasn't easy, for he kept his business going the whole time, but he was motivated to do it. Three years, and he had caught up with those of his fellows who stayed in school the entire time."

The idea was foreign to Robinson, who had been in school all his life, first as a student and now as a professor. But he saw an opportunity to return some of Marta's needling. "And you?" he teased. "Were you ever grib'gahner?"

Marta laughed freely. "Oh, Sab Robinson, I was as restless as they come!"

"And did you travel with your father's caravans during those years?" he asked, leaning back in his chair and stretching long legs before him.

Marta watched him appreciatively. There was such a casual grace to him. How athletic! How male. His blond hair shone in the sun, and little lines crinkled around his eyes and mouth when he smiled. "That was when I married Retneyabo, of course," she answered.

The smile disappeared from Robinson's face. "And how old were you?" he asked in disbelief.

"Thirteen," Marta replied. "That is the usual age for a *sib-batnai,* a child-wife."

One look at his startled face and Marta sighed. "Did you learn *nothing* of our customs before you came?" she asked.

"There is not much available," he defended. "Not even a copy of your Manifest Revelations."

Marta shrugged. "We prefer not to be the object of scrutiny by the unenlightened," was her explanation.

Then she launched into the marriage customs of the Innantans, following guidelines set down by the Holy
Ones. There were many kinds of contract marriages,
with six grades of husband and six grades of wife. Either
sex could have more than one spouse, but there were
strict limits on the number of children allowed. Those
were fairly recent; there was limited arable land on the
continent, and the Holy Ones were concerned lest the
people should overtax the resources of their world. So
each woman was allowed only two children, with which-
ever husband she chose. A marriage contract always
specified who would retain custody of the children if and
when the contract was terminated.

A *sib-dhrusna,* for instance, had several husbands of
equal status to herself, but on an almost revolving basis.
This kind of wife was preferred by men who traveled
much—she was available while they were in town, and
someone else's worry while they were away. Children
were nearly always left in the care of their mother in
such a marriage, since their paternity was uncertain.

A *sib-nurah,* however, was a subservient wife—that is,
of lesser status than her husband—and children of such
a marriage usually stayed with their father. When that
happened, however, the father had to have a *sib-apafa,*
a mother-wife, to care for the children. It was unthinkable for a child to have no proper mother. The sib-apafa
was also responsible for running her husband's household, and her contract was a lifetime one.

Having more than two children became a status sym-
bol for a man. He had to be wealthy enough to support
not only the children, but multiple wives, since one must
be a sib-apafa. When Retneyabo was an up-and-coming
merchant, newly named kukhoosh, his sib-apafa Adni
urged him to seek a child-wife to give him additional
children. A child-wife was particularly expensive, since
once she had borne her children she became a sib-hinan,
and her husband was required to sponsor the rest of
her education.

"That is how I come to be in this enviable position,"
Marta told her gape-mouthed listener. "The kukhoosh

is obliged to sponsor me for as long as I wish to stay at the University, and then to start me in a career. And now he is considering taking yet another sib-batnai,'' she added proudly. "So you see, he is very, very rich.''

"So I gather,'' Robinson managed, quite taken aback by the frank nature of the arrangements she had just discussed. Then his eyes widened as he remembered an olive-skinned cherub he had spotted in Retneyabo's garden the day before. "At his house yesterday, I saw a little girl—maybe six or seven years old. Was she—?''

Marta beamed, pushing her chair back from the table and coming to her feet. "My daughter,'' she said proudly. "I have a boy, too; he's ten. But he was out sailing with his older brother.''

"Half brother, you mean,'' Robinson guessed.

Marta shrugged and headed for the stairs. "We don't distinguish. A brother is a brother.''

Robinson followed her as she trotted down the exterior staircase to the street. "And Retneyabo's other wife—Adni?—she isn't jealous of you?''

Marta laughed. "Why? I'm hardly ever there. I live at University now. Besides.'' She smiled fondly. "A sib-batnai has only the status of a child in the household, and most of us become like daughters to the sib-apafa. That is how it is with Adni and me. I call her Mother, just as my children do.''

Robinson shook his head as he followed her through the crowded street. "There's not a woman on my world who would go for that kind of arrangement,'' he declared. "I can't even date two different girls at the same time without them turning into raving maniacs.''

"That's because you don't have everything spelled out in a contract,'' Marta admonished.

"I think there's more to it than that,'' Robinson murmured.

"Well . . . some sib-apafael can be jealous,'' Marta had to admit, "in spite of their contracts.'' Her own mother Haghir—that is, her father's sib-apafa who raised her—had been one such. Marta's birth mother Shaylah was a sib-nurah whom her father took along on caravan, prop-

erly leaving his mother-wife at home to manage the
household and raise the children. Shaylah was beautiful
and seductive, something of a legend in the bazaar. It
frightened Haghir that Marta's father took the same sib-
nurah every year when he went out with the caravans.
She was afraid he would want to bring her into the house
and keep her there.

But Shaylah, a poor but practical woman, had other
ideas. One year when Marta's father went to make his
seasonal contract with Shaylah, her brother told him that
she had contracted with another caravaner as his *sib-lur,*
a lifetime wife, with an option to become his sib-apafa
if she proved a suitable mother and manager. Though
Marta was too young to remember, only six or seven at
the time, she had heard often enough from gossipy old
drovers how despondent her father had been. Haghir,
however, was elated, and that much Marta *did* remember. From then on Haghir always went to the bazaar
and chose her husband's sib-nurah for him.

Marta did not trouble the Unbeliever with that tale,
however. All she said was, "Jealousy is frowned on. The
Holy Ones can hardly forbid it, any more than they can
forbid covetousness or lust, but they do forbid acting
upon it."

Half a kilometer from the spice shop, they approached
an intersection where a fountain splashed into a shallow
pool. Children of all ages were wading in the fountain,
and mothers squatted nearby, resting and gossiping.
There were also a number of women in colorful shifts
which fell to their toes but left arms and neck bare. "The
wife market," Marta pointed out. "Sure you don't want
to shop a little?"

"Not today," Robinson declined with a wise smile
which said he wasn't going to succumb to her teasing.
"And is there also a husband market in the bazaar?"

Marta snorted. "The entire bazaar is a husband market," she replied. "The men move around; these women
shop by staying in one place."

Robinson had to concede the logic of that. But he

hadn't made his point yet. "If a man like Retneyabo can have two wives," he pressed, "can a woman—not a sib-nurah, but one who has a lifetime contract—can she have a second husband?"

"It depends on the contract," Marta replied, weaving her way through half a dozen sheep being herded down the street. "A sib-apafa, no—she's expected to devote her time to her children and her household affairs. But a sib-lur, yes. She can take a temporary husband of lesser status, but any children would belong to her life-time husband. And such an arrangement is expensive." Marta held out an arm to keep Robinson from stepping in an unsavory deposit on the street.

"It is more common," she continued, taking his arm and steering him around the little pile, "to find a rich widow taking a *sab-bitnai,* a child-husband, or a *sab-hinon,* a student-husband. I know one widow who sup-ports three student-husbands. She is considered a very charitable woman, to share her wealth with three Uni-versity students." Marta smirked. "Of course, if you saw her, you would understand why her husbands spend so much time on their studies."

Again Robinson could only shake his head. "I thought the Children of the Second Revelation were a very fund-amentalist religion," he marveled. "Multiple wives are an ancient custom, but I'm frankly surprised about the multiple husbands. I didn't expect such a . . . shall we say, progressive, development."

They were at the fountain now, and Marta was scan-ning the crowd, looking for her hirelings. "There is a very simple explanation," she told him, climbing up on the low wall of the pool to get a better look. "The Sec-ond Revelation came to three Holy Ones—and one of them was a woman." She frowned a little as her search produced no results. "That boy should be here by now. I hope I didn't make a mistake."

"He probably just got sidetracked," Robinson sug-gested, determined to bring this conversation around to his personal concern. "So how about you? In your status

as a sib-hinan, are you allowed to take a second
husband?''

"Only if I am willing to give up my financial support
from the kukhoosh," she replied, still scanning the
crowd. "And I'm not—look!"

Even as she spoke, there was a sharp cry from a
nearby shop where a knot of people seemed involved in
a scuffle. "That's Tookh!" Marta cried, and she bolted
for the open doorway.

Robinson was hot behind her, fending off a wake of
bodies that Marta pushed aside in her haste. "Wait!" he
called after her. "Marta, for Pete's sake, don't—"

But Marta was already inside, diving into the fray.
Two men had hold of Tookh, who looked about to faint
from pain, while two others looked on with vicious grins.
One had a piece of firewood in his right hand like a club.
Marta snatched up a crockery jar by its open mouth and
swung it two-handed toward the club wielder; it smashed
across his skull, shattering to bits and sending him
sprawling. Without waiting to see if he got up, she leapt
on the back of another brute and locked her right arm
around his neck in a choke hold.

Robinson burst into the shop to see one man down
and Marta riding the back of another like a monkey.
The boy Tookh sagged against a wall moaning, with two
mean-faced men in trousers and open blouses leaving
him to move in on Marta. With a guttural cry, the Unbeliever launched a vicious kick at the knee of the closest
one and was rewarded with a howl of pain as the man
went down. Then he turned to the remaining man, lowered his shoulder, and charged.

Marta saw the two of them go down, but she had no
time to feel any relief at Robinson's aid. Even as the
man she straddled tried to claw her from his back, three
more strong-arms emerged from the back of the shop,
their faces twisted by cruel mocking smiles. "Ho-ho,
Sibna!" one called. "Does the hawk fly at a bull?"

Glancing up, she recognized the speaker—Kadnar,
one of Paun's roughnecks. "To pluck out his eyes," she
snarled, curling her toes and slamming the hard edge

of her sandal savagely at the kidney of the man she was strangling.

The two men with Kadnar pounced on Robinson, tearing him off his opponent as Kadnar circled behind Marta. "Even if you bring the bull to his knees," he said, "you can't escape the fowler."

Marta sank her teeth into the pawing hand of her victim, then suddenly released him as he howled in pain and lurched forward. Pushing off from his back, she dropped to the floor and landed nimbly in a crouched position, facing the speaker. "I see no fowler, Kadnar," she hissed. "And I know I can geld an ass like you!" Then she feinted quickly toward his groin, and as he pulled his hips back instinctively, she locked her fists together and swung them in a double uppercut to his jaw.

Kadnar staggered back but did not go down, and Marta knew she was in trouble. One of the others had Robinson's arm twisted behind him and had forced the Unbeliever up against the wall near Tookh; two more were closing in on her from behind.

Suddenly a hand appeared on Kadnar's shoulder, and he was spun away like a toy. Ibna loomed over the scene.

"Go home," Ibna said simply.

The man holding Robinson released him; the two behind Marta stopped their advance and slowly backed away. The hand-bitten one snarled, but he, too, retreated. Flanking Ibna in the doorway were four tough, stringy drovers. Marta straightened up and inhaled deeply, then cast a fierce look at Kadnar. "Take that piece of garbage," she said, indicating the man she had brained with the pot, "and get him to Infirmary. They can send his bill to Paun."

Kadnar signaled to his men, who picked up their fallen comrade and melted out the back door of the shop.

Marta turned to the proprietor, who skulked behind a counter in the far corner. "You keep poor company," she informed him, fishing in her belt for a coin. "But I will pay for the pot I broke. Here." She flipped the coin in his direction. "My patron is as generous as yours is unworthy." Then she turned and stalked out.

Outside in the sunshine they regrouped. "Are you all right, Sab Robinson?" Marta asked, brushing at the dust on his blouse and ignoring the pain in her own ankle. He had handled himself well for a scholar more accustomed to trading insults than blows.

"I'll be sore for a few days," he promised, still panting a little, "but that's about it. They didn't seem bent on injuring me."

"They weren't," she said bluntly. Not a single blade had appeared during the fight, which spoke to their true intentions. "But the boy is not so lucky, I think." She turned to Tookh, who was being partially supported by one of the drovers.

"Broken arm," Ibna pronounced.

"Ai," Marta hissed, clicking her tongue as she made a visual examination of the injured limb. "Those motherless sons of jackals." Taking the boy's face in one hand, she turned it right and left, checking his pupils. "Three-legged swine," she muttered. "Bottom-feeding *lastimaki*. Pray they don't meet *me* again."

"They followed me from the olive oil shop," Tookh whimpered, his face pale and sweaty from the pain. "I saw them, and I thought to duck into that sweet shop. I thought it would be safe."

"No place is safe from such manure-eaters," she maintained, adding several choice phrases in her native tongue.

"They were waiting for you," Tookh continued. "They told me to call out to you, but I wouldn't do it. They hit me, but I still wouldn't. So the one with the striped blouse took a club and . . ."

"And broke your arm to make you cry out," Marta finished, pushing his sweat-dampened curls back from his forehead with a gentle hand. "Is that the one I brained with the jar?"

A faint smile colored the boy's lips.

"Then justice is served." She turned to the drover who stood by them. "Take him to Infirmary, tell them he is a client of Kukhoosh Retneyabo. I will come by later to square things away."

Now fear filled Tookh's eyes. "I can still come, can't I?" he asked anxiously. "To Dhin M'Tarkhna? It's only a broken arm. I can beat the donkeys with my other hand, they won't know the difference."

Marta exchanged a look with Ibna. Then, "We can't let Paun win, not even in such a little thing; it would shame our patron. I'm going to hire a medtech anyway, you can be his first patient. If the doctor at Infirmary says it won't endanger you, you can come."

As Tookh and his companion started off down the street, Ibna turned to Marta. "Shall I find another drover?" he asked quietly.

"No, no, you'll injure the boy's pride," she replied just as softly. "Get a cook, though—a woman. A pair of hands weaker than his, but an extra pair nonetheless."

A broad smile appeared like a rift in the giant's beard. "Any kind of a woman?"

"As long as she can cook," Marta admonished.

Ibna turned to his drovers. "Come, children, let us see which of Makutna's women can cook." Grinning like a pack of dogs, the men moved off toward the farside of the plaza.

Marta turned her steps in the opposite direction, and Robinson fell in beside her. "I thought you said there was no prostitution here," he chided.

"There's not!" she defended. "They are seeking a sib-dhrusna, a wife who will contract with each of them. Makutna charges a steep commission, but he screens his clients very carefully—on both sides. Ibna is a man of discriminating taste."

She tried to walk normally, but they hadn't gone ten paces when Robinson noticed her slight limp. "Are you hurt?" he demanded, catching her arm and hauling her up short.

Marta looked up into those blue eyes, blazing with concern now, and made an impatient face. "I landed wrong when I jumped off that mongrel's back," she dismissed. "It's just a little sprain. The best thing is to walk it off." Pulling away from him, she plunged back into the stream of humanity that flowed along the streets of the bazaar. But she walked gingerly, her eyes constantly scanning the faces around her. Paun's men could be anywhere.

Robinson slipped into her wake, but he no longer followed blindly; he, too, watched the people around them with suspicion, carefully checking their surroundings for possible hiding places and escape routes. "You hadn't really planned to hire a medtech, had you?" he asked after a few moments.

Marta was nettled more by the embarrassment of her own incaution than by the pain in her ankle. "An oversight," she said brusquely, for it truly was. "I should have thought of it before. Foolish to go into Dhin M'Tarkhna without a medtech."

They walked on in silence. Then he ventured, "You didn't know Paun was going to get this rough, did you?"

Marta shrugged, but her characteristic nonchalance was gone. "It was a delaying tactic, that's all," she said firmly. "Fortunately, Paun knows better than to cause an interstellar incident by doing serious injury to an Unbeliever. Innanta does not want that kind of attention."

He was quiet a moment longer. Then, "Define serious," he said.

Marta sighed. "They want to frighten you. Don't let them. It would have been a simple thing for them to cut you, or break one of *your* bones, to slow down our expedition—but they didn't do that. Even Paun knows there are limits."

But as she limped on toward the tentmaker's shop, Marta remembered Kadnar's words and knew that kidnapping was well within those limits.

CHAPTER 5

"Jinka is not so beautiful as that today," Ari whispered to Mohat as his father waxed on about the glory of that oldest of cities. *"It's got lots of crumbling buildings, and the harbor stinks, and it's full of pickpockets and thieves."*

Hassan heard the remark. *"Ah, but I speak of its golden age,"* he pointed out. *"Long before Mimma and Sedet Narashi rose to be the great centers of commerce they are today. In those days, the caravans went from east to west and back, and not the other way around."*

"What happened to make it change?" the boy wanted to know.

Hassan gave a knowing smile. *"Marta happened, my son. Marta happened."*

When the last tail of the last donkey had disappeared over the rise, Marta breathed a sigh of relief. She tapped two words into her pocketpad—UNDER WAY—and hit the transmit key. The message would be received by Innanta's single communications satellite, locked in orbit over the continent, and bounced back down to the College of Indigenous Life. That done, Marta tucked the palm-sized unit into a storage compartment in her electric cart, where the fabulously expensive little piece of equipment would sit for the next four months. Barring emergencies, there would be no more communication from her team to the College until they returned with their information. She didn't want Shipner's team to be able to locate them from their transmissions.

Glancing at the Unbeliever on the seat beside her, Marta saw that he did not share her relief in leaving the hill town of Ballabim behind them. He did not know how she had sweated out those last couple of days in Jinka, posting Retneyabo's guards surreptitiously near Robinson's apartment and her own, setting Ibna to keep constant watch over their supplies and equipment until departure. Their first night on the road, she had hardly slept for keeping one eye on the innkeeper and the other on his burly nephew, wondering if Paun had bought one or both of them. Even in Ballabim, where they stayed at the home of her father's cousin, she insisted that one of her own people stand watch at the security monitors. What Paun had tried once, Paun might try again.

Robinson, however, knew only that the beds at Ballabim had been soft and the food succulent. On the trail, there would be only sleeping mats and travel rations. He looked positively grumpy.

Marta turned the ignition switch and put the little cart in gear. "You are not happy, Sab Robinson," she remarked as she steered the vehicle back onto the roadway, following the vanished tail of the vanished last donkey.

He shot her a sideways glance. "I'm fine. I just don't understand why we aren't at the head of the column, instead of eating the dust at the end like this."

"I'm not concerned for what's ahead of us," she replied, powering the woven sides of the cart up high enough to block out the dust of her own wheels, but not so high that they restricted her vision. "But what may be following us—that I am concerned about."

Robinson grunted, but after a moment he gave a backward glance. It was futile; between the hanging dust and the glare of the rising sun, there was no way to see anything on the trail behind them.

"Don't worry, though, we aren't going to eat the dust of the donkeys in front of us," she promised. "That is for Ibna's drovers, who will alternate their positions along the train as they travel so that no one man swallows too much dust. No, you and I," she said with a sudden dazzling smile, "are going to take a little detour." And with that she dropped the sidescreens from the roof and gunned the small electric motor.

There were three main caravan routes leading out of Ballabim. One bore to the northwest, through the rugged foothills where the Maknial Mountains plunged down toward the sea. The people of this region were well-known for their artistry in dyeing and weaving. Merchant caravans regularly brought them cereal grains and manufactured goods in exchange for their textiles.

The southern caravan route snaked southward through the rolling hills for two hundred miles before bending sharply to the southwest. There in the temperate reaches of the continent, it serviced a hundred small towns and villages. At any given time of the year one was likely to encounter a different caravan every forty or fifty miles, as likely to be motorized vehicles as traditional camels. It was the most heavily traveled of the three routes.

The central track which Marta and her entourage followed struck almost due west for nearly a thousand kilometers, into the Western Desert. It zigzagged a bit through the southern roots of the Maknial Mountains just where they rimmed the infamous Dhin M'Tarkhna, the Valley of Desolation; but then it stretched back out into a featureless track that bore on through the high sandy desert to the sea.

It was on this trail that Marta had bounced through the springs and autumns of her childhood, first in a sheltering *sudha*, a boothlike structure mounted on a camel, then astride a camel or a donkey of her own. Schooling was for the blistering summer months, when one needed the shelter of buildings and the cooling sea breeze, or for the raw winter months, when a fire and a warm robe made reading a pleasure. But during the moderate seasons young Marta, like her father, could hardly be contained by bricks and mortar, stone and wood. It was the School of Life for Marta, pestering the drovers with her questions, wrestling in the dirt with other children, hunting among the rocks for fool's gold, peeking into the tents at night to learn the secret ways of men and women. As her father's unofficial apprentice, soon she knew every landmark in a terrain which confounded the untutored eye, knew just how far a camel or donkey could travel in a day, knew to an ounce how much water must be carried to make each leg of the trip. She waded in the Western Ocean at one end of her journey and the Eastern Ocean at the other.

But at eleven she had suddenly sprouted womanly features, and her father would take her no more among the rough caravaners. "Why?" Marta protested vigorously. "No one would *dare* to touch me."

"That is exactly why," her father had retorted. "It is cruel to tease an animal with food it cannot eat."

It was a lesson Marta never mastered. As rapidly as she learned to accept her new feminine traits, she learned to capitalize on them. In her father's house, servants walked into walls; gardeners clipped the wrong plants; stableboys misstepped into camel dung. Everywhere young Marta glided, male eyes trailed after her until her mother wailed that disaster was unavoidable. Something had to be done.

It was then that Marta's father spoke to her of the young but influential Kukhoosh Retneyabo, who sought a child-wife. "He is a good man and devout; fair with his clients and generous to his friends and family," he told her. "No doubt he will be the same with his wife." Mother was more effusive—what an honor, to be even considered by the great kukhoosh! He had garnered great glory already, and was sure to gain more. Wealth beyond measure! Influence at the highest level. Marta could hope for no better husband in the entire universe.

Mother's zeal did not impress Marta, but Father's quiet confidence did. There was nothing he didn't know about caravaning; that made his judgment unfailing in her eyes. If Father thought Retneyabo was a good choice, then he was.

But Marta was not the only girl being considered. They were invited to call on Retneyabo at his estate, along with three other girls and their parents. "Oh, I shall snare him, never fear," Marta assured her mother.

(She would never dare speak so brazenly to her father. Pride was a sin.) And she practiced her most seductive looks in the mirror, rehearsed a half dozen remarks filled with innuendo, and polished the nails of her toes a brilliant red.

"Modesty!" her mother begged, but Marta only laughed. None of the men on the caravans cherished modesty, and those were the only men Marta really knew.

The big day came, and Marta arrived at the kukhoosh's fine house in Jinka—for he had not yet acquired the estate down the coast—dressed in her finest woolen gown, bleached a brilliant white, and dainty sandals of white leather. She looked her competition up and down as they awaited the great Retneyabo, and saw nothing that worried her. They sat primly in their latsa chairs in the garden, speaking only when spoken to, fidgeting with their beads and having their hands slapped for their trouble. Marta lounged in her chair, looking around at the lush trees and shrubs, exclaiming over the profusion of colorful flowers, and taking thinly veiled jibes at the other girls.

Adni came to greet them first, and Marta instantly liked the kukhoosh's sib-apafa. She was lovely and round, with plump cheeks and two chins, and her voice was like music. It made Marta feel warm inside when Adni greeted her, and a large smile splashed across the young girl's face.

Then Retneyabo himself appeared, and while the other girls blushed and made polite bows, Marta looked him over with frank curiosity, so that her mother threw an elbow into the young girl's ribs to remind her of her manners. Marta winced and gave her mother a small pout before she made a most elegant half bow, the epitome of respect; then she glanced up from under her long lashes to see how the kukhoosh liked it. He gave her a sly wink, which she took to mean he liked it very much, indeed.

The kukhoosh visited with the parents briefly, then he asked each of the girls one or two questions. He tried to catch Marta not paying attention, for she had become fascinated with a bird roosting in a nearby tree. Marta had never seen a bird in a tree before, since there were none native to Innanta, and the only ones brought along by the settlers were fat fowl which waddled on the ground. But this was a rare songbird, which Retneyabo had somehow managed to get imported—what a clever man he must be, to get that approved!—and its bright yellow breast had caught Marta's eye. She had not lost the conversation, though, so that when the kukhoosh directed a question to her, she answered quickly and accurately—then brazenly asked *him* how he'd gotten such a bird. His curling black beard split in a smile. "The All-Gracious has been generous," was all he said, and went back to his questioning of the other girls.

When Adni called for refreshments, Retneyabo excused himself, and Marta immediately lost interest in the proceedings. While the others chewed on tasty *minim* and crunched little pickled peppers, she slipped away into the garden and began to inspect all the exotic plants the kukhoosh kept. There was a peach tree, its fruit just beginning to ripen, and a strawberry plant spilling out of a marble planter. Now, that was something you didn't see just anywhere. There was a shrub she didn't recognize full of yellow blossoms and emitting the most *heavenly* fragrance. And as the chattering voices faded behind her, she came upon a patch of the softest, greenest grass she had ever seen. It was thick as a carpet and green as emeralds, and Marta couldn't resist kicking off her sandals and dancing barefoot on this lush mat. Then she sprawled herself upon it, inhaling the pungent odor of the blades, and rolled over onto her back to gaze up at the blue sky in contentment.

After a moment she became aware that someone was watching her. Glancing up she saw Retneyabo standing on the path, his hands clasped behind his back and his keen brown eyes taking in her antics. "Not a very modest posture," he observed.

Marta got slowly to her feet and stood insolently staring back at him. "I'm not a very modest girl, I'm afraid," she said frankly.

Still he stood with his hands behind his back, watching her. Marta was accustomed to having men watch her, but there was something different about the way Retneyabo looked at her. It was as though, she realized with a shiver, he was looking not *at* her but *inside* her. *Well, this is what I am,* she thought, *and you might as well know it. That way you won't be disappointed later.* So she sauntered slowly across the green grass and stood directly in front of him, looking up into his examining eyes.

He was a tall man, though at thirty-three not yet as portly as he would later become. As he returned her gaze, Marta felt something she could not describe; she was suddenly aware of his maleness in a way she had never experienced before. It made her heart race, and her blood surged outward toward her skin in a delicious flush.

Had he felt it, too? Perhaps, because, "It isn't proper for you to be alone here with me," he reminded her.

Marta shrugged, a shifting of her shoulders which made the folds of her dress do enticing things across her young body. "You're not a man to behave improperly," she said with confidence. "And even if you did, you're honorable enough to rectify it with a marriage contract. And that's what I want, anyway."

"Someone ought to marry you, that is certain," he replied, still looking down at her with his hands clasped behind his back. "The All-Giving has granted you an extra portion of carnality, and it would be a sacrilege to waste it."

It was one of the Manifest Revelations that humanity's sexual nature was a gift in which to rejoice, not a liability to be overcome. Being a devout man, the kukhoosh arranged an immediate wedding; and although the contract Marta's father signed insisted that there be no intercourse for the first six months—for his daughter's tender years worried him, and he thought to give her a gradual introduction to such mysteries—Retneyabo knew a variety of other ways to give and take pleasure with his new bride. Marta partook of them all eagerly, and gave thanks to the All-Giving for the attentions of such a resourceful husband.

Marriage and childbearing did little to cool Marta's rambunctious nature, however. So with her newborn son in a sling at her breast, Marta accompanied her father—now Retneyabo's client—on a caravan to the west. Such permissiveness on the kukhoosh's part—letting his infant son venture into the desert—raised more than a few eyebrows, but the journey occurred without incident. Furthermore, it so enlivened Marta's spirits that the scandalous event was repeated after the birth of her daughter two years later. Then, with the girl weaned and both children in Adni's care, Marta spent an entire year as her father's assistant before returning to Retneyabo's house to resume her studies.

Having fulfilled her part of the bargain by bearing the kukhoosh two healthy children, Marta now moved to the status of a sib-hinan, a student wife; and with careful motivation from Retneyabo, in two years she qualified herself for University. After two semesters of study, she went with five other students and three faculty members on a field trip to the Maknial Mountains in search of *radakits,* a grublike creature which inhabited the bark of *taliyeko* trees normally, but which had suddenly attacked domestic coffee plants with devastating consequences.

The group made significant finds in their field lab, but found themselves imperiled when their guide came down with *adjeni* fever. It was Marta who diagnosed the raving man, instructing everyone to rub their skin, head to foot, with the leaves of the *bura-bura* vine. A toxin in that plant's leaves killed the eggs of the tiny insects which carried the fever. Then she built a travois, loaded the sick man on it, attached it to a donkey, and started boldly down the mountain to the north in search of a village where proper medicines might be found. Two weeks later she reappeared and guided her party back down the southern side of the mountains to where they had left their electric carts, and thence home again.

Thus began her career as a wilderness guide. Now here she was, at twenty-four, a seasoned veteran of caravans and field expeditions, guiding yet another party into the Western Desert. Propelling her cart up a sandy rise, she stopped it with a lurch and sat looking down with satisfaction on the train of pack animals and drovers carrying their equipment westward toward the rim of Dhin M'Tarkhna.

Turning to her companion, she grinned impishly. "Aren't you excited to be under way, Sab Robinson?" she asked.

He waved away the dust which swirled around them, seeping in through the woven sides and transparent screens which now enclosed the vehicle. "I'd be more excited if I had a filtration mask," he grumbled.

"You complain like an old woman!" She laughed. "See now, if we drive along the crest here, we can jump back down onto the trail ahead of the donkeys. Then we can go ahead to the first resting place to wait for them."

"If you don't tip this thing and get us killed first," he retorted.

Marta laughed again and threw the cart into gear.

"And so they left beautiful Jinka behind and traveled into the Western Desert," Hassan said, then paused to take a drink as though the upcoming passage parched him already. "There the sun grew fierce in the sky above them, scorching the pale skin of the Unbeliever; and the sand cut through their garments like shards of glass."

Ari nodded to himself. Yes, that was just what the sand felt like! He felt a strong kinship with the legendary Marta. "Yet they persevered," Hassan continued. "Marta assured her companion that all would be well, 'For the All-Knowing watches over us,' she told him, 'and protects us from harm.' Then she recited aloud from the Manifest Revelations of the Holy Ones, and their pain was eased and their minds were made at peace . . ."

It was their third night on the trail, and Marta was beginning to be genuinely irritated. From morning prayer to evening prayer, their days had been uneventful—and from evening prayer to morning prayer, as well. Though Marta turned her most charming smiles on the Unbeliever, all he did was complain about the fiber sleeping mat and the tasteless food. After the sweltering day, when at last the wind died back to a cooling breeze and the sunset's iridescent flames lit the western sky, couldn't he find something else to speak of? Oranges, yellows, reds, and all shades in between surged along the dust-filled horizon with a glory so palpable it almost sang. Didn't something surge within him, too?

It certainly surged within Marta. As the day's heat fled from the baking earth into the cloudless sky, and the tiny native life-forms creaked and chirped for joy, she would sit with Sibna Egthassa, a faculty member who accompanied them, and gaze up at the panoply of stars. Kobanan, another graduate student, would stretch out on the warm earth with his head in Sibna Egthassa's lap and tell them stories about the constellations. "Sab Robinson, come join us!" Marta would call.

But, "No thanks," the Unbeliever would reply. "I'm beat." And off he would go to his tent.

What was wrong with the man?

Now, on this third night, Sibna Egthassa turned to Marta after the Unbeliever had gone. "Doesn't he like you?" she asked.

"I don't know what's wrong with him," Marta growled.

"Have you explained to him what the Holy Ones say about sib-hinans?" Kobanan asked. Kobanan himself was a sab-hinan, one of three student-husbands of the infamous widow Marta had told Robinson about.

"I'm sure I did," Marta grumped. "We were in the bazaar, and I explained that the status is more like a child . . ." But they had been interrupted by the fight. Had she finished?

Marta glanced at Robinson's tent and wondered how she could broach the subject without being *too* obvious. After all, it was forbidden to force their ways upon the

Unbeliever. And he had repeatedly turned down the temporary wives in the bazaar, so perhaps . . .

Still, she decided to make one more attempt. Crossing to his tent, she called softly, "Sab Robinson, are you comfortable?" If he would only come to the door of his tent . . .

From within came a heavy sigh. "Yes, Marta, I'm fine, thank you."

If she had believed he meant it, she would have been highly insulted. But it had the ring of politeness, and not truth. So she offered once more. "If there is anything I can do for you, my tent is just across the way."

Cecil Robinson lay on his mat, staring wide-eyed at the ceiling of his tent and trying desperately to will the restlessness from his loins. *She's married,* he reminded himself. *Married, married, married. And to whom? Your patron, no less! The man who brought you here! The man who is going to make you the most famous zoologist of this age.*

But God, she was beautiful! Even in her desert gear: baggy trousers and tunic which protected her delicious skin from the scorching sun. Even with grime on her elegant cheekbones and sweat darkening the brim of her hat, the woman was positively alluring. With fire in her dark eyes she trudged up and down the line of men and beasts, admonishing this one, laughing with that one, cautioning the boy Tookh to drink his water sparingly. Then, as though this were a pleasure trip to the beach instead of a grueling trek into the wilderness, she'd jump back into her electric cart and race up the precipitous side of a rock outcropping at breakneck speed, there to scan the landscape and laugh at Robinson's trepidation.

If only she didn't tease him so mercilessly! How many times during the day did she glance his way with sly eyes, as if to say, *Aren't I a delectable creature? Don't you wish you could have me?* How many times had she reached out to straighten the flap of his tunic or playfully add a streak of dust to his sweaty face, and sent volts of electricity crackling through his body? Didn't she have any idea what that did to him?

Of course, she did, he thought in disgust. She knew *exactly* what she was doing to him. She was playing him like a tightly strung fiddle, and he sang helplessly along. This had to stop. This had to stop! It just wasn't fair for her to taunt him like this.

Leaping up from his mat, he charged toward the tent door. He'd tell her, that's what he'd do. He'd just tell her that she had to back off, or he'd do something that would inspire that fellow Ibna to separate his head from his body. And Robinson didn't intend to receive his Ashdod Prize posthumously.

At the door to her tent he hesitated, overwhelmed by thoughts of how she would look in moonlight . . . No. He could do this. He had to. "Marta," he called softly.

At first there was no answer. Then abruptly the tent flap was flung back, and there she stood.

In the privacy of her tent, she had obviously stripped out of her clothing for sleep; but hearing his voice, she had carelessly thrown her tunic back on. It barely reached to her thighs, and he saw for the first time the firm, slim legs that he had tortured himself imagining. Furthermore, she had not belted the garment; it hung loose, closed in front only by its own weight. Every rational thought and good intention Robinson had possessed fled precipitously.

With a flick of her head, Marta motioned him inside, and he obeyed. There he stood staring at her, completely speechless.

Then suddenly she was in his arms, her mouth fastened on his, and he was clutching her desperately. Had she moved first, or had he? Did it matter? The heat and hunger in her kiss were all too obvious.

Finally she pulled her lips away and he gasped for breath.

"What took you so long?" she demanded, her arms locked around his neck and her silken legs wrapped around his waist. Now, how had she gotten into that position? He didn't know. He didn't care.

"I—But you're married," he stammered, his beleaguered brain kicking out this one phrase.

"I am a sib-hinan," she explained impatiently. "When my husband is more than a day's travel away, my vow of fidelity is abrogated. Didn't I tell you?" She planted another passionate kiss on his mouth.

"But—your religion," he stammered. "Doesn't—I mean, won't your god strike you dead for this sort of thing?"

Marta laughed and licked at his ear. "It's all right," she whispered. "Since sib-hinans are often absent from their spouses, the Holy Ones have declared we can make impromptu arrangements." She buried her fingers in his thick blond hair. "It is not healthy, you know, to go unfulfilled for long periods of time."

Robinson still didn't understand it. But he was through asking questions.

CHAPTER 6

"Remember, my children," Hassan told the two boys, "the All-Giving provides for our every need. While Marta and the Unbeliever journeyed into the desert, the All-Merciful sent clouds to shade them by day, and rain to cool their faces and replenish them by night. And when danger approached, he sent a winged messenger—"

"An angel?" Ari squealed in astonishment.

"An angel, yes," Hassan affirmed. "With eyes of fire and lips like glowing embers. His beard was the blazing sunset in the west, and in his hands he carried a bolt of lightning. 'Beware,' the angel told them. 'Beware, for those you fear come upon you. Rise up and go as the All-Hallowed commands, by a path that I shall tell you . . ."

They were six days out from Ballabim when Marta discovered they were being followed.

"How do you know?" Robinson asked, bewildered by the suddenness of her statement. The two of them were trailing behind the column by half a mile, saved from most of the dust by a cooling southeasterly breeze which wafted the plume of their passage toward the impending Maknial Mountains.

By way of answer she held out a small insect which she had pinched off her tunic. It looked like a yellowish brown mosquito. "Camel gnat," she told him. "Native insect which originally infested the fibrous flowers of the *tadjesk* tree—until we came, and it developed a taste for camel hair." She flicked the pest out the open side of the car. "It cannot venture beyond ten kilometers from its host. Tadjesk trees are coastal, and you may have noticed we have no camels with us."

Pulling off to the side, Marta looked back over the trail behind them and considered. Uncomfortable, Robinson glanced back as well.

"They've probably been with us for a couple of days," she decided. "Just keeping track of us, is my guess. It's too soon for Shipner to be out of Infirmary."

Robinson slouched down in the seat. "You don't know Shipner."

"No, but I know our native viruses and bacteria," she replied. "The series of inoculations you received upon arrival took two weeks, did it not? He will require the same." But she saw the darkness that had settled over Robinson's face.

"I'll send Gladnas and Mettikapu back tonight to spot their camp," she told him, shifting the cart back into gear and starting down the trail. "Perhaps we can divert them somehow."

At nightfall the two spies slipped out of camp, and within two hours returned to report that, indeed, three men on camels were camped beside the trail about a kilometer to the east of them. They carried no equipment, slept in the open, and kept their cooking fire very small and smokeless. At Marta's instruction, the spies had not ventured close enough to overhear conversations.

"If they are only travelers, they will overtake us tomorrow," she told Robinson. "If they do not, we can assume they are spying on us."

The following day brought no contact with the three strangers.

"So what do we do now?" Robinson asked as they ate their evening meal of fresh flat bread smeared with goat cheese. He hated the cheese—it was strong, smelly stuff which tasted on the verge of being rancid; but his stomach rumbled too much to refuse.

Marta shrugged. "We go on. There is not much else we can do, even if we wanted to."

Robinson studied her face in the starlight. What a maddening creature she was! So perversely logical one moment, so inexplicably mysterious the next. "So we just let them follow us till we find the dinka-chak," he challenged, "so they can tell Shipner and he can move in and reap the rewards for all our hard work."

There was a warning light in Marta's eyes as she flicked her glance his way. "I didn't say that," she said quietly. Seated nearby, Kobanan and Egthassa shifted uncomfortably.

Robinson tried to modify his tone. "He would do that, you know," the Unbeliever explained in a more neutral voice. "Wouldn't think twice about it. He'd call that clever, rather than unethical. You have to realize, in most of the universe, scholars compete with each other for funding, and the program with the most credits gets the most money. It can get pretty ruthless. And Shipner? There's nothing he likes better than snatching success away from someone else."

"We go on as we have," Marta repeated evenly. "Until we reach the Maknial Mountains."

Something told Robinson it was time to shut up, so he did. But later that night he picked up the subject again.

They lay side by side on their sleeping mats, panting and dripping with sweat, waiting for the arid night air to dry them. There was no water for washing on this trip; chemical towelettes were used to scrub off the worst of the trail grime, and Innantans in general took the position that sweating was healthy, not unclean. Certainly Marta was unfazed by the presence of perspiration on his skin, or her own. It diminished her appetite not one whit.

She had done a particularly fine job of exhausting him that evening, but as he contemplated how full of surprises she was, it reminded him of her veiled comment about the Maknial Mountains. "So when we reach the mountains," he asked, "then what?"

"Then I will take you to Nabor's Nest," she replied, "and find out if open air and the light of a full moon will make you even more virile."

The thought caused a stirring he did not think was

possible at that moment. But he persisted. "And what about the three men following us?"

"They can't come."

Robinson laughed in spite of himself.

Finally she rolled over and looked at him in the darkness, reaching out to let one hand trail over his chest hair. "We'll go up into the mountains and lose them," she told him. "Then, while they are searching for us, we'll slip down into Dhin M'Tarkhna. By the time they find the spot where we left the rim, the wind will have blown away all evidence of which way we went. They won't be able to tell your Soln Shipner a thing."

With that she rolled over onto her stomach and went promptly to sleep.

The southern slopes of the Maknial Mountains were a forbidding place, dun-colored ramparts of baked earth creased by gullies and almost devoid of vegetation on their lower reaches. Marta sent Kobanan and Egthassa ahead in the two carts, with one of Ibna's men to show them where there was a cave large enough to shelter the vehicles. They would proceed on foot to a rendezvous point.

The rest of them trekked up into the mountains, along paths that only surefooted donkeys could negotiate, and before the end of the first day Marta had secreted half her animals in another cave, along with two drovers. Before daylight she sent Mettikapu off with a pair of field glasses to make sure the camel riders were following; he reported that they had, indeed, left their animals tethered below and were coming after the scholars on foot. Satisfied, Marta began to move laterally across the slopes toward the west, drawing the spies after her.

On the third day they came to a spring, where they found Kobanan and Egthassa waiting for them. Ibna set up a full camp, and they settled in to observe Sabiss. Robinson did not complain at this delay, luxuriating in the free use of water and the consumption of a genuine feast: roasted chickens, a savory vegetable stew, and baked sweet pudding. A good burgundy would have set it off to a tee, but he settled for cool, fresh water and the ever-present coffee.

The following day the Innantans spent in prayer and recitations from the Book of Books and the Manifest Revelations of the Holy Ones, and in dozing languidly in the shade of a dozen trees growing beside the spring. After moonrise, Marta led the Unbeliever off to a crown-shaped pinnacle, where a slab of rock some four meters across was ringed by jagged spires: Nabor's Nest. When they returned to the spring about an hour before dawn, Robinson was shocked to find the camp deserted, the donkeys and drovers gone, and the two tents they had erected empty.

"What happened?" he demanded.

"I sent the donkeys ahead," Marta replied. "And most of the others." Ibna and Gladnas materialized out of the shadows and began silently disassembling the two tents. "They must reach the rockfall before Paun's men realize they've been duped. Come now, we must move quickly," she directed, collapsing a segmented tent pole and binding it with a cord. "We will go in another direction, to lay a false trail. Then we'll double back and meet the others at the rim. All we need is a day to drop out of sight in Dhin M'Tarkhna; then they'll never be able to find us."

For all of that day they traveled without stopping until at nightfall Marta called a halt and everyone collapsed, scarcely pausing to doff their packs. But two hours later she had them up and moving again, a relentless taskmaster who drove them on until they reached the shelter of a rock overhang only a hundred meters above the caravan trail, where they found the rest of their party. Three hours of sleep, and Marta grabbed the forelock of the lead donkey, guiding it down a sheer sheet of rock, across the caravan trail, and down another stony slope into the valley called Dhin M'Tarkhna.

The terrain was littered with boulders, which had, over the eons, tumbled down the sides of the Maknials and into the dry lake bed below. But there was no soil to speak of, and hardly enough dust to take the imprint of a hoof or sandal. As the sun rose scorchingly· hot in the sky, they found the remaining donkeys clustered in the meager shadow of a house-sized rock, along with the two grinning drovers. "It happened just as you said, Sibna," one reported proudly. "They walked right past our hiding place without turning off the trail. We waited for a day, then came here."

The other man pointed to a mound of stones just beyond the shade line. "We're cooking," he announced. "It should be ready by nightfall."

Marta praised them in terse but sincere phrases. "For the next few days we turn our days and nights around," she instructed everyone. "We travel when it's cool and dark, we rest when the sun neither comforts nor conceals us."

After inspecting all the animals herself and making sure their supplies had survived the hasty descent, Marta dropped wearily to the ground beside Robinson, who had stretched out with his head pillowed on a rolled-up mat. "What will Paun's men do if they can't find our trail?" he asked.

"When," she corrected. "Not if. They will have to go back to their kukhoosh and heap insults upon my name for having outsmarted them. And Soln Shipner will have to find the dinka-chak on his own."

"Good." Robinson scratched at the stubble of beard he hadn't had the time to remove in two days. "So it will take them, what, a week to get back there? By camel? And another week to return here . . ."

"Oh, it will take them longer than that," Marta assured him. "They may have difficulty locating their camels." She took the canteen from her waist and sipped sparingly at its contents.

Robinson cocked a blond eyebrow. "Oh?"

Marta closed her canteen and gestured toward the mound of stones radiating heat in the midday sun. "I suspect one of them is cooking right there."

*   *   *

Fourteen days later they reached the area where Marta and her colleagues had discovered the dead dinka-chak eighteen months earlier. There was no sign of the nomad and his family, who had moved their goats elsewhere long since; but they found the spot where those hardy individuals had pitched their tents and proceeded to make camp there. It was in the lee of a limestone uplift, once a piece of lake floor, so it provided some shelter from the omnipresent wind. There were a few twisted shrubs nearby, too, which indicated a seasonal water source.

When Marta had given all her instructions to Ibna for construction of the camp, the four scholars set out to scout the surrounding territory. Carefully Marta pointed out to the others several landmarks by which they could get their bearings: "See that high ground there? The reddish patch? Now look behind you: there is Mount Silm n'Hraffah on the horizon. If you draw a line between those two, our camp lies along it. And when you get this close . . ." She picked up two loose stones and strode to where a patch of bare limestone provided a clear slate. There she placed her two rocks, the smaller one beside the larger pointing toward the camp. "Wherever we go, we will put markers like this, to help guide us back."

"Why don't we just paint an arrow on the limestone?" Robinson asked.

"Because the sun will fade it," she replied, "and the wind and the sand will scour it away in a couple of weeks. I think we'll be here longer than that."

By nightfall Marta had oriented her companions to the topography and given them basic instructions in keeping track of where they were, and where the camp was. Robinson sorely wished for a simple homing device, or some basic communications equipment, but no such electronics were to be had. "Besides," Marta consoled him when he voiced such a wish, "that would make it easier for Paun's expedition to find us."

That night Marta slipped out of her tent, leaving the

exhausted Unbeliever sleeping soundly inside. She was too excited to sleep. Overhead the stars glittered dispassionately in the ice-black sky, all the brighter for the absence of a moon. It was early autumn now, and the wind had lost its fiery breath at sundown. Marta climbed to the top of the limestone uplift which protected their camp and looked off to the west. The bowl of Dhin M'Tarkhna stretched uninterrupted for another two hundred kilometers before it crept upward to a low range of hills, where hardy trees and shrubs grew along the gullies, and herds of sheep and cattle could once more be found. Less than fifty kilometers beyond those hills lay the sea, abounding with life that offered sustenance to the Children of the Second Revelation.

"Is that where you came from, the sea?" Marta asked quietly of the dinka-chak she believed must be somewhere near. "Did it spit you up onto those hills an eon ago, and did you tumble down this side into Dhin M'Tarkhna? Or have you been here from the time when water covered this valley? Were you a swamp creature first, jumping from place to place, that you developed such powerful hind legs? Or did you run across mudflats to escape your enemies and hunt your prey? Ah, little one," she sighed, "you and I must meet soon, I think. And when we do, you must give me answers."

Everyone participated in the search for the dinka-chak. Marta had a map of the area—incomplete, but she quickly sketched in enough landmarks to make it workable, then divided it into sections and assigned each piece to a team. Only three or four people were left in camp at any given time to prevent a surprise visit by Paun's men, if they should happen to stumble across it. In three days they had crisscrossed all the land within ten kilometers of their camp.

"One more day," Marta announced as she came back into camp that evening. "If we find no trace of the creature tomorrow, we will spend Sabiss here, then move on to another location."

"Where?" Ibna asked, a frown puckering his scarred face.

"To the southwest," she replied without hesitation. "Toward the hills. From the undigested bits we found in its belly, the dinka-chak feeds on *grik m'chook* and sandslithers—when it can't get goats. The sandslithers are everywhere, but the grik m'chook go up into the hills during the summer. We'll work our way in that direction."

Later on in her tent with the Unbeliever, both of them too weary and warm even to lie touching one another, she was less confident in her demeanor. "In truth, it could be anywhere." She sighed, stretched out on her mat, waiting for the temperature inside the tent to drop enough so that she would want to pull up a blanket. "The one we found could be far outside its native element. It might have been eating the grik m'chook and sandslithers because they were the only things available."

"Thank you for those words of hope and encouragement," Robinson groaned, lying on his own mat beside hers. "I thought you knew what you were doing."

"I do," she affirmed. "But I don't know what the dinka-chak is doing."

"What I'd give for an aerial survey," Robinson moaned. "A nice satellite picture with infrared. A motion detector."

"When the All-Giving desires us to be dull and weak and ungrateful," Marta sniped, "then our lives will be made easy."

It shut him up, as she had planned it would. He did not dare to criticize her god, or her religious beliefs. Nor did he wish to learn any more of them than he had to. Marta frowned, knowing that sooner or later he would transgress, perhaps grievously.

But it was part of the Manifest Revelation that the Children of the All-Hallowed not carry their teachings to those who did not desire to learn. They could impart such laws and customs as would keep an Unbeliever from embarrassment or harm while in their company, but under no condition were they to request that he or she participate in religious study, prayer, or other forms of worship. When the All-Powerful stirred a person's spirit, he would ask.

Soon she heard Robinson's gentle breathing and turned to look at him in the darkness. He looked almost foolish in repose: hair tousled, mouth slightly open, an insignificant nose, and eyebrows that were practically invisible. But wakeful, he still set her heart to pounding. His keen blue eyes sparkled with intelligence and desire, his mouth quirked in an appealing smile, and he said things which both tried her patience and made her laugh. Best of all, with only the subtlest encouragement, he fell happy victim to her seductive charm. He would climb any rock, brave any bramble hedge, if she promised to make it worth his while, and she was flattered. There was not much she could not get him to do, Marta thought contentedly, as long as she used the right bait.

Even as the thought came to her, Marta cursed herself for a fool and realized what she needed to do the next day.

"Then Marta took a cage of wood," Hassan said, *"and prayed to the All-Powerful, who turned the wood into stone. Next she chanted the blessing over fire, breathed in the smoke of that fire, and blew it into the cage of stone. Then she took the cage which had been so blessed, and set it upon the hard ground of Dhin M'Tarkhna. There she offered up her praise to the All-Hallowed, though the sun raged in the sky above her, sucking the life from her bones . . ."*

"Today we hunt differently," Marta announced as all the searchers filled their canteens and packed bread and cheese for the noon meal. "Sibna Egthassa, you and Kobanan go southwest; find the highest piece of ground in your area. Take one of our chickens—" Marta waved a hand at the crate of live chickens which had been brought to provide fresh meat for the expedition. "Tie its foot to a stake, and drive the stake in the ground beneath a bush a hundred meters or so from your location. Then"— she flashed them a broad smile—"wait. Let us see if dinka-chak will come to us."

She gave each team a similar assignment, to find the point with the best vantage, stake out a chicken, and wait. No traps, but recorders; first they wanted to study the creature in its natural surroundings, record its behaviors, document its habitat. Later on they would think about live-catch traps.

The strategy lifted everyone's spirits. Robinson's eyes fairly crackled with excitement as they set off for a pock-marked rock shelf a good seven or eight kilometers to the northwest. There they set up an awning to shelter them from sun and wind, securing it to the ground on one edge with heavy rocks, since the limestone would not allow stakes to be driven. Their hapless chicken was tethered in the meager shade of a *brimma* bush on the leeward side of their shelter, and they plopped themselves down on the unforgiving surface to watch and wait.

"Much better than tramping over the sand and rock," Marta said as she piled her long hair on top of her head and jammed her field cap over it. "Don't you agree, Sab Robinson?"

"I thought you liked tramping all over the desert," he replied, stretching out his long legs in front of him. "And it's all right for you to call me Cecil, you know."

"I'm honored," she replied truthfully, "but I'd rather not get in that habit. It might slip out when we were in company, and that would be disrespectful."

Robinson had noticed that Innantans did not call each other by pet names or even nicknames, nor did they indulge in public displays of affection. It seemed odd to him that although Kobanan and Egthassa shared a tent, and presumably shared more than that in private, he still called her Sibna. "So it's disrespectful to call me by my given name, but it's not disrespectful to, uh, tickle my fancy till the cows come home?"

She shot him a sidelong glance. "Would you rather I didn't?" she challenged.

"Oh, I'm not complaining," he hastened. "It's just that

I'm—well, surprised, constantly, by the value system here. Not too many fundamentalist religions allow a woman to carry on with a man who's not her husband." He glanced at the sun climbing steadily toward its zenith and wondered if it was too warm already to request a demonstration.

"No, but there are many that allow a man to do as he pleases," she retorted, "while a woman is deemed depraved for merely enjoying the act of copulation, even when it is lawful." She trained a pair of field glasses on the tethered chicken. "Ours is an enlightened religion, where women hold equal status with men, and everyone is permitted to experience the gift of sexual pleasure. Although," she admitted, "that is one of the doctrines which raised the anger of our parent religion, so that the Children of the Second Revelation were forced to flee here to Dray's Planet."

Then Robinson had to ask the question that had nagged at him ever since he started this fiery affair. "Does Retneyabo know that . . . you and I . . . ?"

Marta gave a throaty laugh. "The kukhoosh is no fool, Sab Robinson."

"And he doesn't . . . mind?"

Marta turned her head to look curiously at the Unbeliever. "Sab Robinson," she said patiently, "if the kukhoosh didn't approve of you, he would have told me so very plainly and recommended someone else."

That raised his eyebrows. "He has to preapprove all your lovers?"

Marta laughed; she couldn't help it. "It's not like I have hundreds!" she exclaimed. "And no, he doesn't have to preapprove them. But he is a wise and farseeing man; I would be foolish not to listen to his counsel."

The Unbeliever knit his eyebrows together as he considered that. Then, "You have great respect for him, don't you?" he asked sincerely.

"Of course!" This Unbeliever could be incredibly slow about some things! "He is Retneyabo, a legend in his own time for his sharp mind, his brilliant career, his un-flagging devotion to the Children of the Second Revelation. His father, too, was an important kukhoosh; but Retneyabo made his own way, acquired his own client base, amassed his own fortune, long before his father passed into the Everlasting Presence of the Most High, and left half his estate to his son."

Robinson reached over and caught her proud chin in his hand, looking straight into her eyes. "But you respect him on a much more personal level than the rest of the world, don't you?"

The question puzzled Marta. "I know him on a more personal level," she replied. "He has been my *sab-n'ak-hba*, my father-husband, for nearly half my life. He took a wild, restless girl and channeled her into productive, fulfilling directions. And in that whole time, Sab Robinson, he has not been wrong once. Not once."

Marta raised the field glasses to her eyes once more and trained them on the chicken, but Robinson took hold of them and pulled them away. His penetrating blue eyes held hers as he asked, "Do you love him?"

Marta tugged the field glasses free. "Love," she scoffed. "You Unbelievers speak of love as though it were magic of some kind. There are as many kinds of love as there are marriages on Innanta. More than that. A man can love his father, his brother, his son, and each of three wives, and love them all differently. A woman can love her father, and her father's sib-apafa, and her husband, and her husband's sib-apafa, and her teachers and her lovers— Where does duty stop and love begin? When does caring cross some invisible line and become love?" She fixed the field glasses determinedly on the distant chicken. "If I tell you I love my patron, it probably means something very different to me than it does to you. So let us not speak of it when we cannot agree on a definition."

Robinson sighed and stretched out with his head pillowed on her firm thigh. "You're right," he admitted. "It would be like trying to explain color to a blind person."

They were silent for several moments, each pondering the cultural gulf between them, each sure his or her way was superior to the other's. Marta sat with her jaw set and her field glasses trained on their target, while the Unbeliever drifted toward sleep in the energy-sapping midday heat. Finally Marta tapped his shoulder gently.

"Sab Robinson," she asked, "would you like to look at a live dinka-chak?"

CHAPTER 7

"The smoke of Marta's breath was as sweet perfume, and the blessings she spoke were a pleasant fragrance which enchants and bedazzles the mind of the beast. And lo! the dinka-chak came to that place," Hassan exclaimed, *"and made its nest in the cage of stone. And all the people gathered around, and gave praise to the Most High, and the dinka-chak crooned contentedly to its young . . . "*

The creature approached the chicken furtively, darting from the cover of one scraggly bush to another across the rocky ground. Its mottled skin glistened in the sunlight, and while it was nearly invisible in the dappled shade of the desert scrub, it was hard to miss as it raced across the intervening open patches toward its prey.

Marta ran the recorder while Robinson watched transfixed through the field glasses. "Look how fast that thing is!" he exclaimed in an excited whisper.

"It came from the northwest," Marta observed. "Perhaps we have been too far south here."

Just then the creature attacked, and the two scientists watched in fascinated horror as the dinka-chak went straight for the neck of the squawking bird, almost ripping the head off with its razor-sharp teeth. The carcass of the hapless chicken kept flapping its wings and pumping its legs, but the dinka-chak hung on like a bulldog until those reflexes faded. Then with a swipe of one short foreleg it opened up the chicken's belly and began to feed.

Robinson's stomach turned as he watched the grisly feast. He had never observed a predator in the wild before; the ruthlessness of the dinka-chak's kill bothered him much less than the sight of it tearing bloody strips of flesh and stringy innards from the warm body of the still-struggling bird. Beside him, Marta was calmly recording the event, intent on holding the camera steady. He swallowed several times and tried to be clinical in his observations.

Marta, who had helped caravan cooks butcher chickens as soon as she could be trusted with a knife, was not the least disturbed by the dinka-chak's behavior. But other things did disturb her. "It keeps looking around," she pointed out. "As though it expected something else to come steal its kill. What could do that? There is nothing in the desert large enough to threaten it."

"Another dinka-chak," Robinson replied.

"The skin is very shiny for a desert animal," she continued. "See how it catches the sun? Not good camouflage, except in the shade. And look at the bright orange patch under its chin. The other one didn't have that."

"Maybe this is a male," he suggested.

Suddenly a flash of movement caught Marta's eye and she turned the recorder toward this new development. Another dinka-chak was sneaking up on the feeder. In short bursts it streaked toward the meal it detected, and as it came onward, the first creature grew more and more agitated. Finally the intruder rushed at the feeder with a shrill screeching. The defender rose up on its hind legs, puffed out the orange patch under its chin, then gave a lame squawk and fled. The intruder pounced upon the dead chicken, but before it tore a single morsel from the carcass, it lifted its pointed snout to the sky and gave a series of almost chirping cries. Then it launched into its dinner.

In a moment there was a scurrying through the sparse desert vegetation as four more dinka-chaks made their entrance. They, too, moved in short bursts, but there was no challenge this time for the kill. The four simply joined the victorious dinka-chak in dining on the mangled remains, now and again giving a short chirp of contentment before tearing off and swallowing down another hunk of flesh.

"She called them," Marta breathed. "She called them to come and share with her. They must be her children."

There was great rejoicing in the camp that night. Sundown marked the beginning of Sabiss, so a feast was already prepared when Marta and the Unbeliever returned with news that their quest had been successful. Everyone looked at the recording they had made, even Ibna and his men, and the four scholars chattered excitedly about the proper strategy from this point on.

It was decided to search further to the northwest, since that seemed to be the direction from which the six animals had come. They would try following any tracks that had been left; but given the rocky nature of the soil, and the constant wind sweeping over it, they did not expect to find much—especially since they could not go out again until after Sabiss.

"Don't you ever make exceptions to the Sabiss rules?" Robinson asked Marta later that evening as they lay curled together on her mat.

"In cases of life and death," she allowed. "This is hardly a matter of life and death."

"But this find is so monumental," he began to protest.

Marta silenced him with a finger on his lips. "We must keep all things in perspective," she admonished. "It is important, yes; but to honor the All-Hallowed is more important. Our finding the dinka-chak at all is a gift from the All-Giving's generous hand; should we therefore neglect to render thanks and praise?"

Robinson sighed and surrendered. There was no point in arguing with religious types.

So all the next day he fretted while the other members of the expedition prayed and read their holy book and spoke together of the nature of their god and of the teachings of their holy ones. Robinson wondered if Soln Shipner, who must surely be in hot pursuit of them by now, was having similar troubles with his expedition.

Finally sunset came, the requisite prayers were finished, and Marta issued instructions for the following day's activity. Her mind, Robinson noted, had not been entirely on her god during this mandatory rest. The four scientists, accompanied by Tookh, would leave in the morning with one donkey to carry their equipment and supplies. They would try to track the dinka-chak to its lair, while Ibna sent men scouting in the same general direction for possible campsites. When all assignments were made, the travelers packed their gear, and as soon as morning prayers had been completed, they set out.

They found the ravaged remains of their chicken near the rock shelf; hardly a shred of soft tissue was left, and most of the bones had been cracked and broken in the frenzy. Tiny insects called *ennirel* crawled over the leavings. But of the dinka-chak's presence they could find no trace. On they went until nightfall, when they made camp in the shelter of a *cirrahn* bush.

Early on the second day they reached a low ridge where the limestone floor of the ancient lake bed had cracked and a section had risen some five meters. The layers of compacted sediment, colorful in their striped pattern of dark and light earth tones, were riddled with crevices and small caves worn by the wind. "Too bad it faces the southwest," said Kobanan. "It could provide us with good shelter for a camp."

At the base of the uplift, loose sand had mounded up, and numerous plants were growing. "Sandslither habitat," Marta observed, for the legless vertebrates fed on the stalks and seeds of such flora, and they liked to burrow into the sand at night to insulate themselves from dramatic temperature changes.

But as Kobanan pointed out, it was of no use to humans. So they hiked parallel to it in a generally northeastern direction for half a kilometer before Marta hauled up short and stared back at the wall of sedimentary rock. "Grik m'chook would hide in such caves, would they not?" she inquired of no one in particular. Grik m'chook were native animals the size of a field mouse which curled themselves into a ball and rolled across the landscape, protected by bony plates on their hides.

"Perhaps," Egthassa agreed. "The caves would provide them with shade, the plants with food."

"Dinka-chak feeds on sandslithers and grik m'chook," Kobanan realized.

"We could walk for days in the wilderness and not find dinka-chak's lair," Marta said firmly. "But we may well have found his dining room."

Three days later they knew they had found more than that. Lying on their bellies atop the uplift, the four scientists trained their equipment on the desert floor below and discovered a very curious thing about the dinka-chak. They liked to roost in trees. Two kilometers to the southwest of where they had first approached the ridge, Marta and her expedition found a copse of *limiar* trees, a thorny native species, clustered around a small spring which smelled faintly of sulfur. A colony of twenty-six creatures lived there, sleeping at night in the forked branches of the limiar, venturing out during daylight hours to hunt up and down the length of the ridge. Occasionally one or more would strike out into the desert, but mostly they stayed close to the spring and home.

Ibna located a spot nearly five kilometers from the dinka-chak spring, where erosion had cut a defile through the uplift, providing an area that was sheltered from sun, wind, and prying eyes. "Kukhoosh Paun's Unbeliever will never find us here," he boasted to Marta. A source of water would have made the spot a perfect camp; but as it was, they were back within two kilometers of the caravan trail, and half a day's journey to the west was an oasis with a year-round well. Marta immediately dispatched two men with six of the donkeys to refill all their water containers.

The nights were growing quite cool now, and Marta was glad to snuggle under the covers with Robinson. But during daylight hours she rarely had his attention. For the next several weeks, whenever he was not up on the ridge studying the dinka-chaks through field glasses, he was watching recordings of them or making copious notes on his voicewriter. Sometimes she would interrupt him, though, with questions.

"Which of our fish do you think they resemble?"

The Unbeliever replied that they did not resemble any of the Drayan marine species.

"Then where did they come from?"

In exasperation he pointed out that there could have been an entire evolutionary line leading to the dinka-chak, but that all the intermediate species were extinct. After all, there had obviously been a few climate changes in Dhin M'Tarkhna over the eons, since what had been a lake was now a desert.

"Do you think they warrant their own class, then?"

"Of course, they do," he growled. "But what that class is, I can't know until we locate the intermediate fossils. I can't determine class or subclass or order on the basis of one species." He clicked on his voicewriter and began to dictate the observed dominance of the female within the dinka-chak social order.

"We have never seen fossils of anything resembling these creatures," Marta interrupted again, and Robinson clicked his machine off impatiently. "Then again," she admitted, "no one has ever searched Dhin M'Tarkhna for fossils."

So while Robinson kept vigil atop the ridge, a restless Marta began to prowl the length of that uplift, searching its strata for evidence of the dinka-chak's ancestors. Before she had spent even a week at this task, however, Ibna called her away. The two of them disappeared into the desert toward the southeast and did not return for two days. Immediately thereafter she dispatched a drover and one donkey up the steep track to the caravan trail, but she refused to tell Robinson why until the entire group had collected for the evening meal. Then: "Shipner has arrived," she announced.

An oath escaped Robinson's lips. The others looked at him askance—even the drovers. He apologized quickly, and Marta went on.

"He's found our old camp," she told them, "and he

has set up his own camp there. I doubt he will be able to find us here, except by accident. But he has set out live-catch traps everywhere."

She had sent the drover to fetch one of their electric carts, which was hidden a good week's travel back along the caravan trail to the east. Shipner had no carts with him, so she intended to maximize her advantage by having at least one cart at her disposal in case a hasty return to Jinka was required.

"But it may be that he does not necessarily plan just to trap a creature and flee with it," Marta continued. "Indeed, I would be surprised if he did that. He is a scientist; like us, he will want to study it first, particularly in its native habitat." Robinson nodded agreement. "It may be he plans to catch a dinka-chak, then release it and follow it back to the colony," she suggested. "We must all be very careful not to be seen at our work. We don't want to give him any extra help in finding his quarry."

It was on the crest of the uplift that they were most vulnerable, so Ibna's men began to construct a blind for the scientists. Before it was finished, however, an impatient Robinson sought out his guide.

"I need a live specimen," he said without preamble.

Marta, who was going over their supplies to see how long they could afford to stay, stopped and eyed him critically. "It would be better to wait until nearer the time we leave."

"It's near enough," he insisted. "We've got more 3-D recordings than we can study in six months. Next spring we'll come back to observe mating rituals, if they have any. But I want one or two live specimens, and then I want to head out of here."

Marta studied his face until he began to shift uncomfortably. "You're afraid of Shipner," she said finally.

"Hell, no, I'm not afraid of him!" Robinson snapped. "I just don't want him to beat us back to Jinka with a live dinka-chak."

Marta considered chastising him for his profanity, but

she decided to let the infraction go. "He will not get back before us," she promised.

"How do you know?" he demanded.

Now Marta's patience was tried, for she was not accustomed to having her word questioned. But Robinson was an Unbeliever, unfamiliar with their culture; he expected falseness and perfidy of everyone. That was the way of his world. So she bit her tongue and answered. "For one thing," she said with measured tone, "he's a full day further into the desert. Gladnas and Mettikapu are taking turns watching him; we will know when they break camp and get out ahead of them."

"You'll know what Shipner wants you to know," Robinson grumbled, but he did look somewhat mollified. "He's a blasted Nechtanite, and they're sly devils. Sneaky. Those live-catch traps he's setting out, I wouldn't bet he's planning to follow his captive back here. He may have in mind to take the money and run, so to speak. Back to his kukhoosh. Back to publish a paper as the discoverer of this unique life-form."

Marta considered that. She didn't know how any reputable scholar could publish a paper without having studied the creature in its habitat, documented its behavior, traced its ancestry—but Robinson had a point about getting back to Paun with a live dinka-chak and announcing its discovery. "We can send one or two drovers back with the 3-Ds we have so far," she suggested. "I know Sibna Egthassa wants to keep up the observation, make more recordings; but it wouldn't hurt, I suppose, to have a dinka-chak in captivity. There are many tests we can run here in camp with our field lab, and as you say, we will be prepared in case Shipner does decide to move."

Now a broad grin broke out across the Unbeliever's face. "Exactly!" he exclaimed. "They're so like saurischians, I can't wait to have a closer look at their metabolic readings. The fact that they are warm-blooded is a key element in the paper I want to write, and I need all the supporting data to throw in Shipner's face."

"And if he challenges your conclusions?" Marta

goaded. "As he challenged your previous paper? Will you fight him again?"

Robinson hesitated, eyeing Marta carefully to see what kind of answer she was expecting. "If he leaves me alone," Robinson said cautiously, "I'll leave him alone."

From that, Marta suspected that the brawl at the dinosaur expo had not been as even a match as Cecil Robinson had led her to believe. No, the Unbeliever, strong and athletic though he was, had taken a drubbing at the hands of the Nechtanite.

It made Marta wonder what kind of man Soln Shipner really was.

Capturing a dinka-chak for study was not quite as easy as they had hoped.

First they tried baiting their traps with sandslithers, but there was no way to tether the snakelike creatures inside the trap. A couple of attempts with carrion quickly showed that dinka-chak was not a scavenger; it had no interest in prey it had not killed or stolen from another dinka-chak. There were only four chickens left now, and the cook was not at all happy when Marta appropriated one for bait. But it was effective, at least. Within thirty minutes they had their dinka-chak.

And before they could transport it back to camp, it had chewed its way right through the slats of the wooden trap. It also gave Ibna a nasty bite before it scurried off over the burning rocks.

Another chicken went into a reinforced trap, another creature was caught, and Marta shot the captive dinka-chak with a tranquilizer before they approached it. This time they made it successfully back to camp, but the dinka-chak never wakened from its stupor; it expired soundlessly in its cage.

Now the four scientists puzzled for days, trying to decide what had killed it. There were not so many in this colony that they could afford to kill a few more finding out what kind of tranquilizer to use. While they puzzled, young Tookh worked on a project of his own. Two days before Sabiss he proudly presented his creation to

Marta: a wooden trap with its bars carefully wound up and down with *metkhiss* vine. The tough desert creeper was as resilient as steel cable when it dried. "Not even *Tyrannosaurus rex* could chew through that," the lad boasted, for Robinson had been filling his head with stories of Earth's dinosaurs.

Robinson was skeptical, but Marta was impressed. "You can't imagine how tough this plant is," she insisted to the Unbeliever. "The nomads coil it into sheets, glued together with *rinrin* sap, and they use it for all kinds of things: donkeyboards, travois, sandals. This could work."

Tookh also suggested that instead of baiting the trap with a chicken, they try putting the dead dinka-chak inside. Lacking an orange patch under its throat, the recent captive was dubbed female, the kind that called its young to share food. By playing a recording of such a female's "dinner call," the boy ventured, they might lure some younger dinka-chaks who would then want to investigate the corpse in the trap.

"It couldn't hurt to try," Marta whispered to Robinson. "You should have seen the look on Cook's face when I took the second chicken. Who knows what she'll cook into the stew for us if she thinks we are wasting her provender."

So Marta turned on her most charming smile. "Tookh, what a brilliant boy you are!" she exclaimed loudly. "Cook, I want you to prepare an especially fine feast for us tonight. Roast a small goat. Not only is tomorrow Sabiss, but if this plan works, we shall soon be on our way home and won't need to ration our food supplies."

The happy cook grinned from ear to ear and reached for her best butchering knife.

Most of the 2-D and 3-D recordings had been sent back to Jinka with the two drovers who had been dispatched after the discovery of Shipner's camp, but Egthassa and Kobanan were diligently making more. After checking through several hours of recordings, Marta and Robinson found an audio clip which contained what they believed was a call to dinner, and out they went to set up their trap.

It was late afternoon by then, and both the sun and the wind were fierce. "I thought it was supposed to get cooler in the fall," Robinson complained as they huddled behind a squat boulder, trying to keep as much of their bodies as possible out of the stinging sand.

"This *is* cooler," Marta replied, fastening one side of a square cloth around her neck and pulling the other up over her head from the back, holding it out away from her face to serve as both windbreak and sunscreen.

Robinson tried to use his hands to effect a similar screen. "I hope Shipner is having the same rotten luck we are," he grumbled.

"Luck has nothing to do with it," Marta preached. "The All-Wise sends us these adversities to make us strong." Then she closed her mouth firmly and tried to ignore the grit that had blown into it as she spoke.

Robinson, too, discovered there were grainy particles in his mouth. After trying unsuccessfully to spit or wipe them out, he surrendered to the inevitable, and he, too, kept silent to avoid swallowing any more sand.

But his mind would not keep quiet. Three weeks now, maybe four, and he would release his first paper on the dinka-chak. It would have to be very cursory—there was so much more study to be done on these creatures—but, by God, it was going straight to the editor of the *Journal of the Interstellar League of Zoologists,* and neither Soln Shipner nor anyone else was going to stage a coup on this! In fact, he would ask Retneyabo if there was any way the kukhoosh could use his influence to suppress any transmissions Shipner tried to send offworld. This was Robinson's find, and no underhanded, obnoxious freak like Shipner was going to cheat him out of his shot at an Ashdod Prize!

He had the paper half-written, and the rest of it was all worked out in his mind. Once he'd described the general anomaly of the dinka-chak, he'd start his comparison of it to a theropod of the saurischian order: the skeletal structure, the bipedal movement, the three-part pelvis. He'd point out all the similarities, make his case for convergent evolution. Then he'd start in on the known metabolic processes of the dinka-chak, things which could not be conclusively known about dinosaurs, and he'd pose that most intriguing question: could the similarities run the other way? Might these chicken-lizards-with-nasty-teeth provide them with a glimpse of how the mysterious dinosaurs had once lived and moved and had their being?

And Shipner could scream forever about there being no data to support such a conclusion, the theory would be out there—and it would have Cecil Robinson's name on it.

"There was much rejoicing in the camp over the capture of a live dinka-chak. There was dancing and feasting and making merry long into the night, and the song of the dinka-chak blended with the songs of the Faithful in honor of the wondrous planet to which the All-Gracious had brought his children. Marta herself stood before the others and offered her thanks to the All-Giving for the great gift of the dinka-chak, a sign of the secret gifts this world holds for the Faithful. And she vowed to take the dinka-chak quickly to her husband and patron, the Kuk-hoosh Retneyabo, so that all might know and rejoice in this revelation of life . . ."

The smell of roasting meat drifted out of the defile and greeted the two scientists as they returned at sundown with one captive dinka-chak in Tookh's trap slung on the end of a pole. It shrieked and squawked its displeasure in such piercing tones that nearly the entire camp turned out to greet them, and Tookh was almost beside himself with excitement. "It worked, it worked!" he cried as he danced about, waving his broken arm in the air. "I knew it would!"

Evening prayers were particularly joyful that night, heralding the Sabiss and giving thanks to the All-Giving for the capture of the live dinka-chak. Robinson couldn't remember when he'd felt quite so giddy without having consumed a drop of alcohol. Both Gladnas and Metti-kapu joined in the celebration, for they could not be expected to work on Sabiss; and since not even Paun's hirelings would think of breaking the Sabiss laws, Shipner's expedition was not going anywhere, anyway.

Finally, as the fire died down and the temperature plunged, everyone crawled off to their beds. Cook rewarded Tookh by adding him to her rotation of husbands and taking him off to her tent. Kobanan and Egthassa consoled one another for the fact that the imminent end of this expedition meant each would soon being going back to a contractual spouse who was not nearly as exciting as they had found each other. And Marta made Robinson wonder how he would survive back in Jinka knowing that her amazing skills would not only be denied him but squandered on the overweight, overage Retneyabo. As she brought him to the brink of madness, he hoped fervently that there was some religious law she'd forgotten to tell him that would allow them to continue their liaison back at the University.

After what seemed a very short night, Robinson was roused by the gentle chanting of men and women engaged in morning prayer. Light had barely begun to filter through the walls of the tent; Marta had gone from beside him, and he could hear her push aside the tent flap to stand outside where she would lift her hands to the graying heavens. Then her voice joined the soft, singsong chorus of worshipers offering their thanks and praise: "Gracious is the Most High, and wise is the All-Gracious, for by the hand of the All-Giving does the sun rise once more upon the—

"Motherless son of a two-headed goat! May a thousand biting insects infest his tent!"

CHAPTER 8

Robinson leapt from his mat and snatched up his trousers, pulling them on as he stumbled toward the tent door. What in the world could have set Marta off at this hour? It was not the first time he had heard her launch into a spate of insults like this—it was what devout Children of the Second Revelation used instead of profanity—but he had never heard her quite so vindictive.

"May he swim in a pool of goat manure!" Marta shrieked, as Robinson burst forth from the tent. "May he go naked through Dhin M'Tarkhna at midsummer! May the fiends of darkness pluck out his hairs one by one!"

He saw in an instant what made her so furious, and he cursed in more succinct terms than hers.

The dinka-chak and its cage were gone.

"Shipner!" he spat.

"Paun!" hissed Marta.

A quick investigation told them that several recordings of the dinka-chak colony were also missing. Sibna Egthassa burst into tears.

"May his testicles turn to dust," Marta growled. "Only an Unbeliever would do such a thing."

"It wasn't an Unbeliever who jumped us in the bazaar," Robinson felt compelled to point out.

"It is Sabiss," Marta snapped. "Not even Paun's men, foul as they are, would travel from their camp to ours on Sabiss. May the punishment of the All-Just fall on him who did!"

Robinson didn't ask what the punishment for Sabbath-breaking was, but he hoped sincerely that it involved excruciating physical pain. "I don't suppose there are any tracks?" he asked, checking the ground around the base of the tripod from which the cage had hung, to give the dinka-chak the sensation of roosting to which it was accustomed.

Marta shrugged. "The ground is too rocky here, and too well trodden by our own feet, to give any evidence of a thief's passage."

"Well, at least we know where he's headed." Robinson turned back toward the tent. "Let me get dressed and we can go after him."

He had his hand on the tent flap when her voice arrested him. "We go nowhere until dark."

Robinson stopped and turned to stare at her incredulously.

"It is Sabiss," she reminded him. "A day for rest and prayer. We will conduct no search on a holy day."

He stomped back up to her, barely controlling his fury. "Are you going to let him get away, get back to Jinka ahead of us, steal the glory for Paun, because you don't want to travel on a holy day?" he demanded.

"He will not get back ahead of us," she asserted. "He cannot make the journey without supplies, and he cannot have carried enough on his back to get him to Jinka. He has to go back to his camp. Besides—" Marta lifted her chin arrogantly. "If he is any kind of scientist, he will want to see the dinka-chak colony for himself before he leaves Dhin M'Tarkhna."

Robinson glared at her for a moment, then he blew out a huge breath he hadn't realized he was holding. "You may be right," he admitted. "Shipner's as dogmatic as they come. He knows images can be falsified and data invented. He won't make a claim, even to your Kukhoosh Paun, based on one specimen and recordings that we could have altered." He rubbed the back of his neck ruefully. "Now I wish I *had* doctored the images."

"So," Marta concluded, relaxing a little herself. "At dark we will go after him. Now I will finish my prayers."

"Pray for your god to strike Shipner with a bolt of

lightning," the Unbeliever grumbled and he turned back toward the tent once more.

"It is a sin to pray for anyone's death," Marta admonished, resuming her posture of supplication. "But I will pray that the nettles and thorns of Dhin M'Tarkhna clutch at his ankles and gouge his flesh until I can lay hands on him myself."

"Great was the sin of the dark Unbeliever," Hassan intoned fiercely, his face a scowling mask. "To travel upon Sabiss is a sin against the body, the mind, and the spirit, for the All-Hallowed has given us this day of rest as a time of renewal and rejoicing. And great was his sin in stealing the dinka-chak, a prize for which he had not labored. And great was Marta's wrath, when she saw what he had done.

"But with the charity of the All-Merciful," Hassan went on in softer tones, "Marta spared the life and limbs of the Unbeliever Shipner. Taking only the wisdom which the All-Wise granted her, she approached his camp in reconciliation, to reason with him, as it is fitting for the Children of the Second Revelation to reason with one another, and with the Unbeliever . . ."

Concealed by the sketchy foliage of a cirrahn bush, Marta, Robinson, and Mettikapu looked down into the camp of Paun's Unbeliever. They had traveled all night, slept only a couple of hours, then pushed on to arrive here just before noon. Slithering to this vantage point, they could now survey the tents and donkeys through their field glasses. Only three men were visible, and Marta didn't recognize any of them. They considered what to do.

Robinson suggested the obvious approach: wait until dark, then sneak into Shipner's camp to steal the dinka-chak back. But Mettikapu advised against it—all three of the men they could see carried energy rifles. No doubt that was because they expected a reprisal, and they were prepared to defend their possession of the dinka-chak.

"Why didn't *we* bring our energy rifles?" Robinson asked Marta petulantly.

"I will not sink to Paun's level," she retorted. "The rifles are for defense only. We will use cunning instead of force."

Mettikapu suggested they try bargaining with Shipner, but both Marta and Robinson scoffed at the notion. "We have nothing to offer," she told the drover. Then suddenly her eyes went unfocused.

"If we knew where the creature was," Robinson mused, "we might be able to create a distraction for their guards, then slip in and snatch it." Looking at Marta for confirmation, he noticed the glazed look on her face. "What?"

"I know what to do," she said decisively, rising to her feet.

"What?" he repeated.

"I'll go talk to him," she said simply. "Once inside their camp, I'll see what I can learn: where the dinka-chak is, how it is guarded, and what their plans are. When I have the information, I will return to you, and we can make an informed plan."

"Are you crazy?" Robinson demanded. "You think they're going to let you just walk into their camp and look around?"

"They don't have a choice," she replied hotly. "I am the wife of a kukhoosh; no one of Paun's men will dare to lay a hand on me, or my husband will see that he is prosecuted under the law and loses certain body parts that no man wants to be without."

Robinson stared at her a moment, then turned to Mettikapu. "Is she serious?" he asked.

Mettikapu nodded. "They'll know there are witnesses; they won't dare harm her."

"Well, even if they don't, they're not going to let you just look around!" Robinson protested.

Now Marta turned sly seductive eyes on him. "Aren't they? You will find, Sab Robinson, that I can persuade men to grow quite careless with their secrets."

* * *

Marta was challenged before she was within a hundred meters of the camp. "I come to speak with Soln Shipner," she informed the armed thug, brushing haughtily past him. He turned and followed her, but he did not interfere with her progress.

Three other men rose to gawk at her as she strode through the camp. They were rough-looking veterans of the desert, with a cruel cast to their features. Yet they kept a respectful distance, now and then glancing out across the empty terrain where they knew others must be watching this brazen woman.

In the center of the cluster of tents and equipment Marta stopped. A young-looking man came out of a supply tent and stopped upon seeing her. Her eyes narrowed in contempt as she recognized him. "Fadnar."

Her former colleague managed a trace of a smile. "Marta." His eyes glittered with mingled defense and embarrassment. It was he who had stolen data files on the dead dinka-chak a year ago and taken them to Kukhoosh Paun. "How are you?"

"Well enough," she replied in a flinty voice.

He bridled a little at her tone. "I hear you have found a new companion for your travels," he said in a voice tinged with bitterness.

Oh, and was he angry still, because she wouldn't continue their relationship when they returned to Jinka? Had he really believed she would break the law? What a fool, to let his injured pride send him running to Paun. "I am not here to discuss my traveling companions," she told him haughtily; then added, glancing at a nearby donkey, "Nor yours." Fadnar glared at her. "I've come to speak with Soln Shipner. Where is he?"

From behind Marta came a deep, gruff voice. "Here."

The man had come out of a tent just behind her. Marta let her face slip back into its seductive mask, then turned slowly, deliberately—

—and gasped aloud.

Soln Shipner bore no resemblance to the handsome Cecil Robinson, nor to any other Unbeliever Marta had ever seen images of. He stood before his tent with arms

akimbo, fists planted on hips that were girdled in a swath
of faded green plaid reaching past his knees. A huge
knife hung in its worn scabbard from his waist, but the
kilt was the only garment he wore. Legs, arms, chest,
and feet were bare, and every inch of them were covered
with bold, black, abstractly serpentine tattoos.

Even his face was tattooed, with fierce lines warring
across his beardless cheeks and beak of a nose. Dark
eyes blazed from deep sockets, like animal eyes glowing
from the depths of caves—caves decorated by mystic
runes. His hair was a writhing mass of thin, ropelike
braids coiling back on themselves and fixed to one another with wooden picks. He was the most fearsome
thing Marta had ever seen.

Noting her fright, Shipner parted his lips in a wicked
smile. "Greetings, Princess," he said in a voice so deep
it seemed to rumble up from his abdomen. "You're earlier than I expected; you must have traveled all night."

"I want my dinka-chak back," she blurted, then cursed
herself for a fool. What a stupid, witless thing to say!
This was a powerful man, accustomed to making people
quail before him. She had to show him she was his equal.

To make matters worse, he laughed at her, a great
booming laugh like Retneyabo's, but derisive in a way
her husband never was. "If you can find your dinka-chak
here," Shipner chortled, "you can have him."

"Have *her*," Marta corrected. "You will have noticed
that it is a female."

"Is it?" The smile was gone now, but the mocking
lingered in his eyes. "Had I seen your dinka-chak, no
doubt I would have noticed; but as you see, Princess, it
is not here."

"I am not a princess," Marta told him pointedly. "We
do not have royalty among the Children of the Second
Revelation."

"Oh, don't you?" His voice was heavy with sarcasm.
"Raised in luxury, the pampered child who got everything she ever wanted, married to a man whose fortune
and family are as old as this planting itself—the only

thing you lack is the title, Princess, and I give that to you." He sketched a caricature of a bow before her.

Hot anger rose up in Marta like a desert wind. This was not the introduction she had intended. This man treated her like a child, called her by a child's title—and no doubt she looked like a child just now, and a very dirty one at that. Oh, to have her house garments and her jewelry and her dainty sandals—but something told her Soln Shipner would not succumb to such finery the way Cecil Robinson had.

Perhaps her desert garb was better, after all. Marta drew herself up, knowing that her regal carriage would shine through the dirtiest of rags, and she deliberately softened her eyes. "You are mistaken, Sab Shipner," she replied in a smooth voice. "I am a veteran of the caravans, not a pampered child. Do you imagine I could have reached you here at this hour if I were some delicate creature accustomed to being waited on?"

Now he ran an appraising eye over her form, but it was just that: appraising. There was no trace of a leer. "They told me you were tenacious," he said finally. "A desert rat. And so you are." He grinned, and his large teeth seemed yellow in that tattooed face. "So scurry back to your own camp. There's nothing here for you." Shipner started to turn away.

"Do you know how to care for a dinka-chak?" Marta demanded.

He stopped and turned slowly back to her.

"If you don't care for them properly, they die," she improvised deftly. "We've studied them for weeks, and we still lost one through carelessness. Can you afford to have your only specimen expire?"

He considered this a moment. Then his lip curled in a slight sneer. "Do you propose to share your information with me, Princess?"

Marta slid into her most coy and bewitching half smile. "I haven't decided," she baited, with a flirtatious flick of her long eyelashes. "Why don't you ply me with some food and see if I'll talk?"

Shipner snorted contemptuously. "Don't waste your

simpering smiles on me, Princess. I find you as plain and
unappealing as all the other women on this planet. Soft,
sentimental, and singularly stupid." He gestured to
Fadnar. "Get the princess some food. And let me know
when she's gone." Then he turned and disappeared into
his tent.

Seething inside, Marta had the strong urge to tear
Shipner's camp apart, starting with the tattooed man's
tent; but she knew about how far she'd get in that endeavor. Paun's men didn't dare harm her as long as she
was civil, but the minute she resorted to violence, they
would be justified in subduing her by whatever forceful
means appealed to them.

Instead she went to the door of Shipner's tent, which
was open to allow the air to circulate as the day grew
ever warmer. "If the dinka-chak is not here, then," she
purred, "you don't mind if I just have a look around
your camp, do you?"

"Be my guest," he said flatly. "Search the entire place,
if you like. You won't find it."

Marta turned to Fadnar with a smug smile, then began
to inspect the camp thoroughly.

According to Gladnas and Mettikapu, there were nine
men on the expedition. Counting Fadnar and Shipner,
there were six here now. Not unusual, that three should
be off somewhere at this hour of the day. But it raised
the possibility that one of them had the dinka-chak at
another location.

Crates of equipment were stacked in the center of the
camp, covered on the windward side by a heavy tarpau-
lin, and there were five tents: one for Shipner, one for
Fadnar, and two for the drovers; the fifth held supplies.
A careful inspection revealed no place where the creature might be hidden without danger of suffocating it. It
was truly not here, as Shipner had claimed. Then where
was it?

While she searched, Marta tallied Shipner's supplies
very carefully. Water for six, maybe seven days. They
would have to get more soon, and since the seasonal
springs of this place would not bubble to the surface

until winter rains replenished them, that meant Shipner would have to send someone to the oasis just west of where she and Robinson were camped. There were plenty of travel rations—dried meat, parched grains, etc.—but for fresh meat, only three goats and half a dozen chickens. They were not equipped for a long stay. Shipner must have counted on appropriating her research.

With one donkey as well as three men absent, the stolen dinka-chak could be only one of the things that had been carried off. A supply of water and food, for instance. How long was Shipner prepared to keep the dinka-chak at another location, where he himself could not study it?

They would have to watch this camp closely for the next few days. Given his limited supplies, Shipner might, indeed, make a run for Jinka—although he would have to get water first. Or he would have to go visit the dinka-chak soon, or have it brought back to his camp, in order to glean the information he needed. There was no point in him sitting in the middle of the desert doing nothing but consuming his supplies. Yes, they would have to watch the camp very closely.

The three of them were not equipped for an extended stay either, however. She and Robinson would have to go back and send Gladnas out here with supplies for himself and Mettikapu. In the meantime . . .

Marta turned a cold smile on Fadnar, who had been dogging her heels as she inspected the camp. "Sab Shipner said something about food for me?"

Fadnar found her some bread and cheese, which she ate slowly, watching Shipner's men as they lounged around the camp idling the time away. "Which one is the guide?" she asked Fadnar.

"I am," he replied, thrusting out his jaw.

Marta laughed. "Paun is not so big a fool as that."

His eyes blazed. "It is *Kukhoosh* Paun to you, and regardless of what you think, I am the guide for this expedition."

Marta made a rude noise but said no more about it.

Apparently the guide was not in camp right now. He was probably the one guarding the stolen dinka-chak.

Marta looked the drovers over again, trying to decide if there was one who might be tricked into telling her where the creature was being kept. But Fadnar was watching her like a hawk; he was not going to let her try. It was barely past noon, and already she seemed to have reached a dead end. Was there truly nothing to do but go back?

When she had finished her meal, Marta rose and stretched luxuriously. "I will speak to your pet monster again, I think," she told Fadnar casually; then she strolled to Shipner's tent, coughed politely to announce her presence, and went inside.

Soln Shipner sat cross-legged on a rug, watching something on a flatscreen. Some of the stolen recordings, perhaps? He did not even glance up as she came in, as though her presence was of no concern to him. Marta walked over to his sleeping mat and stretched out on it.

After a moment he remarked, still without looking up, "I did not ask you into my tent."

"I slept very little last night," she replied. "I have to rest for my journey back."

"Rest outside."

"Impossible." Marta settled herself more comfortably on the mat, letting the exhaustion of her night journey catch up with her at last. "I intend to sleep until dark, and there is no place that will stay shaded that long."

"Sleep in one of the other tents, then," he growled.

"Nonsense," she scoffed. "Fadnar cannot be trusted, and a sibna cannot be seen sharing a tent with such base men as Paun hires."

Now he turned and cocked an eyebrow at her, a movement which made the tattoos on that side of his face appear to crawl like snakes. "But it's all right to share *my* tent?"

"You're a respected zoologist," she replied airily. "No one in Innanta would think that amiss. Although," she admitted, "I doubt Sab Robinson will be very happy."

"Robinson!" Shipner exclaimed. "Is that insolent pup nearby?"

"Near enough to see your camp," she allowed.

"Ha!" Shipner returned to his studies. "In that case, Princess, stay as long as you like."

When Marta woke, it was to the sound of evening prayer, and she was surprised that she had slept so soundly. The tent was dark, and the flaps had been lowered to keep out the approaching night. Soln Shipner was curled up asleep on a rug; it occurred to Marta that between his trek to and from her camp, and studying the information he had stolen, Shipner had probably not slept much himself. With his pale skin and black tattoos, he looked like a patch of dappled shadow on the floor.

Marta sat up quietly and looked around her. Where was that flatscreen he'd been using? Ah, there is was. Silent as a cat, she leaned across the sleeping man and picked it up.

Retreating to the sleeping mat, Marta screened the recording still in the machine. It was a text on the history of Innanta. Even Shipner hadn't been so bold as to view the stolen recordings with her in the tent.

"The Second Revelation your Holy Ones claim to have received," came Shipner's deep voice. "It reads remarkably like a treatise on morality written by a certain doctoral candidate at the University of Elakrish about three hundred years ago."

Marta was startled but refused to show it. "The All-Wise may choose any vessel to use," she replied. "It was the Holy Ones who recognized the Voice of the Voiceless One and proclaimed it to the Faithful."

Still lying on his side with his eyes closed, Shipner snorted. "Is that how you explain such blatant plagiarism."

Marta bit back a hot retort. Such sacrilege did not deserve comment. Instead she rose to her feet. "And what do you call stealing another scientist's research?" she asked bluntly.

Shipner rolled onto his back and grinned up at her,

amusement dancing in his dark eyes. "Scientific research is a war, Princess," he told her. "Or at the very least, an ugly competition. And I am a warrior. I do what is necessary to win."

Marta made a rude noise and tugged her tunic straight, snugging her belt around it. "You won't win, Sab Shipner. Not this time. You don't know enough about that dinka-chak to keep it alive all the way back to Jinka."

"But I don't have it, Princess," he mocked. "I told you that."

"Of course, you have it," she said simply. "No other motherless son of a cockroach would violate Sabiss to take it from my camp. Not even these slime-sucking excrement eaters that Paun has hired to accompany you." She added, "And that includes Fadnar."

"They did seem quite aghast at the notion of traveling on your Sabiss," the Nechtanite admitted.

"Only tell me one thing," she demanded, shaking out her crumpled desert cap and jamming it down over her long hair. "How did you even find my camp? It is not visible unless you walk almost the entire length of the ridge."

"I am blessed with this great nose, you see," he answered, tapping what was, indeed, a proboscis of admirable proportions. "I sniffed out your fire and your Sabiss feast."

Marta grunted; she hadn't thought of that. "And have you found the dinka-chak colony as well?"

"I have." He propped himself up on one elbow. "I'm looking forward to visiting it in the daylight. Do you mind if I use your blind?"

Marta tried not to look surprised that he knew about the blind. How long had he been watching their camp? "I'm afraid I must decline," Marta responded. "I don't relish cleaning your blood off the recording equipment if Sab Robinson finds you in it."

Shipner chuckled softly. "The day that young upstart can draw my blood is the day your Martyrs rise up from the dead."

The irreverence was too much for Marta; she started for the tent door. She had just parted the self-adhesive closure when Shipner's voice stopped her cold.

"You know the dinka-chak is not a desert creature."

Slowly Marta turned and stared back at him.

"They live by that spring because they have to; they need far too much water to have evolved in the desert."

It nagged too close to Marta's own feelings for her to object. Instead she said quietly, "The camouflage is wrong, too—such shiny skin. And the skeletal structure . . ." Her voice trailed off in the darkness.

"Someone has invaded your world, Princess," Shipner said softly, "and left you an odd little gift."

The moon was high in the eastern sky yet when Marta reached the rendezvous and found Robinson standing watch. "Have a good time?" he growled.

"The food was good," she replied evenly. "And even the company was . . . interesting. But the dinka-chak is not in the camp."

"And for that you wasted yourself on that—"

"Sab Robinson," she interrupted sharply, "the only thing wasted in that camp were the hours I spent sleeping undisturbed. I went there for information, and I got it. How I got it is of no concern to you. Now, wake Mettikapu and let us be on our way. The dinka-chak will not be brought back into camp until they believe we are gone."

Once Mettikapu was awake, Marta filled them both in on her speculation about the location of the dinka-chak. "But they have to either bring it back into the camp," she insisted, "or Shipner will go to it. And I think I have planted enough doubt in his mind about its survival that he will take the time to study the colony before he makes a run for Jinka."

She instructed Mettikapu to stay behind and keep watch on Shipner's camp, promising to send Gladnas to his aid. As soon as there was a sign of the missing creature, the men would signal that message using a mirror, and Marta would come back with reinforcements for a quick raid. Their drover should be back soon with the electric cart; once they had the dinka-chak, it would be a quick trip back to Jinka for her and Robinson.

It was midnight when Marta and Robinson headed back for their camp. They traveled until dawn, then stopped to rest in the meager shade of a ranran bush. Marta dozed off, then lurched to her feet when a shadow fell across her. Reaching instinctively for the knife in her belt, she had scuttled back several paces before she realized Soln Shipner was laughing at her. "Up, children, up!" he roared, which sent Robinson scrambling to his feet, also. "Are you going to sleep all day?"

Robinson swore profusely, and for once, Marta didn't blame him.

"I'm on my way to the dinka-chak colony," Shipner boomed. He had donned a poncholike garment which fluttered wildly in the desert wind, and there were heavy sandals on his knobby feet. "Won't you join me?"

"The only time I'll travel with you," Robinson growled, "is when I have your tattooed hide for a blanket."

But Shipner only snorted contemptuously. "You can't even insult me creditably. Among my people, it is a great honor to have one's skin tanned and passed on from generation to generation."

"To discolor your flesh in this way is an abomination," Marta felt compelled to say. "It dishonors the body the All-Hallowed gave you."

"Drivel." Shipner spat on the ground in contempt. "I withdraw my invitation, Princess; I would perish from boredom listening to you quote your holy book. The company of skeets and sandslithers is more appealing to me." And off he hiked across the desert, quickly leaving Marta and Robinson behind.

When they reached their own camp at noon, Marta was discouraged to find that the others had been unsuccessful in capturing a second dinka-chak in her absence. She quickly dispatched Gladnas to join Mettikapu with supplies, well aware that Soln Shipner might be watching the whole affair. There was no help for it, though. She could not leave the poor man out in Dhin M'Tarkhna without water and food. Then she sent Tookh down the caravan trail to watch for their returning electric cart, warning the drover to hide it out of sight in the hills and return to the camp on foot.

At the appointed times, Marta watched the southern horizon for mirror flashes relaying messages from her two spies. But for three days no good news arrived. Occasionally she would see Soln Shipner crouched on the ridge, watching the dinka-chaks and making notes, but the tattooed man ignored their camp. She had no idea where he slept or what he used for food, but as long as he was on the ridge, he was not running for Jinka.

It was with mixed emotions, then, that Marta received the news that Shipner had been seen leaving the area, headed back across the desert for his own camp. In desperation they set out Tookh's second trap one more time, using only an audio recording as a lure, praying mightily that another dinka-chak could be persuaded inside.

Then, just before sundown, two important events occurred. One was the arrival of a caravan carrying shells and seaweed rope and other products of the Western Coast to markets in the east. The other was a signal from the two spies outside Shipner's camp: the stolen dinka-chak had been found.

"But the Unbeliever was deaf to the voice of the Most High," Hassan recalled, *"for his heart was granite like the cliffs of Dhrusil-matkhashi. He refused to return that which he had stolen, saying that it was a free creature and did not belong to any one person. So Marta went away angry and determined to do Shipner some harm.*

"But the All-Merciful does not desire us to do harm to one another, not even to the Unbeliever. So the All-Powerful sent a great cloud of dust to hide the dark Unbeliever's camp. For three days and three nights it was hidden from the eyes of Marta and her companions, and they stumbled in darkness."

Ari shivered, knowing all too well how awful it was to be caught in a dust storm. Here inside the tent it was nice, though. Some of the people had gone off to their own tents to sleep, and others had fallen asleep right here, lulled by Hassan's voice. Mohat was one of them. He was curled up around a pillow, his breath whistling gently in and out, for the dry air bothered him. Even Ari felt that some of that desert dust had gotten into his eyes.

Hassan had noticed Mohat sleeping, for he smiled, took one last drink of water, and signaled to those still awake to leave quietly.

"Oh, you can't stop now!" Ari whined.

His father gestured for him to keep his voice down. "It's late, Ari. Tomorrow is Sabiss, we can continue the story then."

"But we're right in the middle," Ari complained.

"You don't want Mohat to miss any of it, do you?" Hassan reproved.

No, that was true. Mohat had been so caught up in the story, it was only fair to wait until he was awake again. Still . . . "Do you have to leave them in the middle of a dust storm?" he asked reproachfully.

Hassan chuckled. "They'll get out of it, don't worry. The All-Merciful is about to bless Marta with some startling new knowledge . . ."

CHAPTER 9

Robinson was incensed that Marta would not leave immediately to recapture the stolen dinka-chak, but she knew there was no need. Shipner's expedition was running low on water, and the nearest source was the dinka-chak spring, which smelled foul and was constantly watched, or the oasis on the caravan trail, just to the west of Marta's camp. If they waited, Shipner would come to them.

In the meantime, they had guests. A caravan from the renowned western village of Rahoub had met some of Ibna's men drawing water at the oasis, so an invitation had been extended for the travelers to pitch their tents with those of the scientific expedition. Tonight they would eat and sing and tell stories, for that was the courtesy of the trail, and Marta would not think of breaking it. Nakkasali, leader of the group, was a friend of her father's and a client of her husband's, and Marta knew him to be an excellent storyteller.

So with a fire crackling merrily in the deep darkness of the ravine, they ate and drank until they were surfeited. Robinson grumbled and sulked, but Marta ignored him. Kobanan had just finished regaling their guests with a retelling of the expedition's flight through the Maknial Mountains, leading Paun's men a merry chase, when Nakkasali turned to his hostess.

"And what is it again that you are seeking here, which the wily Kukhoosh Paun also seeks?" Nakkasali asked Marta.

So she explained again about the "chicken-lizard" which had appeared so mysteriously in Dhin M'Tarkhna.

Then, for the first time on this journey, she voiced her
misgivings, the nagging suspicion which Soln Shipner had
fed: "They don't look or behave as one would expect a
desert creature to look or behave. But I don't know
where they could have come from."

"Perhaps from Dhrusil-matkhashi," suggested Elir,
the younger of Nakkasali's two sons who traveled with
him. He was about twenty-five, a slim young man with
a rectangular face.

Tiny cold fingers tickled the back of Marta's neck.
These people spent their days fishing the ocean between
Innanta and the desolate continent of Dhrusil-matkhashi. But perhaps he only meant it figuratively, for
"dhrusil-matkhashi" translated literally as "land beyond
the gates."

"They are from beyond *my* gates, anyway!" She
laughed.

"No, I mean the continent," Elir insisted.

Marta shook her head in bewilderment. "Dhrusil-
matkhashi is barren," she said, as much to reassure herself as to argue with Elir. "It is a wasteland. Nothing
grows there."

Elir and his brother exchanged a glance. "Certainly
we have never seen anything different," the elder,
Shemir, admitted. He was nearer thirty, with their father's brawny build. "The rock cliffs of the eastern shore
rise up three hundred meters in the air, and though we
have sailed our vessels three days' journey up and down
that shoreline, we have never seen a place where a boat
might land. So it may be as you say."

"But we have heard sounds," Elir added. "From the
tops of the cliffs. Roarings and screechings."

"I have told you before," their father admonished. "It
was the groaning of the earth you heard. Stone against
stone. A boulder splitting away from the cliff. You're
lucky you weren't killed when it let go and fell into
the water."

But sober Shemir shook his head. "No, Father. This
was a sound like a bull bellowing, or a sea panther

squealing. It came again and again. Everyone heard it. And it came from the cliffs."

"An echo," Nakkasali insisted. "A sound from the sea bouncing back off the cliffs." His usually merry face was drawn in hard lines.

"As you say," Shemir demurred.

But it was clear that neither son believed that.

Robinson excused himself to answer a call of nature, but then he drifted down the ravine toward its mouth and stood staring out at the night sky. How immense this place was! The unchecked reaches of space soared overhead, and the ghostly star-shadowed land stretched away from him to a horizon obscured in darkness.

Framed there in what seemed like the doorway to eternity, he breathed deeply and tried to set his thoughts in order, to focus on the problem at hand. The problem was the dinka-chak, he reminded himself. Not Marta, not Shipner, but the dinka-chak. It was so saurian in its characteristics!

This was the kind of discovery he had come seeking when he left Melius: a life-form to amaze the zoological community. He had not known then what form it would take, but now it was clear: a creature had evolved on an Earth-like world, with traits so very like those of a complex Terran species that the theory of parallel interplanetary evolution leaped forward an epoch. Quasi-saurian, he called the creature in his paper. Like begets like; Earth-like Dray's planet evolved pseudo-fish, pseudo-mollusks, pseudo-crustaceans—and the quasi-saurian.

But just where had it evolved? Here in Dhin M'Tarkhna, in the dying, drying remains of this once-great sea? Or across the water on a continent the natives had never seen? Robinson had not missed the fire that ignited in Marta's eyes when Elir told his tale. She was captivated by the prospect that other life-forms dwelt in a place thought by scholars to be dead. He knew what was on her mind without asking. She wanted to seek the origins of the dinka-chak on Dhrusil-matkhashi. She wanted to see for herself the Land Beyond the Gates.

Somewhere at the back of his mind, it nagged at Robinson that Elir was probably right; the dinka-chak had probably floated across the choppy waters on a piece of driftwood a hundred or more years ago. He knew there ought to be a fossil record of its evolution, and the chances were slim that such a record was here in Dhin M'Tarkhna but simply had not been stumbled across. Somewhere in the back of his mind, Robinson knew that there might be more wonders in Dhrusil-matkhashi than anyone on this expedition could imagine.

But then he told himself the first lie: it didn't matter. Whether the feisty little creature had evolved here or there, whether there were bones embedded in this limestone or not, whether this continent or another had spawned the creature, it did not matter. What mattered for Cecil Robinson, Ph.D., was that it was a quasi-saurian, a creature so like a Terran species that it was frightening. What mattered was that he, Cecil Robinson, would be the first person to break that news to the Interstellar League of Zoologists. What mattered was that his paper, "Implications for the theory of convergent evolution on a planetary scale resulting from the discovery of quasi-saurians on Dray's Planet," would be a seminal work read and debated for centuries to come. That was what mattered.

Marta fairly ran to Robinson when she saw him returning. Their guests had retired, and the three Innantan scientists had clustered near the fire discussing the startling revelation of bestial sounds coming from Dhrusil-matkhashi. "Sab Robinson, did you hear?" she exclaimed, catching at his arm in her excitement. "Life on Dhrusil-matkhashi. Life where the Holy Ones said there was none. Do you know what that means?"

"A busy and prosperous future for the College of Indigenous Life," he replied with a touch of humor.

She missed it completely. "Rahoub is only two days from here by electric cart. If we left, even by noon tomorrow—oh, we'd have to stop for Sabiss, but even so—"

"Are you crazy?" he demanded. "Go to Rahoub *now*?"

"But we are so close!" she insisted.

Robinson took her firmly by the shoulders. "Listen to me. Our mission is to get all our data, all my research, and one live dinka-chak back to your husband. That's what he wants. That's what he's going to get. That other continent has been there for eons; trust me, it isn't going to sink into the ocean overnight. We take care of the dinka-chak *first*." He released her arms slowly. "*Then* we can talk about chasing over to Dhrusil-matkhashi." *After I have my paper published. After I get my invitation to speak at the annual conference of the ILZ. After I have rubbed a few noses in my success.*

"But we can send the dinka-chak back with Sibna Egthassa," she argued, as she had just argued with the two at the fire. "Retneyabo will have his glory."

Robinson leaned in to lecture her. "He wants more than glory, and you know it. That's why he brought me in. He wants interstellar corroboration—all that rot about needing an outside expert was just that, rot. Yatzahl knew what he had—he just needed someone who wouldn't balk at sending his paper for publication offworld, wouldn't be afraid to draw the similarities between dinka-chak and dinosaur in front of the interstellar community. It's my guts Retneyabo wants, as much as my knowledge. I can't go running off to the other side of the planet with you. Not till I've seen this paper published." *I can't get that far from the uplink to the communications satellite.*

Marta's shoulders sagged, for she knew he was right. Sibna Egthassa had said much the same thing. "Before you build the house, you must lay the foundation," she had counseled, using an old proverb. Kobanan's concern had been more worldly. "Marta, if there is anything over there, either the Holy Ones were mistaken—may the All-Merciful forgive such a sacrilegious thought—or they really don't want us to know about it. And if they really don't want us to know about it . . ."

It was too much for even Marta's agile brain, to con-

template either the ignorance or the perfidy of the Holy
Ones. It had to be a mistake. It had to be a misunder-
standing, or a misinterpretation . . . Retneyabo would
know. Yes, Retneyabo would make sense of it. "All
right," she relented. "We will get the dinka-chak and
return to Jinka. We'll need fresh supplies, anyway, and
a different team—I doubt we could get Ibna onto a boat.
But we will go there, Sab Robinson. We will go beyond
the gates of Innanta, and see what is to be found."

He drew her close to him then, smiling, and bent to
press his lips to her ear. "Wild horses couldn't stop you,
my little whirlwind," he whispered, chuckling.

Marta was so excited, she didn't notice that he hadn't
included himself in the declaration.

Nakkasali was in no rush to move from his encampment before Sabiss, so their guests lingered for two more
days. Robinson spent his time almost exclusively with
his voicewriter, editing and reediting his paper, adding,
expanding, documenting. He even worked through Sabiss, much to Marta's horror; but he declared that Soln
Shipner was most assuredly working on *his* paper, and
Robinson would gladly commit greater crimes than
Sabbath-breaking to keep one step ahead of Shipner.

The instant the sun set on Sabiss and evening prayers
were concluded, Marta sent Ibna, Tookh, and another
drover to lie in ambush at the oasis to the west of their
camp. Then she led Robinson quietly out of camp and
across the silent, shadowy flats of Dhin M'Tarkhna
toward Shipner's camp, hoping to meet up with Gladnas
and Mettikapu, who would be on their way back to her if
the tattooed man and his entourage had begun to move.

"Now, where did I leave off?" Hassan asked the group
gathered once more in his tent.

"The Unbeliever Shipner had stolen the dinka-chak,"
Ari replied quickly, *"and Marta and the other Unbeliever
were going to get it back."*

"Ah, yes," Hassan said with a smile. It delighted him
to see the rapt attention of the two boys. Somehow, the

old stories always looked fresh through the eyes of the young. And it had certainly improved Ari's disposition. Suddenly the landmarks of the stark terrain were of interest to him. He wanted to know the name of this mountain and that rock formation, and if Marta and the Unbeliever might have rested there.

"*From the rising of the sun to its setting,*" *Hassan picked up, repeating a little of the previous night's tale,* "*Marta spoke with the Unbeliever called Shipner. And the blessing of the All-Hallowed was upon her speech, so that all who heard her were moved by it—all but Shipner, whose heart was granite like the cliffs of Dhrusilmatkhashi. He refused to return that which he had stolen, saying that it was a free creature and did not belong to any one person. So Marta went away angry and determined to do Shipner some harm.*

"*But the All-Merciful does not desire us to do harm to one another, not even to the Unbeliever. He sent a great cloud of dust to hide Shipner's camp. For three days and three nights it remained hidden from the eyes of Marta and her companions, and they stumbled in darkness. And when the dust settled, lo! There came a caravan from the west . . .*"

Marta and Robinson lay flat on their bellies behind the meager screen of a cirrahn bush, watching through a night scope stripped from one of the energy rifles, as the train of donkeys ambled across the sandstone floor of Dhin M'Tarkhna. They had met up with her two spies a couple of kilometers back and gotten a report that Shipner was moving in a beeline for the caravan trail, on a heading that would bring him out no more than ten kilometers east of the defile. Under cover of darkness, she and Robinson had scurried ahead to confirm the report.

"Missing three men and four donkeys," Marta observed as she watched the column come on. "They must have sent the others for water, as I predicted."

"Great!" Robinson crowed. "Divide and conquer,

right? So let's jump them now, while it's dark. Before their waterboys get back."

But Marta was frowning. "I don't think that's Shipner."

Robinson's spirits sank. "What do you mean?" he demanded. "Who else could be out here?"

"Oh, it's his expedition," she qualified. "But the one in the lead there, the one wearing the kilt and strutting along, I don't think that one is Shipner."

Robinson snatched the night scope away from her to look for himself. "He's painted like Shipner."

"Soot from the fire, perhaps," Marta suggested. "To make this one look like Shipner. But he isn't wearing that huge knife Shipner had. And the walk is wrong."

"Wrong how?"

Marta took back the scope and studied the man again. It was more a feeling than anything else . . . ah! "Boots!" she exclaimed triumphantly. "He's wearing boots. Shipner was barefoot in camp and wore only sandals when we met him in the desert." It seemed the Nechtanite scorned apparel which covered up his tattoos. Marta wondered wickedly what manner of markings were hidden beneath his kilt.

"He might have boots, as well," Robinson pointed out.

But Marta shook her head. "In Dhin M'Tarkhna, a man travels faster in boots than in sandals. If Shipner owned boots, he'd have been wearing them earlier, for the sake of speed. Wrong footgear, wrong knife—that man is not Soln Shipner. I don't recognize who he is— maybe he's the guide who was hiding out with the dinka-chak."

"Then where's Shipner?" Robinson asked.

Marta was scrambling to her feet. She no longer cared if they were seen. "Going for the water himself," she guessed. "And he'll have the dinka-chak with him, ready to make a run for Jinka on his own. He may even have located our solar cart! Come on, we have to get back."

The sun had not slipped very far over the eastern horizon when Marta and Robinson clambered up out of

Dhin M'Tarkhna onto the caravan trail and thankfully found Kobanan waiting with the electric cart. If Shipner had planned to steal it, Kobanan had either beaten him to the vehicle, or his plans had gone awry.

Moments after reaching the trail, she and Robinson were bouncing along the rocky track at full speed. Even so, they arrived at the well half an hour after their adversaries.

Ibna had done his job well, though, wily man that he was. Two men sat securely bound at his feet, four donkeys with empty water containers tethered nearby. "One slipped away into the mountains!" he called out as Marta and Robinson approached.

Marta leapt from the cart and quickly checked the faces of the two captives. "Was the other one painted?" she asked.

Ibna frowned; he did not understand.

"Was his face marked?" Marta repeated impatiently. "Black marks on his face, his hands, his feet—"

"Yes, yes!" cried Tookh eagerly. "He wore a head-cloth pulled across his nose, and long sleeves and pants, but I saw his feet—I thought at first they were muddy. Then I looked at his eyes, and there was black all around them!"

"I thought he was a black-skinned man," Ibna grumbled.

"Did he have the dinka-chak with him?" Robinson demanded, climbing out of the cart to join the knot of people.

"He carried something," Ibna replied. "I thought it was a water container, but the cage could have been inside—it was that large."

Robinson turned to his guide. "Now what?" he asked her. "Follow him up into the hills?"

Marta chewed her lip as she considered the alternatives. Shipner had the dinka-chak, yes, but he had no water—or at least, not enough to get him back to Jinka. There was none in the mountains along this stretch of the trail, not at this time of year. Later, when the rains fell, yes, but now? "He must have water," she said

aloud. "The dinka-chak must have water. I think . . ."
Her mind raced ahead. "Ibna," she commanded, "let
these two men go. Let them fill their water jugs and
rejoin their expedition—the Manifest Revelations forbid
depriving any creature of water in the desert, and the
rest of Shipner's expedition will be dangerously low by
now."

Robinson stared at her, but Ibna nodded soberly and
directed Tookh to release the captives.

"They must have water, Sab Robinson," Marta repeated. "Shipner must have water. So we will let these
men take all the water they need, and you and I will
help them carry it to their train. Do you understand?"

A light kindled in Robinson's eyes. "Ah. You think
he'll come to his own train to get water."

"They must have a rendezvous point arranged," she
reasoned. "Shipner will have to find them, at any rate."

"And we'll be there when he arrives," Robinson deduced with a smug smile. "Ready to trade—water for
the dinka-chak."

"Well . . ." Marta hedged. "Not exactly . . ."

Soln Shipner stole through the dry and brittle scrub
on the lower slopes of the Maknial Mountains, careful
to break no branch and dislodge no stone as he passed
from shadow to afternoon shadow. Not that any of these
stupid Innantans could have tracked him this far. His
early route, yes, because he had needed first to put distance between himself and any pursuers. But then, sure
of his lead, he had begun to take more care, and his
tracks had disappeared.

For all the good that does me, he thought ruefully as
he made his way closer to the caravan trail. He had
lavished the last of his water on the ungrateful creature
in the cage an hour ago. Vicious thing! But it would
perish more quickly than he, and Paun had specified a
live animal. Retneyabo already had a dead one; to top
that, a living specimen was necessary.

When his meager supply of water had run out, however, so had his options. He'd studied maps of this trail

and the surrounding mountains carefully before leaving
Jinka, and he knew there were no water sources within
his reach, except the oasis which Marta's people held,
and the sulfurous dinka-chak spring which was also
closely watched. There was no help for it; he would have
to join up with his expedition if he wanted water.

The ambush at the well hadn't surprised him. In fact,
he had expected trouble. But he hadn't expected the
cleverness of it, nor that it would be more than he could
handle. They had climbed up the rim in darkness, he
and his two minions and their four donkeys, approaching
the watering hole in the gray morning light. There was
only one lone guard there, and he was having trouble
staying awake by that time. No reinforcements were in
sight. Easy enough to jump him.

But, of course, there had been others out of sight,
lying under woven mats concealed by sand and loose
rock. They popped up at the guard's signal, energy rifles
covering the intruders. Shipner had taken advantage of
the one's youth and inexperience to cast sand in his eyes
and break for cover with the dinka-chak, charges from
the rifles shattering rocks behind him. Easy to get
away himself.

Easy, but pointless, since he could not go much further
without water.

A thin stream of smoke caught Shipner's eye. His
party? The princess? Or perhaps that caravan he'd spotted before he left the dinka-chak colony, on the move
after their Sabiss stop? One could always hope . . .

Creeping nearer, he saw that it was his own expedition, camped on the caravan trail; one tent had been
thrown up, and three of his men sat outside it. There
was something odd about them, though—ah, yes. Their
hands were tied; and lolling in the shade of a taliyeko
tree was Cecil Robinson, an energy rifle lying carelessly
across his knees. A scowl started to form on Shipner's
brow, but then he saw that Robinson leaned against the
wooden chassis of one of Innanta's ungainly but efficient
solar-powered carts.

Slowly a smile spread across Shipner's face. Now, this

had possibilities. To sneak into camp, replenish his water, and make off with the vehicle would certainly leave egg on the young zoologist's face. But . . . the ambush at the well had taught him not to underestimate the craft of the princess. Robinson was undoubtedly not the only one of Marta's expedition waiting in the camp— how many could be inside that tent?—and one of them, surely, would have been smart enough to disable the electric cart to prevent its theft. Well, then . . .

It was time to bargain. He held the trump card, after all: the dinka-chak. He would do much as Marta had done, walk boldly into the camp and demand water. He'd read the Innantans' holy books; they could not refuse him water. And as long as he didn't have the dinka-chak with him, they would have to let him go or give up any hope of retaking it.

Glancing around, Shipner spotted a cleft in the rocky slope near a bura-bura thicket which would suit his purpose. He tucked the dinka-chak's cage carefully inside, then covered the opening with some dried foliage. Brushing away any marks of his presence from the area, he circled around to another quarter before he straightened up, refastened an unruly braid which was dangling in his face, and sauntered casually into the camp.

His own men met him with worried and embarrassed countenances; Fadnar's in particular looked as black as a storm cloud. Shipner paid them no mind, nodding a greeting and heading straight for the water barrels.

Robinson drew himself up as Shipner approached. "Well, hello, there, Soln," he greeted with insolent cheerfulness. "How nice to see you."

Shipner only harrumphed, for his throat was too dry to attempt speech. Opening the spigot on a water barrel, he let the precious liquid stream into his empty canteen, then lifted the canteen to his lips and took a long, quenching drink. Finally, "Good evening, Dr. Robinson," he said. "Changed sides?"

Robinson laughed. "No, actually," the blond man replied, "I was just waiting here for you to show up and surrender the dinka-chak to me."

"Dinka-chak?" said Shipner. "What dinka-chak is that?"

"The dinka-chak you stole from my camp." There was more of an edge to Robinson's voice now.

"The dinka-chak is a wild creature," Shipner told him. "It has no owner and therefore cannot be stolen except from its own kind, and you did that, not me."

"Horseshit," said Robinson flatly. He had made the amazing discovery that not every word classified as profanity on Melius was considered profanity by the Innantans—only those relating to a deity or a deity's prerogatives, and certain words making light of sanctified acts or institutions. References to animal excrement were not included.

Shipner grinned at him, took another swig of water, then nodded toward the vehicle and asked, "What's wrong with the cart?"

"Power's disconnected," Robinson informed him. "I was kind of hoping you'd slink in here and try to steal it, just so I could see the look on your face when it wouldn't start."

Shipner chuckled. "Did you think of that all by yourself, or did the princess help you?"

"The princess?" Robinson raised an eyebrow. "Now, who would that be?"

"The young lady you were screwing rather noisily when I slipped into your camp about a week ago." Shipner expected some reaction to that, and he got it, but not from Robinson. Fadnar came to his feet explosively. "Sit down, Fadnar!" Shipner snarled, and the boy sank back down. What a wretched lot of lackeys Paun had secured for him!

"Oh, you mean Marta," Robinson replied easily. "Yes, she can be quite a distraction. And I must admit it was her idea to unplug the power cell and pocket the connector. She's a sharp little number, that one."

"Poor taste in men, though," Shipner observed, and he noted with satisfaction that Robinson's smile grew a little frosty. "Where is the princess? In the tent?" If she had the connector in her pocket, it was she with whom he should be negotiating.

"No, she's not here," Robinson told him.

"Oh?" Shipner studied him curiously. He was too calm, too sure of himself. In previous encounters, Robinson had been volatile, lashing out with as little forethought as he gave to pulling his research together. Now he acted like a man holding four aces. What was going on? Shipner turned to look at his own men, and the smile slid from his face. "Fadnar, where is the princess?"

"She went back up the trail," the young man told him. "A couple of hours ago."

A couple of hours! But why would—

Suddenly Shipner whipped around and looked back up the slope to where he had earlier crouched concealed, peering down at the camp. Surely she hadn't been waiting up there, watching his approach— Oh, yes, surely she had. The woman knew he would have to come down from there for water, and that only a fool would bring the dinka-chak with him into camp . . .

As if summoned by his fears, Marta appeared from the shadow of a shrubby *chakmo* tree, carrying the dinka-chak cage in one hand. She waved merrily and started down the steep slope toward them. "You're very clever, Sab Shipner," she called as she came on, her eyes on the treacherous ground beneath her feet. "I lost you momentarily when you crossed the last ridge, and by the time I got you in my sights again, you no longer had the dinka-chak."

Shipner tensed. If he waited until she was a little nearer, then lunged at her, he might get the creature back and get away. She was unarmed, and Robinson wasn't likely to fire at him and risk injuring her or the dinka-chak. "Dinka-chak?" he bluffed. "I had no dinka-chak, I told you."

"Not after I lost you," Marta agreed, puffing a little with the exertion of descending the slope. "But I knew it had to be around there somewhere," she continued, "so I opened my water bottle and shook it around a little. They can smell water, you know, the dinka-chaks."

The creature in the cage squawked, whether in protest of the rough ride or affirmation of her statement, it was hard to say. "Sure enough, she started to make a terrible racket, and then she was easy to find." Marta stopped at the edge of the camp and put the cage down. "I doused her and let her drink, and then she was much happier." The dinka-chak gave a disgruntled chirp by way of disagreement.

"How lucky for you, Princess," Shipner replied as he carefully refilled his canteen. "And for the dinka-chak. How do you suppose it got up there?" He wondered if the canteen would be enough for him to make it back to Marta's camp, where they would not be expecting him, and where he could steal enough water to go on. Or should he pretend to fall in with them, wait until they got nearer to Jinka—no, Marta would never trust him. But if he had the creature—

Just then a huge, bearded Innantan pushed out of the tent—it was the guard from the well, and he had a large coil of rope with a loop at one end. He toyed idly with the loop as he eyed the painted man, as though measuring him for a fit. Shipner knew he had lost.

The tension slid out of the Nechtanite's bunched muscles like water seeping away into the sand, and Shipner stooped to pick up a rolled sleeping mat from the stack of supplies near his feet. Without a word he pulled the binding cord and spread the mat on the ground near the fire.

"What are you doing?" Robinson asked suspiciously.

"Getting some rest," Shipner growled. "I've been on the trail for twenty-four hours, and unless you plan to give me a ride to Jinka in your electric cart, I have a long journey yet ahead." He stretched out on the mat and closed his eyes. "So if you'll excuse me . . ."

Before Marta and Robinson could even exchange a startled glance, Soln Shipner was asleep.

CHAPTER 10

"But Marta discovered his ruse," Hassan told his listeners, *"and leaving the imposter, she followed the Tattooed Man into the mountains. For three days and three nights she tracked him; then she found him sleeping in the shade of a taliyeko tree. Quietly she slipped up to him, slid the dinka-chak's cage out from under his hand, and ran away in the darkness. The creature sang its joy at being reunited with the brave Marta, and all around, it seemed the voices of creatures everywhere joined in the song. So Marta returned to her husband, the great Kukhoosh Retneyabo, and brought him all honor and glory."*

They were enjoying dinner at Retneyabo's seaside estate. At least, Marta was enjoying the dinner. She lounged on cushions at the low table, dressed once more in her flowing white gown with the nails of her bare feet polished bright red and three exquisite toe rings winking in the lamplight. Her daughter Rakkela cuddled next to her, feeding her bits of seafood and ripe olives, while her son Yari sat at her elbow pestering her with questions about the expedition and the dinka-chak and the scary tattooed man, Soln Shipner.

Robinson found it unnerving to think that these youngsters belonged to her. Oh, to be sure, they didn't call her Mother—that title was reserved for Adni—but her features shone from their faces: Yari's bright, inquisitive eyes, Rakkela's long lashes and dark, curling hair. Even more unnerving was looking at Retneyabo, seated there at the head of the table like a smiling, benevolent patriarch, and knowing that tonight Marta would be with *him,* offering up those same pleasures Robinson had so lately enjoyed . . .

And she'd been so *heartless* about it! In their breakneck flight back to Jinka, the two of them had taken turns driving the solar cart so they could travel straight through the night. At Ballabim they were met by Retneyabo's retainers, for as soon as they had left Shipner and his gang safely behind, Marta had used the pocketpad to send word of their return to the College of Indigenous Life. From Ballabim there were other drivers, but again they traveled through the night. Robinson and Marta slept in the backseat of the cart, the dinka-chak on the floor between their feet, and Robinson had only wanted to hold her while they slept, but she declined. "No more, Sab Robinson," she said firmly. "We are within a day's journey of my husband now. I must honor all the terms of my marriage contract."

If only she'd sounded regretful! A sigh, an apology— but no, just this matter of fact, "No more." Robinson felt like a cast-off shoe.

"You put the connector in your pocket!" Yari was exclaiming in delight. "How clever you are, Marta! Then what happened?"

"I went up into the hills above their camp," she told him, "and simply waited for him to come. But he managed to give me the slip once, and hide the dinka-chak."

"Hide it! Where?" the boy demanded.

"Oh, he was clever," Marta said with obvious praise in her voice. "He tucked the cage into a cleft of rock behind a thicket, then arranged branches over the opening so that you couldn't tell it from the rest of the foliage in the fading light. He's a smart one, that Sab Shipner."

"But how did you find it?"

Robinson stared grimly at the fruit concoction in his glass and wished mightily that it were a stiff belt of rye whiskey. Why wasn't the boy asking *him* about their adventure, anyway? You'd think they had an Unbeliever to dinner every day of the week . . .

As though sensing his jealously, Marta continued: "Sab Robinson kept Sab Shipner distracted in the camp while I searched. I just sprinkled water around, hoping the dinka-chak would smell it and make some noise—and that's just what it did." She shot a smile in Robinson's direction. "But it was Sab Robinson and Ibna who made sure Sab Shipner didn't get away and try to steal the creature back."

Seeing the glowering look on Robinson's face, Adni now entered the conversation to pull the focus back to her guest's area of expertise. "How soon will your paper be published, Sab Robinson?" she asked. Adni herself held an advanced degree in economics, and her thesis was still cited by undergraduate students of that subject, so she knew the importance of publication and the glory it brought.

"It was released on the University network this morning," Robinson told her proudly, "and printed copies will be distributed in all the major cities starting next week. I submitted a more elaborate version—since I had to explain more of Innantan zoology—for uplink to the communications satellite this afternoon. At this time of year, it should have been transmitted directly to the Portal. They'll shoot it through on the first ship, and by tomorrow noon it will be in the hands of the editor of the *JILZ*." *And I'll be by-God famous. What do you think of that, Yari?*

Adni raised her eyebrows. "Transmitted this afternoon?" She shot her husband a curious look. "So quickly? I was sure the mazhel would debate it longer than that."

Robinson blinked. "Debate it?"

"Any transmission that goes beyond our gates," Retneyabo explained, "must have the approval of the Holy Ones. But I have the ear of Mazh Nrin, who believes as I do, that this discovery is blessed. He will shepherd it through quickly. It may be—a week or two, but I'm sure the delay will be no longer than that."

Robinson felt his stomach turn. "Shipner could be back here in two weeks."

But Retneyabo laughed. "Have no fear on that count, Robinson. Were he to magically appear this evening,

Paun does not have the influence necessary to get any writing of his transmitted ahead of yours. Our Holy Ones understand the ways of scholastic publication, and they are incorruptible; they will not allow one man to gain or lose because of the order in which they issue their approvals."

"Don't worry, Sab Robinson," Marta chimed in. "I'm sure you'll have confirmation of your paper's receipt by the ILZ before we leave for Dhrusil-matkhashi."

"Ah-ah-ah," Retneyabo cautioned, waving a pudgy finger at her. "I have not made my decision yet as regards funding an expedition to Dhrusil-matkhashi."

Marta did not pursue the topic; she knew she would have to provide Retneyabo with much more information than she had been able to sketch out for him in the past two days. More research to find historical references to the continent, chasing down maps of the channel, perhaps a visit to the fishing villages of the Western Coast—

"I appreciate your wanting to include me," Robinson said carefully, "but if I've concluded the work you brought me here to do, patron, I would like to return to my homeworld now to continue my study of the dinka-chak recordings. I anticipate there will be some . . ." He cleared his throat. "Some speaking engagements requested. I would like to spread your glory beyond the gates of Innanta by telling them of your patronage, and how you made this discovery possible."

Marta's face fell. *Then she does care,* Robinson thought with satisfaction. *She did want me to go off on expedition with her again, to be with her again . . .*

Retneyabo frowned momentarily, then gave a heavy sigh. "I am sorry to hear you say that, Robinson," he said. "There is much work yet to be done in studying the dinka-chak, and I had hoped you would remain to assist us. Now that the initial discovery has been credited to my college, we will have the exclusive right to further investigation, and there will be no more trouble from Paun's creatures. We could set up a more permanent— meaning more comfortable—base for you next spring— build a road down into Dhin M'Tarkhna . . ." A lift of his eyebrows indicated that this was an attempt to lure Robinson into staying.

Robinson thought about a cozy shelter in the ravine, a lab with proper equipment, and Marta in his bed . . . He shook his head, smiling. "Thank you, but—I think your own scientists can do that best. I've opened the road, established the connection to Earth's dinosaurs, which is what you wanted from me. I think now we are both best served by my being back in the larger scholarly community." *Guest speaker at the annual conference. Invited lecturer at a paleontology symposium. Ashdod Prize . . .*

"As you wish," Retneyabo conceded. "I will see the provost tomorrow about processing your request for transport back to Melius. I'll let you know when there is a ship available for your passage. But in the meantime, I hope you will plan to give a symposium? To present your paper? Before you go."

A chance to do a dry run on his presentation, polish it up a bit for the Big Show. "I'd be delighted, patron," he said with a dazzling smile.

"But what about Dhrusil-matkhashi?" Ari squeaked as his father concluded the recitation.

"Tomorrow," Hassan promised. "I will tell you more of the story tomorrow." His throat was dry, and his eyes burned from the dryness.

"While we travel?" Ari asked eagerly.   .

Hassan furrowed his brow sternly. "You don't want Mohat to miss any of it, do you?"

Mohat threw Ari an indignant look, and the boy cried, "Oh, no! But can't Mohat ride with us, instead of with his mother, tomorrow?"

Hassan sighed. "I have much to do tomorrow, Ari," he explained. "I can't be telling stories when there's work to be done."

Mohat tugged on Ari's sleeve and gestured quickly. "Oh. Mohat wants you to tell the story again," Ari told his father; but Mohat shook his head and gestured once more, impatiently. "No, no, he wants me to tell him the

story again. Tomorrow, Mohat? Oh, yes!" the boy exclaimed happily. *"I'll ride with Mohat and his mother
tomorrow and tell him the story again."*

Hassan smiled. Now, that was more like it. Two boys,
traveling across the desert in a caravan, telling each other
stories, acting them out, playing amongst the rocks and
tents—that was why he'd brought Ari along. To experience the old ways of doing things, to know the land as
his ancestors had known it, to live the legends and the
history of his people. The Children of the Second Revelation must never lose touch with their past, their heroes,
or their imaginations.

Hassan's smile softened as his eyes shifted to Mohat. It
would do the Silent One good, too. That had not been
part of Hassan's plan when he agreed to take the boy and
his mother along on this caravan, but he suspected now
that it had been part of Kukhoosh Sridr's plan. A wise
man, and a clever one, was Kukhoosh Sridr.

"But tell me first," Ari pestered as the others made their
way out of the great tent, "did Marta and the Unbeliever
go to Dhrusil-matkhashi?"

"Oh, yes," Hassan assured him. "Marta went forth
unto the Land Beyond the Gates; and the Unbeliever followed her joyously."

Marta glared at Robinson across the living room of
his faculty apartment. It was a month now since they
had returned from Dhin M'Tarkhna, and the Unbeliever
had presented his paper that afternoon in an outstanding
symposium at the University. The hall had been packed,
the questions directed to him afterward had been astute
and challenging, and Robinson had been brilliant in his
responses. Perhaps he would actually win that Ashdod
Prize he wanted so badly.

But when she went to congratulate him afterward—
and, she must admit, to try to seduce him into staying—
he had brushed her off. Hurt, angry, she was here now,
inappropriate as it might be for a married woman to be
alone in an apartment with a single man. Dressed once
more in her student clothes, seduction having been re-

buffed as a means of getting what she wanted, Marta
was back in her accustomed posture of making decisions
and giving orders.

"How can you not want to go back and study the
dinka-chaks this spring?" she demanded of the Unbeliever.

Robinson, who was busy packing, shot an angry glance
at her. It was hardly the first time she had hurled the
subject at him since the dinner at Retneyabo's, where
he'd announced his intention to return to Melius. Usually her tirades revolved around Dhrusil-matkhashi, but
the theme was the same. How could he not want to go?
What kind of scientist was he? Robinson was well tired
of it—especially after this afternoon's symposium. "Me!"
he barked. "What about you? Are you going to surrender Dhrusil-matkhashi to keep studying the dinka-
chak?"

A pout clouded Marta's features, which might have
amused him if his stomach hadn't been tied in knots
over the symposium. "The kukhoosh has not yet said I
may go to Dhrusil-matkhashi," she admitted. "It flies in
the face of the Holy Ones' teachings, you see, and so
there could be unpleasant consequences to sponsoring
such an expedition. If we cannot go there, you should
certainly come with me back to Dhin M'Tarkhna."

Her high-handed attitude was not what he needed just
now, and Robinson was profoundly glad that he would
be departing in a few days. There was a medical shuttle
on its way back from an emergency trip to the GenOrg
mining colonies—an outbreak of something-or-other,
and with the critical serum delivered, there was no reason the shuttle couldn't divert to Dray's and pick him
up on the return voyage. He would miss the unexpected
turns of her mind, the leaps of her imagination, and he
would certainly miss their erotic adventures—but he
would *not* miss her nagging. He was reminded of a message he had seen scrawled on the wall of a men's room
somewhere: No matter how good she looks, someone
else is tired of her shit.

"Look, I've told you," he repeated none too patiently.

"I have to go back to defend my paper. There are going to be questions about my research, just as there were at the symposium today: challenges to my assumptions, attacks on my conclusions. If I have to get every transmission off-planet approved by your Holy Ones, it will take weeks to respond to each one." Including the one that was never voiced today, the one Robinson knew would come in the most public forum possible. "I need to get back to where communications are better, to where lab equipment is more sophisticated. It's necessary to my career." *And I want to accept my Ashdod Prize in person—and thumb my nose at Soln Shipner, damn his tattooed hide!*

Shipner had shown up at the symposium, dressed as always in his worn kilt and nothing more. He'd walked in just before Robinson started, given him a cold smile, and then stood at the back of the auditorium for the entire presentation. Just stood there, arms folded, eyes mocking. Robinson had kept waiting for him to raise his hand, a signal to the moderator that he wanted to ask a question at the close of the presentation. But Shipner had not moved from his posture of contempt. There was a hand here, a hand there, and finally a flood of questions at the end; but still no response from Shipner. Nothing. Robinson knew the man did not agree with his conclusions—Shipner never agreed with *anything* that broke with conventional teaching. So why hadn't he said anything? Why hadn't he challenged the amount of research Robinson had done, the quality of the lab work, the speculative nature of this association with dinosaurs?

Marta clicked her tongue in impatience, unaware of any turmoil but her own. "You need to collect more data on the dinka-chak," she charged, inadvertently treading on a sore spot. Robinson knew this would be the general reaction from the scientific community.

"Yatzahl said he'd send me copies of further research," he replied doggedly, telling himself that was good enough. "I wish I could take the dinka-chak specimen with me, but Yatzahl won't release that to me." He tucked several data disks into his valise. "Not that I blame him," he grumbled. "Who knows if the poor thing would even survive space travel?"

Marta marched across the room to burn her gaze directly into Robinson's face, something she could only do because he had sat down at his flatscreen to download more files. "There could be a whole continent full of quasi-saurians," she grated at him between clenched teeth. "Dinka-chaks and dinka-chak cousins, and all those intermediate evolutionary creatures we know have to exist somewhere! You could take a shipload of specimens, and who would care?"

"There could be nothing on that continent," he pointed out perversely. "Surely there were early surveys of the planet, before your people were granted their charter. Do you think your Holy Ones just made up the notion that the place was barren?"

Marta ground her teeth in frustration, for those were the same objections Retneyabo had raised, and Sab Yatzahl. She had no more answer for Robinson than she'd had for them.

A hearty knock at the door relieved her of trying to reply. "It is I, Robinson!" boomed Retneyabo's familiar voice; but something in it sounded off to Marta's ear. Something of his usual joviality was missing . . .

"Brilliant lecture today, Robinson, absolutely brilliant!" Retneyabo congratulated the Unbeliever as he was admitted to the apartment. His bodyguard, as always, waited outside the door. "It will take three weeks to peel that smile off Yatzahl's face. Of course, it was a very kindly disposed audience," he cautioned, "which you are not likely to find offworld, but all the same, I found your arguments very convincing. So did the Dean of Biology, and he is not easily impressed."

Retneyabo paused and looked pointedly around the room at the furniture. Robinson hastily invited him to sit down.

As the kukhoosh seated himself, Marta tried again to imagine what problem had really brought her husband here, but the possibilities were too broad, and nothing in his face or demeanor gave it away. Retneyabo never gave anything away until he was ready. Fortunately, he came quickly to the point.

The smile faded slowly from his broad face as he looked at Robinson, who was seated now in a chair across from the kukhoosh. "I'm afraid I have bad news, Robinson," Retneyabo said gently. Marta knew that tone; she held her breath and begged mercy of the All-Hallowed.

Robinson froze in his chair.

"The mazhel have decided it is not in the best interest of the Faithful to have news of the dinka-chak spread to other worlds."

Robinson's sun-darkened face blanched white. Marta's jaw fell.

"Your paper will not be transmitted back to the ILZ," Retneyabo said succinctly. "Furthermore, you will not be allowed to leave us. The knowledge you have acquired must stay within our gates. I am afraid, Sab Robinson, that you are stranded here on our planet." Then he added, whether by consolation or to pour out every last injustice, Robinson didn't know: "And so is Soln Shipner."

Retneyabo stood on the balcony of his town house and wished fervently that he were back at his seaside estate. He badly needed the bracing sea breeze and Adni's quiet comfort to ease his spirit. But there was much for him to do in the next few days, and he could not afford the luxury of traveling back and forth to Jinka from his estate down the coast.

The decision of the mazhel had been as much a shock to him as to Robinson. He had spent years building up to this, cultivating the right people, establishing the proper precedents. When they approved his request to bring in a guest professor, he was sure the climate was right and that he had the confidence of the mazhel. There had been objections in the Council of Kukhooshel to publishing Robinson's work off-planet, but that was to be expected. It was the same old hard-liners, objecting on the same old principle: no traffic with the Unbeliever.

But it was not their decision to make; the decision of what ought and ought not to be published offworld rested solely with the Holy Ones. Historically, the Holy Ones had always ruled that the Unbeliever was not bound by Innantan law, but by the laws of Unbelievers. That law allowed Robinson to publish.

But this time, their decision had gone the other way. "When he came to us," they said, "he came within the realm of the Faithful and promised to abide by our laws." Then they produced a document Robinson had signed accepting residence on Dray's Planet as a gift from the mazhel. Residency constituted citizenship, they said; he had surrendered his rights as a Meliusan citizen and was now subject to the wishes of the mazhel.

Retneyabo was sure that a Meliusan attorney could argue that point and win eventually, but it would take so many years to negotiate the case that Robinson would be long dead before it was decided. In the meantime, when the University of Northsea bothered to inquire about their absent professor—if they bothered to inquire—they would be shown the signed document and told Dr. Cecil Robinson had accepted a permanent staff position with the University of Innanta. It was unlikely they wanted him back badly enough to investigate further.

How Robinson had raged at this betrayal! Retneyabo didn't blame him. He, too, was enraged, although on a less personal level. This decision meant two things for the kukhoosh: one, that he did not have the influence with the mazhel that he'd believed he had; and two, that his dream of opening a door to limited commerce between Innanta and the outside had run into a significant roadblock.

Who was responsible? Mazh Farbo? Paun's influence over the mazh was increasing; but even so, could Farbo sway the rest of the mazhel to her side? She was highly respected but relatively young for a mazh. Retneyabo needed to know exactly what had gone on during the debate, what allegations were leveled, what points made, and by whom. His messenger was even now waiting in the courtyard of Mazh Nrin, bearing Retneyabo's note begging humbly for an audience.

And what about this story that had Marta so excited, that there might be animals on Dhrusil-matkhashi? He had glanced through the file Marta brought him that evening with all the official references to Innanta's second continent which could be found in the mazhish literature. "Uninhabitable," was the word used. School texts said "barren" or "sterile" or "wasteland," but the mazhish literature was carefully consistent: uninhabitable. For what reason? Nothing was specified.

Yet if the continent were not a useless or even dangerous place, why had the mazhel allowed that perception to continue? Did the current mazhel even know why the mazhel of past centuries had classified Dhrusil-matkhashi as uninhabitable?

Too many questions, and Retneyabo did not like any of the possible answers.

Just then Marta came out from inside, dressed in a tantalizingly filmy house garment. Ah, what a delicious sight she was, even with that frown darkening her brow. He beckoned to her to come into his arms.

Standing with her young body close to his, Retneyabo could feel the tension in her and knew she was too agitated by all this to be very playful tonight. He was agitated himself; but he had taken concrete steps today to locate the source of his difficulties, and that helped immeasurably. Marta was a woman of action; he must give her something concrete to do, as well.

"I have a task for you, my wild one," he murmured in the growing darkness. "I want you to plan another expedition—just plan it—and like the last one, very quietly, very discreetly. Take all winter to plot it out, everything from your transportation to your supplies to your personnel. Present your plan to me, your cost estimates, your justification. But don't enact anything until I tell you."

Marta caught her breath. "An expedition? To—?"

"To a place you have never been," he said quietly, a small smile coloring his lips. "To Dhrusil-matkhashi."

                        *   *   *

Mazh Nrin was a tailor. Like all the mazhel, he supported himself with a trade, so that he might stay in
touch with the lives of common people, and so that he
need not be financially dependent upon others, a condition which could influence his thinking.

Also like his fellow mazhel, Nrin was very careful
about choosing his clientele. Many people vied for the
honor of being a mazh's client, and it was necessary for
a mazh to select those who were devout and of noble
purpose, or once again he might be subject to corrupting
influence. Nrin counted among his clients three University professors, four musicians, nine shopkeepers, eight
tradesmen, ten factory workers, two merchants, eighteen
construction workers, sixteen primary school teachers,
three sib-nurahs, and only one kukhoosh.

Retneyabo had first come to Mazh Nrin as a young
man of nineteen or twenty. Nrin had consented to see
him because his father was a good man; but he was not
impressed by the polite but zealous young trader. "You
do good things for the wrong reason," he said bluntly.

"Better than to do bad things for the right reason,"
Retneyabo quipped.

But Nrin shook his head. "When you can explain to
me why that is not true, you can come back."

It was eight years before a humbler Retneyabo once
again gained an audience with the tailor.

"A caring heart will strive to correct an errant deed,"
said the young merchant. "A good deed can never correct a blighted heart."

They talked for long hours then of Retneyabo's struggle, not to become prosperous and respected, but to be
fair and generous. They spoke of the risks, of not financial but emotional investments. Finally Nrin put a hand
on the young man's shoulder. "You are your father's
son," he said. "Let me make you a shirt."

Sixteen years had passed, and Nrin had made some
very fine garments for Kukhoosh Retneyabo. Now here
was the prosperous merchant in his shop again, and as
they looked over a selection of fabrics, Retneyabo had

many questions—few of them dealing with the cloth. "Do not the Manifest Revelations tell us," Retneyabo was saying, "that the Faithful must not force their ways upon the Unbeliever?"

"Indeed, they do," Nrin agreed.

"Yet we force the Unbelievers to stay among us, when they do not desire to do so."

"That is different," Nrin explained. "Belief in the Most High cannot be forced, any more than one can be forced to like the taste of a particular food; and without that belief, the outward motions are meaningless. But we do require that those Unbelievers who sojourn among us do not behave in such a way as to corrupt the Faithful; likewise, when we feel their departure endangers our refuge here in Innanta, we must prevent that."

Retneyabo spread his hands. "How can sharing this great scientific discovery endanger the Faithful?" he asked.

Nrin cocked an eyebrow and gave Retneyabo a knowing look. "You know very well the kind of attention this discovery would draw. That is why you orchestrated it. You have been caught, that is all."

Retneyabo grinned, for he knew Nrin was a moderate when it came to isolationism. The old mazh was of the opinion that such things as more advanced medical equipment and regular shipments of hard metals would surely not corrupt the soul. "And would this attention be so bad?" he asked the old man.

Nrin sighed deeply. "I must tell you, Retneyabo, I found it hard to object when Mazh Sodat presented his concerns. It is good to share Knowledge; but there are many without Knowledge who are fascinated by these creatures, these extinct animals called dinosaurs. It is not the attention of true scholars I mind, but the attention of curiosity-seekers. My heart is uneasy at the thought of what commotion this dinka-chak may cause beyond our gates."

Retneyabo frowned and fingered a fine blue brocade. "It was Mazh Sodat, then, who suggested the Unbeliev-

ers be detained." Sodat certainly would command the
respect of his peers.

"Sodat was one of many who voiced concern over the
release of this information," Nrin qualified.

"And Mazh Alaria?" Retneyabo questioned. "Was
she also in favor of withholding Robinson's paper?"

"You don't want the brocade," Nrin told him, setting
aside that bolt of fabric. "Here. Feel this twill. Nothing
better for a winter coat." He unrolled a length of burgundy cloth. "Alaria thought it would be better if Sab
Robinson studied the dinka-chak further before he reported on it to the ILZ."

"So they all danced around it, eh?" Retneyabo
guessed. "No one wanted to be accused of squelching
Knowledge, but no one wanted this information to go
beyond our gates."

Nrin sighed heavily. "The twill is easier for me to
work with," he said honestly. "My fingers grow weaker
with age; I suggested the twill for my convenience, not
because it suits you better."

They are afraid, Retneyabo thought. *They recognize
the fear in themselves and know it for what it is. They
wonder if their decision was truly just.*

"The twill is fine," Retneyabo said. "For now. Perhaps
another winter I will choose a brocade."

"It is not an irreversible decision," Nrin agreed. "We
can consider it again later. One of my apprentices is
getting very good. Perhaps next year I will let him work
on a coat of yours; his fingers are stronger than mine."

Retneyabo took the old man's gnarled hand. "Your
fingers are as strong as the All-Wise means for them
to be."

Nrin patted his client's beringed hand, then turned
and picked up the twill. "I should have the coat ready
in about three weeks," he told the kukhoosh.

Retneyabo started for the door of the shop, then
stopped and turned back. "Mazh Nrin," he called to the
tailor, "what do Holy Ones say today about Dhrusil-
matkhashi?"

Nrin turned on him with startled eyes which narrowed quickly with suspicion. "Why do you ask?"

Retneyabo smiled and spread his hands. "I seek Knowledge."

"To what purpose?" the tailor demanded, and Retneyabo's smile faded. It was unlike the mazh to take that tone with him.

"My sib-hinan has just come back from the West," he explained. "She heard strange tales about sounds coming from Dhrusil-matkhashi."

"Tell her to forget them," Nrin said bluntly. "Forget she heard them. And for the love of the Martyrs, do not let her repeat those tales at University!" Then the tailor turned on his aging heel and shuffled out of the room.

Marta sat on the floor of her University apartment with books and papers scattered around her, staring at the notepad in her hand. On it was a list of equipment they might need for an expedition to Dhrusil-matkhashi: tents, mats, and blankets; lots of rope for climbing the cliffs; traps, cages, and specimen boxes for the creatures they hoped to find—but after that she was stymied. What they would need depended on what they would find. What kind of climate did the western continent have? What kind of terrain? Would it be a moist jungle, requiring machetes to hack their way through? Snow-capped mountains, requiring sleds and skis to move across? Inland seas, making boats necessary?

There was simply no way of knowing what to expect. The only clue she had was the dinka-chak, and that was a poor clue, indeed. "Suppose that the dinka-chaks did come from Dhrusil-matkhashi," she'd proposed to Robinson. "What does that tell us about the climate there? The terrain?"

"You could find an assortment of environments," he'd growled back at her. He was working at the University now, continuing the research with Sibna Egthassa, but he was not happy. After a moment's thought, he'd added, "There's probably more water there than here. Fresh water. And trees—they roost in trees, not on rocks."

Marta waited patiently while he brooded a while longer.
"Not too cold," he hazarded, "because they prefer the
valley to the mountains. Moderate to warm, I'd say. And
prey animals—they're carnivores."

It was not much for Marta to go on. Trees—so bring
axes, to chop firewood if nothing else, but possibly ham-
mers and saws to build things they might need, or to
clear a path through a woodland. And insect netting,
because if there were animals, there could be biting insects. But what else? A boat? Robinson could sail, so a
small sailboat might be good to have. But to haul it all
the way up a cliff face . . .

There had to be more information, there just had to
be! If only she could get an educated guess . . . Sibna
Egthassa hadn't had anything more to offer than Robinson. Who else had studied the dinka-chak enough to—

Soln Shipner sat cross-legged on the floor of a one-
room rental, intent upon a flatscreen sitting on a plank
that was propped up by two mud bricks. A small brazier
burned in the center of the room, for the first of the
winter rains sluiced in sheets against buildings and trees
outside, and the room was chilly. Shipner wore only his
faded kilt, seeming not to notice the temperature.

Marta shivered inside her oilskin cape, but whether it
was from the dampness or the sight of those tattoos
snaking over his body in the flickering light, she wasn't
sure. She had read his dossier before coming—not that
it told her much beyond his academic credits. Nechtanites were notoriously close-mouthed about their personal
lives. There was precious little written on the warrior
sect itself, either. But she had learned that Nechtanites
were Nechtanites by choice, not by birth, and the first
tattoos were not applied until the choice was made, usually in adolescence. No two Nechtanites bore the same
tattoos, and although there were some discernable patterns, no one knew what those patterns meant—or
rather, no one who knew was telling.

"Well, well, Princess," Shipner said without looking
up, "what brings you to my humble abode?"

It was humble, indeed. Paun must have cast him off with almost nothing, for the room was hardly three meters square and furnished with no more than the brazier, a couple of rugs, the makeshift table, and two or three crates. "It looks as though your patron did not take very good care of you," she remarked.

"Oh, I have resources enough," he replied easily. "My needs are simple."

Still he had not looked up from the flatscreen. Marta was tempted to make herself more noticeable, but she wasn't dressed for it, and she didn't think Soln Shipner would be impressed, anyway. Instead she shook the water droplets from her oilskin and took two steps closer to the painted man. "I want to ask you a question," she said bluntly.

He was scrolling through images on the flatscreen. "Ask away," he invited in that absentminded way professors and parents have when they're involved in something else and are really only listening with half an ear. Or less. Marta decided that if you could get past the wildly braided hair, the tattoos decorating his face, and the fact that he was sitting cross-legged on a dirt floor, Soln Shipner looked very professorial just then, wrapped up as he was in the contents of his data files. All he needed was a pair of half-spectacles perched on that jutting nose.

"What kind of place do you think our dinka-chak comes from?" she blurted, like a silly schoolgirl trying to ask the teacher if he thought the moon was made of goat cheese. At least she had not mentioned Dhrusilmatkhashi. Shipner need not know where her thoughts were headed.

It was a moment before Shipner finally turned and regarded her, and there was nothing professorial about the way those dark eyes bored into her. But she stood under his scrutiny, confident as always that no man could find anything there to fault.

"What kind of place, as in what planet?" he asked after a moment.

"No, no," she said hastily, "I mean—what kind of

climate, what kind of terrain, regardless of the location
in the galaxy? Wet? Dry? Cold? Hot?"

His search of her face continued. Eventually he turned
back to his flatscreen. "A wetter climate than any you
have in Innanta," he said decisively. "Probably with
standing or running water: bogs, streams. More moisture
in the air. A leafy place, I should think, judging from the
dappled camouflage of its skin, replicating light and
shadows. Plants like trees, of a moderate to tall height
with branches strong and rigid enough to provide roosting. Smaller animals for them to prey on; larger animals
from whom they must hide—thus the skin camouflaging."

Marta nodded; that was not much more than Robinson had told her.

But now Shipner was gazing pensively at nothing, his
mouth resting against one fist. "I don't quite understand
why they shun the mountains, though," he said, almost
to himself. "Unless they need the heat, for some reason.
It could be they come from a swampy place—and yet
they are so efficient in stalking over dry ground . . ."
He harrumphed softly. "Dry ground, moist air . . . heat
and shade . . . a caldera, perhaps, with some active geysers. Hmm, that might explain why they prefer that sulfurous spring to the purer water of the well at the oasis.
They might need the sulfur for some metabolic process;
or perhaps it is only the familiarity of the smell and the
terrain that draws them."

Marta nodded absently. "Dhin M'Tarkhna does resemble a caldera, except that its rocks are sedimentary
rather than volcanic."

He glanced up at her, stirred from his meditative state.
"Of course, this is sheer speculation about a caldera,"
he qualified. "Much like Robinson's flight of fantasy in
comparing the dinka-chak to dinosaurs."

The remark took Marta by surprise. "Don't you think
the dinka-chak resembles a small theropod?" she asked.
"A velociraptor, or some such?" The similarities had
been obvious to her, and Yatzahl had agreed.

"Resembles, yes," Shipner replied. "Only a fool could
fail to see the resemblance. But that's on the outside.

The collared peccary resembles a wild pig on the outside, but in fact it is more closely related to the rhinoceros. We have no idea of a dinosaur's inner workings and never will; saying that the metabolism of a dinkachak tells us what the metabolism of a dinosaur might have been is a classic piece of Robinsonian wishful thinking. We are scientists; science is about proof, and he has none."

Marta, who was always more about fiery possibilities than about bald facts, was disappointed in Shipner's attitude. Her face fell, and she rustled the hood of her oilskin up over her mass of hair. "He's only proposing a theory," she defended. "One has to start with a hypothesis, before one can prove or disprove it. *That* is what science is about." She started for the door. "Thank you for your time, Sab Shipner."

She had her hand on the latch when he asked, "Are there active geyser fields along the eastern coast of Dhrusil-matkhashi?"

CHAPTER 11

Marta froze in her tracks. It was a moment before she could calm her pounding heart enough to reply. Even then her voice shook just a little. "Dhrusil-matkhashi? Why do you ask about Dhrusil-matkhashi?" She hadn't slipped and mentioned it, had she? No, no, she was sure she hadn't.

"It's almost certainly where the dinka-chak originates," Shipner said.

Marta gulped, glad her back was to the Unbeliever. Hang the man, how did he know? Had he heard something, some rumor in the bazaar, of her interest in Dray's second continent? Or had he actually come to this conclusion based on the evidence at hand? "I thought you said they were not from Dray's Planet," she said carefully.

"That was one theory," he admitted. "But while the thrust of Robinson's paper is blatantly unsupported, he did successfully prove that the dinka-chak is native to this planet. Similarities in cellular structure, cell reproduction, enzymes, etc., all indicate a very rudimentary but undeniable relationship with other life-forms spawned here. Yet there is no trace of its evolutionary line on this continent; that leaves only one alternative."

Now Marta turned slowly to face him, her face drawn into a mask—a rather pale mask, true, but a mask just the same. "Dhrusil-matkhashi is uninhabitable," she said, carefully using the term found in the mazhish literature.

Shipner snorted. "By whom? Not by dinka-chaks, I think." He picked up a data disk from the floor beside him and slid it into the flatscreen. "Now, if we look at a map of the eastern coast—"

In a single motion Marta was across the tiny room and kneeling beside him, gazing dumbfounded over his shoulder at the image on his flatscreen. "Where did you get that?" she cried in wonder. The screen showed a diagonal slash of coastline running north-northeast to south-southwest and bending around to break up into a mass of islands.

"Not from your University library, certainly," Shipner replied drily. "For a people dedicated to Knowledge, your holy ones are rather selective about what they allow their people to see."

Marta didn't even hear the criticism. She was looking at a northern boundary, which was nothing more than a latitude line. How far north did the continent really go?

"This is actually in the Universal Library," Shipner told her. "I requested it before I accepted Paun's invitation to come to Dray's Planet. The map is based on a photograph, the only one taken by Captain Dray's original probe that shows any of the larger continent. Most of it was obscured in cloud at the time the probe passed by," he said, pulling up the original photograph and pointing out the swirling white masses in the image. "But you can see the outline of the eastern coast right here. And based on that—" He shifted back to the map. The details were sketchy, indeed: a couple of elevation markings, a polar ice cap to the south, and the distance at various points between Dhrusil-matkhashi and the western shore of Innanta.

"But it shows no mountains, no rivers," Marta observed in disappointment. Ah, what a help that would have been!

"All obscured by cloud cover," Shipner explained. "One of the reasons the second survey probe, the one which actually touched down, was put down on this continent—they could see what kind of ground it would be landing on. But look how the coastline of Dhrusil-matkhashi matches so closely to that of Innanta across the channel. It's quite likely that once they were a single landmass, separated now by water."

"Then Dhrusil-matkhashi must be very similar to Innanta," Marta blurted. "The same foliage, the same—"

"Not at all, Princess!" Shipner laughed. "The separation could have been eons ago—perhaps during an ice age, when all of this section was covered by glaciers so that no life survived here. No, this map tells us very little that is useful. But this one . . ." He brought up another image and laid it over the first. It filled in depth markings for the channel between the two continents. "Your own geologists have sounded the ocean with their rather primitive equipment and found this classic trenching pattern." He enlarged the area to show how the ocean floor dropped almost in steps toward the center of the channel. "This kind of formation is generally found when two continental plates are pulling away from each other: the resultant gap is filled in by magma oozing up from the planet's core. Stretch, fill, stretch, fill—consequently, this is not an area of high volcanic activity."

Shipner reduced the image to its original size, then tapped the eastern coast of Dhrusil-matkhashi with an index finger oddly devoid of tattoos. "These cliffs, though," he mused, "are said to be granite, by those who have sailed close enough to know. Granite is an igneous rock, the product of volcanic upheaval. If it did not flow out of eruptions to the east"—here he tapped the channel—"it therefore follows that it must have flowed out of eruptions to the west." Now he tapped the interior of Dhrusil-matkhashi. "Long, long ago, perhaps. The area may be quite dormant now, with no trace of those ancient volcanoes."

"Except, possibly, a collapsed crater," Marta added. "A caldera."

Shipner leaned back from the screen. "Idle speculation. Pissing in the wind."

His vulgar expression brought Marta back to herself, jerked out of an almost conspiratorial mode, and she withdrew a little. "As poor as that map is," she said with forced coolness, "it is better than any I have seen of the channel and coast opposite. May I have a copy?"

"Of course," Shipner replied immediately. "Unlike your holy ones, I unilaterally support the free exchange of scholarly information." A sly smiled quirked his mouth. "Except, of course, when it is superseded by my contract with an employer. That is not the case here, however; I will drop by your College with this disk, where you can make a copy. I haven't the proper equipment here to transfer files to a data sponge."

Marta nodded and rose to her feet. "I thank you, Sab Shipner. I know the faculty of our College of Geology will be interested in it." She started for the door.

"What will you do if you find a jungle there?" Shipner asked abruptly.

For a second time, Marta was arrested in her tracks. She turned back slowly. "A jungle where?"

"When you visit Dhrusil-matkhashi."

"Dhrusil-matkhashi is beyond our gates," she stated flatly. "It is not a place for the Faithful to visit. My curiosity was intellectual, Sab Shipner. Knowledge for the sake of knowledge."

"Admirable," he allowed, and Marta thought she had escaped. But as she turned toward the door again, he told her, "To find your way in a jungle, to survive there, is very different from guiding an expedition through a desert. A warrior must take his training in many environments, and believe me, I know. Different skills are required, different ways of thinking. It would be very dangerous to venture into a jungle, or a forest, or a swampland, with a guide who only knew mountains and desert."

A cold sensation that had nothing to do with the storm outside crept down Marta's spine, raising gooseflesh where it passed. "I'm quite aware of that, Sab Shipner," she said quietly; and with one hand firmly holding her hood in place, Marta opened the door and stepped out into the rain.

* * *

Only half the number of tents had been pitched this night, for it was warm and calm and a blanket by the fire would do for most of the drovers and laborers. Even Hassan had declined to pitch his great tent, preferring to spend the night under the glittering black ceiling of the Tent of the Most High. Ari was looking forward to it himself, although no amount of pleading could convince Mohat's mother that her son should sleep outside, too. Poor Mohat, his mother coddled him so. "Ah, she has reason to be protective of him," Hassan pointed out to his disappointed son. "It's not just that he can't speak; he's not used to the desert air, either. It is just possible that his mother knows what's best for him."

"He does, too, speak," Ari grumbled. Having mastered a great deal of the complex system of gestures by which his silent friend communicated, Ari was impatient with those like his father who had not.

But when the evening meal was done and people settled back to hear more of the story, Ari was surprised to see Mohat's mother come to sit near her son for the storytelling. Ari hardly ever saw her sit among the other members of the caravan in the evenings.

Hassan was surprised, too, and glad. She was a figure of some political importance, and Kukhoosh Sridr had asked Hassan to be sure she felt welcome. So he smiled at her before surveying the rest of his audience, and he chose the opening of his story with care. "This is the tale of Marta and the Unbelievers," he began. "It is one of the most beloved of the Children of the Second Revelation, for it tells how she ventured beyond the gates of Innanta to a land that none had seen before, and how the hand of the Most High was upon her. It tells of Marta's courage and fortitude, and of the respect that the Faithful have for the many gifts which the All-Giving has provided. It tells of Marta's respect for creatures unknown to her, and the joy with which she embraced their existence. It tells how the Unbeliever . . ." Here Hassan hesitated, selecting his words carefully. "How the Unbeliever found a place among the Children of the Second Revelation; and although it was never his home, he was content."

Hassan winked at Ari. "Of course, it is a tale of treachery and deceit, as well, and many brushes with death; but we know how the All-Just deals with that, don't we?"

Finally he began. "One day the Most High said to Marta, 'O Woman of the Faithful, sail into the Western Ocean and across her depths, and go to Dhrusilmatkhashi—the Land Beyond the Gates. Take with you one who is not among the Faithful, that even the Unbeliever might know of my awesome power . . ."

Cecil Robinson bent over a microscope studying a drop of the dinka-chak's blood. It was like working in a museum, here in the lab he'd been given at the College of Indigenous Life, without the full range of computerized equipment he was accustomed to having. Outside the rain thrummed against the eastern windows, as it had off and on for the last two weeks. It seemed impossible that this was the same planet where just a few short months ago he had lain parched and sweating in the broiling heat of Dhin M'Tarkhna, with Marta impishly promising pleasures his heat-fatigued body could hardly accept. That was another place, another age, another Cecil Robinson. That Cecil Robinson had been on his way to an Ashdod Prize. This Cecil Robinson was stranded on a primitive world, cut off from his home, his culture, his hope of interstellar preeminence.

With a rush of air the door to the lab burst inward, and an oilskinned figure blew in with a fine spray of moisture, shaking and stamping to dispel the droplets from arms and legs. It was Marta, of course, stopping in for her afternoon chat. She worked for Yatzahl in the mornings and had class until four; then she always came directly to the lab to see how he was doing. "What news from the dinka-chak world?" she asked brightly as she shucked her dripping oilskin and hung it on a hook by the door.

Robinson looked up and thought that she was just as beautiful as always, with damp curls clinging to her smooth brown skin. "Their white cells, if you can call them that, behave much the same way as yours and mine," he replied without enthusiasm, "despite the density of the cell walls. They just gobble up foreign bodies with amazing efficiency." He would like to gobble her up, just one more time.

Marta brought a footstool over and stood on it so she could peer in the microscope, too. Robinson inhaled discreetly; she was wearing that perfume again, the stuff made from some pseudo-mollusk called a *kirim*. It was light and tingly and made him think of green apples and tangy lemons.

"Hungry little monsters," Marta observed, then turned and sat on the table facing him. "How did it go with the provost?" she asked.

It was a sore reminder of his fruitless morning meeting. "How do you think it went?" he asked with a thinly veiled snarl.

Marta sighed. She'd warned Robinson that Retneyabo had already done everything that could be done to get permission for his guest professor to return home; but then, she could hardly blame the Unbeliever for wanting to try himself.

"The kukhoosh has not given up," she assured him. "He says the decision is not irreversible, and he will try again next fall to—"

"Next fall!" Robinson erupted.

"It is not wise to push too soon," she hedged. Sometimes she was afraid Robinson did himself more harm than good by going around Retneyabo and appealing to officials who had already given their answer and could hardly go back on it so quickly.

Robinson's face looked darker than the skies outside.

"Oh, Sab Robinson, don't lose heart! Retneyabo can move mountains, given enough time," she promised. "Just do what you do best—continue to study the dinka-chak—and he will do what he does best—which is manipulate things to get what is necessary."

Robinson rubbed a hand irritably over his clean-shaven chin. "I don't suppose I could get an audience with one of these mazhel," he grumbled.

"No, I don't think so." Marta heard him curse under

his breath and chose to ignore it. The last thing he needed was a reminder that he was among foreigners. Instead she turned coy. "I know a way to keep your mind off it until the kukhoosh can fix things," she tempted.

Robinson's gaze trailed unbidden across her damp tunic. Oh, he could think of a few things that would make his exile a little sweeter: setting up a still in his apartment, finding a little casino near the harbor, and tucking Marta between his sheets three or four times a week. But such activities were either impossible or extremely dangerous. He had been informed that the penalty for manufacturing alcohol was the loss of three digits—fingers or toes, the mazh's choice. As for fooling with another man's wife, he was afraid even to inquire about the penalty.

Marta lowered her voice. "Retneyabo pretends he hasn't made up his mind yet, but I can tell," she whispered. "I'm going to Dhrusil-matkhashi this spring."

"Have a nice trip," he replied glibly.

She gave an exasperated sigh, putting both hands on her hips. "Sab Robinson, I need a senior zoologist on the team. Someone knowledgeable in evolutionary patterns. Someone who isn't terrified to tempt the displeasure of the mazhel."

Robinson remained unmoved. "Try Shipner," he jabbed, "I hear he's available."

Marta's jaw jutted out momentarily, then retracted smoothly. She slid off the table, and let her hands brush across his chest. "But I want someone pleasant," she whispered seductively. "Someone tall and handsome and . . . entertaining."

It was the first time she had touched him since their return; Robinson sucked in his breath. "Well, that leaves out Shipner," he admitted.

But how could he leave Jinka? The planet's only launchpad was here. If something were to break—if Retneyabo stirred something loose somewhere—he wasn't about to be half a planet away, scaling cliffs that were three hundred meters tall.

"Please, Sab Robinson," she entreated in a breathy voice.

After all, there would be no incentive for Retneyabo to keep trying to get him off-planet if he weren't right there to catch the next shuttle. No, no, he needed to stay here and keep applying pressure. He'd petition the mazhel. He'd go back to the provost. Anyone who had any influence in the nation of Innanta was going to hear from him.

"Cecil . . ." she purred, deliberately using his given name for the first time.

Oh, God, she wanted him, and not just for his scientific expertise. Oh God, oh God—

"I want a guarantee," he said abruptly, catching her hands which insisted on playing with his blouse buttons. "A guarantee in writing, that if I go along on this fool's errand, Retneyabo will get me off-planet somehow—legally or illegally."

Marta's eyes grew wide, and her jaw dropped in outrage, all sympathy vanished. "He has said he will do all he can!" she snapped. "You need no more guarantee than that."

"I can't believe there isn't someone who can be bribed," Robinson replied bluntly, pulling away from her and pacing to the window. The rain was letting up, but the skies remained gray and ominous. "I don't believe everyone on the planet is incorruptible. I'll bet Kukhoosh Paun could find someone to subvert. You tell Retneyabo I want guaranteed passage off this rock—legal or illegal—before I agree to go to Dhrusil-matkhashi." Outside a low rumble of thunder boiled up and faded. Robinson knew he had no leverage, and his speech was as likely to offend Retneyabo as convince him, but he was desperate. He wanted to go home.

"A plague of pustules on your ungrateful hide!" Marta swore, charging across the room to snatch up her oilskin. "You don't deserve a patron like Retneyabo! Had he not already given his word, I would tell him you are not worth his efforts." With that, she jerked the oilskin on over her head and stalked out of the lab.

Now I've done it, Robinson thought in mounting panic. *Oh God, oh God, what am I going to do? I have to get off this planet somehow . . .*

Marta stomped off across the rain-drenched courtyard, feeling as stormy as the weather. How dare he! A written guarantee! This was not decadent Melius, this was Innanta, and all its inhabitants were Children of the Second Revelation! Hadn't he learned anything about them? Was he such a stranger to honor that he did not recognize it when he saw it?

And to suggest that Retneyabo *bribe* someone—now, that was a tactic worthy of Paun! Nor had such tactics succeeded, for Soln Shipner was still here. He had come by the College only days after her visit to him, to deliver the promised map of Dhrusil-matkhashi's eastern coastline. He had scared Yatzahl's secretary half to death with his wildly braided hair and tattoos, demanding to see Marta and rejecting Sab Yatzahl's polite invitation to see the dinka-chak display which was under construction.

When Marta took him to one of the study rooms to make the data exchange, he had regarded her through slitted eyes. "So when do you leave for Dhrusil-matkhashi, Princess?"

"No such expedition has been approved," she replied coldly.

His reply was that wicked yellow grin. "I didn't ask if it had been approved," he rumbled in his deep voice, "I asked when you were leaving."

"And I'm telling you, there is no expedition!" she replied hotly, and that was true, to a degree. Her planning was all theoretical; the thing did not exist until Retneyabo gave his go-ahead.

Shipner treated her to the dialectical word for camel dung. "For a culture that claims to revere Knowledge," he growled, "you are a singularly incurious lot. I can't believe it's been over two hundred years, and no one has gone there before this."

"You don't understand," she defended. "When the

Holy Ones of the first generation named it 'Land Beyond the Gates,' they weren't just saying it was unknown; they were saying it was unwise to go there, just
as it would be unwise for the Faithful to leave the sanctuary of Dray's Planet."

Shipner made a rude noise.

"Survival in Innanta has never been easy," she persisted. "We had our hands full with just one continent
to explore and develop. Why take on a place that was
labeled uninhabitable?"

"And now you have population control," he returned.
"Women are sterilized after two children. Yet you still
hide your eyes from a landmass which, at the very least,
is equal in size to that you now occupy. So what if it is
barren? You know how to plant. You know how to fer-
tilize and irrigate. The land there can't be any worse
than that godforsaken hole you call Dhin M'Tarkhna.
But no, you won't even go look at it."

No Unbeliever could understand what it meant, to
learn that the Holy Ones might have been . . . inaccu-
rate. It was like discovering the world was round, and
not flat, and that perhaps there was no edge after all . . .
"Some have gone there," she said quietly.

He glanced at her sideways.

Marta had found the stories in an obscure volume
called *Tales from the Western Fishing Villages.* They
might be fables, of course, or warped versions of the
truth, but . . . "In the ninety-seventh year after landing,"
she told Shipner, "when villages began to sprout up on
the Western Coast, two brothers climbed the cliffs of
Dhrusil-matkhashi to see what lay atop them. They
never returned."

His eyes, which had been suspicious at first, narrowed
with interest. Marta continued. "From one of the southern ports, a ship set sail to see if the coastline of Dhrusil-
matkhashi was any friendlier to the south and west," she
said. "The ship never returned. And there are other stories of people who tried to breach the coastline and
were lost."

There was a brief pause as Shipner weighed her

words. She finished copying the file and returned his disk to him. "So it is a frightening place," he dismissed as he tucked his disk into a leather pouch dangling in front of his kilt. "It only means you shouldn't go alone."

"I'm not going at all!" she snapped, and tried to tell herself it wasn't really a lie, not at this point. Then, seeing Shipner was not inclined to leave, Marta started to exit herself.

"Is Robinson going with you?" he asked her retreating back.

Marta turned and asked with feigned innocence, "Going where?"

Shipner laughed, unprovoked by her continued denial. "He won't be any help, you know. He can't take care of himself anywhere they don't accept credits for food and sell drinks from a machine."

Marta gave him a condescending smile. "I wouldn't take him for that purpose."

"Ha. One of your donkey drovers would do for *that*," Shipner replied. "And probably do a better job." Then he hitched up his kilt and crossed to where she stood, smirking down at her over that goodly nose. "For this trip, Princess, you need someone with a warrior's cunning, not a playboy's appetites," he advised.

With a final grin, he had gone on his way chuckling.

That was ten days ago, and Marta had been unsuccessful in discarding the incident from her mind. The truth was, Shipner was right. She needed a crew of men who knew how to handle themselves in strange situations. Robinson was strong and reasonably courageous—but he didn't know the wilderness. He didn't know any kind of wilderness. Marta herself knew only one kind: desert. The men she could find here in Innanta might know desert or mountains or ocean, but did any of them know swamplands? Forests? Geysers? Wild beasts?

Pondering her dilemma yet again, Marta found her steps turning toward Shipner's rented room. As the tattooed man had so broadly hinted, he himself was the one person on Dray's Planet best qualified to venture into uncharted territory. As a Nechtanite, he had under-

gone rigorous survival training in a variety of climates
and terrains. He'd done fieldwork in all kinds of wilderness environments throughout his career. He had crossed
long stretches of Dhin M'Tarkhna without a guide; he'd
made his way through the Maknial Mountains quickly
and quietly when fleeing pursuit, gliding in and out of
shadows and thickets while she watched, amazed.
Shipner was exactly the kind of man she needed on
this expedition.

But she wanted Robinson. She wanted him for purely
selfish reasons, and because he had never worked for
Paun. Paun's hirelings were not known for their integ-
rity, and this expedition could be life and death.

Marta paused in front of his weathered door. Could
she trust Shipner with her life?

Could she afford not to?

Finally she knocked.

"Well, well, Princess," Shipner greeted her as she entered. He was seated at his flatscreen again, cross-legged
on the dirt floor. The single window in the room was
open today, and its meager light spilled in along with a
cool draft. "Have you come to your senses, then?"

"There is no expedition," she insisted doggedly.
"Yet." Shifting uncomfortably, she pursed her lips and
asked, "But if there were such an expedition . . . would
you be interested in coming?"

"Why, Princess!" he mocked. "Are you offering me
a job?"

Marta's temper flared. "You can be sure my patron
would be more generous, and more trustworthy, than
yours has been!" she snapped, for the room was no better equipped than it had been before, and now it was
downright cold.

His voice was surprisingly quiet when he responded.
"Paun was generous, in a manner of speaking," he said
tonelessly. "We value different things, Paun and I."

Marta eyed him curiously in the dim light. Was that
pain, hiding there behind those dark eyes?

"To answer your question," he went on, "I would be
interested, yes. Will I do it? That's another question. I

have just learned that an ore freighter left the GenOrg colonies last week; it will pass near here around twenty-five forty-three twelve Standard. If your mazhel can be made to see reason, I could be on that ship. Do you plan to be back from your little adventure by twenty-five forty-three twelve?"

"Well . . . *if* I were going," Marta hedged, pacing a little to keep her feet warm, "I would leave in the spring when the weather breaks and plan to stay three or four months, depending on conditions."

"Yes or no, Princess."

Marta gulped. "Yes. If we get back at all," she added drily. "The history of that is not good."

Shipner grunted. "In that case, I will think on your theoretical proposition, Princess," he told her.

"Yes, I know you have so many competing offers, Sab Shipner," she retorted, "and so much to consume your time here until that ship arrives. I shall wait with bated breath for your reply." No wonder Paun had cast him off—the man was insufferable!

Shipner's soft laughter followed her out of the room.

Marta was in the lab to try once more to enlist Robinson for the expedition when Shipner arrived to accept her offer.

Robinson was brooding, for he'd had yet another fruitless meeting with yet another official who he hoped could get him off-planet somehow. Marta was urging him once more to be patient, to let Retneyabo handle it, when the door opened behind them.

"I'm not a patient man," Robinson was saying. Snarling, actually.

"And that's the trouble with your research, Robinson," the painted man sang out as he strode in, tugging off the poncholike garment which was all he ever wore in addition to his kilt. "You haven't the patience to do the exhaustive studies required." He tossed his poncho carelessly on a nearby table.

Robinson's eyes narrowed, and his lips curled back. "What are you doing here?"

Shipner rubbed his hands together as he glanced around the room. "Looking over the facilities of my new employer."

"New employ—" The word died on his lips as Robinson turned accusing eyes on Marta. "You didn't—!"

Marta tried her best to feign innocence, but it wasn't in her repertoire. "He has survival training," she defended. "And besides, I need a senior zoologist, and you have been so stubbornly refusing . . ."

Shipner was inspecting a lab table. "Archaic," he muttered, "absolutely archaic. Stone Age. Worse."

"Oh, and I suppose you're going to share *his* tent," Robinson hissed.

Marta's mouth flew open in indignation, but before she could find words, Shipner interjected. "Save your petty jealousy, Robinson," he advised. "I'd rather sleep with a she-ass than take one of these Drayish females to bed. There's not a woman on this planet to interest a man of my discriminating taste."

Now Marta spun on this new attacker. "Baboon!" she snapped. "Unspeakable jackal! Carrion-eater! Bottom-feeding—"

Shipner cocked an eyebrow at Robinson. "Is she always like this?"

"Sometimes she's even more creative," the younger man assured him.

"Do you go back on your word?" Shipner demanded of Marta.

Marta stopped mid-invective, nonplussed. "What?"

"You offered me a job. You aren't going back on that because I have a low opinion of your sexual appeal, are you? Or is this expedition about bed partners?"

"If it were," she huffed, "I would never have approached you!"

"Then tell me about your plans for the expedition, and I'll tell you what's wrong with them." He was inspecting a microscope constructed of glass and highly polished wooden tubes. "Barbaric," he murmured in fascination. "Ingenious, but barbaric."

"I haven't finished my plans," Marta replied archly.

"And I haven't got funding or approval, so this is still theoretical."

Shipner grinned wickedly at her. "Well, theoretically, I'm coming along. So if you want me to look over what you've got so far, you know where I live." He turned his yellow smile on Robinson. "You were wrong about the dominance of the dinka-chak egg-layer, by the way," he said bluntly. "The throat-patched ones you call males will stand up to the *smaller* egg-layers; it's a matter of weight, not gender." He cast a mischievous glance back at Marta, then said in an aside to Robinson, "Unlike yourself."

Robinson came off his lab stool, but Shipner was walking away laughing. He picked up his discarded poncho, tossed it deftly over his head, and walked out into the soggy winter gloom.

The Unbeliever rounded on Marta. "How could you ask that cretin to go to Dhrusil-matkhashi?" he hissed.

"You told me to," she reminded uncharitably.

"But I wasn't—"

"At least *he* didn't ask me for a written guarantee!" she jabbed.

Robinson closed his mouth and drew back. Turning his back on Marta, he paced to the other side of the lab, then turned and paced back.

"I'll come along," he said quietly. "As long as we can be back by twenty-five forty-three twelve Standard."

It was the same date Shipner had given. So Robinson knew about the ore freighter, too. Marta hesitated, knowing that the date of their return might be beyond her control. "That is my plan," she hedged.

"Good." Robinson drew a deep breath. "Just tell Shipner you've withdrawn your offer."

Marta balked. "I can't do that."

The Unbeliever's eyes grew dangerous. "What?"

"I made him an offer, and he accepted," she said stubbornly. "In Innanta, that is a contract, and it cannot be broken. And besides, I need him. I don't know what kind of terrain we'll find. He has survival training, he's done fieldwork in all kinds of wilderness conditions . . ."

She could almost hear Robinson's teeth grinding. Finally he said, "All right. But I'm the senior zoologist."

"There is no senior and no junior," she said quickly, seeing a storm brewing. "You are both members of my team. *My* team." And before he could object, she, too, donned her coat and left the lab.

Outside, Marta closed her eyes and leaned back against the door. A light drizzle was starting up, and the leaden skies made no promises of sunshine in the near future. The courtyard was sloppy with mud. "All-Merciful and Benevolent One," Marta prayed fervently, "what am I going to do with *two* of them?"

CHAPTER 12

"So great had been the triumph of Marta's return with the dinka-chak," Hassan told his listeners, *"that even the Unbeliever Shipner came to her and swore loyalty. So now Marta could not choose between the two Unbelievers; and so she took them both. And Shipner and Robinson became as brothers, for such is the will of the Most High, that scholars should regard one another in this way. So Marta went forth from Jinka, across the waters of the Western Ocean to the place called Dhrusil-matkhashi, to see what it was that lay beyond Innanta's gates. With her went the Unbeliever Robinson on her right hand, and the Unbeliever Shipner on her left; the Light and the Dark, hers to command . . ."*

By the time the winter rains broke, Marta was as prepared as Shipner's experience and Retneyabo's money could make her. Robinson had taught her the rudiments of free-climbing rocks—such climbing aids as pitons and carabiners being nonexistent on Dray's Planet—using the cliffs below the kukhoosh's seaside estate as a training ground; but it was clear to Marta that she would have to leave any serious climbing to experts. They either had to find a reasonable beach to the north or south of the precipitous coastline, or she would have to wait patiently below while Robinson and Shipner scaled the heights.

Shipner had helped her hone the list of supplies, and they included such oddments as a water purifier, hammocks, a folding sailboat, a small wind-powered generator, fishing line, and a radio beacon. Marta hadn't located this last item yet, but she was hoping to do so in Mimma, where a small amount of delicate manufacturing was done from scarce native metals. Her medical kit was also extensive: antibiotics and antitoxins of all kinds, adrenaline and other stimulants, even anesthetics and a few surgical supplies in case of extreme emergencies.

Retneyabo gave his final approval, and Marta began to assemble her crew. She consulted with one of Retneyabo's sea-captain clients, and with his help selected four men of tough mettle and varied background, known for their cool heads in desperate situations. Finding no medtechs to her liking, she reluctantly took Shipner's word that between his first-aid training and a comprehensive emergency medical diagnostic/reference program he'd brought from offworld, Shipner himself could handle most situations. On a balmy late-winter morning, they all stood on a pier in the harbor, ready to slip quietly away to the southern port city of Mimma, where the bulk of the supplies would be garnered, and from which they would depart for Dhrusil-matkhashi.

Marta and the two zoologists were in hooded kaftans, doing what they could to conceal their identities and keep rumors at a minimum until they were gone, at least. She had refused to let Robinson commission the manufacture of any pitons or carabiners for the possible climb, even at his own expense, because there were no rock faces on Innanta steep enough to warrant such tools and the craftsman might guess where they were headed. It was not competition from Paun that Marta feared; rather, she was just a little squeamish about going against the counsel of the mazhel. Not that this trip had been forbidden, for it hadn't—and as long as no one knew about it, it wouldn't be.

A chill went through Marta, then, when someone hailed her from the shore and ran out along the wooden planking toward her. She was trying to slip unobtrusively behind several of her hirelings when Robinson said, "Look, it's Tookh!"

It was indeed the scrawny youth who had accompanied them to Dhin M'Tarkhna. He had grown inches over the winter, and the nutritious food at the residential school he'd attended had added flesh to his bones, although he was still gangly as a foal. "Sibna Marta!" he called joyously as he panted to a halt in front of their group. "I went to the College yesterday looking for you, to see if you would go to Dhin M'Tarkhna again this season, and they said I might find you here."

Marta forced a smile while grinding her teeth, vowing to find out who had directed the boy to the harbor. "Yes, Tookh, we are about to take a sea voyage," she said with artificial lightness to her tone. "Sibna Egthassa is taking the expedition to study the dinka-chaks. I'm sure she'd be delighted to have you along."

"Oh, no!" the boy cried. "I want to come with you, wherever you are going." He craned his neck back to look up at the tall mast of the ship floating in its dock beside the pier. "Are you going on that? I've never been on a ship before!"

"Just a journey to Mimma," she dismissed. "I'm really not looking for any help, Tookh. I'm sorry."

Tookh's face fell. "Oh." He searched the faces of the hired men, hoping for someone who would put in a good word for him. "You have—what, five? six? Are you sure you couldn't use one more? I'm very smart, you know," he reminded her. "I thought of using the metkhiss vine to reinforce the cage—"

Just then he saw Shipner's tattooed face under the hood. "All-Powerful protect us, it's him!" he exclaimed, edging himself between Marta and Shipner and reaching instinctively for his knife. "The painted one!"

Marta bit back a laugh and put a restraining hand on Tookh's arm. As though he could protect her from Shipner! She'd seen the knife the boy carried: a pitiful six-inch blade of flint. It was hardly a match for the fifteen inches of steel that Shipner wore prominently on his belt. "It's all right, Tookh," she assured him. "Sab Shipner has left Paun's employ and is coming with us on this journey. He's on our side."

Tookh looked uncertainly from Marta to the malevolently decorated Unbeliever.

Shipner favored the lad with his yellow grin. "We have met before, I think," he said. "You are the budding warrior who held a rifle on me at the well." Shipner chose not to mention that it was Tookh he had given the slip by throwing sand in his eyes.

"Yes, and he's the only one who identified you for me," Marta felt inclined to point out. "He saw the tattoos on your feet, when no one else noticed."

"Sharp eyes and a quick mind; you'd better snap him up," Shipner advised.

Marta scowled at him. It was one thing to insult her and Robinson, quite another to hurt the boy's feelings. "I have my crew," she said sourly.

"Actually, you're short one," the Nechtanite reminded her. "No medtech, remember?"

What was he trying to do? "He's not a medtech," Marta growled.

"But I might be one day," Tookh put in hopefully. "I like biology and chemistry—I might go into a medtech program when I finish secondary school." His dark eyes pleaded with her.

"Tookh, you don't even know where we're going!" Marta protested.

"It doesn't matter!" he cried passionately. "I can be useful, and you don't have to pay me. I'll work for my keep, no more. The kukhoosh has been more than generous already."

"I'll teach him some first aid," Shipner offered, "and how to use the EM program. That way if I get injured, there will be someone to sew *me* up."

"I will gladly sew you up," Marta hissed at him, "starting with your mouth." Then she turned back to Tookh. "I appreciate your offer, Tookh, but I really need highly trained—"

"Oh? You've got Robinson," Shipner sniped.

"Hey!" Robinson objected.

"The boy will probably do better under hardship conditions than this hothouse excuse for an outdoors—"

"You overblown asshole," Robinson snarled, taking a malevolent step toward the Nechtanite. "If you think—"

Tookh shouldered quickly between them. "Sab Robinson, Sab Shipner," he interceded. "You must be brothers now, and not quarrel. We are on the same side, as the Sibna says."

"If you were my brother, I'd kill myself," Robinson growled at his rival.

"Kill *yourself?*" Shipner taunted. "What, no courage for fratricide?"

"Scholars, scholars!" Tookh pleaded, then turned grinning to Marta. "You see?" he declared triumphantly. "You do need me, to keep these two from each other's throats!"

"You're hired!" Marta snapped, her patience gone. "Everyone, onto the ship!" She stormed up the gangplank to escape the lot of them.

They had not been at sea half an hour, though, when she cornered Shipner on the foredeck. "Why did you do that?" she demanded. "Back me into taking Tookh along?"

He was leaning against the foremast, paring his fingernails with that monstrous blade. He gave a negligent shrug. "Every young warrior needs an adventure," he said.

"What if he panics under stress?" Marta pressed. "He could jeopardize us all. What if his ignorance or his haste proves fatal? This adventure might very well cost him his life!"

Shipner sheathed his knife and looked her straight in the eye. "That, Princess," he said with deadly calm, "is the nature of war."

In Mimma, Marta went straight to Retneyabo's agent, a man named Hagiath, and set him to tracking down the desired radio beacon. In the meantime, she established her credit with the local merchants and located the rest of the supplies she required, then turned her attention to hiring a ship. She found the captain of a small cargo vessel who was familiar with the Western Ocean and was willing to undertake the commission without knowing exactly where Marta wanted to go. Hagiath approved the woman, who was a veteran sailor with a fine reputation, and they loaded everything aboard. As soon as Hagiath succeeded in locating the beacon, the eight adventurers embarked.

Only when they were well out to sea did Marta tell the ship's captain their destination. The captain raised her eyebrows but declined to comment. Retneyabo's agent had paid in copper ingots, half in advance; the other half was due after Marta and her entourage were picked up at the end of the expedition. The captain was not about to risk losing that second fare by questioning her client's business.

They sailed around the southwestern bulge of Innanta and through shallow seas toward the deeper channel which separated that continent from Dhrusil-matkhashi. Shipner was true to his word, giving Tookh instruction in rudimentary first aid and showing him how to work the computer program for emergency medical procedures. Tookh was thrilled with the responsibility, an ardent student. Marta shook her head over Shipner's tutelage of the boy. "I would never have guessed you for the type," she told Shipner bluntly.

"You have Robinson for a pet," he told her indifferently. "The boy is mine."

Then Marta began to worry that Shipner, who had such disdain for Drayish women, had an unnatural interest in Tookh. Wasn't it common, among warrior cults, for the men to use each other disgracefully? She was sure she had heard that in one of her sociology courses. Robinson, when asked, professed no knowledge of that proclivity in Shipner, but still Marta worried. Such an abomination would not be tolerated. She'd slit his Nechtanite throat herself if there were any evidence he practiced such depravity.

Incensed, she marched straight off to demand an answer of Shipner himself. He was standing at the starboard rail, leaning over and staring down into the waters. "Curious sea plants," he observed as she came up beside him. "Either they're very tall, or the water is very shallow here."

He looked so much the professor, absorbed in his observation of the natural world, that the wind went out of Marta's challenge. "Sab Shipner," she said uncomfortably, "I need to ask you something." Her tone caused him to look up. "I noticed when I read your file that . . ." She hesitated, feeling terribly awkward. What if she was wrong? To accuse a man of such perversion . . . "That there is no mention of a wife or children. I don't know what the Nechtanite customs of—"

"If this is a proposal of marriage," he interrupted, "I decline. Nechtanites do not marry."

Marta's jaw dropped, not sure whether to be outraged by his assumption or stunned by the rejection of matrimony as an institution. "Don't marry?" she echoed in amazement.

"Our lives are too often violent and brief," he continued, peering back down at the sea plants in intent curiosity. "Living in nuclear families isolates us. We prefer to live in communities, where all the adults care for the children, and men and women can mate with whomever they perceive will give them superior offspring." He paused to grin at her. "Or a superior tussle." He turned his attention back to the plants. "Maybe they aren't anchored at all. You do have some plant species like that, don't you, that survive as floaters? Just drawing their nutrients from decomposing matter in the water?"

Marta tried to sort through the implications of what he'd told her and apply them to her concerns for Tookh. "Do you have any children, Sab Shipner?" she asked.

"There were twelve in our community when I left," he told her. "But I assume you mean have I personally fathered any. Three or four," he said. "That I know of. Why?"

"I just . . . I wasn't sure . . . if Nechtanite men ever . . ."

He looked at her inquisitively. "I've never seen you tongue-tied before, Princess."

Marta's face burned. "If you commit abominations with other men!" she blurted.

Both his eyebrows shot up. "The practice is not un-known among Nechtanites," he admitted. "*I* don't. Was that your question?"

Marta didn't know if she was infuriated more by her own embarrassment or Shipner's lack of it. "I just wanted to be sure," she defended. "The way you have taken to Tookh."

He laughed, of course, which made her blush even more furiously. "There are men who would challenge you to combat for that," he remarked. "No, Princess, just because I have no interest in your bed doesn't mean I have an aversion to women in general. My interest in Tookh is that of a mentor. It is the Nechtanite way for older warriors to tutor the young—a concept Robinson never seemed to grasp."

Her fears relieved, Marta deemed this a good point at which to escape the encounter. It wasn't until long after-ward that she wondered what he meant by his remark about Robinson.

Finding a suitable beachhead was as daunting as Marta had been led to believe. Everywhere they sailed along the eastern coast of the Dhrusil-matkhashi, they were confronted by towering cliffs soaring hundreds of meters into the air, usually bolstered by jagged rocks protruding from the surf. The further north they went, the more forbidding it got; after five days they turned around and ran south, hoping to do better.

Finally, after twelve days of skirting the dangerous breakwaters, they came upon an area that gave Marta some hope.

Had there been fog that morning, they would have sailed right past it; but the rising sun shone brightly enough that a vertical shadow appeared on the massive stone wall just astern of the ship—a fissure. Closer in-spection revealed that a chunk of the cliff a hundred meters thick had split away from the mainland, forming a pillarlike island. The channel separating this island tower from the continent was plugged on the northern end by a massive rockslide which did two things. One, it blocked off the sea from the north, creating a harbor with a rocky beach. Two, it had left the cliff face on the continent side with a sloping face.

Having sounded the area from small boats and deemed it free of submerged boulders, they brought the ship in closer to the tiny bay. When the captain had gotten as close as she dared to the little beach, Shipner slipped over the side and swam for shore, where he proceeded to strut over the rocks in his bare feet, staring up at the cliff face.

Marta and Robinson followed in a boat. By the time they reached the tattooed man, he was nodding his head in approval. "It will do," he said. "We can use the beach as a staging area for our gear. Robinson and I will go up the cliff face here, anchor pulleys up above, and send ropes down to haul up the cargo." He grinned at Marta. "If you're good, we'll bring you up, too."

Marta turned pointedly to Robinson. "What do you think, Sab Robinson? Is the rock climbable here?"

Robinson stomped around the tiny beach for himself, using field glasses to inspect the slope above and muttering about pitches and cracks and fall potential. He tried it out by climbing five or six meters up the granite wall, then had to agree with Shipner's analysis. "Unless there are some surprises further up," he told Marta, "we should be able to free-climb the whole thing. It may take us all day, but there are no verticals that I can see from here, and plenty of cracks, so it should go fairly quickly."

"Tomorrow morning then," she decided. "At first light. I'll see the gear gets unloaded and netted for transport while the two of you climb."

So it was that noon the next day found Marta waiting with their crew and the gear on the jumbled rock fragments which comprised the beach, watching anxiously as the two men maneuvered their way up the rock wall. Both had packs on their backs and chalk bags around their necks, with tubes leading to water bottles so they only had to turn their heads to drink. Robinson had purchased custom-made leather slippers in Jinka to protect his feet from the sharp edges of granite while allowing him to slide his foot into a crevice in a "foot jam" or curl his toes in a "toe jam." Soft leather gloves without fingers protected his hands, which likewise must slide into cracks in the rock and wedge to support his weight as he searched for his next handhold.

Shipner climbed barefooted and bare-handed, and he was now fifty meters higher than his younger colleague.

Marta could never tell from looking at Soln Shipner just how old he was; her eye was always baffled by those tattoos. Judging from the dates of his published papers, he ought to be nearly forty Standard; but watching him climb, Marta could almost have believed him younger than Robinson. She didn't know if it was his extra years of experience or his Nechtanite upbringing that caused him to outstrip his colleague.

By late afternoon, however, Marta was profoundly glad the tattooed man was so tireless. He reached the top as the light began to dim in the deep crevice of the harbor. Affixing a sturdy pulley in the ground above, Shipner tossed a rope down to Robinson, who climbed easily up the last weathered stretch. Then, working together, they began hauling up men and equipment. Marta and Tookh were the last to go up, their belts clipped to ropes, walking up the cliff like two-legged spiders while the last light faded from the sky. As they neared the top, they went to their knees, and strong hands reached down from above to haul them up the final meter. Stars sparkled overhead and a quarter moon shed its light on the scene when at last she stood and looked out across the continent of Dhrusil-matkhashi.

At first she could only stare, gasping for breath after her climb, too winded to speak. Finally she croaked, "It's *alive*!"

Dhrusil-matkhashi was, indeed, very alive. Ground cover resembling grasses clung to the soil even in this exposed place, and fifty meters beyond, rolling downhill to the northwest, was a dense stand of treelike vegetation with a canopy so thick it blotted out the stars. Over the sound of the wind came a chorus of creaking and chirping—insects, or some kind of night creatures. Whatever else it was, Dhrusil-matkhashi was no wasteland.

It was colder up here than below, and Marta shivered as she gazed at the foreign landscape. Robinson slipped an arm around her shoulders. "Looks like you were right, Marta," he said quietly.

Suddenly Shipner was in front of her, thrusting a water bottle at her. "Drink," he commanded. "Get the dust from your throat. Then say something to your men—they look ready to climb right back down."

Marta glanced over and saw that they were indeed eyeing the wooded terrain warily, like men who expected monsters to pop out at any minute. She gulped a mouthful of water, then called out crisply, "Dakura! Set up camp and get a fire going. Tookh, find some rolled oats and boil them, we'll have hot food." Not only would the fire warm them, but Marta had no assurance that the men's fears weren't founded; a roaring fire would, she hoped, keep any curious creatures at bay until morning.

Shipner was now rummaging through one of the packs. Marta pulled away from Robinson's comforting arm to see what the tattooed man was up to. He was unpacking their radio beacon. "We'd better test this," Shipner said as she approached, "and make sure it works."

Its solar battery was weak but sufficiently charged to emit a brief burst. On the ship below, the captain had a receiver; she fired off a flare to indicate their transmission had been heard. When the battery was fully charged, the signal would easily reach Mimma, where a second receiver was in the hands of Hagiath. Marta would start it up when the expedition was ready to return.

Later that night, no one slept much despite their exhaustion. The Unbelievers were not as fearful as the Innantans, for they had seen many strange places and many unaccustomed climes. But for Marta the moist air, the unfamiliar sounds, and the nearness of the dense forest were enough to set her skin to prickling. She felt isolated in her hammock, trapped like a fly in a spider's

web, and wished desperately that she were on the solid
ground where she could cling to Robinson, drawing comfort from his warmth and his nearness. But Shipner had
advised them it was not safe to sleep on the ground until
they knew what creatures might crawl or slither into
their tents.

When dawn came at last, they all stood at the cliff's
edge and watched as, far below, their sturdy ship hoisted
a single sail to catch a light breeze that sang through the
rock cleft. Then it inched its way out of the narrow inlet
and back into the open sea, where the sails blossomed
like cerus flowers, and the ship moved swiftly away to
the east.

Afterward they all gathered in one tent with their
steaming coffee to plan a course of action. Shipner
wanted to build a stockade around their encampment
first thing, fencing the promontory off from the forest,
where unknown dangers might lurk. Marta saw the wisdom of that, but she was anxious to start exploring. She
hadn't come all this way to sit in her tent and shiver.
Finally it was agreed to put four men to work securing
the camp, while the scientists and one hireling scouted
the nearby territory. Tookh volunteered to explore with
them, but Marta was firm: Dakura was older, cagier.
Tookh would stay and work on the stockade.

They took two energy rifles, one for Dakura and one
for Robinson, and Shipner unsheathed his long knife—
"To blaze a trail," he said. But as they stepped out of
the tent into the open, Marta saw the way he eyed the
dimly lit woodland, and she knew very well the warrior
in him was prepared to do more with that knife than
hack away encroaching vines.

For her part, Marta took one look at that shadowy,
ominous place and decided they would inspect the clearing around their camp first. This took less than thirty
minutes; the grasses held little beyond an occasional
loose rock and a few beetlelike creatures munching contentedly on the narrow leaves. The work crew was using
the loose rock to construct a low wall, but they were
obviously reluctant to take their axes to the forest for

wood. It was up to her, then. Marta gritted her teeth and turned her attention once more to the unsettling forest, approaching its boundary cautiously.

Marta was no stranger to trees; there was a large wooded area on the landward slope below Retneyabo's estate. But these pylons of vegetation—oh, call them trees, it was what they most resembled—were unlike any Marta knew, towering thirty to forty meters in the air on trunks one to two meters thick. Around their impressive bases grew head-high shoots of greenery with feathery leaves, and a tangle of creepers shading from deep purple to green to pasty gray-white.

More than anything else, it was the darkness that disturbed her. The canopy above was so dense, and the entwining brush so tall, that very little light filtered to the forest floor beyond the easterly fringe. Accustomed to desert skies, where the barriers to sun, moon, and starlight were rare, this close, humid darkness made her skin crawl. She knew only one way to deal with it. She glanced at the three men with her. "I will go first," she announced.

Marta took a determined step forward, but Shipner's hand on her shoulder hauled her back. He looked down at her with a patronizing scowl. "You are a child of the desert," he chided. "What do you know of woods?"

Her chin came up. "I am the leader of this expedition!" she declared.

"Then lead with your head," he retorted, batting the heel of his palm none too gently against her forehead. "Not with your pride."

Marta's cheeks burned, but she had no answer. Robinson tried to step in on her behalf. "If she wants to go first—"

"Shut up," Marta snapped. "Dakura," she said, "what do you know of trees?"

Dakura shrugged uneasily. "How to climb them, that's about all."

She turned to Robinson. "And you? How is your woodcraft?"

The blond Unbeliever looked none too happy about

having been told to shut up; but he answered, "I've camped in the woods a couple of times. But I've only hiked trails, I guess. Given we don't know what any of this foliage is—"

Marta didn't let him finish. "And you, Sab Shipner? You, I suppose, are a great Nechtanite woodsman."

"I told you, a warrior must know all kinds of terrain," he replied with an arrogant indifference. "How to blaze a trail and how to hide one; how to keep from going in circles . . ."

"A regular Junior Scout," Robinson muttered.

"Then this is what we will do," Marta said firmly. "Today, we will go no further than shouting distance into this forest. Sab Shipner, you will teach us essential woodcraft: what dangers to watch for, how to find our way. Then tomorrow we will go farther, each taking a turn at leading. We must all be able to do it. The ignorance of one endangers us all."

Shipner regarded her with an appraising eye for a moment, then broke into a wicked grin that made Marta's flesh prickle almost as much as the dark forest did. "Very well, children," he chortled. "Class is in session."

Shipner's method of instruction was clearly designed to embarrass his students, and Marta noted irritably that these were not the tactics he had used when teaching Tookh first aid. To school his erstwhile trainees in woodcraft, Shipner started with a terse lecture, after which he led the three others into the fringe of the woods, where he set up scenarios which called for them to use the information he had just imparted. But of course, he hadn't told them quite everything. No matter what they did, he knew something else that twisted or negated their response, and each scenario ended with: "—and you're dead."

How, Marta wondered irritably, had he managed to gain tenure as a university professor with such tactics? But then, he was a research professor; perhaps he didn't teach classes at all. It was probably the only reason one of his students hadn't killed him years ago.

They saw no creatures during this session, although

there were rustlings in the undergrowth from time to time, and swaying branches where there was no wind. Shipner had scouted the immediate area carefully before he began his training exercises, and Marta noticed that his eyes continually raked the foliage above and below them, his ears cocking this way or that—even his great nose could be seen to quiver as he tested the air around them. His mouth admonished Dakura to watch where he put that hand or risk losing it; it jeered at Marta for driving her knife tip so deep in a tree bole that she could hardly get it out ("I was pretending it was your fat head and got carried away," she growled); it laughed unkindly at Robinson when he turned suddenly and knocked his head against a branch that hadn't been there a moment ago. (Shipner was holding it to the precise level of contact.) But even as that rude mouth harried them unmercifully, his eyes and ears and nose worked for their protection. And his own, of course.

Marta did her best to emulate his watchfulness, although she wasn't sure exactly what she was watching or listening for. Her gaze tended to travel along the ground, for all Drayan land animals of her acquaintance were small, crawly things; even the dinka-chak was barely half a meter tall. So with her attention elsewhere, she wasn't quite sure what Robinson had done, for which Shipner was taking such pleasure in chastising him, when Robinson decided he'd had enough.

The fair-haired zoologist stood with his arms folded across his chest, glaring down—how was it Marta hadn't noticed before that Shipner was half a head shorter than his fellow Unbeliever?—at the painted man, his face bristling with anger and three days' growth of a beard he'd decided not to remove. "Listen, jerk-off," Robinson snarled. "If I hear that one more time, *you're* the one who'll be dead."

"Ha!" goaded Shipner, stepping up to the challenge. "You have no more data to support that than you have to support your wishful fantasies about dinosaurians."

Robinson's hands came to his sides, curling unconsciously into fists, and Marta made to step between the two men; but something stopped her cold. "Hold very still, Sab Shipner," she said quietly, "or he may have more data than any of us wants."

Shipner's expression did not change, but he went stock-still while his eyes began to make a careful circuit. There was nothing ominous in his field of vision, but he saw where Marta's gaze was fixed over his head, saw that Dakura's was there, too, calculated the angle and slowly bent his knees. Marta unsheathed her knife, stooped, and cut through the stalk of a fernlike plant which was at hand. Then, still with slow and careful movements, she extended the stalk up over Shipner's head. "When I tell you, step toward Dakura," she instructed softly.

"Now!" she barked, and Shipner sidestepped as directed, drawing his blade with one swift motion, while Marta swatted at the tendril snaking down from overhead. The thing curled tightly around the fern and was jerked from its overhead perch as Marta's swing continued toward the ground and away from the four humans. She saw only a flash of green and brown tangled in the greenery before she released the stalk and danced away from it. A small thud sounded as it hit the ground.

Then there was a blur of black and white and flashing steel as Shipner struck, cleaving the thing in two. Marta gasped, more from the swiftness of his stroke than from any fear for herself or the creature. Shipner recoiled quickly and stood poised for another blow, but the thing only twitched a few times and then began to uncoil. Shipner's eyes raked the branches from which it had come—up, oh yes! one must learn to look up—but they found nothing threatening there. A long moment, and another, and he slowly relaxed his stance.

Dakura had his energy rifle fixed on the thing in the fern, but although it continued to twitch occasionally, Marta was reasonably sure it was dead. Shipner approached it slowly, prodded it carefully with the tip of his long knife, then knelt to pry it loose from the entangling fronds attached to the stalk. Marta came, too, curious to see what it was.

"Dakura, please keep an eye on the overhead branches," Shipner said casually. "And Robinson, be a good boy and see that nothing jumps us while we examine this thing."

Marta saw Robinson stiffen at the insult and the instructions, but she wasn't about to offer to trade places with him—not just yet. "I just saw it snaking down from above you," she told Shipner. "I couldn't tell if it was a vine or an arm or just what, but I didn't think it would reach down like that with innocent intent."

"Maybe it thought those braids on your head were cousins," Robinson suggested snidely.

Shipner ignored him, busy examining the two halves of the thing. "Huh. Legs," he grunted, pulling them back from a clenched position against the body with the tip of his knife. They were short, stubby affairs, compared with the meter and a half length of the creature. The tiny claws looked better suited to climbing trees than inflicting damage on enemies or prey.

Marta was using her own knife to examine the muscular tendril she had seen first. It was four or five centimeters in diameter, broadening a little as it neared the legs, narrowing to only two centimeters at the tip. Finding no head or other feature of note, she turned her attention to the other piece of the creature, neatly severed by Shipner's blade, and there she found a shorter extension with a very definite face on it: eyes, blunt snout, and a wicked-looking mouth.

"Ah, teeth," Marta commented, prying the jaws apart enough to see sharp ivory-colored projections. "Not very friendly-looking. We were probably wise to destroy it first and ask questions second."

Shipner's face split in a grin, vastly amused. "The warrior's creed," he said.

Robinson was growing impatient, so Marta rose to her feet. "Have a look, Sab Robinson," she invited. "I'll keep watch."

The first thing Robinson did was unclip the recorder from his belt, focus it on the creature, and start it. Then he and Shipner did an impromptu postmortem, speculated on the creature's possible relation to sandslithers (none), and promptly dissected it. When they had located organs, nerve ganglia, and a sophisticated vascular system, they finally rose, Robinson pausing to wipe the brownish fluid which served as blood from his hands onto the dirt. Shipner simply used his kilt.

"Well, I'm hungry," said Shipner cheerfully. "Let's go back to camp for some lunch."

When they returned to the forest that afternoon, they discovered more of Dhrusil-matkhashi's creatures, for the carrion-eaters had descended on the remains of the tree-creeper. A quick recording and they were ready to set off again, using a standard procedure which Marta dictated. Whoever led watched the forest in front of them; the person in second position watched overhead; number three scoured the left flank and number four the right. In that manner they proceeded a hundred meters into the woods, turned right and walked another hundred meters, then returned to the clearing. They saw one or two things scurrying away through the underbrush, heard a snorting sound flee from their passage, and encountered a cloud of flying insects which did not bite or sting but were unpleasant to inhale.

Having encountered no large aggressive life-forms, they felt more at ease that night as they sat near the campfire, eating sparingly of their provisions. "I wonder if the tree-creeper is good to eat?" Shipner speculated, eyeing the piece of leathery goat jerky in his hand.

"How is it that the creatures here have teeth?" Marta wanted to know. "And legs? Nothing native to Innanta has either one, and even the marine life does not have what you'd call teeth, only some cartilaginous projections. Why should they show up here, and not elsewhere on the planet?"

"Nothing in your oceans is as sophisticated as that tree-creeper," Shipner replied. "I would say the marine life and the land dwellers of Innanta are from a second evolution."

Marta raised her eyebrows. "A *second* evolution?"

Robinson turned and stared at his painted colleague a moment; then he grunted affirmation. "You could be right," he agreed. "It would make sense. If Innanta were once attached to this continent, some kind of geologic upheaval must have caused this piece of ground to raise up and Innanta to sheer off. If that happened before any sophisticated life-forms had evolved . . ."

"Or if the upheaval were severe enough to cause Innanta to sink," Shipner suggested. "Imagine if seawater flooded Innanta and everything drowned—plants, animals—even insects would have lost their food source and perished. Then eventually the land rose again, and creatures crawled out of the sea to become the species you have there today."

"In the meantime, a shift in the salinity of the ocean could have killed off the marine species that gave rise to the life-forms on Dhrusil-matkhashi," Robinson added. "A mass destruction of marine life happened on Earth at least once, and it's been documented on a couple of other worlds. Or a temperature shift might have done it, or some other catastrophic event. But the fact is, what we've seen here puts Dray's Planet much further along in the evolution of its life-forms than we previously believed."

"Tomorrow we should set out traps," Shipner suggested. "Where a creature as complex as the tree-creeper exists, doubtless there are many more life-forms."

"We need to look for water, too," Marta pointed out, "or this will be a very short expedition."

"We're more likely to find animals near a water source," Robinson added.

Shipner grunted agreement, then rose and stretched. The pale skin between his tattoos caught the firelight, making the designs seem to flicker and dance. "We'll make an early start," he announced. "Robinson, you take the first watch."

"*I* set the watches," Marta hissed at him.

Shipner sprouted his wicked grin. "Oh? Did you have another use for Robinson during the first watch?" he baited. When she did not respond, except with a daggered look, Shipner rolled his neck and shook out his arms. "Well, give me the last watch, Princess," he told her. "Old men like me dislike being wakened in the middle of the night."

Suddenly, over the quiet cacophony of chittering and clicking which had been a soothing backdrop for their conversation, there came a great, high-pitched screech. Even Shipner froze in his tracks at the sound of it, and the Innantan men rolled their eyes in terror. All the hair along Marta's neck and shoulders rose on end. Then the sound died out; in its wake the absolute silence was deafening.

Great Maker of All Things, Marta prayed fervently, *is that what I have come to find? Why did it shriek so? Was it in pain—or was that savage sound its hunting cry? Which is it, prey? or predator?*

And which are we?

CHAPTER 13

"And so," said Hassan, "they climbed up the mighty cliffs of Dhrusil-matkhashi, hand and foot, like lizards scaling a garden wall. When they reached the top, behold! a fair and prosperous land stretched before them, filled with growing things, overflowing with the gifts of the All-Giving, just as the angel had foretold. Marta raised her hands and gave thanks to the Creator God; and her song was as the song of the celestial host, so that the words of her mouth moved even the Unbelievers to thanks and praise."

"I have never seen an Unbeliever give thanks and praise to the Most High," Ari interrupted.

His father looked him sternly in the eye. "You have not seen everything there is to see."

Marta found Shipner outside their makeshift stockade, going through a series of slow, controlled movements in the waning starlight with his long knife in his hands. She had gone back to bed after her watch but been unable to sleep, her mind turning over a series of questions about the creatures they had encountered in their first three days of exploration. Since Robinson was still sleeping soundly, she had slipped out of their tent and sought out Shipner for his expertise.

It surprised her to find him so far outside the crude barrier. When she and Mahanna kept their watch, they stayed inside, near the fire, watching out over the fence into the darkness, but never going there. Lekish was still inside, tending a pot of porridge, but Shipner had moved ten meters outside the gate, off to the left. Marta peeked through a crack in the stockade, then stepped outside and watched, fascinated, as with his right hand he swept the blade in a slow arc across the sky, then clasped it in both hands and extended it upward, and finally sank into a crouch with the blade still held overhead. In the shadowy clearing, his tattooed body took on an eerie tone.

"Sab Shipner?" she called softly.

He did not break from the rhythm of his movements or acknowledge her presence.

"What are you doing?" she asked frankly.

He was down on one knee, his other leg extended before him, and he leaned left to touch his blade to the ground. "I do not disturb you at your prayers, Princess," he said as he returned the blade to center, then leaned to the right. "Do not disturb me at mine."

Marta's mouth fell open in amazement. For a moment she could only stare; then abruptly she snapped her mouth shut, turned on her heel, and marched back inside the stockade.

The fortifications had progressed rapidly, once the men had learned they could venture to the edge of the forest without being attacked by wild beasts. It was a simple wall and ditch, with the wall made of sharpened poles sunk in the ground and interwoven with an assortment of vines and stalks. It was starting to look impressive, but Marta sometimes wondered if the rickety structure would actually keep anything out.

"It is only one line of defense," Shipner had assured her. "The ditch is another, and beyond the ditch will be our best hope: a row of brambles and dried vegetation which we can set afire. The ditch will keep the blaze from spreading back to us in our stockade."

Marta had snorted in response. "I can just see a horde of tree-creepers scampering across the clearing on their stubby legs, and before we can rush out to light the fire, they'll hop the ditch and swarm over our little stick fence to chew us up while we sleep."

"Would you rather there was nothing between us and them?" he'd challenged, and Marta conceded the point with her silence. At least the wall and ditch gave an illusion of safety.

So far their limited exploration in the near environs of the forest had revealed nothing which acted aggressive enough for them to fear an attack. The creatures they saw seemed either puzzled by the strangers, unable to decide if these odd-smelling bipeds were friend or foe, or they shrank from any contact. The team had made recordings of several species, which they watched back at camp and which the two Unbelievers argued over continually. But the terrifying shriek of their second night had not been repeated, nor had they seen any tracks of animals that looked large enough to give them trouble.

One of the happiest discoveries they'd made was the presence of a spring-fed stream not far away. That had been Marta's greatest concern, that there would be no fresh water on Dhrusil-matkhashi and they would be forced to terminate the expedition when their supplies ran low. The water tested safe, if a little high in mineral content, and the course of the rivulet gave them a fruitful direction for hunting wildlife. Today they would mount a recorder along its bank to see what sorts of things came to drink in their absence.

Since the first day's episode with the tree-creeper, Shipner had left off harassing the novice woodsmen, though he continued to instruct them and point out any foolish actions. His tone was short and gruff, but rarely jeering. It was as though he had amused himself that day, and now it was time to stick to business. But he still goaded Robinson at every opportunity about his pet theories, about his scholastic reasoning, about his lack of experience. Tookh had on several occasions fulfilled his promise by stepping between them, and in his absence, Marta had done it herself more than once. To her mind, Soln Shipner was intentionally picking quarrels by being arrogant, unfeeling, and downright rude.

She peeked back through the loosely woven stockade to watch him. What he was doing looked more like a series of martial-arts exercises than any kind of religious ceremony. Before long he finished, sheathed his long knife, and swaggered back into the stockade, where he helped himself to water from a canteen.

"What god do you worship?" Marta asked with frank curiosity.

"There is only one god," he said simply, putting the canteen away on its peg. "It is people's understanding of God that varies: male or female, one being or many, benevolent or indifferent." Shipner picked up two or three sticks of wood and crossed to the fire with them.

Marta followed. "And what is your understanding of the All-Hallowed?" she pursued.

"Deep," he replied, settling back on his heels as he added the fresh wood to the coals. A flame sprang up almost instantly, and its light danced off his face and bare chest, giving the tattoos a life of their own. Marta watched the writhing black lines in fascination until Shipner glanced in her direction. "If you have nothing else to do, Princess, start the coffee. And don't add any cinnamon to it."

Then Shipner rose and posted himself just outside the gate, patrolling back and forth, searching the darkened forest with his senses as dawn leaked into the sky behind them.

Late that afternoon they met their first real challenge.

It was the day before Sabiss, and Marta was urgently trying to get the two Unbelievers to hustle back up the stream to camp before dusk. Dakura had not come along; he was by far the best cook of the group, and Marta had put him in charge of their Sabiss meal. It would be a meager feast, for although they had tested a few of the plants in the area and found them edible, they had a very low nutritional content and didn't taste very good. Dried stores cooked into a soup was the best they could manage.

After stopping to examine the tracks of a new creature, and for Shipner to cut samples of bark and leaves from a different kind of tree, they were now in danger of being caught in the forest when darkness fell. This troubled Marta on two counts: one, they didn't know what predators might come out at night; and two, it was forbidden to travel on Sabiss, which began at dusk. She was in the lead, moving along at a good clip, when she ducked under a low-hanging branch and startled a creature at its evening meal.

Marta stopped in her tracks, and for a moment the two just stared at each other. It was nearly a meter tall, sitting on its haunches with its head raised and pointed in her direction. The head was hammer-shaped, with a crest of some kind jutting back from the crown. The neck was thick and only slightly elongated, the forearms longer proportionally than the dinka-chak's, and the tail was long and muscular. It was definitely a carnivore, for clamped in its mouth was a stringy piece of flesh just torn from a carcass at its feet.

The two stood frozen, too surprised to react, until Robinson ducked under the branch and came up beside Marta. "I'll be damned," he whispered, just as Shipner appeared on the other side.

The numbers were too much for the creature. It let out a shriek and fled into the forest.

"Did you see that?" Robinson exclaimed joyously. "My God, it looked like a cross between an allosaur and a hadrosaur, only smaller."

Shipner had bent to examine the creature's kill. "A fast classification for a fleeting glimpse, and no idea of its bone structure."

"I wasn't classifying it," Robinson replied testily, "I was just describing it. A comparison of physical appearances, not a reference to its taxonomy."

"We shall name it after you," Shipner goaded. "Bunkosaurus."

Robinson clenched his fists, but Marta laid a soothing hand on his arm. "Did you see how large the eyes were? Is it nocturnal, do you suppose? Just coming out at dusk to stalk its prey—"

Her speculation was cut off by another shrill scream from the direction in which the creature had fled. The hair rose on Marta's arms and neck as it recalled the screech they had heard on their second night, and she looked questioningly at Robinson. "Is that what we heard . . . ?"

"Too high-pitched," Shipner asserted, rising and looking after the creature. The scream sounded again, a terrible squalling that faded abruptly.

"What do you suppose," Robinson asked uneasily, "makes a creature like that cry out?"

Shipner looked back at his two companions and grinned. "Let's find out!" With that, he started into the woods after the beast.

"Are you nuts?" Robinson demanded, following reluctantly. "What do you have, a death wish?"

Marta caught his arm. "Let him go," she hissed. "Why should you be as stupid as he?"

Robinson hesitated, torn. "I've got the energy rifle," he said after a moment. "All he has is that oversize hunting knife. Stay here." He started after Shipner.

"Oh, certainly, stay here with the wild animals and a smaller knife than he has!" Marta snapped, following Robinson. "I say leave him to his fate. You're too noble, even for me."

"Noble, hell," Robinson growled. "I'm not going to let him accumulate enough material to steal the Ashdod Prize from me!"

They didn't have to go far. Shipner had hauled up short by the trunk of a scarred tree, and he motioned them to stay back. Marta crept forward and peered around his shoulder.

Twined around the tree trunks just ahead were velvety-looking vines with huge pink flowers more than half a meter across. In its haste, the creature had stumbled into this mass of vines and was now sprawled among them, struggling feebly. It was not the vines themselves which hindered it, but the pink flowers. Two had snapped shut on its forelegs, another on its neck, a fourth on its tubular crest. Other blossoms were swaying now, bending to affix themselves to haunches, back, tail. A faint whimpering noise came from the beast.

"They're *eating* it," Marta breathed hoarsely.

Shipner nodded. "Like a Pradnarian lamb-eater, or a Venus flytrap. A carnivorous plant."

Marta studied the vines carefully, noting the buds of unopened flowers twisting around a tree trunk. Her heart jumped. "There are vines like those on the other side of the stream, where we went yesterday," she said in a small voice. "Only the flowers weren't open."

"So right, Princess." Shipner turned and started back the way they'd come. "Not mature yet? Or still digesting their last meal?"

Marta shuddered involuntarily at the thought of how near they had come to death without even knowing it.

When they reached the stream again, Shipner paused to poke at the late predator's victim. "This is one of those quadrupeds we saw earlier," he pointed out. "See the plate-like scales along its neck?" Grabbing it by the tail, he hoisted the torn carcass aloft. "Good chance to study this one." Then he flashed Marta a wicked grin. "When we're through, we can roast it for your Sabiss meal!"

"Sabiss!" Marta exclaimed in dismay, trying desperately to see a sun well hidden by the dense foliage. "Come! Hurry! We must get back to camp!"

The others were already at prayer when Marta and the Unbelievers broke out of the trees, and the light was fading fast. Distressed that she was so close to transgressing Sabiss, Marta quickly handed off her equipment belt to Robinson and stopped there at the forest's edge, raising hands and voice immediately in the prescribed ritual.

Shipner cocked an eyebrow at her. "Better to move inside the stockade, Princess," he advised.

Marta paused at the end of a sentence. "I do not bother you at your prayers," she parroted. "Please do not bother me at mine."

Shipner sighed wearily. "Innantans," he told Robinson, "are not very practical."

"I've noticed," Robinson replied dryly. "Never mind, I'll stay here and keep an eye on her."

Shipner snorted contemptuously. "And who's going to

keep an eye on you?" he asked. "Here, take this," he said, shoving the animal carcass at Robinson. "Stand very straight, Princess."

Marta gave a short gasp as Shipner seized her around the hips and lifted her off the ground. But she kept chanting doggedly, even as Shipner marched across the clearing and deposited her inside the wooden fence. Behind her, she could hear the two zoologists discussing the four-toed foot of their specimen as she sang of the justice of the All-Hallowed, and the last bit of daylight faded in the west.

It was hardly the first time Mazh Nrin had sent an apprentice around to ask Retneyabo to come for a fitting. But it was the first time he'd done so when Retneyabo was not having a garment made.

"I have this beautiful new fabric," Nrin explained when the kukhoosh arrived. "It made me think of you."

"Oh?"

"Many things make me think of you lately," Nrin admitted.

Retneyabo waited patiently for the old man to continue. "How is your wife Adni?" Nrin asked after a moment.

"Thriving," Retneyabo replied. "A little arthritis in her knees, but she doesn't complain. Much."

"A good woman, Adni," Nrin approved. Then, "And your wife Marta?"

Retneyabo hesitated. How much did Nrin know? "She's off adventuring again. You know how she is. New places, new things. The young!" Retneyabo laughed heartily.

Nrin did not laugh. "She courts danger," he said pointedly.

Retneyabo's laughter subsided. Nrin was a wise man, well respected among the mazhel, but he was not necessarily in touch with the comings and goings of the citizens of Jinka. "What kind of danger?" he asked.

Instead of answering, Nrin shuffled over to a table where bolts of cloth were heaped and tugged one out of the stack. "This is the one," he said. "There is so much green in it. I like green, I think it is a good color."

Retneyabo joined the mazh at the table. "Do you know where Marta is?" he asked softly.

"Do you?" the mazh returned.

Retneyabo considered, not whether to answer, but how. He'd received word from his agent in Mimma, who had heard from the ship's captain, that Marta and her party had scaled the cliffs of Dhrusil-matkhashi and signaled their safe arrival at the top. He would have no word now until the radio beacon signaled their desire to be removed. Was any of this known to the mazh? And if so, how?

"The last word I had," he said finally, "on the seventh day of the month of Tekar, she stood on the cliffs of Dhrusil-matkhashi."

Nrin sucked in his breath. "That is what I feared."

"How did this knowledge come to you?" Retneyabo demanded. "And why does it make you fearful?"

Nrin shook his head, clearly disturbed. "There are rumors in the streets. My boy brings them to me. They are all three gone, your wife and the two Unbelievers. They seek Knowledge, but no one knows where. One can only speculate. It was you yourself who told me where. Before that I did not know." He unrolled the bolt of cloth. "Here, let me see how this looks on you."

Retneyabo was in no mood to have yards of fabric draped over him just now, but he held out his arms obligingly and waited with patience for the old man to come to his point. Nrin threw one end of the cloth over Retneyabo's shoulder and spread it out across his broad chest, tucking it here, gathering it there with his hands. "Green," he muttered. "Yes, green."

"Why is green significant?" Retneyabo prodded carefully.

"Green is the color of growth, of prosperity," Nrin said obliquely. "Everything you touch prospers, my son." He shook out more yards of the fabric. Then, "Dhrusil-matkhashi is green," he said quietly.

Retneyabo barely concealed his start. "A green place,

eh? And prosperous? Filled with plants and animals?" he guessed.

Nrin's voice was barely audible. "So it is said."

Retneyabo quieted his pounding heart. "Said by whom?"

Nrin's eyes flickered to the kukhoosh's, then looked quickly away as he tugged the cloth off the big man's shoulder and began to roll it back onto the bolt. "Many years ago," he recounted, "in the fourth generation after the Martyrs, a mazh sailed to the southern coast of Dhrusil-matkhashi to see what was there. After he passed the towering cliffs, he came to a region of dangerous rocks and reefs. Beyond that he found a swamp, and through the swamp he came to a mighty river. There at last he saw the land he had come to see. It was green and verdant and filled with living things."

Nrin drew a great breath. "Making his way up the river, he found excellent grazing land and large stands of trees for lumber. There were veins of coal breaking the surface of the land, and rocks bright with iron ore and other signs of minerals. Along one tributary he found a swampy place where oil lay on the surface of the water in thick black pools. There in the Land Beyond the Gates were treasures in abundance."

Retneyabo's eyes crackled, but he kept silent.

Nrin sighed heavily. "But when he tried to return with the news, many hardships befell the mazh. His ship was cast up on rocks, and most of the crew drowned. They put together a raft from the wreckage and paddled back toward Innanta, but a creature came out of the sea and swallowed up one of his companions. Finally, when they were within sight of land, a great wind capsized the raft, and only the mazh was washed up on the shore. Everyone else was lost, and he himself was badly injured.

"When finally he reported to his fellow mazhel, they were concerned by these signs. They prayed fervently, and the All-Hallowed spoke to them, directing them to keep the treasures of Dhrusil-matkhashi a secret. It was better, they decided, for the Faithful to labor in subduing Innanta—then they would never forget how dependent we are upon the Most High. It is good for the Children to labor, and not to have a soft life."

It was all Retneyabo could do to keep from shouting, *You fools! Iron ore. Petroleum. Land for planting and for grazing—were we not meant to harvest the bounty of this place for the glory of the All-Giving, from whose hand it surely comes?* But he bit down hard and managed to bring himself under control. If the Most High had revealed to the mazhel that these treasures were to remain a secret . . .

"Why do you tell me this?" Retneyabo asked, tight-jawed.

Nrin gave another great sigh and sank down on a little stool in the corner. He looked frail and bent, as though he had carried a heavy load for far too long. "Time passed," he said wearily. "Some of the mazhel felt the secret was best kept by silence, and so they said nothing of it to their successors. Some, however, passed the secret from one generation to the next, always with the precaution that this treasure must not be allowed to corrupt the Faithful. But they made one mistake; they believed themselves to be incorruptible."

Now Retneyabo's eyes widened in alarm. "Are you saying there are mazhel—now—who take advantage of this treasure?"

Nrin nodded sadly. "Perhaps three generations ago, three adventurous young mazhel made an expedition to verify the richness of Dhrusil-matkhashi. Having done so, they decided—among themselves—that it would be of benefit to the Faithful to bring just a little of this wealth back to Innanta. Some tall trees for ship masts. A little coal, to power the kilns of a modest ceramics factory. It seemed harmless.

"But as time went on they were seduced by the possibilities of these resources and grew more bold. They dug out iron ore and brought it secretly to an island where they built a smelter. They shipped out coal to fire the smelter. It became such a huge task that they brought in partners, some of their most trusted clients. The steel they produced was divided into small batches and sold

surreptitiously as black-market goods, reaping a huge reward. This money was used to fund infirmaries, to purchase those few medical supplies which are approved for
import—some of the steel was even used for manufacture of communications equipment and other things we
need so badly, need to keep us from being dependent
on the Unbeliever. There was so much good that came
of it . . ."

Tears glistened in the old man's eyes. "But it was
wrong. It was wrong because we kept it for ourselves,
and we let the Faithful believe a falsehood: we let them
believe that Dhrusil-matkhashi is a wasteland. We tell
our women to limit their families so that we do not overtax the resources of this poor continent, when we know
very well the bounty of the All-Giving is so close at
hand . . ."

Nrin lifted his moist eyes to Retneyabo. "I did not see
the harm, long ago. I kept nothing for myself, as you
can see—I have always earned my living by the sweat
of my brow. But the others . . ." He ducked his head.
"I finally opposed them. They told me I spoke against
the will of the All-Powerful. They said it was the will
of the Unknowable that this should be done, and they
threatened to discredit me if I tried to expose them—
oh, it has gone on so long, you see. It is difficult to see
that a thing is wrong when it has gone on so long . . ."

Nrin trailed off. Then slowly he clambered to his feet,
blew his nose in a large handkerchief, and cleared his
throat. "We let others call us Holy Ones," he said with
rather more firmness, "but we do not hold to the same
standards we demand of the Children."

Retneyabo took several moments to absorb this confession. Then he asked, "How is Marta in danger, then?
From these mazhel and their clients?"

Nrin nodded. "If she comes back and exposes the deception—especially if people learn the Holy Ones
themselves have profited from the wealth of Dhrusil-
matkhashi . . ."

Slowly Retneyabo nodded. He understood all too well
the social and political upheaval that would follow.

"Thank you, Mazh Nrin, for telling me this. I am honored by your confidence. I will take steps to protect Marta, without bringing dishonor to the mazhel."

Mazh Nrin shook his head sadly and shuffled toward the back of his workshop. "We have dishonored ourselves," he said tiredly. "May the All-Knowing be as lenient with us as you are, my son."

"In the times before Marta," Hassan told his listeners, "Dhrusil-matkhashi had been a barren place where nothing would grow." Hassan knew as well as the rest of his listeners that the fossil record showed Dhrusil-matkhashi had supported life for eons before the Innantans arrived, but that bothered him not at all. It was the way the story was told, and would continue to be told. *"But the All-Compassionate saw how the Children of the Second Revelation were faithful in their devotion, and so took pity upon them, for the land where they dwelt was a dry and harsh land. The All-Gracious made the trees of Dhrusil-matkhashi to grow, and placed minerals in its soil, and watered it with many rivers. Then, when the land was full of plants and animals, the All-Powerful called forth Marta and the Unbelievers to discover it there . . ."*

Cecil Robinson frowned in concentration as he studied the chart he was constructing on his flatscreen. No, he couldn't really make a case for the unidillo—as they called this pig-sized armored quadruped—being related to the *maknook,* the "walking-stewmeat" quadruped that Shipner had brought back to camp for their first Sabiss feast. Any common ancestor they'd shared must have been twenty or thirty iterations back.

For a month now they'd been observing and recording the wildlife of Dhrusil-matkhashi, never going more than half a day's journey along the stream so that they could return to the safety of their stockade by nightfall. And what a wealth of data he'd amassed! Six separate varieties of tree-creeper identified, a host of small, lizardlike creatures they simply called "skitterers," several bipeds with balancing tails, the slower, four-footed herbivores,

and even two or three kinds of life-forms with amphibious traits.

Shipner was still referring to them by obvious differen-
tiators: carnivores, herbivores, insectivores, omnivores;
bipeds, quadrupeds; three-toed, two-toed, five-toed. He
even referred to one group as "tube-crested," because
jutting up over the crowns of their skulls like a crest
were a pair of tubes connected with their breathing passages. But did he draw any connection between those
crested animals and certain duck-billed hadrosaurs? No.
As a scientist, the man had no imagination. No vision.
No intuition. His ideas were so rigid and his thinking so
hidebound that he couldn't see what was right in front
of his beak of a nose.

Robinson had made the leap of recognition the instant
he first saw the dinka-chak, and every new species they
discovered here only helped corroborate his theory.
Dray's Planet, as a world, was the nearest thing to
Earth's twin of any planet charted in this arm of the
galaxy. Mass, composition, distance from its sun, atmosphere, rotation—*everything* lined up within a couple of
thousandths of a percent of Earth's conditions—except,
of course, that further out along the galactic arm, planets
were younger. So given the nearly identical conditions,
life on Dray's Planet had evolved in a nearly identical
fashion—only it was younger. One had to be a fool—or
a stiff-necked, intransigent dogmatic—to refuse to acknowledge it.

At first he'd thought the dinka-chak might be a last
remnant of quasi-saurian development, an evolutionary
leftover from a class that died out as the desert enveloped Innanta. But here on Dhrusil-matkhashi, he'd discovered the truth: they were in the heart of the Innantan
equivalent of the Age of Dinosaurs! Why, just look at
the unidillo with its armored hide and its single hornlike
projection—it had ceratopsian written all over it!

Robinson had learned to keep such observations to
himself, however. Glancing across the compound, he saw
Shipner at work on his own research notes. Sorting, no
doubt—the man was forever sorting: by this joint, by

that bone, by kind of teeth and number of digits— It was important work, of course, and Robinson would get to that end of it eventually, but it never ceased to amaze him that the vaunted Dr. Soln Shipner had missed the big picture entirely. Missed it? Refused to look at it! Robinson had pointed it out, and Shipner had scoffed.

Well, let him sink in the mire of his own inflexibility. Having beaten Shipner to the conclusion, Robinson now had only to beat him off this godforsaken planet . . .

If he could get on that freighter—hell, two months to the Portal, maybe another two weeks till a communications ship or something jumped through—the time would be well spent reviewing all this data he was collecting: sorting, digesting, extrapolating. By the time he passed through the Portal, his analysis and conclusion would be ready for transmission to the *Journal of the ILZ,* and they wouldn't *dare* hold it up by having it refereed. Who was qualified to referee it, anyway? As long as Soln Shipner was left well behind . . .

"Sab Robinson, look!"

Robinson looked up into Marta's smiling face and for a moment didn't care what she was holding up for his inspection. God, she was beautiful! Those sparkling eyes, that full mouth . . .

Close beside Marta was Tookh, holding a woven basket with its lid tied on firmly. "More skitterers," the boy announced. "One's got a red collar and four toes. That sounds like another new species, doesn't it?"

The boy's enthusiasm always made Robinson smile. Marta had been reluctant to let the teenager come along on their forays into the wild, concerned for his safety, but it did no good to make him stay behind. He simply wandered about the forest on his own, collecting samples of insects and grubs and such, which he presented to Marta with the utmost pride. She'd finally had to let him come along with her, just to keep an eye on him.

Today she had gone with him into the near forest while the two Unbelievers worked on compiling their notes and reviewing the images from the recorders. It made the boy doubly proud that he and the Sibna had captured these creatures together.

"A red collar and four toes, eh?" Robinson said. "Yes, it sounds like a new one to me, although our resident naysayer will probably disagree out of sheer orneriness."

"Oh, not when I show them to him," Tookh boasted. "He likes me."

It was true, and Robinson didn't understand it any more than Marta did. Shipner went out of his way to be rude to everyone else in the camp, but he was oddly careful of Tookh's feelings. Not that he was never sharp with the boy, particularly if Tookh was careless in tramping through the forest, but the reprimands were always brief and—for lack of a better word—paternal.

Tookh was not the only one who had learned to capitalize on this anomaly. "Why don't you show them to our painted pain in the posterior, then?" Robinson suggested to the boy. The midday sun was warm, and the Unbeliever's attention had been suddenly arrested by little beads of sweat trickling down Marta's collarbones headed for . . . "He'll take the time to look at all of them, if you ask him."

Tookh grinned and trotted eagerly toward Shipner with the basket of skitterers.

Robinson turned back to Marta. "Are you through playing in the forest for today?" he asked slyly.

Marta's eyes went suddenly smoky and her smile softened into a seductive curving of her lips. She ran a moist pink tongue over them to heighten the effect. "In the *forest,* yes," she agreed. "I think I'll go into the tent and . . . wash. Hm?"

Robinson closed up his flatscreen and rose from the packing crate he'd been using for a chair. "Mm, sounds like fun. I'll even get the water for you."

"Oh!" Tookh cried as he dumped the contents of his basket into a mesh cage at Shipner's feet. "Sibna, look! I think the red-collared one is eating the speckled one!"

Marta chuckled. "You go ahead and get the water," she told Robinson, "I'll be right there. I must see this phenomenon or hear about it in detail later this evening." She let her fingers trail across his chest in a promise, then went off to see Tookh's skitterers.

They kept a supply of water in barrels inside the compound. Those barrels sat out in the open, so that at this time of day the contents were reasonably warm. Robinson drew a bucketful and headed for the tent he shared with Marta. Since water for bathing was not normally in large supply on the expeditions she led, Marta was making the most of this luxury. And with her gift for creative seduction, Robinson was anticipating a scintillatingly hedonistic diversion.

"Ah! The great warrior prepares to do battle again," Shipner called, seeing Robinson draw his bucket of water. "It is fortunate that nothing seems inclined to attack this stockade, for at the rate you wage the carnal war, Robinson, you must be in a state of perpetual exhaustion."

Marta, who was kneeling near the Nechtanite with Tookh, fired him a daggered look that would have killed a lesser man at a hundred meters. Tookh looked up from the skitterers and frowned a little.

"Jealous, Shipner?" Robinson goaded.

"What, do you imagine I have any interest in such an insipid, inornate, facile female?" Shipner laughed. "A Nechtanite would not so degrade himself as to mate with such an undistinguished person."

"Sab Shipner," Tookh said quietly, "it isn't right for you to say such things."

But today, Shipner's charity toward Tookh seemed to be forgotten in his malice toward Robinson, for his tone lost none of its taunting edge as he addressed the lad. "See this?" he said, pointing to an elaborate design on his chest. "This is the badge of my manhood trials. Only when I earned this was I allowed to touch a woman. And then—" He grinned mirthlessly at Marta. "She had a knife in her hand. Remember, Princess—" The grin disappeared in a flash. "That which is so freely given away has no value."

Robinson truly thought she would launch herself at

Shipner and scratch his eyes out. But whether it was Tookh's presence or the sudden darkness of Shipner's face, she did not, though her chest heaved with the effort of controlling her compulsion for violence. At last she drew a great, cleansing breath, threw her shoulders back, and exhaled audibly. "Ah, now I understand, Sab Shipner," she said in a voice dripping contempt, "what gives you such a vile humor. You indulge in pleasures so seldom that your body is polluted with unspent passion. What a pity that you are stuck here on Innanta for the *rest of your life*—" Her lip curled in evil satisfaction. "—where all the women are beneath you." Then she rose, turned, and strolled—no, fairly slithered with bewitching, sinuous motions—into her tent to await Robinson.

CHAPTER 14

Marta watched the little stream gurgle and splash its way through the trees, disappearing as the ground dropped rapidly to the west and north. The day was warm and the air still, here where the treetops met thinly over the narrow cut of the stream. Behind her, the two Unbelievers were bickering again, this time over a serpentine track in the soft ground beside the water.

"It's another tree-creeper," Robinson insisted. "Look, here are the little scratch marks from its feet propelling it along."

"This is not a drag mark," Shipner argued. "It's as though the animal rolled over the ground, hunched up its back, then rolled forward again."

"So maybe the tree-creeper doesn't slither," Robinson came back. "We've never actually seen it move on the ground." They had been here for six weeks, and still they found more to argue about than to agree on.

"There's no reason for a creature to do this," Shipner puzzled. "Some desert snakes move like this, yes, to keep from boiling their blood on the hot desert sands. They lift their coils to cool them, almost walking across the ground on those coils. But temperature is not a problem here, even if the creature should be ectothermic . . ."

"Snakes have scales to slither on," Robinson pointed out. "Maybe the skin texture of this animal doesn't let it slide easily."

Marta came back and brought her boot down firmly on the print they were studying. Both men looked up.

"A house tree would hold two sleepers, with room left over for gear, yes?" she demanded.

Tookh had been the first to discover a species of large trees with trunks that were split open and hollow inside. He called them house trees because the hollow interior was almost as big as the two-meter-by-three-meter hovel in which he'd grown up.

Robinson stood up, wiping his hands on his tunic. "So?"

"We could camp overnight in them," Marta said, "with a fire at the opening and a guard, and be reasonably safe."

The two men exchanged a look.

"I want to see more of this place," Marta said bluntly. "We've been here six weeks, and we've hardly penetrated the forest at all. We haven't seen any dinka-chaks. We don't know how far this forest goes." She nailed Robinson with a look. "I want to find out what else is here."

There was silence for a moment.

"I want to catch a spaceship," Robinson replied with equal bluntness. "Its nearest point to this planet is seven weeks from now; I intend to be back in Jinka where the only shuttleport is, and your husband better damn well have found a way to get me on it."

Shipner said nothing, but his hard eyes gave her no encouragement. He, too, knew exactly when that freighter would be available. Marta gauged them both.

"That gives us two and half weeks," she said finally. "Two and a half weeks in, two and a half weeks out. Three days for our ship to reach us, seven days to make Jinka, four days to spare. All right?"

"Only if you're ready to meet the author of that scream we heard when we first got here," Robinson pointed out. "You may have noticed a lot of the predators in this forest like to hunt at dusk."

But a slow smile curved Shipner's lips. "Come, Robinson, where is your sense of adventure?" he goaded. "Will you go back to Melius and say, 'We don't know what lies in the interior because we were afraid to venture there'?"

"As long as I'm alive to say it."

"Then Sab Shipner and I will go, and take Dakura instead of you," Marta said with decision. "And you can explain to the ILZ why your research does not include any data from our trip to the interior, and Sab Shipner's does."

For the next five weeks, Robinson wondered why he let his testosterone get the better of him that day.

It took Retneyabo three weeks to figure out which mazhel they were, but it gradually became clear. Mazh Tabla lived modestly, but his client Kukhoosh Surim made a fortune, supposedly from his copper mines in the south. Upon inspection, it was shown that the mines had been producing only a poor grade of ore for the last ten years. Surim should have been a pauper.

Mazh Tabla's mentor had been Mazh Hokoffna, who had been a toolmaker specializing in medical instruments. When one looked at the quantity of steel tools and instruments produced by Mazh Hokoffna and Mazh Tabla, it seemed excessive for the amount of scrap steel that was available on Dray's Planet after so many generations. The steel had to have come from the secret smelter and refinery.

Hokoffna had passed into the Eternal Presence of the Most High, but his good friend Mazh Elkniar was still living, although he was now blind and unable to practice his art of creating tiled murals. But he lived comfortably, supported by his children and apprentices—comfortably enough to keep three sib-hinans. Three! There had to be money coming from somewhere else.

Elkniar's protege was Mazh Kummel. It was hard to find any evidence for Kummel's involvement other than his association with Mazh Elkniar. But one of his clients, Kukhoosh Serai, had a thriving shipping business, and those ships made occasional journeys through the southwestern islands. The villages on those islands scarcely harvested enough kelp and sea creatures to survive; they had no surplus to sell to Serai; yet that was what his ships claimed to carry.

So there it was: the miner who knew how to collect

and refine the iron ore; the ships that freighted the iron ore to and from the smelter; the toolmaker who slipped the medical instruments into circulation—and all of them profiting from the sale of Dhrusil-matkhashi's resources. As for Mazh Nrin's involvement, though Retneyabo would not inquire directly, he learned that Nrin had once had a friend, a fisherman, who brought the meat of large creatures to market, claiming they were marine animals he called *wali*. But no one had ever seen a live wali, and no one else ever seemed to catch them.

Tabla, Elkniar, Kummel. Retneyabo looked at the three now seated in chairs on the rooftop of the College of Holy Studies and sighed in satisfaction. The glances Tabla and Kummel had cast at each other at his appearance only confirmed Retneyabo's belief. Blind Elkniar sat with a sullen frown on his face.

"Ah, how gracious of you to receive me!" Retneyabo boomed as he approached the trio.

Tabla put on a stern face at this greeting; Kummel blanched. "Who's that?" Elkniar demanded irritably. "That doesn't sound like Nrin."

"I am Kukhoosh Retneyabo," the kukhoosh introduced, bowing his forehead and touching it to the hand of the aging mazh. "I have the honor to be a client of Mazh Nrin the tailor."

"I know who you are," Elkniar snapped peevishly. "Where is Nrin?"

Tabla lifted his chin. "Somehow, I don't believe Mazh Nrin is coming," he said in a high, pinched voice. It matched his pinched face.

"Ah, you are wise indeed," Retneyabo said pleasantly. "Mazh Nrin is not well."

Kummel's pale face flushed; Tabla's eyes narrowed. "Oh?" said Tabla. "We hadn't heard."

"Nor shall you, except from me," Retneyabo replied, seating himself across from them. "It is his heart that is not well. He carries something in it that gives him pain."

Elkniar waved that aside with a palsied hand. "I did not agree to meet with you, Retneyabo. For Nrin I came here—I owe him that much. But not you." The old man struggled to his feet, assisted by Tabla. Kummel rose as well.

"Aren't you the least bit curious why I have approached you?" Retneyabo asked easily.

"He who must approach in deception," said Elkniar, clutching at his cane, "has nothing of merit on his lips." The three mazhel started across the roof for the stairs.

"Deception—now, there is an interesting topic," Retneyabo called out pointedly. "I could call for a meeting of the Council of Kukhooshel without deception or subterfuge, and I'm sure they would be interested in what I have learned about Dhrusil-matkhashi."

Jittery Kummel stopped short, inadvertently holding Elkniar back. Tabla turned around to face Retneyabo once more. There was a long moment of silence.

It was Elkniar who finally spoke. "What do you want, Retneyabo?" he demanded. "Do not play word games with us. Speak plainly and be done with it."

Retneyabo's face grew hard, and he leaned forward in his chair. "Plainly, then," he agreed. "You have been keeping the wealth of Dhrusil-matkhashi from the Children of the Second Revelation. Keeping it from them, and profiting by its exploitation."

Elkniar banged his cane loudly on the floor. "Not so!" he hissed. "We do not profit from it. Innanta profits from it."

"And how is it you pay the tuition and upkeep for three sib-hinans?" Retneyabo asked quietly.

The old mazh's mouth was set in a grim line, but he did not answer.

Tabla strode up to the kukhoosh. "What do you want, Retneyabo?" he demanded.

Retneyabo had thought about that much in the last three weeks. Here was a great bargaining chip. He could have three very powerful men in his camp on the issue of trade with the Unbelievers. He might get Cecil Robinson's passage off-planet, and Soln Shipner's, too, for that matter. He could certainly demand Marta's protection. What exactly did he want?

"I want what is good for Innanta," Retneyabo said

firmly. "I want the riches of Dhrusil-matkhashi to flow freely into this country."

"We are not a country, we are a people!" Tabla retorted. "And to pour such wealth upon our people so suddenly would ruin the economy, ruin the lives of the Faithful! You would be ruined, Retneyabo, if every ship's captain could sail to its southern coast and load up whatever it pleased him to take, bringing it back here to sell. Your goods would drop in value; you would be beggared."

"Not," Retneyabo pointed out, "if the ships' captains were my clients."

Kummel, who had been silent until now, seized upon this. "Is that what you want? To share in the trade?"

"I want," Retneyabo said patiently, "for the level of medical care on this planet to improve. I want women to be able to bear as many children as pleases them. I want a place where the poorest of the poor can go and make a living by the work of his hand and the sweat of his brow. I want the truth about Dhrusil-matkhashi made known."

"Impossible!" Elkniar raged. "Impossible! That would make liars of the mazhel!"

Retneyabo's thin smile was as cold as ice. "No, Mazh Elkniar, you have made that of yourselves."

The old man advanced on the kukhoosh, in spite of Kummel's halfhearted efforts to restrain him. "We do what is best for the Children of the Second Revelation," he rumbled in a voice that quavered as much from age as from anger. "Nrin knew that once. He has lost the vision."

Now Tabla turned to the other two. "Kummel, why don't you take Mazh Elkniar home? I believe that I can reason with Kukhoosh Retneyabo and persuade him to change his mind."

Kummel threw his colleague a doubtful glance, but he took Elkniar's arm firmly. "Come, Elkniar," he said soothingly. "Tabla will deal with this."

"In all things it is necessary to seek the will of the Most High," Elkniar preached. "I have devoted my life to seeking it. Dhrusil-matkhashi is not a place for the Faithful to inhabit!"

Retneyabo weighed the old mazh carefully and decided that Elkniar truly believed what he said. He was Nrin's contemporary, and like him a somber and resolute man. But these other two—they were a different generation. They were a different kind of mazh. Kummel was leading Elkniar away now, almost patronizing with his placating words, and Tabla—

Mazh Tabla pulled up a chair across from Retneyabo and sat down. "I think, my son," he began in conciliatory tones, "that we are largely in agreement: we both want what is best for the people of Innanta. Where we differ is on how to achieve that."

The kukhoosh eyed the mazh carefully, waiting for him to explain.

Encouraged, Tabla leaned forward a bit. "You are right," he said, "the wealth of Dhrusil-matkhashi should be used to benefit the Faithful. But to throw the continent open—" He shook his head, softly clicking his tongue. "Devastation. Only in small bits and pieces can we bring these resources into Innanta without creating chaos."

"And what chaos it would create in your bank account," Retneyabo observed, "if just anyone could go there and bring the resources back."

Tabla frowned and shifted slightly in his chair. "We mazhel have not benefited personally from this traffic," he insisted, "but we have had to take a few of our clients into our confidence in order to add these resources effectively to the Innantan economy." Steepling his fingers together, Tabla added, "You are a merchant yourself, Retneyabo. You know that it would be unnatural for a trader not to sell his goods for a profit. If our clients were suddenly to offer their goods at reduced prices, it would be bad business. A balance must be maintained."

Retneyabo smiled benignly and said nothing.

"However, since you are now privy to the secret," Tabla went on hesitantly, "perhaps you could join us. If you wanted to send, say, one ship a year to Dhrusil-matkhashi and bring back . . . timber. Or salt. Or even copper—I understand there is a large deposit breaking the surface only two or three days' sail up a river from the coast." Tabla's smile was a simple baring of teeth. "Or perhaps you will find something even more interesting."

"Like a dinka-chak?" Retneyabo inquired evenly.

The mazh's brow furrowed. "That was an unfortunate accident. One of our captains picked up a nest of eggs, thinking he could sell them as goose eggs, but as he sailed along the western coast of Innanta, they hatched. Vicious little things. It was all right when they gobbled up the mice they found in the hold, but then they started on the rigging. He threw them all overboard." Tabla managed a ghost of a smile. "Apparently they can swim."

The silence stretched between them. Finally Retneyabo stirred. "Your desire to add to the Innantan economy is commendable," he said. "And no doubt I could make a tidy profit from helping you. But tell me, what good does it do me if I cannot buy replacement knees for my wife? If the Dean of my College must struggle with computer equipment that was ancient two hundred years ago? We need full use of the hard metals and petroleum reserves that Dhrusil-matkhashi may have to offer."

Tabla stroked his beard thoughtfully. "There is another alternative," he said slowly. "It would take a generation or more to develop the resources of which you speak. By the time we can manufacture plastic knee joints, your wife will be past all pain, in the Everlasting Presence of the Most High. But you could have such things—medical supplies, sophisticated electronics—in only a year or two, if we were to allow the purchase of such from the Unbelievers."

Retneyabo fought back a smug smile. "You would give me license to trade offworld for these things?"

Tabla coughed delicately and cleared his throat. "It would have to be very limited, you understand. And very discreet. But perhaps . . . once every three years . . . ?"

The smile would not stay off his face now, although Retneyabo kept it very small. "So once a year I could send a ship of my own to Dhrusil-matkhashi to harvest its—resources—and once every three years, I could make a purchase of manufactured goods from the Unbelievers, is that right?"

"The first I grant you now," Tabla agreed. "The second . . . I will have to win the approval of my fellow mazhel; but I believe it can be done."

Retneyabo pushed himself out of the chair and to his feet. "Mazh Tabla, I see that you truly have the good of the people of Innanta in your heart. It is for this reason that you were called by your fellow mazhel to be a mazh, and to interpret for us the Holy Writings, and to seek to know the will of the Most High for the Faithful." Retneyabo bowed solemnly. "I salute your great wisdom."

Tabla waited until Retneyabo had started for the stairs. Then, "There's just one other thing," he called after the kukhoosh.

Retneyabo turned back with a questioning look. "Yes?"

"There is a rumor," Tabla said, "that your sib-hinan has taken an expedition with two Unbelievers to the southwestern islands. She would not, by chance, have gone to Dhrusil-matkhashi by mistake?"

Retneyabo smiled broadly. "Marta does not make mistakes."

"It would be unfortunate," Tabla told him, "if she should bring back any report of that continent. Very unfortunate."

"I understand completely," Retneyabo assured him. Then, bowing once more to this far-thinking mazh, he left the roof.

Robinson clung with all four limbs to a brittle branch nearly ten meters above the forest floor. "Whose idea was this adventure, anyway?" he growled, looking at his companions perched on similar branches just over his head.

Below them, a group of large beasts ambled between the trees, scratching their sides against the bark and bending to nibble at some fernlike undergrowth here and there. They had four slender legs and graceful tails that switched back and forth as they moved. The tallest stood a good two meters high at the shoulder; three young ones looked about half that height. At one point the serpentine neck of the leader craned up like a periscope, and its head swiveled around in the direction of the humans; but it seemed unimpressed by the three strange creatures roosting in a tree. Eventually they moved on.

Robinson heaved a great sigh and picked his way carefully back down to the ground. The trees were not so tall here as they had been near the coast, but the lower branches were still mostly dead sticks, as likely to snap under a man's weight as to grant him passage upwards. *Just another one of the little adventures,* he thought sourly, *of living with Marta.*

Only the three of them had come on this journey. Marta was reluctant to risk the lives of her hired men on what was admittedly a dangerous foray into the unknown. "Great," Robinson had grumbled. "You're willing to risk me, but not them."

"You are a scientist," she replied. "You take risks for the sake of Knowledge. They were hired to do a job, and they do it as best they can under difficult circumstances; but it is unnecessary to ask them to leave the encampment. Unfair and unnecessary."

They would travel faster, she said, with only the three of them, and she was probably right. But he would have liked the extra protection of a few more bodies with weapons. Robinson carried their only energy rifle while Marta carried the recorder. Shipner, like the other two, wore a backpack of supplies, but he refused to carry anything except his knife. "A warrior's hands should be free," he declared.

Free hands had made him the first one up this tree, reaching back to haul Marta up after him and leaving Robinson to make his own way. Now he dropped to the ground beside the younger zoologist. "Herbivores," he noted. "They probably haven't much to fear from predators, at their size. Did you notice they had no plating or spikes?"

"They could well have great speed, too," Marta added, aiming the recorder at a pile of droppings one of the creatures had deposited. "Did you notice the proportionally long legs? Almost like a giraffe."

"This is ridiculous," Robinson protested, uncapping his canteen and taking a drink. "We're gathering more data than we can hope to analyze, and there's no depth to any of it. I say we turn back now, capture some live specimens, and blast the hell out of here." They had been trekking further and further into the forest for two weeks now.

"Sab Robinson, I do not appreciate your profanity!" Marta reminded him irritably. "If you are to stay in Innanta for any length of time, you must curb your tongue or risk losing it!"

"Back in Innanta, where I have a soft bed and clean clothes and food that doesn't bite back," he growled, "I'll undoubtedly do a much better job. But out here, where I have to make my bed in a tree and be careful the local fauna doesn't squash me like a bug, I get a little testy!"

In fact, this was the first time they had encountered animals of such large proportions. The majority of creatures they had spotted so far were the size of dogs, some large, others toy-sized. Most were solitaries; these tall quadrupeds were the first animals they'd seen moving in a group. But they took no chances with anything they encountered; if the beast didn't flee upon seeing them, it was up the nearest tree until it lost interest and moved on. They'd gotten quite good at climbing trees.

Robinson dropped his lean frame onto the ground and dug his notepad out of his backpack. Reluctant to bring his flatscreen or voicewriter into the woods, he'd settled for the old-fashioned paper notebook and pencils Marta provided for him. Now he made a quick sketch of the creature they'd just seen, noting several of its characteristics.

Shipner was doing the same. "No crest on this one," he observed aloud. "No visible armor, either. With legs like that, it either relies on speed or sheer size for protection. Three toes showing in this track—if there's a fourth, it's shortened like a dewclaw. That seems to be a dominant trait on this continent. Marta, do you have a location?"

Marta consulted the pedometer she wore strapped on her ankle. "About four kilometers beyond where we camped last night."

"Less ten meters for the climb up the tree," Robinson mumbled.

"And what's the reading on your recorder?" Shipner prompted. Marta rattled off the number showing on the recorder cartridge. Both scientists noted it in their books.

"Ready to move on?" Marta asked, stepping out to take the lead.

"Not quite," Robinson replied, still scribbling in his notebook.

Shipner scowled at him. "What, are you making notes on its skeletal structure? Do you have x-ray vision?"

"I don't need x-ray vision to see which way the joints bend," Robinson told him. "Or the size of the skull in relation to the body. There are certain assumptions that can be made."

"Such as?"

Robinson folded his notebook with a snap and tucked it into his backpack. "I'll be happy to send you a copy of my paper. Just as soon as it appears in the *Journal of the ILZ.*"

Shipner's lips curled slightly. "Afraid to debate your assumptions?"

"No, I just don't give a rat's ass for your opinions, that's all."

"You'd rather be proved a fool in front of the whole galaxy, I suppose."

Marta stepped between them. "If you're going to

argue," she said impatiently, "can you at least argue
while moving in a forward direction?"

The two men favored each other with a parting sneer
and turned to follow Marta through the forest.

Yetta cleared his throat softly, not wanting to disturb
the kukhoosh if she were in the midst of prayerful meditation; but she glanced up immediately. "Yes, Yetta,
what is it?"

"I spoke with Zaradin, patron," he told her. "He has
reached an agreement with the captain of the privateer.
They will pretend they had previous instructions to pick
up the two Unbelievers and divert into orbit over any
protestation of the Orbital Authority here. They will demand assurance that their passengers are not ready to
be picked up before they go on to GenOrg in search
of . . . whatever it is they are in search of. We can send
a shuttle up before they go, on the pretext of forwarding
further payment for Sab Shipner's passage here."

The kukhoosh nodded. "Good," she said. "Then provided our passenger shows up on time, all will be well."

"He knows the timetable," Yetta assured her. "And
the consequences for failing to fulfill his contract." With
a short bow he faded from the room, leaving Kukhoosh
Paun to her contemplation.

Paun was a large woman, both tall in stature and
large-boned. A slight widow's peak in her dark hair com-
plimented a strong nose and wide-set eyes, so that in
her youth her countenance had been characterized as
"noble," and she as a handsome woman. Age and bitterness, however, had given her face a pinched look, with
an almost permanent frown puckering her dark eyebrows. She had never taken a husband of equal status,
for she didn't truly believe any man was her equal; and
though she took a *sab-nurah* from time to time, she
found their character so deficient that she never kept
one for more than a few months.

Yet she surrounded herself with men: male body-
guards, male clerks, male accountants, male servants.
Some said she didn't want any female hirelings showing

her up in beauty, which was not hard to do; others said
she liked having power over men, forcing them to obey
her will. In fact, she simply felt more comfortable around
men. Her father had been her mentor; she had learned
business at his knee. She had no patience for the docile
members of her sex, and those who had the wits and
wisdom to rise in power were her adversaries. That left
very few women for whom Paun felt any affinity.

Sometimes Paun envied beautiful women who used
their charms to make fools of men. But her way was
better, and Paun knew it. Wits and cunning, knowledge
and power—those were her tools, and Paun wielded
them with a merciless hand. The only thing they had not
been able to get her yet was a College to sponsor, but
that would come. That was a secondary objective at this
point. There was one thing that Paun wanted much,
much more than the honor of being patron of a College.

She wanted to step on Retneyabo's head to get there.

Robinson was in the lead when the tree-creeper
dropped off a branch and wrapped itself tightly around
his neck. The energy rifle slipped unnoticed from his
grasp as he seized the creature with both hands, trying
to pry it off his windpipe, hardly aware that it had
clamped its vicious teeth into the back of his head. Instinctively Marta reached for the thing, thinking to tear
it loose from the Unbeliever, but Shipner's hand hauled
her roughly back. Even as she shrieked in objection, he
stepped up behind Robinson with his knife drawn,
slipped the blade between the necks of man and beast,
and yanked outward.

The tightening muscles of the tree-creeper fell slack,
and Shipner flung the serpentine body aside. But the
mouth remained locked on its prey, and Robinson
clawed frantically at the dangling neck.

"Hold still!" Shipner barked, and when Robinson in
his panic did not obey, he seized the younger man
around the chest, pinning his arms to his sides. "Hold
still!" he repeated, and in a moment Robinson calmed
down, although he panted heavily through clenched

teeth, more from the terror of his attack than from the pain he still endured. Shipner released him slowly. "Let me look at this."

"Get if off," Robinson grated.

Shipner examined the way the teeth had sunk into the thick tendon just next to the medulla oblongata. "Ingenious," he murmured. "You know, I think these fangs retract. The creeper extends them, like a cat its claws, so that it's almost impossible to shake or pry loose—"

"Marta!" Robinson snarled.

"Let me see, Sab Shipner," Marta interceded quickly, gently but firmly pushing the Nechtanite to one side. "Sit down, Sab Robinson."

Robinson sank slowly to the ground, groping with his hands for adequate balance as he sat. Marta knelt behind him, studied the clutching teeth a moment, then used a stick and her knife to pry the creeper's jaws apart. The lower teeth came loose first, and then she carefully extracted the uppers and cast the severed head aside. Blood welled up from the wound instantly, and Marta let it ooze and drip while she fished in her pack for first-aid supplies. They had not found any of the tree-creepers to have poisonous bites, but just in case, it was good to let the wound bleed freely.

A few snips cut away the hair from around the wound; then she applied antiseptics and a bandage. "There," she pronounced when she had finished. "That should do it."

"That and about six days of bed rest," Robinson grumbled.

Marta responded by handing him a paper of pain relievers, which he tore open with shaking hands and swallowed down.

Shipner was now examining the dead creeper's mouth. "Ingenious," he repeated. "You know, snakes are able to dislocate their jaws in order to open them wide enough to swallow prey. This creature does not—presumably it tears its prey into manageable bites with those teeth—but it does have—"

"You know, Shipner, I don't really want to hear about it right now!" Robinson warned loudly.

Shipner gave him a wicked grin, but held his tongue.

"I have an idea," Marta said, trying to change the subject. "Why don't we eat now, so Sab Robinson can rest a bit, and then after lunch we will—"

"I have an idea," Robinson broke in. "Let's go back."

Marta clamped her mouth shut and counted to ten, then reminded herself that it was the pain talking.

"Come on, it's been two weeks," Robinson continued. "That's close enough, isn't it? Let's just turn around now and head back."

"Three more days," Marta coaxed. The stream had grown and deepened, picking up speed as it splashed between trenchlike banks, and the foliage was changing. She felt sure that they were entering a different geographical or climatological zone, and she wanted to see what it was. Surely this forest must end somewhere.

"Marta, you aren't going to find anything in the next three days that you haven't found in the last," Robinson protested. "Let's just turn around now."

Marta threw a quick glance at Shipner. "We can set up our camp early tonight," she compromised. "Or, I know—we'll go on today and tomorrow and the next day, but on the third day, you can stay in camp while Sab Shipner and I go ahead a bit; but we'll come back to the same camp that night before Sabiss, so it will be like being a day back on our journey."

Now it was Robinson's turn to look at Shipner. "Don't you want to go back?" he demanded. "Hell, we've already got more recordings than we can study in a lifetime! What's the point?"

For a moment Shipner was silent, and Marta held her breath, afraid he was going to side with Robinson on this. But finally he said, "We promised her two and a half weeks. I'll go on for three more days." Robinson made a disgusted sound, and Shipner frowned. "We agreed," he repeated quietly.

Marta drew a breath of relief, then quickly put her arms around Robinson and hugged him. "It will be all right, you'll see," she promised. "Tomorrow or the next day we'll make some incredible find, and you'll be glad we went on. You'll write it up in a paper and be famous for it."

Gradually his arms came around her and he returned her embrace. But even as he clung to her, he hissed, "I hate this place."

Robinson's statement disturbed Marta. That night as she lay curled up beside him in the sanctuary of a house tree's capacious hollow trunk, she turned the matter over and over in her mind. How could he hate it? Wasn't Dhrusil-matkhashi a zoologist's dream? A continent full of new life-forms, a brand new ecosystem, offering the chance to study and create an entire evolutionary taxonomy—how could he hate it? Every turn of the river, every track in the mud, gave him something new to wonder about. Didn't it excite him? Wasn't this what a scientist lived for?

Then Marta discovered an amazing thing: she *loved* this place. With all its dangers, with all its hardships and inconveniences and stinging insects and frightening sounds—she *loved* it. The wonder of it all, the exhilaration of being the first person to encounter a given species, the heady power of naming each one, the challenge of understanding them and their place in this biosphere— She wanted it to go on and on. Each day an adventure, each sunrise an opportunity . . .

Too excited by this revelation to sleep, Marta crawled out of her leafy bed and stood in the dark opening of the tree. Shipner was standing watch, the energy rifle crooked carelessly in his right arm as it always was when the others slept, his eyes raking the forest in all directions. She could hardly make him out, for the light and dark of his tattooed body blended smoothly with the dappled moonlight of the forest.

Marta called his name softly, and he left his station to come stand beside her. It was like standing beside a shadow, but one with heat and smell and substance. She lifted her face to look up at the shadow-man in his shadow-world. "Do you hate it here?" she asked bluntly.

"In the forest?" he asked. "No, I was raised in a forest."

Marta shook her head. "I mean—here," she said gesturing with her arms. "This place. Dhrusil-matkhashi."

Shipner shrugged. "There is no point in hating a place where you are," he said. "You must live there, and cope with it."

Is that all he was doing? Coping? She couldn't believe that. "Do you really want to go back to Valla?" she persisted. "Leave Dray's Planet, leave all this for someone else to explore?"

For a moment he stared down at her, then he shifted his eyes back out to the forest, and she could not see what was on his face. Finally, "I have wanted to leave since your holy ones forbade it," he told her. "A curious contentious streak in my nature. I dislike being told I cannot do a thing."

"And so you will leave us," she said, "walk away from all the adventures and the challenges of this place, just to prove you can."

Shipner grinned down at her. "Will you miss me, Princess?"

"You are a scientist," she accused, disappointment edging her voice. "How can you not want to stay?"

His face went suddenly cold and hard in the moonlight. "I am a warrior, Princess," he snapped. "Never forget that."

CHAPTER 15

The next morning Robinson's wound was only swollen a little and gave no evidence of infection, so they went on, but the trio was quiet and subdued. The hard granite of the eastern shore had gradually been replaced by softer stone, and the stream was cutting a deeper channel through it. That, along with a drop in elevation, gave rise to thick vegetation at the water's edge, so they had to leave the marshy shore for higher ground. There they bushwhacked their way through thickets of dense cane-like stalks entangled with tenacious vines.

Near noon, there was a squealing and a crashing in the brush ahead of them, but there were no trees sturdy enough to support their weight; so the trio had to stand their ground and wait in trepidation while the ruckus drew rapidly nearer. Shipner, long knife in hand, slung off his backpack to free himself for action, and the others followed suit. Robinson brought his energy rifle to bear, dialing its beam down to a small and deadly diameter. Marta gripped a large staff she had cut to help push the encroaching branches out of her way.

What burst through the dense undergrowth was not a monster, though, but a half dozen wild-eyed creatures the size of sheep, galloping on their hind legs, pebbled brown hides glistening with sweat. They swerved around the humans like runners avoiding a puddle, dropping occasionally to all fours as they maneuvered. Then they disappeared with squeals and bleats into the forest behind the scientists.

For a moment the trio stood panting while their adrenaline levels dropped and their pulses slowed from frantic to merely agitated. Then, "What *were* those?" Marta gasped.

"A better question," replied Shipner, glancing in the direction from which the creatures had come, "is, what frightened them?"

In the dead silence that followed his remark, they could hear a feeble scuffling not far away, followed by a forlorn sound reminiscent of a honk. Shipner crouched low and advanced toward the sound, signaling Robinson to circle around from the other side. Marta considered her options, then snatched up all three packs and slunk along well in back of Shipner.

Tangled in the pernicious vines was one of the creatures, its sides heaving and its eyes rolling in terror. It had a small, graceful crest which doubled back down toward its head, and large, soft eyes. As Shipner loomed over it, it gave another plaintive little honk, and the Nechtanite sat back in astonishment. "That sound did not come from its mouth," he marvelled. "How does it do that?"

"The crest," Robinson said almost impatiently. "It uses the tubular crest as a resonating chamber. Like a hadrosaur."

Shipner frowned, then bent cautiously to examine the creature. It honked again.

"I think you're right," he admitted. Then, "Ah, little one, what have you done to yourself?" he asked softly. Its forelegs, though smaller than the rear, had short, stubby toes with blunt claws which showed they were used more for walking than for grasping, and it was painfully obvious that one of the legs was broken. "Can't help you, little one," Shipner sighed, then with a quick movement, he sliced its neck. The creature jerked once and sagged into lifelessness.

Now they listened carefully for what might have been pursuing the creatures, but no sound reached them. Shipner even scouted forward twenty or thirty meters, but returned to report no danger in sight. "They may have been spooked by a noise, or a smell," he told the others. "Stay watchful, though." Then he knelt beside the dead creature and began to cut away the entangling vines in order to get a better look at it.

"Four-toed," Shipner observed. "But with three toes fused on the hind feet, and the fourth one so reduced as to be useless. And look at the size of the gut—I'd say that's for processing roughage, wouldn't you?" He looked up at Robinson.

Robinson had handed off the energy rifle to Marta and fished out his notebook. He was writing industriously, but he made no comment.

"Well, we'll know when we get to the teeth," Shipner answered himself. He turned back to the carcass. "Three, six, nine—eleven? Yes, eleven ribs, that's an odd number."

Robinson knelt at the creature's head, pulled the jaws apart to look inside, then made more notes in his book. Shipner, beside him, glanced at the pad; Robinson turned to put his body between Shipner and the notebook. "Herbivore?" Shipner prompted.

"I'll let you make your own assessment," Robinson said coolly.

Shipner bent and checked the teeth on the creature himself. "Herbivore, all right. You know, we haven't seen a cud system on any of these animals. Then again, that's a mammalian trait, and these are not mammals." He waited a moment, but Robinson refused to rise to the bait. The younger zoologist was busy examining the crest. "Of course, we don't know for sure the crest is hollow," Shipner goaded. "We'd need an x-ray—or I suppose we could hack it open to find out."

Robinson gave him a cold smile. "If you like."

Shipner moved his examination to the tail. "Classic balancing tail," he said. "Probably what allows it to use bipedal motion for bursts of speed." Eyeing Robinson slantwise, he added, "Of course, it might be used as a club, in defensive fighting. Or territorial disputes with others of its kind."

Robinson said nothing.

Shipner sat back on his heels. "You have no opinions today?" he growled.

"I have lots of opinions," Robinson replied. "I just choose not to share them with you." He continued making his notes.

"Afraid I'll prove them wrong?" Shipner challenged.

"No, I just don't see the point in previewing my observations for you. You can read them in my book."

"Oh, now it's a book," Shipner sneered. "I suppose you're already drawing up terms for its publication, calculating what your royalty will be."

"I'll autograph a copy for you," Robinson offered drily.

"Haven't you ever heard of the free exchange of scientific information?" Shipner challenged.

"Haven't you ever heard of the *theft* of scientific information?" Robinson shot back. "You took our dinka-chak and our recordings in the desert—how do I know you won't do the same now?"

"Because we both have the same employer!" Shipner snapped. "And because what we've found on this continent is bigger than a war between two petty kukhooshel!"

Marta's head came up. She did not like hearing Retneyabo referred to as petty, and she might have objected, but the argument rolled on without her.

"What we've found here is bigger than the whole damn planet!" Robinson retorted. He tried to examine a foreleg and found to his irritation that it was still tangled in a piece of vine.

"Then why the big secret of what you put in your notes?" Shipner demanded. "The life-forms of this place are going to rock the whole biological community back on its heels; what does it matter who collected the data, who made the observations?"

"It matters to my career!" Robinson snarled, clawing away the vine that thwarted him. "It matters to my tenure and my salary and my recognition within the scientific community!"

Marta had had enough. "Oh, please stop this," she sighed wearily. "You sound like children."

Shipner snorted derisively. "Oh, yes, children," he agreed, bending back over the dead creature to flex its hip joint. " 'Can you tell me what time it is?' 'No, it's my chronometer, get your own.' 'But I don't want your chrono, I only want to know what time it is.' 'Not until I have a copyright on this particular microsecond.' Your problem, Robinson, is that you see science not as a means of understanding the universe, but as a tool for your personal aggrandizement—"

It all happened too fast for Marta to intervene. The vine was still in Robinson's hands; he reached over and wrapped it around Shipner's neck with murderous fury. Startled, Shipner reached first for his own constricted throat; but then both hands snapped back over his head and found purchase on Robinson's tunic. With a powerful forward lurch he flipped Robinson over his shoulder and slammed him on his back beside the carcass. Robinson, the wind knocked out of him, lost his grip on the vine and Shipner was free. In the flash of an eye, the painted man had his attacker's head locked in his left arm, and that wicked long knife at Robinson's throat.

Marta tried to scream, tried to rush forward, but before she could do either one, Shipner had flung the blade point down on the ground beside him, pushed Robinson over with his face in the dirt, and was holding him there. The younger man struggled furiously for a minute, then gradually his struggles lessened until he gave up and lay panting and subdued.

Shipner let him lie there for several moments. Then, "Can I let you up now?" he asked coldly.

"Yeah," Robinson croaked.

Cautiously, Shipner released his hold on his colleague. Then he retrieved his knife and got slowly to his feet. "Don't test my reflexes like that, boy," he growled. "You could have been dead." Slipping the knife back into its sheath at his waist, the Nechtanite turned and took the energy rifle from Marta's limp hands. "You don't mind if I carry this, do you?"

Marta was weak with relief. "Sab Shipner," she whispered hoarsely. "He didn't—I'm sure that— Praise be the All-Hallowed you are both all right."

Shipner snorted contemptuously. "The day hasn't

been, that I had anything to fear from someone as soft
and weak as Cecil Robinson. And fortunately for him,
our Nechtanite creed forbids a warrior from killing
someone who is so obviously mentally deranged."

Robinson was struggling into a sitting position. "Why,
you son of a bitch, next time I'll—"

"Next time," Shipner snapped, spinning to stab a
warning finger at Robinson, "I won't hesitate to break
an arm or two to keep you from running amok. Do
you understand?"

Robinson nodded, pale and mute.

Snatching up his pack, Shipner turned on his heel and
started picking his way through the underbrush. "I'm
tired of this animal," he said. "Take some recordings of
it, if you want, then let's move on."

Marta moved silently along between the two men, less
worried about the danger that might lurk around them
than the danger which loomed large and heavy between
them. She was going to have to turn back, probably in
the morning. Robinson was clearly at the end of his
rope, and Shipner continued to egg him on, baiting him,
goading him into one conflict after another. Why? He
was patient with Tookh, tolerant of the others, but with
Robinson he was constantly picking fights. Why wouldn't
he leave Robinson alone? And was there any way she
could get him to do so?

Wrapped up in her gloomy thoughts, Marta hardly
noticed that the vegetation here was growing thinner,
with large patches of blue sky visible between the tall
stalks. Then suddenly they were in a meadow of knee-
high grasses, with the forest behind them, and Shipner
had stopped in his tracks.

Marta drew up beside him and gazed out toward the
horizon. The ground sloped noticeably to their right—
the creek must be there, nestled below the level of the
surrounding land. But it was the vista ahead that took
her breath. Less than fifty meters beyond the forest's
edge, the land stopped abruptly. In the far distance was
a horizon of tall cliffs and taller mountains, and in be-

tween lay a vast river valley carved through colorful layers of sandstone, limestone, and other sediments, back down to the granite which underlay the whole region.

Marta walked until she stood at the very rim of the canyon, gazing down a slope more forbidding than the steep northern rim of Dhin M'Tarkhna, and greater in length by tenfold. Water roared nearby; she turned her head and saw the stream careening off the edge of this vast cliff, tumbling fifty, a hundred meters over the rocks, then splashing through a rocky granite defile to crash another fifty meters straight down. Mist rose from the narrow waterfall in a constant spray.

Far below, a wide river coursed its lazy way through the relatively flat land. There was movement on the valley floor: shadows of clouds drifting silently upstream, groups of animals grazing . . . "Herd beasts," she said aloud.

Robinson stood to one side of her, Shipner to the other. She hadn't noticed their approach. "Look at them, grazing down there," she said numbly. "Herd beasts. Hundreds of them."

Robinson slipped off his pack and pulled out a pair of field glasses. "They look like sauropods," he said, focusing on the animals below.

"If it has four feet and a tail, it looks like a sauropod to you," Shipner grumbled softly, too softly for Robinson to hear. Then he raised his voice. "Look. More of our crested friends."

Marta turned to the left to see where he pointed. There in the meadow with them stood eight or ten of the sheep-sized creatures like the one with the broken leg. Some had raised themselves on their back legs to stare at the intruders; others were on all fours, cropping the lush grass. None of them showed any sign of fear.

Turning her gaze out over the great canyon once more, Marta sank wearily to the ground. "Just let me be here for a while," she sighed in resignation. "Tomorrow we will turn back, but just let me be here for the rest of the day, to fill my heart with this sight. It will be enough, for this journey."

There was a moment of silence following her remark. Then Shipner mumbled something about going to look for a suitable campsite, and he wandered off along the rim. Robinson settled to the ground near Marta and reached out a tentative hand to touch her arm. They were quiet for a long time. Then, "It's just that I have to get back," he apologized. "If I'm going to . . . if I'm going to *do* anything. I've got to be on that ship and—"

Marta shushed him gently, taking his large white-palmed hand in her own tiny brown one. They sat there, hands clasped, until the dazzling red ball of the sun began to slip behind the mountains in the far, far distance.

Shipner had found a shallow limestone cave in the canyon wall about twenty meters below the rim. When he came to fetch his two companions down the steep and slippery slope to its shelter, he had already made rough preparations in it. A small fire crackled at the broad opening with a kettle steaming over it, and grass was mounded in two heaps toward the back. Marta changed the dressing on Robinson's wound first, saw that it was healing well, then inspected the concoction bubbling over the fire.

It was a simple soup of barley and beans and lentils, with a little dried mutton shredded into it, and none of the hot peppers that Shipner liked so well and Robinson hated. It seemed almost like a peace offering, as though he realized his own culpability in the day's drama, and Marta was curiously touched by this. The three of them ate in silence, watching the stars come out, gazing with fascination at the roaring waterfall that foamed and frothed its way down the stone embankment and into oblivion somewhere on the rocks below.

When they had finished, Shipner rose, picked up the energy rifle, and announced that he was going up to the meadow to see if anything interesting came out after dark. "I'll be gone half an hour at least," he said, and vanished silently into the darkness.

Afforded this rare time of privacy, Marta and Robinson wasted no time putting it to energetic use. There had been only stolen moments along the trail, with the sole saving grace being that at the end of the day they were generally too tired to disport themselves lustily, anyway. By the time Shipner returned, they were properly clothed once more and Robinson was nodding off on their bed of grasses.

The Nechtanite said nothing, merely added a few twigs to the fire and stood facing out over the canyon, the rifle balanced casually in the crook of his arm, his eyes and ears searching the darkness relentlessly.

Marta came to stand beside him on the narrow ledge before the cave. She felt as though she were standing on a shelf overlooking the virgin Creation with heaven above and firmament below. Silence enveloped the two of them like a cloak of wonder, and it did not seem empty or awkward in the least. Marta felt a little guilty about breaking it, but there was something she needed to say.

"Thank you," she said in a voice so low and dry that it sounded like the flutter of a bird on the evening breeze.

"For what?" Shipner asked, as though he would take no responsibility for this gift to her.

"For seeing if anything interesting happens in the meadow at night," she responded. "I was very curious about that."

"I thought you might be."

Again the silence flowed around them, a gentle current in the stillness of time. Then, "The river flows south," Shipner observed. "I would have thought it would flow north, because the land we traveled over sloped to the northwest. But down there, it must slope the other way."

Marta hesitated. "We could come back," she ventured, "and find out. Later. After we have returned to Innanta with our discoveries."

But Shipner shook his head slightly. "Time for me to go home."

She wondered again what kind of home he had, this rude, querulous man with the quick mind and the cruel tongue. A community of Nechtanites like himself, warrior-scholars—what were they like? Were they all as intentionally abrasive as he? "Do you miss them, your community?" she asked.

"Sometimes," he said without emotion.

"Well, I'm sure they miss you," Marta offered politely.

Shipner gave a soft, dry laugh. "Not likely." He dropped to his haunches on the ledge, resting as easily in a crouch as he had standing up. "By the time I get back, I expect two of them will be vying for my position on the faculty, and three others will be after my spot as an elder in the community. No, I don't think they miss me too much."

"So why do you go back?" Marta wondered.

"To fight them," he said simply. "I am a warrior. It's what I do."

Marta mulled that over for a while. Then, sitting on the ledge beside him, she asked, "Is that why you go after Sab Robinson the way you do?"

Shipner shrugged. "Probably."

"But you aren't that way with Tookh."

"Tookh is a boy," Shipner dismissed. "He's bright, he's eager, he wants to learn. Robinson—" He shook his head sadly. "Robinson swaggers with a warrior's bravado, but where are his tattoos?" Seeing her puzzled look, Shipner grinned. "It's a Nechtanite saying. It means, where's the proof of his accomplishments? Show me how he's earned his bragging rights."

Marta reached out a finger and touched one of the marks on Shipner's arm. "Is that what these are?" she asked in curiosity.

The painted man gestured toward his upper arm. "That's from the first paper I had published, while I was still an undergraduate. This"— he gestured at his left collarbone—"my wilderness trials in Fjallar, which is a snow desert. And this"— he stroked a spot on his neck—"seventy-two hours of *chukirka,* the prayers you have seen me do. On my back are seven marks representing single combat with seven different weapons—in actual battle, not staged trials."

The thought of that made Marta shudder inwardly. To lighten her discomfort, she asked in teasing tones, "And are there no marks for your conquest of women?"

Shipner flashed her his yellow grin. "Scars, maybe, but no tattoos." But then he grew sober. "It is forbidden for a Nechtanite man to take a woman by force. When we mate, it is customary for the woman to hold a knife in one hand, to show that if she objects to the mating, she has the power to stop it." His lips twisted in a wry smile. "Young Nechtanite men learn early to be considerate of their partners."

Marta laughed softly. "I can see why." Then she mused, "I wonder if I should try that with Sab Robinson, hold a knife in my hand and see what he does."

"In your case," Shipner snorted, "you'd have to give the knife to *him*."

"Now, there you go again," she chided gently. "He is no threat to you, Sab Shipner, why must you go at him so?"

The amusement slid off Shipner's features, and he turned his attention back to the dark river valley below. "Because he should be a threat," he growled.

Marta was surprised. "Should be?" she prodded.

"He has all the tools," the Nechtanite said gruffly. "Quick mind, solid instincts, competitive spirit—but he stops short. He takes a brilliant idea and bats it around with a tennis racquet instead of nailing it to the wall with a javelin."

This was a new insight for Marta; like many of Shipner's insights, it made her think. "Like his paper on cladistics," she guessed. "The one you refereed."

"Cladistics are a convention," Shipner sneered. "He was right to challenge traditional taxonomies, but instead of poking holes in the accepted methods, he left gaping ones in his own. What he proposed was no better than what he sought to tear down."

Marta took a moment to digest this. Then she asked bluntly, "Do you think he's right about the quasi-saurians?"

Shipner's eyes slid in her direction, then slid back to

the darkness. "I think there's an eighty percent chance," he said tightly, "but he's got to *prove* it. Why is he content to *suggest* it, leaving others a mountain of ammunition to attack it?"

At last Marta began to understand some of what was at work in the complex Nechtanite's attitude toward his younger colleague. And as she sat on the ledge beside Soln Shipner, Marta knew she had never respected the man more.

There was no point in trekking down into the canyon for a day only to spend two climbing back out, so they agreed to use the cave as a base camp while they explored the meadow. The crested browsers were still there, so the three scientists spent several hours observing them, making recordings, speculating on what had spooked the animals the day before. The creatures certainly did not seem frightened of the humans. "Because they've never smelled anything like us before," Shipner explained to the others. "They haven't associated our smell with fear."

It occurred to him then to see just how close he could get to the browsers. He walked into the meadow straight toward them, but they began to edge away as he drew near. So he circled around to put himself downwind, on the farside from Marta and Robinson, with the cliff edge forming a third side to the triangle. Then he began to stalk them through the tall grass in his best warrior's mien.

Some sound or movement gave him away, though, for the herd bolted and sprinted twenty meters closer to Marta and Robinson, then settled down to cropping the grass again. Shipner gave up and circled back to join his companions. "It seems they trust a stationary stranger more than one moving toward them," he observed as he flopped down in the lush grass beside Marta.

Marta was going to make a smart remark about the creatures exhibiting good taste in preferring a beauty like herself to a beast like him, but she stopped abruptly when something on one of the browsers caught her eye.

Dropping the recorder, she snatched up the field glasses from Robinson's idle hands to confirm what she saw.

"What?" Shipner asked, noting her sudden interest.

"Third one from the right," Marta said breathlessly, handing him the glasses. "Toward the back. Take a look at his neck."

Shipner looked, but the animal in question managed to shift behind one of his fellows just then, and Shipner could not see its head and neck.

"Here," Marta said impatiently, grabbing the glasses back and handing them to Robinson on her other side. "Can you see it from there? Look, look, the one in back there, the—not the one with the bad eye, but just to the left of him—" She grew frustrated as Robinson failed to locate the proper beast. "Here, here," she insisted, jumping to her feet and dragging him along with her to a better vantage point. "That one, jerking his head up just now and—"

But either her movement or some vagrant scent on the breeze startled the creatures, for they suddenly wheeled and raced fifty meters in the opposite direction, disappearing into a stand of cane.

"What was I supposed to see?" Robinson asked.

"A rope," Marta said emphatically.

Both men swiveled their heads to stare at her. "A rope?" Robinson echoed.

"Well, not a rope, a piece of vine," Marta qualified, "but knotted around its neck like a rope. Like a tether that has broken."

The two Unbelievers exchanged a look. "Maybe," Shipner suggested, "it got itself tangled in a trailing vine and—"

"It was knotted, I tell you!" Marta snapped. "Knotted: tied in a knot."

Shipner opened his mouth to question her again, but thought better of it and closed it without speaking. Robinson peered through the field glasses toward the stand of cane where the creatures had vanished. "Maybe it will show up in the recordings," he said without conviction.

They waited for another hour, but the crested browsers

did not return. Shipner went to explore down into the
canyon a short distance while Robinson opted to study
the valley below from the cliff ledge. Marta stayed with
Robinson, but she spent her time checking back through
the recordings for images to corroborate what she had
seen. She found none.

There was a thunderstorm that night, with blinding
flashes of lightning that lit the sky outside their cozy cave
like a strobe, followed by heavy rains. Marta winced with
each great crack of thunder that rumbled across the valley and echoed off the canyon walls, clinging to Robinson for comfort. Shipner sneered at her. "You shrink
like a child at the noise!" he taunted, but there was
an uneasiness in her breast that the ferocity of nature
only exacerbated.

What did it mean, a vine knotted around the creature's neck? Were there other people in Dhrusil-
matkhashi? Earlier adventurers who had scaled her sea
cliffs and never found their way back? Or were these
people the reason the mazhel had discouraged anyone
from visiting the continent? Were they exiles, heretics,
dangerous criminals? No, such persons would have been
executed, in full view of the population, as an expiation
for sin. They had to be wanderers, people who were here
by accident.

Or . . .

Marta sucked in her breath as another possibility occurred to her.

*Hassan looked over the heads of the two boys to where
Mohat's mother sat silent and attentive. The caravaners
left a little space around her, for she was of high status
and they did not wish to offend her by jostling her elbow
or crowding too near. "And there Marta came upon a
great river valley," Hassan continued. "It was the river
we call Grakkan, 'powerful,' and it cleft the land in two
from north to south. Along its banks are some of the
greatest riches in Dhrusil-matkhashi: iron ore, and coal,
raw petroleum. Great wali roamed in vast herds on either
side of the river, and the grain we call shinnoan grew*

wild upon its banks. And when Marta saw the wealth of this place, she was moved to tears. 'Oh, let us stay forever,' she cried, 'and make our home in this great valley! You two shall be my husbands, and we shall have sons and daughters without number, and they shall never want.'

"But the Unbelievers were afraid, and cried out to her to lead them back to Innanta, to lead them back within the gates. So Marta had pity upon them, for they had no faith and did not trust the All-Powerful, and she led them back the way they had come. But she wept with sorrow to leave such a wondrous place."

"You are ungrateful cowards, both of you!" Marta snapped as she thrust her arms angrily through the straps of her pack. "What kind of scientists are you to walk away from such a place before you have to?"

She had slept badly and awakened late to find the two of them conspiring over their morning coffee. At first she had been thrilled to see them talking to each other, thinking they had resolved to be civil for the duration of the expedition; but as soon as their eyes shifted to her, she knew she wasn't going to like what they had to say.

They had decided, simply, to head back a day early. Spotting the look of defiance in her eye when they suggested the vine was only accidentally caught around the creature's neck, the two of them meant to forestall any fruitless search by leaving the area. Robinson remembered too well how she had pleaded with him to forsake the dinka-chak quest and travel to Rahoub on their last expedition; he wasn't going to risk missing his ship offworld because she insisted on hunting for a browser with a piece of vine caught around its neck.

Shipner had agreed without much coaxing. If he could get back to Valla now, with tales of new zoological lifeforms on Dray's Planet, he wouldn't have to fight to retain his post at the University. If he delayed and somehow Robinson's paper got out—or worse yet, if Robinson himself returned to break the news—he would not be awarded the same merit as if he appeared to be the codiscoverer. Then there would be challenges. Then he would have to fight.

So by the time Marta woke, they were united in purpose, and there was no standing against them. She threatened and lectured and pleaded and called them the most unspeakable names she could, but to no avail.

Midmorning found them tramping along the soggy trail, their clothing soaked from rain that clung to the canes and vines of the place. Marta's anger still burned so fiercely that it threatened to send steam up from her waterlogged tunic. Since Robinson's attack in the cane forest, Shipner insisted on carrying the energy rifle while they traveled, as though Robinson might use it rashly at any moment. The Nechtanite was in the lead again—and since when had the Most High appointed *him* leader of this expedition?—when he slowed suddenly, and exclaimed, "Would you look at this!"

"This" was the remains of the unfortunate browser with the broken leg, which they had left in the forest two days before. The many scavengers of Dhrusilmatkhashi had ravaged the carcass so that what was left resembled a mangled heap of hide, gristle, and wellgnawed bones. Insects swarmed over it, and a few skitterers scurried off as they approached.

"Can we get a recording of this, Marta?" Robinson asked, waving a hand to clear away some of the insects. "I know the bones are out of order, but—"

"Get it yourself!" she snapped.

With an exaggerated sigh, Robinson took the camera from its clip on her belt and, making a face at the odor coming from the remains, moved upwind and began recording.

"Must be tasty meat," Shipner observed, waving his long knife to clear the insects again, and then using it to push the larger bones back into some semblance of their original configuration. "I should have taken a haunch myself, after I killed it. If I hadn't been distracted—" He stopped short.

Marta stood scowling to one side. "If you two try to

kill each other again," she growled, "don't count on me to interfere." *Let the scavengers fight over* their *carcasses, tugging and tussling and—*

Then she saw what had made Shipner break off his comment. One of the hind legs was missing.

Robinson stopped recording as he saw them both staring at the carcass. "What?" he asked in irritation.

"There's a leg gone," Shipner said bluntly. He scowled thoughtfully, then turned and surveyed the cane forest around them with suspicion

"So? Some greedy little carnivore tore it off and dragged it away to chew on it in peace," Robinson replied.

Holding her breath to keep from inhaling insects, Marta bent beside the creature and examined the damaged hip joint. She had seen goats and lambs taken by wild dogs, and she knew the kind of marks that were left by teeth. Pulling back again she said, "This looks a little neat to have been taken by an animal."

Now Shipner squatted beside her and inspected the joint. "Wrenched from its socket, clearly—see the tearing of the muscle? But here where the hide was severed . . ." He shook his head. "A claw might have ripped such a straight line. A very sharp claw, like the dinka-chak has, but larger. Teeth would have left different marks." He stood up again. "It's hard to tell, because the edges have been chewed by insects and such, but a knife would have made a cleaner cut, I think."

"A good steel knife, yes," Marta agreed, "but we have very little steel on this world. A knife of flint, or obsidian . . ."

Shipner's scowl deepened, and his eyes searched the standing cane again. "You are as bad as Robinson, with your wild speculations," he insisted.

Marta gave him a sour smile. "As bad as his wild speculations about quasi-saurians and dinosaurs?" she taunted, recalling his confession that he believed there was an 80 percent chance Robinson was right.

Shipner sheathed his knife and took up the energy rifle once more. "Innantan females are as stupid as they are ugly," he grumbled as he started back along the track. "I must get off this planet and back to Valla, where the women are sane, sightly, and reasonably sensible."

When the cane forest gave over to more treelike vegetation, they were able to get back to the stream, and there they halted for their midday rest and repast. "This must be where we stopped before," Robinson remarked as he slipped out of his pack and dropped it to the ground. "Here are the ashes from our campfire."

Shipner poked at the sooty smudge on the elevated stream bank with his big toe. "Not my campfire," he disagreed. "I bury the ashes. Besides, I don't remember stopping in this place." He frowned.

"Lightning strike?" Robinson asked.

Shipner surveyed the surrounding area with slitted eyes, his nostrils flaring, and then grinned. "Ah. Good guess, I'd say." He pointed out a tree across the water that was heavily charred. Foliage to either side of it also showed burn damage. "Probably a cinder from there blew across and started a small fire here. Good thing the rain was so heavy last night, or there might be a fire raging through here right now." But he continued to scan the forest on all sides.

Disgusted, Marta descended to the stream's edge to splash her face and fill her canteen. Neither man, of course, would admit the possibility that there might be someone else in these woods who could light a fire. No, they, the great zoologists with their Ph.D.s, could not admit that she, a lowly graduate student, and a *woman,* might have been right when she claimed she had seen a piece of vine *knotted* around the throat of that beast. So why even say anything about the fire? Shipner would not believe until presented with concrete evidence. Robinson would not believe because it might delay their return to Jinka. No, she would keep her opinions to herself and—

Something caught in the rocks of the streambed drew her eye.

At first Marta thought it was just a white stone glimmering there in the shallows, odd amongst the tumbled volcanic rocks and chunks of earth-toned sandstone. But she took a closer look . . . and smiled broadly.

When Marta climbed up from the streambed with her prize, Shipner was sitting on a rock worrying a piece of jerky as he continued to scan the woods. She tossed the object down at his feet.

At first Shipner only glanced at it. Then his eyes grew wide and he picked it up. It was very clearly a femur, of a size consistent with the ravaged browser carcass. It was scraped nearly clean, with marks along its length as though it had been gnawed. That could have been done by any predator, of course. But the tips of this bone were both charred, while the remainder of it was white and clean. That part had still borne meat when the femur was exposed to fire or intense heat.

Shipner looked up into Marta's gloating face.

"I have a bone to pick with you," she said.

CHAPTER 16

They made their camp that night in a thick stand of trees well back from the stream edge, for there were no house trees in this section of the forest. Shipner was more cautious than usual, scouting deep into the surrounding forest and setting crude trip wires made of vines and dry branches, to make it difficult for an intruder to catch them unawares. He had studied the thighbone carefully, but he could come up with no other explanation for its condition than the obvious one: someone had roasted the leg of meat, then cast the bone into the river.

But who? As they ate their cold supper—he forbade them making a fire that night—Shipner grilled Marta about the stories she had unearthed telling of people who had attempted to scale the cliffs of Dhrusil-matk-hashi in the past. Could someone have succeeded? A lot of someones? Was there now a colony of Innantans dwelling here in the forest, living off the riches of this land? Perhaps they were the descendants of castaways or renegades, to whom Innanta and her people were only a myth. How would they feel about strangers invading their territory? Did they know the scientific expedition was here? Were they hiding, reluctant to show themselves? Or had they simply not noticed that they had guests?

Marta answered his questions about the stories as best she could, but she knew that he would not find any clues there. Nor did that bother her too much, for Marta had come up with another explanation for the roasted haunch and the knotted vine. She didn't waste it on

Shipner, for she knew he would give it no credence when she hadn't any evidence to support it. But later that night, as she and Robinson lay close together, wrapped in their blankets, she tried it out on him.

"Sab Robinson," she whispered, for Shipner was only a few meters away, taking the first watch, "if some cataclysm had not destroyed Earth's dinosaurs, where would their evolution have led?"

Robinson shrugged. "Hard to say," he murmured back. "Depends on the climatological changes: heat, humidity, nitrogen in the soil. Big sauropods like brachiosaurus could only survive while there were massive amounts of vegetation to feed them. Given an ice age or two, a change in the ratio of oxygen to nitrogen in the atmosphere, and the kinds of vegetation available, most likely it would have been the smaller species that survived."

"And would the more agile bipeds have fared better than the bulkier quadrupeds?"

"Possibly." He shifted in his blanket, trying to find a more comfortable piece of ground. "The bipeds tended to have larger brains in relation to their body size; therefore, they were more intelligent; therefore, they had the best chance of surviving."

"Do you think," Marta pressed, "that they might eventually have evolved an intelligent, self-aware species? That is, a sentient species?"

There was silence from Robinson. Then, "Marta, you don't think—"

"Is it possible?" she insisted.

He hesitated, then sighed. "I suppose it's possible. They were a hugely successful life-form, you know, surviving for millions of years. I've read some papers that speculated on what might have happened if they hadn't been killed off. They might have reached a level where they were . . ."

"Capable of using tools," she finished. "Like knives and fire."

"It's just highly unlikely, Marta," he told her. "Look, don't your Creation stories say that God intervened in history to create human beings? So it's either that, or it was a cosmic accident. A huge one."

"As huge as the accident which created life out of carbon molecules," she pointed out. "Which has happened on a dozen worlds that we know of."

Again he was silent for a time. Finally he said, "If someone cooked that leg, Marta, they were Innantans. Just plain Innantans. How they got here is a mystery, but who they are is not. Now go to sleep."

But Marta could not sleep. Wasn't it possible? Dray's Planet was so like Earth in every aspect. It had evolved carbon-based life-forms with striking similarities to Terran life-forms. Why not sentient life? Not mammalian, as Earth had done when mammals became the default survivors, but quasi-saurian, here where quasi-saurians were obviously the dominant class. Why did the roasters of that haunch have to be Innantans?

Why couldn't they be Drayans?

Marta slept fitfully, her dreams stalked by a nameless, faceless presence which watched her through tall trees, or peered at her from dark caves. As she stood her watch in the hours before dawn, she fought to keep her imagination from wandering down eerie paths, from hearing whispers in the rustling of the branches overhead and deliberate signals in the cawing and hooting of night creatures. She was profoundly grateful when the sky began to lighten and she could wake Shipner to relieve her.

Sometimes at this hour Marta crawled back into her blankets for another half hour's sleep before rising to offer her prayers, but it seemed pointless this morning. Instead she took the energy rifle for safety's sake and headed for the river's edge to empty her bladder and wash her face.

The necessary ablutions completed, Marta stood on the pebbly bank and breathed deeply of the damp, fresh air. Sometimes creatures came to the stream at dawn to drink, but this was a very open section, and Marta could see nothing which looked even interesting, much less

dangerous. There was enough light now that she felt sure
it was the right time for prayers. She could just as well
say them here as back in camp with two Unbelievers
scuffling around irreverently, waiting impatiently for her
to finish so they could move on. So Marta rested the
energy rifle carefully against a nearby rock, lifted her
hands to the heavens, and began to chant.

Blessed are you, Most High,
Maker of the dawn,
Guardian of the light,
Who refreshes the body with sleep
And the spirit with beauty.
Blessed are you, All-Hallowed,
Creator of the stars and planets,
The worlds wherein we dwell
And the spaces in between them.
Blessed are you, All-Merciful,
Who has granted unto your faithful servant
A new day—

Marta broke off with her mouth open, staring across
the stream at the shadowy forest on the other side.
Something stood there among the trees, watching her.
It was more slender than any creature they had seen
heretofore, lacking the thick haunches which characterized the bipeds of this continent, and its shortened forelegs seemed set more toward the sides, as though they
might rotate behind the creature as well as to the front.
It had large eyes and a modest crest, and although the
neck was elongated, it was not nearly as serpentine as
most they had seen here. The hide was a muddy shade
of brown, rough in texture, and there were light-colored
markings across its chest— Markings? Marta fixed on
the row of spots. No, not markings—

"Sab Shipner," she whispered hoarsely, not wanting
to frighten the creature. "Sab Robinson . . . Sab
Shipner . . . Sab Robinson—" Her voice was rising
slightly. "Sab Shipner—! Sab Robinson—!"

*   *   *

Shipner and Robinson both heard Marta's chanting stop in mid-phrase. They exchanged one look of alarm and bolted for the river's edge. As they broke through the last patch of head-high ferns into the clearing they could hear her calling them urgently.

"Sab Robinson! Sab Shipner—oh, no! No, no, no, no, no—!"

Shipner jumped down the slight embankment and landed on her right, his knife drawn, searching the riverbank for some danger. Robinson scuttled down to her left and caught hold of her arm. "What is it?" he demanded.

Marta was weeping. "Now you've frightened it! Oh, no, now you'll never—You won't believe me—!"

"Believe what?" Robinson asked. "What's wrong? Are you all right?"

"It was there!" she sobbed, ignoring his concerns and pointing across the stream. "It was standing there watching me! It had great dark eyes and a short muzzle and—and—"

"You saw a creature?" Shipner prompted her. "What kind of creature?"

"I'm trying to tell you!" she cried impatiently. "It was—oh, maybe two meters tall, I suppose, though it was hard to tell from here. And it stood on its back legs—but it stood *upright,* it wasn't squatting or crouched the way the others look, and it had brown skin and—"

Now Shipner caught her face in a callused hand and forced her to look into his penetrating eyes. "What are you trying to say?"

Marta found she was panting. Angrily she sucked in a deep breath and forced her voice to be even and steady. "It had a string around its neck," she said deliberately. "A string with something on it: teeth or claws or bits of wood, I couldn't tell. But it was a necklace, Sab Shipner," she said firmly. "The creature was wearing a necklace!"

Marta sipped at the strong black coffee and refused to look at either one of them. Shipner hadn't wanted her to build a fire, but she'd made one anyway, and then she'd brewed the coffee just as thick as she wanted it, without regard for their tastes. Now she was sitting on a blanket roll, and she intended to sit there and finish her coffee before she moved one step back toward the coast.

Robinson paced and scratched at his jaw, which was bristling with two months' worth of beard. He paused, leaned wearily against a tree, then turned to look at Marta once more. "It could have been a piece of—"

"It was a necklace," she snarled before he could finish.

"Marta, you were thirty meters away!" he protested. "How could you tell at that distance?"

"It was a necklace," she said doggedly, and sipped again at her coffee.

Shipner stood with his back to them both, feet planted apart and arms folded across his bare chest.

"Okay, what if it was a necklace?" Robinson asked. "What does that tell us?"

"Animals don't adorn themselves."

"I've seen chimps that—"

"Animals don't adorn themselves," Marta insisted. "Unless people teach them to."

"Okay, okay." Robinson resumed pacing. "Say it was a sign of intelligence. What do you want us to do—track it down?"

"If you were any kind of a scientist—"

"We are not prepared to launch a manhunt!" Robinson shouted. "Marta, you will have to come back to do that. We don't have enough supplies. We don't have—"

"We could forage for food!" she snapped. "Food is not the problem. It's that cargo ship that's the problem, the one you're so determined to be on!"

"So sue me!" Robinson rubbed at his face. "Marta, imagine yourself on my planet: a nice place, I think it's really great, but you'd find everything a little strange. Strange customs, strange beliefs. People look at you funny when you walk down the street. Then someone tells you that you can't go home. Ever. You can't go back to see your family, can't ever go on caravan again, can't join the rest of the Faithful in saying your morning prayers. How would you feel, Marta?" His voice was anguished. "How would you feel? Wouldn't you do everything in your power to break free, to get back to where you belong? Wouldn't you turn your back on science, on Knowledge and Beauty and everything else, just to get back home? Wouldn't you?"

Marta felt her heart squeezing in her chest, and she stole a look at the Unbeliever. Before, he had only been angry, and she couldn't see any of this through his rage. Now it was laid out before her, and she couldn't ignore it. He had a right to go home. Dhrusil-matkhashi would not, as he had pointed out before, sink into the sea. She could find others willing to come back with her, lots of them. The School of Anthropology at the College of Sociology was teeming with scholars who'd gladly forfeit home and family for the chance to be in on such an expedition. There was no reason to torment Robinson by depriving him of whatever chance there was that he might make it offworld on this ship.

Unbidden, her eyes trailed to Shipner's broad, taut back. Did he feel the same way? Was going back to his community more important to him than finding a sentient species? "Sab Shipner—"

"Don't ask," he interrupted gruffly. "You won't like my answer."

So. Once more she was alone. Marta swallowed coffee and brooded.

Robinson watched her for a few moments, then tried again to make her see reason. "Marta, I know you think—"

"Let me finish my coffee," she growled.

Finish her coffee? Tomorrow was Sabiss when she wouldn't travel, there were unknown persons abroad in the woods, they were a long day's journey from any house trees, and she wanted to finish her coffee? "Marta, I don't think we have time to—"

"Let her finish her coffee," Shipner barked.

Robinson threw his hands up in the air, stomped over

to his waiting pack, and slumped with his back against
a tree.

Shipner stood with his back to the others and wrestled
with himself. He hated being in the wrong; and the only
thing worse than being in the wrong was *knowing* he was
in the wrong, and keeping on. He was in the wrong now.

Damn the little Innantan wench! It was one thing to
turn one's back on a continent full of the most advanced
life-forms to have evolved outside Terra. That was bad
enough. But to turn one's back on the possibility of sentient life—Damn her! Why did she have to claim it was
a necklace?

If you were a true scientist, she'd said, and the words
had cut deeper than any blade. If he were a true scientist, he'd be across the creek right now, looking for
tracks, going after the creature she saw, whatever it was.
If he were a true scientist . . . But that was the flaw in
the Nechtanite way. It was not possible to be both a true
scientist and a true warrior. Time and time again during
his life, the two ideals had come into conflict. And here
they were, in conflict again: the scientist would have
stayed, but the warrior . . . The warrior had another
agenda. The warrior had a prior obligation.

And he'd let his contempt for the Innantans slip, more
the fool he. Robinson was no problem: Robinson was
an arrogant ass, easy to be contemptuous of, and Shipner
didn't care what fate befell him. Usually. But the boy
Tookh was so eager to learn, to do well, and with the
right encouragement he could be . . . anything. No
scholar could be contemptuous of that. And the
woman—damn her, there was a fire in her spirit that
sometimes put him to shame.

Like now. Childishly stubborn, yet stubborn about the
right thing. They should stay and investigate, she was
right. Yet he would side with Robinson in this, and they
would force her from her purpose, force her to go on
with them. Back to their base camp they would go, and
she would tell the others what she had seen, and how
she had wanted to stay, and he would have to endure
the contempt in the boy's eyes or else justify—

No. No, he would not attempt to justify his wrong-doing. A warrior might lie to any number of people to achieve his objective, but he must never lie to himself. That error was always fatal.

Behind him, Marta poured out the dregs of her coffee and started to pack up her gear. Shipner used a folding spade to bury the ashes of her fire while she hoisted the heavy pack into place and adjusted it. Then he stowed the spade and nodded to Robinson. "Here," he said, tossing the energy rifle to the younger man. "I trust you can keep that aimed in the right direction, now that we're headed back."

Robinson's grin had a cold glitter to it. "As long as you don't get in my way."

Knife drawn, Shipner turned and struck off through the forest for the sea, and the narrow strait that separated this rich, productive land from the harsh deserts of Innanta.

They were three days out of the base camp when they came through a section of forest that looked as though the wrath of the All-Powerful had torn through it. Ferns and shrubs were trampled, small trees snapped, and branches broken to a height of four meters. The ground looked like a battlefield, gouged and bloody. The trio halted at the edge of the carnage while Shipner examined a broken frond, then squatted to study the tracks. "Three days old, at least," he announced. "But whatever did this was big. Very big."

Slowly they moved into the battered swath, eyes sweeping back and forth for some clue as to what had happened here. "Could be a herd of those tall beasts," he ventured as he puzzled over the tracks. "If something had stampeded them."

"The *sratali,*" Marta said, for so she had named the long-necked, long-legged quadrupeds.

"But these—" Shipner pointed out deep scratches in the dirt. "These were made by claws, I think. Long, sharp claws. The sratali have short, blunt claws."

A few meters to their left was an unsightly heap, buzzing with insects. Marta and Robinson kept their distance while Shipner approached it. Poking at the mangled pile with his long knife, he drew back with an exclamation of surprise, then returned to his grisly work for several more minutes. Finally he retreated, rejoining his companions. "That's what's left of a sratali," he told them.

"A baby?" Marta asked, trying not to let her voice tremble.

"No." Shipner uncorked his canteen and took a long swig, as though clearing a bad taste from his mouth. "The head is still there; it's a full-grown adult. The head, the feet, bits of the neck and tail . . . some other pieces . . . Not much."

"Wait a minute," Robinson said. "Are you telling me that mound of stuff"— it was only half a meter high and less than two meters in diameter—"is all that's left of a creature that stood two meters high at the shoulder?" Shipner nodded. "And that something *ate* the rest?"

"Not necessarily," Shipner replied with forced detachment. "It might have been several somethings—a pack. They may have dragged parts of it away. But the bite marks are . . ." His voice trailed off.

"Are we talking a *T-rex* here?" Robinson demanded.

At that, Shipner scowled. "Wrong planet, Robinson. Don't let this insane theory of yours carry you away. And the bite marks indicate something much smaller than a *T-rex.*" He stroked his chin thoughtfully. "Jaws maybe . . . forty or fifty centimeters. Across."

Marta sucked in her breath.

"So we're talking about something five meters tall," Robinson guessed.

Shipner shook his head as though to disagree, but what he said was, "We don't know how long-necked it is. The tracks indicate it's bipedal, and heavy, but it wouldn't have to be tall. It could be shorter and more massive than the classic theropod."

"Oh, that's comforting!" Robinson snapped.

"What does it matter?" Marta interjected. "It's big enough to kill and eat a sratali; that makes it big enough to kill and eat a human."

"Probably with fewer leftovers," Shipner remarked drily.

"Then I suggest we make haste to return to the safety of our base camp," Marta said. "And always know which nearby tree can be climbed to a height of ten meters."

She led the way out of the damaged zone at a trot.

When evening approached, Shipner once more led them back away from the stream, where predators were most likely to hunt. But a house tree no longer seemed adequate protection. Instead he selected a tall, broad-trunked tree with large limbs seven or eight meters above the ground. Cutting down half a dozen saplings, he and Robinson constructed a sturdy platform amongst the branches, which Marta interwove with flexible stalks and vines. Safely ensconced in this lofty perch, they pulled up the rope they'd used for access and tied themselves to their aerial bed. There they spent a brief and uncomfortable night.

In the morning they hurried onward, anxious to put as much distance as possible between themselves and the unknown carnivore—Grendel, Robinson called it, in reference to some folktale Marta did not know. That night they constructed another eyrie and slept a little better, but all three were profoundly glad when dawn arrived.

Because they had twice stopped well before dusk— the time when so many predators hunted—in order to build their lofty sanctuaries, it would take them another day and a half to reach their base camp. "We could press on through the night," Shipner suggested when the weary trio paused for a breather midafternoon. They had been on the move almost continually for more than six weeks.

But Robinson shook his head. "Our luck, some trigger-happy goon back in camp will see movement in the trees and shoot us before he can tell we're friendlies."

He had a point, so Shipner conceded. "We'll find a house tree near dusk, then," he said. "We haven't seen any more evidence of the beast's presence"—he didn't have to specify which beast—"and it's unlikely that it would stalk so near our base camp, anyway. Not enough big game in the area, we've scared it all away."

So they lit a fire that night for the first time in three days and cooked a porridge of oats, raisins, and dates. Robinson marveled that such a concoction could taste good to him, but after three days of camel jerky and figs, it was a welcome relief. Then he and Marta curled up together inside the hollow tree while Shipner took his customary first watch.

" 'As God is my witness,' " Robinson groaned in a mocking falsetto, " 'I'll never eat camel jerky again.' "

"What?" Marta asked in some confusion.

"Nothing," Robinson sighed. "Just a joke. I'm so tired of the food here. And everything else." He reached for her. "Come here."

Marta slipped into his arms and they shared a long and intimate kiss. But she was distracted by worries that he'd pinned so much hope on this cargo ship. "What will you do," she asked quietly, "if Kukhoosh Retneyabo has been unable to secure your passage home?"

"Steal you and hold you for ransom," Robinson replied flippantly, tugging at her tunic to gain access.

"Seriously," she prodded.

"I am serious," he insisted, his hands roaming hungrily over her warm flesh. "I'll keep you locked up with me in a little room somewhere and make love to you night and day, and I'll tell Retneyabo he can't have you back until he gets me a ticket home."

Marta sighed, wishing he would be serious about this. Although she had told him differently many times, there was a real possibility that Retneyabo had not been able to bring the mazhel around so quickly—particularly if they found out he had sent an expedition to Dhrusil-matkhashi. "And if I escaped, and fled back to my legal husband?" she asked. "Then what would you do?"

Now Robinson stopped his playful groping, and she could feel the anger in him. "You would, too, wouldn't you?"

"He's my husband," she reminded him.

"Look, Marta, I don't want to talk about this," he said bluntly. "Let's just pretend that he's done his job, just like we've done ours, okay?" He drew her close again. "Now make love with me," he whispered, "and let's not think about what happens later."

And so, trusting Shipner to remain alert and discreet outside the woody enclosure, they indulged their passions with a quiet intensity, knowing that one way or another, their time together would soon end.

Sleep came more easily after that, though Marta's was troubled by dreams of wandering through a forest that had no end. She was vaguely aware when Shipner woke Robinson to take his watch, then settled himself as far away from her as the dimensions of the tree would allow. *Martyrs forbid,* Marta thought dimly, *that he should cast out an arm in his sleep and accidentally have it touch me.*

When next she stirred to consciousness, Marta was aware of the dawn light seeping in through the breach in the hollow tree. She knew there was something wrong with that, but at first her sleep-numbed mind couldn't remember what it was. Then she realized that Robinson had never wakened her to take her turn at watch. Marta jerked up, peering around to make sure he wasn't in the tree with her. No, only Shipner was there, curled up on his side as usual, his snakelike braids in a wild disarray around his head.

Had Robinson fallen asleep at his post? Or maybe he had not felt sleepy at the end of his watch and chivalrously decided to take Marta's turn for her. Extricating herself from the blanket, Marta crawled to the opening of the tree and peered out. Robinson was nowhere in sight. Maybe he had stepped behind a nearby tree to answer a call of nature—but no, the campfire had been carefully extinguished. Why would he do that? And where was he?

An uneasiness gnawed Marta, and she leaned over to where they had stacked their gear inside the tree last night. There her unease blossomed into alarm.

Robinson's pack was missing. So were all the cartridges of recording they had made on their excursion.

"Sab Shipner!" Marta hissed.

His eyes popped open instantly, though he was a moment in speaking. "What is it?" he asked quietly.

"Sab Robinson is gone." She hated the tremble in her own voice. "I fear we have been betrayed."

It was dawn when Robinson stumbled into the clearing where the stockade stood, that bastion of false security. "Dakura!" he called out. "Mahanna! Lekish!"

They all came running out from their camp, Tookh in the lead. "Where is the Sibna?" Tookh cried in alarm. "Where is Sab Shipner?"

"Back there," Robinson gasped, waving a hand toward the stream. "Shipner was attacked—one of those nasty amphibious things. He managed to kill it, but it tore up his leg pretty good. Marta is staying with him. I was afraid to move him myself. Tookh, you'll need to take the first-aid kit and that medical program. Dakura, Mahanna, you may need to construct a litter of some kind to carry him on. Habbel, take an extra rifle—there's something very big and very nasty out there, we saw its tracks. I just hope it doesn't smell the blood . . ."

"You don't look very well yourself, Sab Robinson," Lekish said worriedly, as the others jumped to obey. "Here, let me help you into the stockade."

"How far back are they?" Dakura asked as he tucked a hatchet into his belt and looped a small coil of cord around it.

"About two hours, maybe three," Robinson replied. "We were trying to come on by moonlight. What a mistake that was."

Dakura clapped a hand on Tookh's shoulder as the youth darted past. "Slow down, boy. We have some distance to go, and we don't need to have you with a broken leg, too." Then the four of them trotted off into the forest.

As soon as they had disappeared into the trees, Robinson turned to Lekish. "Is everything ready?"

"I had the boat out yesterday and went over it," Lekish replied. "We found a small lake to the north of here, so that was a good excuse to make sure the boat was serviceable."

"Good. Let's get to it."

In fifteen minutes they had collected the folding sailboat, water and supplies, all the image recording from the expedition, and several specimen cages with live skitterers and other small creatures. They clipped on harnesses and prepared their ropes for rappelling down the cliffs to the shore, where they would assemble the boat and load their cargo. There was a fresh offshore breeze—perfect conditions for sailing across the channel which separated Dhrusil-matkhashi from Innanta.

"Kukhoosh Paun will have a ship waiting for us in Sedet Narashi," Lekish told him. "It's a little village just northwest of Mimma along the coast. People may ask questions there, but they won't be able to make any trouble, as they might in Mimma."

"Good." Robinson knew it would not go well for him if Retneyabo found out that his Unbeliever had changed sides. Robinson needed to be well away before that happened. "I think your kukhoosh will be quite pleased with the information I've got here."

Lekish grinned broadly. "It will be nice to show up that ass Retneyabo, for a change."

Funny, Robinson thought, how each side thought the other's kukhoosh was an ass. And why not? Like major universities, there wasn't really much difference between them. Each kukhoosh wanted glory, and to be known as a patron of Knowledge and Beauty. Each was willing to spend a fortune to have that at the other's expense. What did it matter to him if Retneyabo was credited with the discovery of Dhrusil-matkhashi, or Paun? What did it matter to him if the College of Indigenous Life was given the mandate to explore, or if a new college were established with Paun as its patron?

What mattered, he told himself again, was that Paun had guaranteed to get him off Dray's Planet. Positively, absolutely, she would buy his way off. She had connections. It would be done. He would go with his research notes, image recordings, and one or two skitterers as proof of the miraculous evolution of life here; and the whole of the inhabited galaxy would be at his feet. Cecil Robinson, discoverer of the first complex, Earth-like creatures of non-Terran origin. Cecil Robinson, landmark author in the field of interplanetary convergent evolution. He'd be the Charles Darwin of this century.

And Soln Shipner could rot in hell, here on this primitive world. He'd fit right in, anthropological throwback that he was. Robinson laughed out loud, imagining Shipner's face when he heard the announcement of next year's Ashdod Prize for Zoology. "Hell, I could be a first-year undergrad, and they'd still give me the Ashdod for this plum," he chuckled.

Just before they went over the side, Lekish ducked into the supply tent and came out with the radio beacon.

"We don't need that," Robinson protested.

"No. But we can't have the Sibna calling for help, can we?"

At that, Robinson balked. "The ship can't get here in time for them to—"

But with a powerful swing, Lekish smashed the boxy beacon against a rock. "No point in taking chances," he said with a grin, tossing the shattered instrument aside.

Robinson stared at the ruined beacon and tried to tell himself it was all right. Marta would be all right here, with Shipner. They'd be safe in their stockade, and eventually Retneyabo would realize they were in trouble and send the ship. Maybe he'd send Retneyabo a message himself, once he was safely offworld.

Yes, that's what he would do. When he was safely offworld.

CHAPTER 17

"But a spirit of Evil came over the Unbeliever Robinson,"
Hassan told them, "and he thought to take for himself the
glory that was not his. He mixed a potion into the food of
Marta and the Unbeliever Shipner, so that they slept a deep
sleep, and he called forth the great beast Grendel to hunt.
Then he slipped away into the darkness and, making a raft
from topo trees, he sailed away from Dhrusil-matkhashi."

"What happened to Marta?" Ari demanded. "Did
Grendel eat her?"

"Mighty Grendel came forth from its lair," Hassan
went on. "It was the largest grendel that has ever lived,
taller than a two-story house, with jaws wide enough to
swallow a camel whole. Through the forest came Grendel,
each step so heavy that it shook the ground, and as it
sniffed the air for food, it caught the scent of Marta and
her companion. But the All-Merciful cast a spell upon it,
so that it could not see her; for she was chosen by the
All-Wise, who would not suffer her to be harmed. And
so Grendel passed by the place where she slept, and went
on to hunt other game that night."

Mohat tugged at Ari's sleeve and gestured frantically.
Ari translated, "Mohat wants to know what happened to
the traitor Robinson? Did he get away? Surely the All-
Just would not allow that!"

Hassan smiled. "The ways of the All-Just are beyond
the comprehension of the Faithful," he replied. "But listen, and I will tell you what happened . . ."

Marta stooped and picked up the shattered radio
transmitter at the edge of the cliff. Trembling with rage,

she voiced a howl that began at her toes and worked its way up to erupt from her mouth in a piercing sound that roared down the cliff face to the ocean, flinging itself against the choppy seas. "May the All-Powerful curse you and your children to a thousand generations!" she shrieked as she hurled the useless beacon out over the water. "May the sea rise up and swallow you whole! May you go to the place of everlasting torment and be boiled in sulfur throughout eternity! May you—"

An arm caught her roughly around the waist and hauled her back from the brink of the cliff. "You can curse him later, Princess," Soln Shipner growled. "I'll even help you, I'm quite good at it. But right now we need to assess the damage."

Marta stood quivering with ill-controlled fury, unable to focus on anything but the pain of her betrayal. "Paun," she hissed. "It had to be Paun. Pray the All-Merciful she gets him off-planet before I find him. I will personally remove every one of his fingernails with a pair of pliers. I will slice his—"

"Princess!" Shipner interrupted firmly. "We need to assess our situation. Stop acting like a jilted lover and remember you are in charge of this expedition."

Marta's eyes of molten lava snapped to his face, but he met them ugly glare for ugly glare. "Or are you truly a spoiled, pampered baby aristocrat," he goaded, "who is not up to the responsibility of leadership?"

Marta's jaw worked. Her chest heaved with the motions of breathing, but no air passed in and out of her lungs. Her hands clenched and unclenched. Finally she gasped one quick draught of air, then another, then a third. "What did they take?" she demanded in a whisper.

"I'll check the supply tent," Tookh volunteered quickly, and dashed in that direction. The others wandered after him to check the cages of animals, the few stacks of crates and barrels, etc., that were left after three months on the continent.

Shipner took his eyes off Marta long enough to make a quick surveillance of the camp. The enterprising Innantans had spent their time fruitfully while the scientists

were absent, using the hollow stalks of a bamboolike
native plant to construct an aqueduct from the nearby
spring to the camp. There were thatched, pitched aw-
nings over all the tents, and small trenches around their
perimeters to provide drainage during the occasional
rains. Outside the barricade, the ditch had been broad-
ened and the excavated dirt heaped up on the farside,
forming a second redoubt with sharpened stakes protruding from it—that looked quite recent. Had these
men also found evidence of the huge predator which
prowled not far away?

There had been little breath spared for discussion
when Dakura and his party reached Shipner and Marta,
who were by that time only an hour and a half out of
camp. It had taken only moments to realize the ruse
which had been perpetrated, and to guess what Robinson was up to; but though they returned with all haste,
there was no hope of catching the traitor.

The reports that came to Marta now confirmed what
they had suspected. The folding sailboat was gone, along
with all the recordings, some specimens of quasi-
saurians, and enough supplies to reach any of a number
of coastal villages on Innanta. Two rappelling harnesses
were also missing, as were sufficient lengths of rope for
two people to make the trip down. Marta was still
breathing raggedly, her fists twitching in futility, as the
men reported back to her. Shipner kept keen eyes on
her, watching for the tiny signs that might indicate an
impending loss of control. The last thing he needed right
now was for her to go over the emotional brink. But his
ploy of shoving responsibility down her throat seemed
to be working. Marta nodded grimly to each report.

"Well, we are not in immediate danger," Marta grated
through clenched teeth. "We have plenty of water, and
food enough for a while. But we will have to be more
diligent about verifying the edibility of native plants.
Even though we cannot signal Innanta, we will be missed
eventually—before winter, certainly. Sooner, if the kukhoosh catches that *dung-eating, camel-mating recreant—*"

"Careful, Princess," Shipner whispered to her. "You just called yourself a camel."

She turned on him with nails clawing, but he caught both her wrists and held them in one hand, tucking her neatly under his free arm, where she writhed and kicked impotently while he strode toward the barrels of water that had been collected inside the stockade. There he dropped her, and before she could launch another assault on him, he upended one of the barrels and doused her thoroughly. She came to her feet sputtering and swinging, but exhaustion was catching up with her. Shipner caught her shoulders and held her, not at arm's length, but at a distance where she could land a few ineffectual blows on his broad chest. It didn't take more than half a dozen before she dissolved into weeping.

Shipner made a sour face, then turned her around and propelled her gently but firmly toward her tent. At the door he paused. "Go lie down," he directed in a low, stern voice. "When you can be strong for these men, come back out. I'll give you one free shot. Any more than one, I'll hit back."

It was midafternoon before Marta had gained enough control of herself to emerge from her tent. Tookh was proudly showing Soln Shipner something to do with a heap of rope he had made from twisted native grasses. Shipner was on one knee, inspecting the creation, when Marta walked up to him. He looked up with glittering, challenging eyes. Marta launched one vicious kick to his ribs; Shipner woofed in surprise and sagged over, clutching his ribs with one hand and propping himself up with the other. She could hear him sucking his breath in between his teeth, biting back a cry of pain. A slow, cold smile spread over Marta's face.

"Tookh," she said calmly, "I want you to give me an account of all that happened in our absence. The unimportant things as well as the important. I have plenty of time to listen to them all." Then she strolled over to the fire and dished up a bowl of stew from the pot simmering there. Suddenly, she was very, very hungry.

Robinson stood on the landing field of the shuttleport, waiting while his few crates of belongings were stowed on the drone shuttle by Kukhoosh Paun's servants. No employees of the Orbital Authority were present. How Paun had accomplished that, he didn't know and didn't care. Nor did he care that this vessel was not a GenOrg ship, as he'd expected, but a privateer, more willing to skirt the law. All he cared was that a ship was waiting in orbit for him, and it was going to take him home.

Robinson had been reluctant to trust Paun—how did he know she wouldn't take his research and just kill him? But at their first meeting she'd asked testily, "Would any of these men serve me if my word were not reliable? Here in Innanta, a kukhoosh's word is her most valued asset, and I would not violate it for spite. I cannot do business if my clients cannot trust my word."

All the same, when he and Lekish reached Innanta safely with their cargo, he'd kept himself armed, prepared for some attempt at treachery by Paun's hireling; but Lekish had laughed at him. "I'm being paid for a live scientist, not a dead one," he told Robinson.

Now Paun's electric cart approached across the sands, and the great lady herself stepped out. "And so you are on your way, Robinson," she observed.

"So I am." The cargo hatch was being sealed; time for him to squeeze into the tiny passenger hold. "Do you have the space-voyage drugs for me?"

Her gaze never flickered. "I regret that we have no such drugs on Innanta. Our chemists have neither the means nor the motivation to make them." She shrugged absently. "Perhaps the ship's captain will have some."

Robinson hesitated. Most cargo crews didn't bother with the drugs; they were lifetime spacers who never left a zero-g environment. "Maybe," he agreed politely, telling himself it would be all right. The voyage shouldn't take more than a few months; his muscles wouldn't deteriorate noticeably in that amount of time. He'd just keep up his exercises, and it would be all right.

Hell, he admitted, *even if I lost two or three percent of my muscle tissue, it would be worth it.*

"You are aware now, Robinson," Paun told him, "that you can never return to Dray's Planet? The mazhel will not be pleased to learn that you have defied them, and they will never grant permission for one as corrupt as you to return."

Robinson managed a wry smile. "I can live with that."

"As you wish, then." Paun nodded toward the shuttle. "Time for you to go. Farewell, Dr. Robinson."

Yes, time to go. And as soon as the ship broke orbit, he'd send a message back to Retneyabo to retrieve Marta. "Farewell, patron," he replied. "I wish you all the glory you deserve for this discovery." He gave a last jaunty wave and climbed into the shuttle.

Paun watched the drone hurtle skyward and pondered what to do with the evidence the Unbeliever had brought her. How could she best use it to her own advantage? Her first thought had been to release it to the public as a great discovery: life on Dhrusil-matkhashi! But as she pondered it, she realized that to do so would be to declare to the people that the mazhel had deceived them. That could be bad. To show up the Holy Ones as false tore at the fabric of Innantan culture, and such disillusionment was always bad for the economy.

Yet Retneyabo must have some plan in mind. Retneyabo knew some way to use this information to his own advantage. For some time, Paun had been making discreet inquiries. Just recently she had learned of his meeting with several mazhel on the rooftop of the College of Holy Studies, a few weeks after his expedition's departure. That must be the key, that meeting. Retneyabo knew something that Paun didn't, and she must find out. She must go to Mazh Farbo, to see what she could learn about the three mazhel who had attended that meeting. She must find out what they had to do with Dhrusil-matkhashi.

*   *   *

Marta stood on the wooden bridge which spanned the ditch surrounding their encampment. The planks of the bridge were short and narrow, set twenty or thirty centimeters apart on their rails, so that one had to step carefully to cross over without falling through the gaps. Nothing bigger than a skitterer could cross it without falling in or breaking through. Shipner tended to chuckle every time he saw the contraption.

Just after Marta and the two Unbelievers had struck off inland, those left behind had heard once again the great animal screeching. It had prompted them to build the aqueduct, to reduce the necessity of leaving the stockade. But all was quiet for over a month, and they grew more relaxed. Then the sound came again, during daylight hours, about a week before Marta's return. That was when they'd improved the fortifications.

The sound had been more distant this last time, which Dakura thought was a good sign, but they went nowhere these days without every energy rifle they had, charged and ready. There had been some other scares: an armored quadruped the size of a small donkey had charged Mahanna, and it took three blasts of the rifle to stop it. Later, a great crashing in the bushes caused Habbel to fire his gun until it was empty at what turned out to be a knee-high *nall* shaking a tree-creeper in its jaws. But no one had seen any sign of a beast the size of Grendel, neither tracks on the ground nor the remains of any large prey animals.

"If it is a cold-blooded creature," Shipner speculated, "it may go into a torpor after eating, in order to digest a large meal."

"And if it is a warm-blooded creature," Marta replied, "it may not. Are you a gambler, Sab Shipner?"

He eyed her with his dark, mocking eyes. They'd had little to say to each other since their return; Marta's kick had cracked several ribs, and Shipner was highly resentful of having to bind them with a cloth wrap which covered a number of his striking tattoos.

As she stood now on the bridge, gazing between the

planks at the shallow ditch below, Marta frowned. It was presently filled with brush, the idea being to set it afire in case of attack, but Dakura wanted to fill it with water instead. Marta didn't see the point in that. Would an animal be less likely to cross a ditch filled with water than one filled with fire? It didn't seem so to her, but then, the fire would eventually go out. All it could buy them was time. Time to go over the edge of the cliff and find sanctuary on the rocky beach three hundred meters below.

The rope contraption of woven grasses which Tookh had been showing off to Shipner turned out to be a ladder. He and Mahanna were now working on it industriously. Robinson had explained to them all about rappelling, and how easy it would be to get down the cliff that way, but none of the Innantans were accustomed to heights, so they were not very comfortable with the idea.

Dakura and Habbel were extending the aqueduct to the edge of the cliff, where they could create an artificial waterfall if necessary. No one really wanted to give up their comfortable camp atop the cliffs for the barren, rocky, sea-splashed beach below; but if Grendel walked out of the forest one day, they intended to be prepared.

Marta decided now that fire was the better option for filling their ditch. Not knowing their enemy, it seemed more logical that fire would deter a creature longer than water. With the dry vegetation already heaped in the shallow moat, they only needed sufficient warning to set the ditch ablaze. Not only that, but to the desert-born Marta, filling a ditch with water seemed a terrible waste of the precious liquid.

It bothered her a little that Shipner had ventured no opinion in this matter. Leaving the bridge, she came back inside the camp and approached the painted man where he sat in the sun, scribbling in his notebook. As usual, he did not deign to look up at her, so she squatted down beside him.

"What have you decided?" he asked after a moment.

"Fire," she replied.

Shipner grunted. "Good."

Marta wondered what she was supposed to make of that. Had he known all along that fire was the right choice, and just waited to see if she would choose correctly? Maybe he honestly didn't know which was better, and wanted her to make the decision so no one could blame him if it was a bad one. Maybe it truly didn't make any difference, and he would have said "good" to either one, just to make her think he knew. She wanted to believe it was the first option.

"Are you a teaching professor, Sab Shipner?" she asked, for she knew that a good teacher would force his students to reason out problems for themselves.

"I teach," he said succinctly, then added, "Students don't like my style very much."

Marta grinned, remembering their first lesson in woodcraft on Dhrusil-matkhashi. No wonder students didn't like his style. Then another thought occurred to her. "Did you try to teach Robinson?" she asked, her smile gone at the painful memory.

He was sketching now in his notebook. Marta recognized one of the crested herbivores. "Habit," he allowed. "Fifteen years in a faculty position will do that to you." To the side of his sketch he began doing a more detailed drawing of the forefoot. "He thought he knew everything."

Yes, that was Robinson, Marta thought. Like Fadnar, that long-ago lover who deserted to Paun. Why hadn't she seen that before? Robinson was full of himself, like Fadnar. Jealous, like Fadnar. And like Fadnar, when he felt his needs were not getting enough attention . . .

"I knew he was weak," Shipner said, as though reading her thoughts. "I didn't think he was that weak, to betray his word to Retneyabo."

"Oh, you are a great one to talk!" Marta hooted sourly. "Who was it stole our dinka-chak and our recordings to take back to Paun?"

Shipner paused in his sketching to give her an exasperated look. "I don't recall giving anyone my word that I would not steal the dinka-chak," he said drily.

"It was theft!"

"Theft is a useful tool," he replied, erasing a line he didn't like and redrawing it. "I have used it more than once to keep my word."

"But you lied to me!" Marta protested. "You denied that you had stolen the dinka-chak."

"I still deny it," he replied easily.

"Why do you persist?" she demanded. "We all know you did it. Why do you endanger your immortal soul by continuing to lie?"

"There's no harm in it," he dismissed, busy with his pencil. "Especially since there is no danger of you believing it."

Frustrated by his obstinacy, she tried again. "Doesn't your god tell you that deceit and deception are sins?"

"Doesn't your law say not to kill?" he countered. "Yet criminals are executed. Context is everything, Princess."

"Don't call me Princess!" she snapped.

"Don't act like one," he retorted.

It was one more insult than Marta could stand today. Jumping to her feet, she strode across the compound and snatched up an energy rifle. "Dakura! Habbel!" she called. "Come along, I want to change the cartridges in our recorders. I will have something to show my husband for the money he invested in me."

Robinson floated through the hatch onto the ship's bridge. They'd been out of orbit for an hour now, and before he did some exercising and settled down to his research, he had to take care of something. "I'd like to send a message back to someone on Innanta," he told the radio officer.

"Sorry," the man replied, "no personal messages allowed. Company policy."

Frowning, Robinson thought for a moment. "It's to my employer—to let him know his cargo is safely en route," he lied. He had to let Retneyabo know about Marta.

"Sorry," the man repeated.

Now something else occurred to Robinson. "Once we're clear of solar interference, I'd like to send some files to the Portal for relay to a scientific journal. It's a business transaction, I'll gladly pay—"

Now the captain interrupted. "With what?" he asked drily.

Robinson balked; he'd left credit accounts behind on Innanta, but they were no good to him now; and he had nothing of value with him except the priceless research notes and specimens. "I have a credit account on Melius," he ventured, but the captain shook his head.

"No credit. Cash up front."

Thieves, Robinson thought. *Company policy, my eye, they're looking to pick up a little something on the side.* "How long till we reach the Portal?" he demanded. The Portal Authority had to accept his Meliusan credit. "Two months? Three?"

The captain gave him an odd look. "Portal?" He shook his head. "We're outbound, son. Headed for the GenOrg colonies to do some trading. It'll be a year before we get back to the Portal."

Suddenly Robinson's legs began to ache.

Paun sat in the library of Mazh Farbo's faculty apartment, pretending interest in one of the mazh's paintings. Having acquired Knowledge in the area of mazhish literature, Farbo was now trying to acquire Beauty in the form of paintings and sculptures. Too bad, thought Paun, that she couldn't acquire Taste as well.

Farbo was pawing through a mound of books, some bound, some on data sponges, some actually on parchment. "And here's another reference," Farbo said, absorbed in her research. " 'The island lies seventy kilometers to the southwest of Dhrusil-matkhashi, but unlike that continent, it is covered with trees and plants bearing fruit.' It seems quite clear to me that the Holy Ones have known the continent to be barren for some time."

It made Paun despair to think that such a fool masqueraded as a Holy One. Farbo might know how to find any given topic or reference in the writings of the maz-hel, but simple truths often escaped her. "That reference does not say barren," she pointed out carefully. "Neither have any of the others. At any rate, that was not my question." Paun struggled to control her impatience and show proper respect for the mazh. "What do the mazhel *today* say about Dhrusil-matkhashi?"

"I do not recall it being mentioned at all," Farbo said honestly.

"Not by Kummel or Tabla, or maybe Elkniar?" Paun prodded. Those were the mazhel her informant said had met with Retneyabo.

"Elkniar? No!" Farbo exclaimed in surprise. "Elkniar speaks only of social harmony, never of such irrelevant things and a barr—an uninhabited continent. As for Kummel, he waxes on and on in abstracts and similes, while Tabla—well, Tabla is fairly straightforward," Farbo admitted. "But I don't recall ever—oh, let's do this," she said, rising with decision. "Let's go see Tabla, you can ask him yourself."

Paun hesitated. "It would be presumptuous of me to—"

"Then I'll ask," Farbo said firmly. "If you want a question answered, go to the source. Tabla has been a mazh for twenty years to my five. He'll know much better than me what has been said in this generation about Dhrusil-matkhashi."

By the time they reached the home of Mazh Tabla, Paun was fairly sure this was a mistake, but Farbo was insistent. "You've walked all this way," she protested, "at least let us greet the mazh. Then, if you do not wish to put your question to him, you can go and I will speak with him privately."

It would have been discourteous to refuse to give the mazh greetings, so Paun had to accompany Mazh Farbo inside.

Tabla was in his workshop, checking the work of an apprentice who was polishing a set of dental tools. He looked up when the two women entered. "My esteemed

colleague," he greeted Farbo. "And the worthy Kukhoosh Paun. What brings two such honored personages
to my humble abode?"

Paun jumped in before Farbo could say anything.
"Mazh Farbo was instructing me in the interpretation of
some obscure passages of mazhish literature," she tem-
porized. "Wanting your opinion on a fine point, she invited me to accompany her here to greet you." Paun
bowed slightly. "It is an honor to be admitted to your
establishment, Mazh Tabla; but as I see you are busy, I
will simply greet you in the Name of the All-Hallowed
and go on my way."

"Paun was asking about Dhrusil-matkhashi," Farbo
offered.

Was that a flicker of anger in Tabla's eyes? Paun
couldn't tell, it was gone so quickly. "I am never too
busy to receive the Faithful," he replied with false humil-
ity. "Please come into my garden; my sib-nurah will
bring us refreshments."

"I would not dream of putting you to such trouble,"
Paun protested.

"And I would not dream of sending you on your way
without giving you at least a cup of water," he returned.
"Please. My garden is well shaded, with a fountain that
sprays a fine mist—most pleasant at this time of day."
He turned to Paun's bodyguard, a hulking brute who
stood respectfully just inside the door. "Please be comfortable in my home," he bade the man, tacitly giving
him permission to find the kitchen and a glass of cool
water or iced coffee.

It meant Tabla expected Paun to stay for a while, and
that did not quiet her unease a bit. With trepidation,
she followed the mazh out of his workshop and into
the garden.

After changing out the cartridges in three recorders
along the bank of the stream, Marta was hot and sweaty
and bug-bitten. She wanted a bath; but the idea of bathing alone in the tent where she had so often taunted
Robinson with her wet and glistening flesh made her

ache once more with his betrayal. No, she was not ready to face such memories quite yet.

But she was so hot, and this oppressive humidity made her skin crawl . . .

Looking down at the cool water in the stream, Marta made a hasty decision. "I'm going to bathe," she announced to her two companions. "Dakura, Habbel, you stand here and watch the woods for any sign of danger. I'll go beyond those ferns there. And if I catch either of you peeking, I'll have an eye for your audacity."

The two men exchanged a look, then shrugged and turned their backs on Marta. She marched on past the ferns, then stripped out of her clothes and boots and waded out into the stream.

The water was only a few centimeters deep and icy cold, for the springs which fed this rivulet were only a hundred meters ahead. Marta cupped some of it in her hands and splashed her face, shivering as the droplets trickled down over her neck, back, and breasts. Next she scrubbed her shins and calves with gritty mud from the creek bottom, then quickly rinsed it off. The mud was cold, too, and it left her lower legs almost numb. She decided to try sand from the bank on her thighs, and that was a little better. Finally she scooped up two great handfuls of damp sand and began to scour her neck and breasts.

She was in the process of rinsing when she saw Shipner standing back in the forest watching her.

He stood like a statue in the dappled light which filtered through the trees, an energy rifle resting casually in his hands, and she might not have seen him at all if it weren't that the shadows flickered and wavered as a breeze stirred the branches of the trees, while the tattoos on his body remained still. He had pointedly streaked dirt and ash across the white bandage tied around his ribs the very first day Tookh applied it, so it acted like an extension of his camouflage.

Marta gasped when she saw him there, but then her anger boiled up hot as she realized he could have been

there for a very long time. Defiantly, she ignored him
and continued rinsing the sand from her body.

As she gouged up handfuls of mud to rub her arms,
however, she could not resist goading him a little. "I
thought you found all Innantan women ugly, Sab Shipner,"
she called to him.

"I find them plain," he replied. "And unappealing.
That is not the same as ugly."

Marta scrubbed vigorously at her arms. "And if I am
so unappealing," she challenged, "why do you stand
there watching me?"

"Why, to guard your life, Princess," he replied soberly. "Beasts care more for how you taste than how
you look. And as for those two guards you brought with
you, their idea of beauty differs from mine. They might
find the sight of your nakedness too great a temptation,
and so I must save them from themselves. And consequently from you."

Marta wasn't sure if he meant that she would harm
them for peeking at her, or that sharing pleasures with
her would damage them. Either way, she knew it was
meant as an insult, and she took it as such.

"How fortunate for them," she retorted, "that you
find me so repulsive."

"Oh, no female body is entirely repulsive," Shipner
drawled.

That infuriated Marta even more. He was watching
her and enjoying it, but insulting her with words of
feigned indifference. *Wise man,* she thought viciously.
Because if you try to touch me, I will kill you.

But she could not stop the words from coming out of
her mouth. "I suppose you would like me better," she
growled, "if I painted myself with those abominable
black markings."

"It would improve your appearance," he agreed. "But
you are not a Nechtanite, and you have not earned the
right to wear tattoos."

Marta stooped over to rinse the muck from her arms.
"I would not pollute my body with such an abomination," she grumbled. "And I do not have to wear my

accomplishments on the outside and flaunt them in front of others. I wear them on the inside, in here," she insisted, tapping her chest over her heart, "which is the only place it matters."

Now Shipner left the shadows of the forest and moved to the bank of the stream. "What an apologist you are." He chuckled.

"I'm not apologizing for anything!" she flared.

That made him laugh merrily. "No, no, Princess, I didn't imply that you were. An apologist is one who argues on behalf of a particular viewpoint. You make a strong case for the plainness of your body."

Marta jerked a finger at herself. "This body has put better men than you in a state of shock!" she snapped.

"No doubt you have slain untold millions," Shipner mocked, wading out to join her in the water. "And if you had but a few adornments . . ." He scooped up a handful of the gritty mud and made two streaks on her shoulder with his fingers. "Like this."

It was not the coldness of the mud that froze her, made her stand rigid, scarcely able to breathe.

"And perhaps one here," he went on, streaking mud across her belly just below her navel.

Gooseflesh sprang up all across her arms and thighs.

"And we mustn't forget," said Shipner, tracing a line from her cheek down her neck and across her collarbone, "the sacred spiral . . ." The line curled down around her breast and came back up to end pointing at her nipple. Shipner stood back to survey the effect. "Yes, much better," he observed with satisfaction. "Now, if only you had earned those marks by your courage and cunning, as Nechtanite women must, you would be almost irresistible."

Then Soln Shipner wiped his muddy hand on his bandage, grinned his yellow grin at Marta, and walked away.

Paun passed a hand across her weary eyes. "That is very interesting, Mazh Tabla," she lied, "but I have taken far too much of your time already." Night was falling; they had said their evening prayers together here

in the garden, and now Tabla was going on at length
about the value of adversity in honing the spirit. It would
be a long walk in the darkness before Paun reached her
comfortable house. "I must return to my home, and not
intrude upon your hospitality any longer," she said a
little too bluntly.

"Nonsense!" Tabla exclaimed, smiling beneficently.
"You and my colleague Farbo will dine with me. I have
sent word to some of my friends; they are most anxious
to join us."

Paun knew very well that this was not the sort of thing
a mazh did fo. a kukhoosh. "You make too much of
me," she responded uncomfortably. "I am but a merchant, a trader in goods, while all wisdom belongs to
you."

"Oh, not all wisdom," Tabla demurred. "Tell me
again how you became interested in Dhrusil-matkhashi."

Paun gritted her teeth, then retold the carefully constructed truth she had fed him earlier. She'd heard rumors that Retneyabo had some interest in it. Whatever
interested such a successful merchant as Retneyabo interested her, as well. But Retneyabo's people were tight-
lipped; she had learned nothing from them.

"So you did not send your own expedition," Tabla
said, smiling.

Paun raised her eyebrows in feigned surprise. "Expedition?" How much did Tabla know of Retneyabo's expedition? What had Retneyabo told him at that meeting
atop the College of Holy Studies?

"Oh, surely you learned that Retneyabo's sib-hinan
has gone off somewhere with the two Unbelievers,"
Tabla pursued. "If you knew of Retneyabo's interest in
this place, it must have crossed your mind that they had
gone to Dhrusil-matkhashi."

Paun smiled back, a cold, strained smile. When in
doubt, say nothing—or rather, admit nothing. "No one
goes to Dhrusil-matkhashi. There is nothing there."

Just then Tabla's apprentice showed two more people
into the garden: Mazh Kummel and his favorite kukhoosh, the mine owner Serai, exchanged familiar greet-

ings with Tabla and Farbo, then greeted Paun with respectful words on their lips but a cold glitter in their eyes. It made her blood chill and run jangling through her veins. She felt as though the garden were closing in on her.

"So, Kukhoosh Paun," Serai said as he seated himself in a chair across from her. "I understand you have been at the shuttleport this afternoon."

All-Merciful, have pity on me, Paun thought. *They know. They know I smuggled the Unbeliever onto the shuttle.* "I needed to send some goods to a creditor offworld," she said tightly. But if they knew about Robinson, they must also know where he had been, and what he'd brought back. Were they in league with Retneyabo on this?

"Very valuable goods, I think," said Kummel, "to require your personal attention."

"Worthless goods!" Paun spat, losing her temper. "Worthless, corrupt goods that are best removed from among the Faithful!"

A brief silence echoed throughout the garden following her outburst.

"Ah, that was not wise," sighed Tabla.

"So you have known all along," Paun challenged them. "You have known that Dhrusil-matkhashi teems with life, and you have kept that knowledge to yourselves. Why?" The unbelievable popped into her head and out of her mouth before she could stop it. "Do you grow rich from its produce?"

"Do I live like a wealthy man?" asked Tabla. "No, no, Paun, you are mistaken about many things. It grieves me to see how you err in judgment." He folded his hands in practiced piety. "I am overcome with compassion for you, and I will pray ceaselessly to the Most High that you be restored to right thinking."

"Right thinking?" Paun exclaimed, startled. For the Children of the Second Revelation, there was Right Thinking and there was Wrong Thinking. Wrong Thinking had only one connotation. "You speak as though I were a heretic."

"My good friend Tabla, I will join you in this," Kummel chimed in quickly, and Paun's heart lurched at the way their eyes slid to one another, as though they had reached a silent agreement. "We will take Paun under our wing and pray fervently for her restoration."

No. She would not sit still for this subterfuge. "I appreciate your prayers," said Paun angrily, rising to her feet, "but I must not continue to be a bother to you. I will not dine this evening, but will go to my home fasting to give thanks to the All-Giving for your concern."

"I do not think it wise for you to return to your home," Kummel said bluntly.

Paun turned dangerous eyes on him.

"I would be delighted," offered Kukhoosh Serai, entering the exchange for the first time, "to provide my worthy colleague with a room in my house, until she has been restored to right thinking." He motioned to his bodyguard, who stood nearby.

Paun blanched, seeing what they intended. "You can't do that. You can't hold me prisoner."

"It is ignorance that holds you prisoner," Tabla admonished. "We seek to set you free."

In desperation Paun turned to Mazh Farbo; but Farbo looked as pale as Paun.

"The people will rejoice," added Kummel, "that one such as yourself has chosen to retire from the world for a time of prayer and meditation, with Farbo to instruct you as you explore the depth of meaning in the Manifest Revelations."

"You can't do this!" Paun shrieked. "Belak!" she shouted to her bodyguard, who was nowhere to be seen. "Bela—" But her cry was cut off by a handkerchief being stuffed into her mouth, and strong arms gripped her from behind.

"You sent Belak away hours ago," Tabla informed her with just the trace of a smile on his thin lips. "It is Serai's man who will escort you to his master's house. Don't worry, you will be quite safe. Serai is most concerned for your welfare. Aren't you, Serai?"

"Indeed, I am," Kukhoosh Serai agreed, as Paun

struggled furiously against the hands that constrained her. "You will be most comfortable as my guest. In fact, I think that instead of just a room, I will provide for your use a cottage I own in the southwestern islands. It is quite temperate there this time of year, and so far from the commotion of Jinka that you will be able to study and meditate undisturbed."

Then Serai's bodyguard hauled Paun bodily out of the garden, while Mazh Farbo followed meekly.

"Poor woman," Tabla sighed, as his wife appeared with a plate of olives, shellfish and pickled onions. "She is quite deranged."

"It is the weight of her sins," Kummel agreed as he helped himself to the simple fare. "We will pray that the All-Merciful grants her relief."

CHAPTER 18

"But how did Marta get home?" Ari asked. "Did she swim? Did she make a boat? Did an angel carry her?"

"Hush, my son," Hassan scowled. "Let me finish. For forty days and forty nights were Marta and the dark Unbeliever forsaken in the wilderness of Dhrusil-matkhashi. Then the All-Knowing whispered of her peril to Retneyabo, the husband of Marta, and he sent a ship to rescue her. But even as the ship sailed, Grendel prowled the land, growing hungry and impatient—"

Retneyabo sat on his spacious white stone terrace, enjoying the cool sea breeze washing over him. It was unbearable in Jinka at this time of year, with the misery of the heat compounded by the misery of high humidity. He was glad to have this place of sanctuary, where a person was not too hot and sweaty to think straight. Or think deviously, as the situation required.

It had been nearly four months now since Marta and her expedition had scaled the cliffs of Dhrusil-matkhashi, and with each day he grew a little more concerned. They did not have enough supplies to stay out this long; but of course, if it were as lush as Nrin intimated, they could have replenished from local sources. Still, he worried just a little. Great would be his relief when Hagiath sent word that Marta had activated the beacon, and a ship was on its way to retrieve her.

It also bothered him that a privateer orbiting Dray's Planet had sent down and retrieved a drone shuttle without his knowledge. He'd made a few such discreet arrangements himself in the past, and it bothered him that he did not know what goods had been exchanged. It particularly bothered him because Paun was on one end of the transaction. What was she up to now?

It was possible, of course, that Paun was completing payment for Shipner's passage to Dray's Planet, as her official authorization claimed. But who would wait a year for compensation? And why all the subterfuge about its delivery? No, something was not right here, and Retneyabo needed to find out what it was.

Adni came out on the terrace to join him. "Ah! It is so clean-smelling out here!" she exclaimed as she eased herself into a chair near his. "Even with the ingenious ventilation system Sab Ragammar designed, the house gets stuffy at this time of year. Close, you know."

Retneyabo smiled and kissed his wife's hand, knowing how her knees must be throbbing in this weather. Yet Adni never complained; she did, however, sit down a lot.

After a moment she said, "I heard something very strange today."

Retneyabo cocked an eyebrow. "Oh?"

"I sent a crate of fresh *skoriss* around to your sister's house—you know how she loves them, and they are so plentiful in the tide pools this year." Adni paused, her brow puckered, and brushed her fingertips thoughtfully across her several chins. "But Hadmiel brought it back. He said the household was in such an uproar, he was afraid to leave it there."

"Uproar!" Retneyabo was surprised. His sister's house was never in an uproar. She wouldn't allow it. Of the two siblings, she was always the more organized, the more demanding. "What kind of an uproar?"

"Hadmiel couldn't get the whole story, of course," Adni cautioned, "but he gathered that the steward had left hastily, and with more property than was appropriate; and half the household staff seemed inclined to follow suit." Adni turned her beautiful, penetrating dark eyes on her husband. "I just can't imagine that happening in her household."

Retneyabo frowned, too. "She won't like it if I interfere," he warned.

"It's not interfering to go pay a visit," Adni pointed out. "Just because she threw an orange at you last time doesn't mean you can't pay a visit. She *is* your sister."

Retneyabo sighed; it hadn't been just an orange, but a dozen of them, fired one right after another by a strong and accurate arm. But he rang for a servant and requested his boat; he must go into Jinka and see about this. If Hadmiel had the story straight, then something must be very, very wrong.

There were no guards at his sister's gate as Retneyabo and his bodyguard passed through; that in itself boded ill. When he knocked, he could hear a flurry of feet inside, and someone peeked out a window before the door finally opened. "What are you doing here?" demanded an old man who was in enough of a dither to completely forget his manners. He carried a sizable stick of wood in one hand, but whether for defense or punishment, Retneyabo could not guess.

"I came to speak with my sister," Retneyabo said patiently. "Kukhoosh Paun. Is she in?"

"Don't you know?" the old man asked crossly. "She's gone into seclusion. Prayer and meditation and all that." He eyed Retneyabo suspiciously. "Did you sic them on her?"

A dozen thoughts popped immediately into the kukhoosh's mind. Paun would never leave her household without making proper arrangements for its care in her absence. Paun would never go entirely into seclusion, but would keep several strings out so she could stay in touch with her business enterprises and keep firm control of her staff. Paun would only do this if she were forced. But who had the power to force her? Some other kukhoosh? One of the mazhel?

"Has Mazh Farbo gone with her?" Retneyabo inquired politely, ignoring the man's accusation. Farbo was too weak a person to perpetrate the deed, but this question might flush more information from the grudging retainer.

"Farbo, yes," the man snapped. "But it wasn't Farbo's idea, I'll tell you that! Had to be one of the others."

"One of the other mazhel?" Retneyabo prodded gently.

"They were at Mazh Tabla's house," the old man growled. "Belak was there—worthless swine. Said she sent him home—why would she do that? Dumb as an ox, that one."

Retneyabo smiled and inclined his head slightly in acknowledgment. "Well, please tell your patron I inquired after her health," he said agreeably, "and let her know that I am at her disposal, if she requires any assistance in this unique situation."

The old man snorted contemptuously and closed the door. The kukhoosh turned away, his smile frozen in place, but inside he was suddenly very afraid. If Tabla were involved in this, that meant Paun's shipment offworld had something to do with Dhrusil-matkhashi. But Paun had sent no competing expedition, of that he was sure; so whatever she had must have been suborned from his own. And if Paun had managed that—What had become of his fair, fiery sib-hinan?

Marta looked down at the stiff, ashen form of Mahanna, his face frozen in a rictus of agony, and knew that she had blundered badly. She'd led these men here in search of life, but they'd found betrayal and death; and she could not put the blame anywhere but on her own shoulders.

They'd known about the amphibious beasts since their first week here, of course: the recorders picked up one attacking an unwary nall as it stooped to drink from a muddy pool near the stream. Robinson described it as a shark with feet, for although it was only half a meter long, it had a fat torpedo-shaped body and a gaping, undershot mouth full of razor-sharp teeth. But Shipner had dubbed it a *pooka*, which he said was a mythical creature from some ancient Earth culture. The pooka, or water horse, was a sly and dangerous thing which lured unsuspecting children onto its back, then carried them to the bottom of a lake, where they drowned.

Mahanna was no child, and this pooka had not carried
him anywhere, but it had rendered him very, very dead.
He and Dakura and Habbel had been hunting along the
stream, hoping to flush a maknook or something else
edible, for their supplies were very low now and needed
to be conserved against a possible retreat over the cliffside. They knew to avoid shallow, muddy pools where a
pooka might lie hidden, but this one was larger by half
than any other specimen they'd seen, and it had lain like
a piece of driftwood among the rocks of the stream,
only half-submerged in the shallow water, as the men
wandered by. Then out it sprang and seized Mahanna's
ankle in its powerful jaws.

All three men had energy rifles, but they were set to
a broad, half-meter field which they jokingly referred to
as a "twenty-mule kick." It might have killed the pooka,
but the overspray would most definitely have snapped
off Mahanna's leg in the process. While Habbel hesitated
and Dakura dialed down his rifle to a more precise
beam, Mahanna lost his balance and fell. Before anyone
else could act, the pooka let go of his ankle and shot
onto Mahanna's abdomen, where it tore open a hole and
began feasting on his entrails. Dakura killed it with one
shot, but it was too late for Mahanna. His comrades
carried him as quickly and as gently as they could, but
he died before they reached the camp.

Marta had seen many gruesome things in her life:
She'd seen the mashed body of a careless drover who
tumbled down a rockslide into Dhin M'Tarkhna, shattered bones protruding from mangled flesh. She'd seen
Ibna relieve a man of his hand for stealing water, and
listened to the anguished moans of the victim all through
the night. She'd seen people dead of heatstroke and of
disease and of stupidity, but she had never before lost a
man who was her responsibility. It rattled her to the
very core.

Innantan custom called for the dead to be buried, but
the ground here would not yield to a shovel for more
than sixty or seventy centimeters. It was the reason their
defensive ditch was so shallow and that earthworks had

to be mounded up to set the stakes of their stockade. Marta would not suffer her man to be laid in a shallow grave that animals might later dig up; and so they chose to wrap him in a rug, weight his body with stones, and cast him off the cliff into the surging sea well away from the tiny beach. Dakura led the prayers; Marta could not. When the others headed rather hastily back to the fortified enclosure, Marta remained on the brink, staring down from the dizzying height at the churning gray waves which had swallowed up Mahanna's body.

She could feel Shipner standing just behind her, off to one side, as though he thought she might get too close to the edge and he would need to intervene. "It's my fault," she said softly.

There was a pause. "How so?" Shipner asked in his deep, gruff voice.

"I brought him here," Marta replied. "I brought him to an unknown place, with unknown dangers, and I sent him out to hunt. His safety was my responsibility."

Shipner moved closer. "You're right; it is your fault," he said flatly.

Marta turned on him with burning eyes. "Do not make fun of me!" she snapped.

"I'm not!" he snapped back, just as angry. "You're a leader—then take the bad with the good. Take the blame with the power. That's the way it works, Princess. Don't pretend to be a leader if you haven't the courage for it."

Hot tears stung in her eyes, but Marta would not cry, not in front of this man. Not when he was right. "I've never lost a man before," she hissed at him.

"Get used to it," he growled. "And unless your self-pity can bring him back, you'd better start thinking about how you're going to keep the rest of your men safe until we get out of here."

Marta didn't want to think about the others now. She didn't want to do anything but crawl into her tent and stay there until a ship arrived to rescue them all. But Shipner was right. She couldn't afford that luxury. So she brushed past him and strode back into the camp.

The others were gathered around the campfire, energy rifles in hand, murmuring together: Dakura, Habbel, Tookh. They looked up as Marta approached.

"I told you it would be dangerous when I hired you," she said bluntly. "I don't know how we could have foreseen this or avoided it. And I can't promise we won't all meet a similar fate. But right now I can't offer you a choice, either." She drew a deep breath. "Here we are, and we must make the best of it until our ship returns. Until that event, we must eat; therefore, we must hunt, and no one will be exempted from this duty. Is that understood?"

Shipner had arrived close behind her. Marta didn't even glance at him. "Dakura, give me your rifle," she commanded. "Tookh, Sab Shipner—it is our turn now. We shall try hunting to the north of the stream, where our presence has not made the local creatures so skittish."

It was not very often that Retneyabo journeyed to cities other than Jinka, but there was no help for it this time. He'd gone straight from Paun's house to his own, where there was a computer uplink, and sent a message to his agent in Mimma: please retrieve my package. But as he sorted through the complexities of the situation, he realized that this was a delicate situation and that certain aspects should not be trusted to his agent.

From a servant who had fled Paun's household, he learned that it was Robinson who had betrayed him, bringing Paun evidence of life on Dhrusil-matkhashi. How she had traced things back to Tabla, Retneyabo didn't know. But whether she had tried to blackmail the mazh, or whether he had discovered her dealings, it was clear that Mazh Tabla had taken swift and extraordinary measures to seal Paun's lips. Rumors flying around the bazaar were that Kukhoosh Paun had been caught in heresy, necessitating her seclusion. But had Paun been provably guilty, she would have been stoned to death in the streets like any other heretic. No, Tabla had gotten her out of the way, but he could not convict her falsely.

Whatever goods Robinson brought Paun had vanished with Yetta, who saw the handwriting on the wall and fled with every asset he could collect. That hardly mattered to Retneyabo, however. What mattered was that Tabla and his cohorts had been swift and ruthless in cutting off any attempt to reveal the wealth of Dhrusilmatkhashi. Would they deal so harshly with him, to whom they had promised a share in the profit? Would his silence be bought, not with merchandise, but with blood?

While he doubted the mazhel themselves could be so blatantly perfidious as to commit murder in order to keep their secret, they had clients who might be desperate enough to do so. In any case, Retneyabo could not wait patiently to see what became of Paun. His Marta, if she were still alive, was in danger the moment she returned from her expedition. If these corrupt mazhel would kidnap and imprison a kukhoosh like Paun, what would they do to Marta?

And what might they do to Retneyabo, if they feared he would expose them?

Going to Mimma accomplished two things. It put him where he could do Marta the most good upon her return. It also put him well out of Mazh Tabla's reach.

It was Tookh, of course, who taught them how foolish they had been to use up the charges in their energy rifles while hunting, to the point that two of the four weapons were always recharging. From one of the hammocks, which all the Innantans had abandoned in favor of sleeping on mats in the familiar way, he made a snare to capture animals, and he spent long hours perched on a tree limb waiting for suitable beasts to pass. Shipner taught him how to conceal the net most effectively, and then they puzzled out how to rig the snare to a bent sapling so that the hapless prey would spring the trap itself, and no one need wait in a tree. All they had to do was come by in the morning and collect their night's catch.

But Marta knew they could not subsist on only meat

and some edible fungus which grew on the trees. Their cereals and dried fruits were gone now, and the few greens and roots they'd investigated in the nearby forest provided virtually no nutrition. Anything that resembled grain would likely grow in a meadow; and other than the clifftop meadow in which they were camped, the only clearing they'd discovered bordered a small lake just to the north.

So one morning she set out with Tookh and Shipner to gather some samples of what grew in that meadow, to see if there were any plants which could provide them with necessary carbohydrates.

To Marta, stepping out of the dark, confining forest into the open meadow was a relief. She relished the sunshine and liked being able to see on all sides of her. But Shipner had the opposite reaction; an open meadow made him nervous, for he felt too exposed. He carried his energy rifle at the ready.

Tookh carried the other rifle, and made a great show of going out in front of Marta, ready to save her from whatever demons might lurk in the grass. Marta referred to the grass as being "waist-high," which made Shipner laugh at her. "That depends on how high your waist is, Princess." He chuckled. It was true; the tops of the grasses hardly brushed over their knees.

Nothing in the meadow looked very promising. It was nearly all the same fibrous stuff that grew at the camp-site—it required more calories to chew than it added to one's system. Here and there a broad-leafed plant lurked, and these Marta dug up and stuffed into her samples sack whole. Even if the leaf was not nutritious, it might be that the root was starchy enough to provide some nourishment. But of seedpods or heads of grain, which she'd hoped to find, there were none.

"How does this stuff propagate?" she demanded irritably.

"Probably by runners from the roots," Shipner replied absently, his mind on the forest at the far end of the meadow. "Terran plants and trees didn't have flowers, you know, until toward the end of the Age of Dinosaurs."

"Maybe by the water the plants will be better," Tookh suggested.

Marta and Shipner exchanged a look. Of course, he was right. Lush plants required more water.

Tookh saw their expression and grinned. "I'll go check," he volunteered, and trotted off toward the lake at the far end of the meadow.

"Be careful!" Shipner called after him. "It might be marshy at the edge. Or the pooka might be lurking there."

"I will!" Tookh called gaily, his energy rifle held out in front of him as he watched the ground at his feet.

"Do you know how many times that boy has made me feel stupid?" Marta sighed softly as she knelt to dig out another broad-leafed plant. "What a quick mind! I hope he can apply it to his schoolwork, as well."

Shipner grunted. "He makes me feel old." After a moment he added, "Then again, a lot of things make me feel old."

Marta laughed. "Oh, come, Sab Shipner. You are what—thirty-eight Standard? Thirty-nine? Even on Innanta, you can expect to reach twice that age. Or nearly."

But Shipner was shaking his head. "Most men might expect that; but I am a Nechtanite."

Marta paused in her digging to look up at him, scrutinizing his inscrutable face. "What does that have to do with it?"

"We are warriors," he said. "We do not live as long as other people."

"Even if you do not fight in wars?" she asked, for that was the only death she could imagine a Nechtanite succumbing to.

He positively glared at her. "All life is a war. But it is not war that kills Nechtanites, it is the challenges. The personal challenges."

Now Marta was truly confused. "You mean your goals? Because you set them so high?"

Shipner rolled his eyes in exasperation. "Personal combat. Duels, if you will. One warrior challenges another."

Marta's eyes widened and her jaw dropped in shock. "You mean you kill *each other?*" she shrieked.

"Not often anymore," Shipner grumbled. "Governments tend to frown on it. But the way to gain place in a Nechtanite community is to face down an elder, either in scholarship or on the field of combat. The fight may not be to the death, but a broken spirit is worse than a broken body." His hands tightened on the energy rifle, and he glared at the forest as though daring it to send some foe at him. "Old warriors who have been defeated usually leave their community, and without our community we lose touch with the Way. Many prefer to seek combat time and again until death finds them."

Marta had completely forgotten the plant in front of her. "And this is what awaits you, when you return to Valla?"

"Not right away," he hedged, avoiding her eyes by watching Tookh at the shore of the lake. "Especially not if I can bring any of this"—he waved his hand to indicate Dhrusil-matkhashi—"with me. Such credentials will keep other Nechtanite professors at bay for a long time. And within my community itself . . ." He shrugged. "This will carry weight there, too."

Tookh disappeared a moment in the tall grass and Shipner tensed; but the boy reappeared a moment later waving an uprooted plant at them. Shipner unclenched his left hand from the rifle long enough to wave back. "And I have learned," he continued, "that if I keep to the older women for mating, the younger men are not provoked as much." He slung a haughty glance in Marta's direction. "Young women are not nearly as interesting as seasoned ones, anyway," he said pointedly. "They lack creativity."

Marta's cheeks flushed, and she yanked the plant in front of her unkindly from the ground, snapping off most of the root. No one had *ever* accused her of lacking creativity! "I don't understand why you want to go back there," she said tightly, rising to her feet and searching around for other likely plants among the grasses.

Shipner's shoulders sagged just a little, but he did not

reply. Marta thought he was going to ignore her; but after a moment or two, he said, "Because it is my obligation. Who will teach the children? Who will open their minds and their hearts and their souls to Nechtan's Way? There are things you cannot learn from books, from images, so we do not even try to capture them in words and pictures. Heart must speak to heart; and where have these young warriors been, what have they done, that they can inspire children to the Way?"

And that's what he has done with Tookh, Marta realized suddenly. *And perhaps tried to do with Robinson, once. His heart has spoken to Tookh's heart, in a way I do not understand, and inspired—yes, inspired Tookh. Not to paint himself and hurl insults at people, as Shipner himself does, but to learn. The medical program, for instance. Woodscraft. Strength. And to explore.*

"It is my duty to go back," Shipner said firmly. "It is every Nechtanite's duty to train up the young warriors, and there are none here." He gave Marta a disparaging look. "You are all too fearful. That's why you are content to listen to your mazhel and have them tell you what you can and cannot do."

Marta's sympathy vanished. "Is it not just another way of learning from our elders?" she demanded. "If a mother tells her child, 'That bug is poisonous, don't touch it,' should the child doubt her and find out for itself? What is the difference between—"

Suddenly a bestial scream tore through the meadow, tightening every nerve in her body to the point of snapping. From the tall reeds and grasses at the side of the lake, a huge beast lumbered to its feet and stood on powerful hind legs, screeching its displeasure at being disturbed. The sound started in its throat and escalated through several octaves before shunting into twisting nasal tubes that pinched it into the screech Marta had heard once before.

Grendel.

It stood five meters tall, with a pointed snout sporting a set of jaws forty centimeters wide and sixty deep. The back of its crested head was also pointed, giving it an

appearance like a pickax. Its hide was a mottled green
and brown, shading to yellow across the breast, and
three meters of muscular tail thrashed back and forth,
wrecking the vegetation around it.

The scream froze them in their places—no doubt one
of Grendel's many hunting tools, to paralyze its prey
with fear. But the instant it took its first step toward
them, all three humans broke from the spell.

"Run!" Shipner thundered, propelling Marta in the
direction of the forest with a broad hand to her back.
"Run!"

Marta ran. The shortest of the three, and unarmed,
she dropped her bag of plants and plowed her way
through the sea of grasses toward the only possible sanctuary, a stand of very tall trees.

Shipner waved frantically at Tookh, who had raised
his energy rifle to draw a bead on the monster. *"Tookh,
run!"* he bellowed. The energy rifles were only good for
three maximum-strength blasts, and Shipner had a sink-
ing feeling that even three would not be enough to halt
a creature of Grendel's size.

But Tookh fired anyway. Grendel screeched again, but
it did not even hesitate as it gathered speed, thundering
around the curving shore of the lake toward Tookh.

Then Tookh ran, too. Shipner took flight himself,
looking back toward the boy as though he could somehow encourage greater speed with his eyes. But Tookh
needed no encouragement now; he ran full tilt toward
the forest.

Seeing there was nothing more to do, Shipner turned
his attention to his own escape. In no time at all he
overtook Marta. "Tookh?!" she gasped, that one word
being all the breath she could spare for her question.

"He's coming," Shipner panted back. "Run!"

They were almost to safety now, or as near as they
could get. One tree at the edge of the clearing soared a
good forty meters into the air, and its lower branches
came within two meters of the ground. Shipner glanced
back once more.

In that brief moment he knew that Tookh would never

make it. The beast was overtaking the boy; he would never reach the trees before those gruesome jaws clamped down on him, snapping through thin flesh and fragile bones. Visions of Tookh being shaken like a rag doll flashed through Shipner's mind, were shoved resolutely aside.

They had reached the tree now. In desperation, Tookh turned to fire once more at the oncoming beast, but it didn't even break stride. Shipner dropped his energy rifle and seized Marta, practically flinging her upwards toward the lowest branch. "Climb!" he ordered.

But Marta, having caught the limb and swung astraddle it, stopped and reached back toward him. "Toss me the rifle!" she demanded.

Shipner knew the futility of that. "You can't—"

"Toss me the rifle!" she shrieked.

With a growl he bent and stanched up the useless weapon, tossing it up to her. "Now, climb!" he commanded, and she did. Shipner followed.

Tookh was screaming in terror now as the creature gained on him. Marta hoisted herself through one, two more limbs and then stopped, taking up a position with her back braced against the trunk. Shipner reached a limb just below her. "Keep climbing!" he barked.

"Not yet," she said doggedly, drawing a bead on Grendel. Merciful Martyrs, but it was fast! The great tail did not thrash now, but arrowed out behind the beast, balancing the towering torso which leaned forward as it ran.

"You're wasting your time!" Shipner shouted. "It's too big! Climb!"

Marta ignored him. If she could hit the creature's eye . . . what a small eye, for such a huge beast! And it moved so fast—

Whooofff! went the first charge. Grendel trumpeted angrily but did not slow its pace.

"Marta!" Shipner growled at her. "Marta, save your charges! You can do nothing for Tookh."

"I can!" she insisted. *All-Merciful, be merciful now. Guide my aim! I will not lose another man . . .* Grendel's

eye was on the side of its head, too small a target to
begin with, and the creature was coming straight at them
so Marta could not get a clear shot. But the mouth . . .
The mouth was open in anticipation. Marta squinted
through the gunsight and targeted the beast's gaping
jaws—

Whoooffff!

Grendel shrieked its bloodcurdling scream and shook
its massive head, but it kept coming. "Climb, Marta!"
Shipner shouted again, for they were only four meters
up in the tree. He had hoisted himself past her on the
other side of the bole; now he reached for her arm to
drag her up behind him.

"One more!" she cried, tearing away from him. "I
owe him; one more, I owe him that much!" *I brought
him here. I brought this child to this place, when I knew
better* . . . Grendel was almost on top of him now, and
they were close enough that she could see Tookh's face
twisted in terror, screaming as the creature stretched out
its neck to seize its prey. Marta remembered how Mahanna had died, remembered the agony frozen on his
face—

Whoooffff!

Tookh pitched forward into the grass, his life snuffed
in an instant by the lethal charge of energy. Shipner
stared at the fallen boy and realized what Marta had
done.

Grendel was on its victim now, tearing at the body
with vicious teeth. Shipner seized Marta's arm and
hauled her upward. "Climb!" he bellowed.

Marta climbed. The spent rifle slipped unnoticed from
her hands as she clambered up through the branches,
past Shipner, up a good ten meters to safety. "Enough,"
Shipner called and she stopped, panting, trying to twist
around so she could look back.

But Shipner stood on the same branch with her, and
he blocked her with his body, pinning her against the
tree trunk. "Don't," he whispered in her ear, arms
wrapped around the trunk on either side of her.
"Don't look."

Clinging to the tree, caught between its firm support and Shipner's sheltering body, Marta began to shake. What had she done? Tears streamed unbidden down her cheeks.

"Hush, Sibna," Shipner crooned in her ear. "Hush."

But Marta could not hush. "It is our law," she sobbed, needing to understand her own actions. "It is our law that we must not prolong a creature's agony, when it is possible to give it a quick death . . ."

It took the beast only ten minutes to devour its prey; then it lumbered off to the lake for a leisurely drink of water and on into the forest beyond, having no interest in the two humans perched in their tree. Still they waited another half an hour to be sure it wouldn't return. Finally Shipner deemed it safe, and he cautiously guided Marta down through the branches to the forest floor.

She stood trembling a moment, then clutched at the tree for support as she wretched violently. Shipner waited patiently till her spasm passed, then wordlessly handed her the canteen from his belt. She swished the water around in her mouth and spat it out on the ground. Neither of them had said a word for a very long time.

"Is there . . . anything left for us to . . . bury?" she croaked.

"You don't want to see what is left," he told her quietly.

Marta wanted to protest that she couldn't just leave him there, couldn't leave the bright boy who adored her so, who trusted her, who—But she had no strength left to protest. Without so much as a whimper, she allowed Shipner to lead her away, back through the forest to their camp.

Dakura saw them coming and ran out to meet them. They had heard the beast's screams, and he started to call out his fear for their safety—then he saw Tookh was not with them. Marta stumbled along in Shipner's grasp, ashen-faced, and one questioning look at the Unbeliever told Dakura everything.

"We were too far away from Tookh to save him," was all the painted man said.

"Ah, Sibna," Dakura groaned, "he has passed into the Everlasting Presence of the Most High." Despite such brave words, his own grief was obvious. "May we all join him at the time of the All-Merciful's choosing."

"Yes, but not today," Shipner interjected. He cast an eye at the sun slipping behind the tall trees. "Let's get that aqueduct shunted over the side of the cliff and start packing up. Tomorrow morning we move our camp to the beach below."

Dakura shot Marta a questioning glance, and she managed to nod her assent; but that was as far as her participation went. Shipner led her to the fire and sat her down. There she stayed while he gave orders to her men, while they offered up prayers for Tookh's soul, while food was pressed into her hands, while darkness stole over the camp.

"Eat, Sibna," Habbel urged her gently when, after the others had finished, he saw the bowl of stewed meat still in her hands. "You need your strength."

Strength. Yes, strength. She needed strength. Slowly Marta took a bite and chewed; it tasted like sawdust. But Habbel kept urging her, another bite, and another, four, five, six— Shipner looked over her shoulder at the bowl. "Enough," he said, and Habbel went away.

The night was cool, and a wind swept over the clifftop. Shipner brought a blanket from Marta's tent and draped it around her shoulders. "Into your tent, Sibna," he whispered in her ear, raising her up and guiding her toward the shelter. "Habbel has the first watch. We will survive one more night here, and tomorrow be safe upon the shore below."

Safe. The word echoed in Marta's aching head as she stumbled into her tent and crumpled onto her knees on her sleeping mat. Safe. There was no safety on Dhrusil-matkhashi, she knew that now. There was no safety in Dhin M'Tarkhna, either, or in Jinka, or even in the protected confines of Retneyabo's seaside estate. If people like Robinson could betray them, if clever boys full of promise like Tookh could be snatched from her keeping, then safety was an illusion. When she did everything she could and things happened beyond her control, then there was no safety at all.

That's when she began to shake.

The shaking was uncontrollable and had nothing to do with the temperature in her tent. Her teeth chattered, and she could not make them stop. *I must stop,* she thought dimly, sitting huddled on her mat. *I must stop shaking like this. Sab Shipner will come in and see me and think I am weak. He will see me and despise me for being weak and frightened, and it's not that.* The blanket slipped from her shoulders unnoticed. *It's not that I'm frightened; it's just that I know at last how powerless I really am . . .*

Moments later her tent flap rustled, then raised, and Soln Shipner entered with a canteen. "Drink," he commanded.

Fluids, Marta thought numbly. *Yes, that's right. Mustn't become dehydrated, very bad to become dehydrated.* So she drank, but her hands would not stop shaking, and she sloshed the water down the front of her tunic. A plague on her hands, why did they shake so? It was over and done. Why couldn't she stop shaking?

Shipner squatted in front of her, picked up the blanket she'd dropped, and drew it around her shoulders again. She clutched it instinctively, for she thought that must be right, too, to stay warm. Maybe she was cold and didn't know it. It was possible that she shivered with a cold she was too numb to feel.

Shipner brushed the hair back from her face with callused fingers, then stroked her cheek gently with his thumb. "It will pass," he said softly.

As if to make a liar of him, her shaking grew abruptly more violent. Shipner's arms went around her, and Marta thought if not for that, she would shake apart. So there he was again, as he had been in the tree, using his strength to cover her weakness. What a coward she must think she was! He would be more than glad to be quit of her when they were finally rescued, she was sure. And she would be glad to see the last of him as well, the overbearing, arrogant oaf— That thought calmed her, and the shivering subsided somewhat.

He did not let her go immediately. "I'm all right!" she hissed. She could hiss through her teeth without that awful shake in her voice.

Shipner pulled away and looked at her with his searching brown eyes. What did he hope to see? "No one does what you have done today and is all right afterward," he told her bluntly. "Except a madwoman. You are not a madwoman."

"Oh, no," she agreed bitterly, turning her head to avoid those penetrating eyes. "Just a coward with no stomach for . . ." She couldn't even put a name to it, the thing she had done. Had to do. Never wanted to do. Couldn't ever do again . . .

His hand caught her chin and forced it back to face him. "Listen to me, young warrior," he said sternly, sincerely, his gaze riveting her. "Courage is not the absence of fear. Courage is doing what must be done, in spite of your fears."

It took a moment for the sense of that to penetrate Marta's benumbed brain, and then her mouth gaped slightly as she understood. Action *in spite* of fear . . .

Shipner saw her foggy mind lock onto the concept and felt a measure of relief. Good. She needed to come to terms with her deed, and the flood of emotion that followed. "Only a fool feels no fear," he told her. "And only a piece of granite feels nothing afterward."

"Yo-you don't sh-shake like this," she stammered by way of objection.

He let go of her chin but trailed the backs of his blunt fingers across her cheek. Why did God design so fragile a package for such a task as this? "Do you imagine I never have?" he asked.

Marta's eyes grew round with wonder. Shipner, grow weak-kneed and shaky? It was a—a falsehood, a thing he made up to make her feel better. Why would he bother to make her feel better? Why wasn't he filled with contempt for her, as she was for herself? She had *killed Tookh*. She had taken the life of another human being—to spare him, yes, but—"I was afraid to watch him die," she whispered in awful confession.

"Yet you did not let that fear paralyze you." Shipner's voice was rough with deeply felt emotion. "That is courage, Sibna. *That* is what makes a warrior."

A warrior. In Soln Shipner's vocabulary, there was no higher compliment. Marta searched his face in disbelief. A warrior? He called her a warrior?

Shipner read the amazement in her eyes and wondered how he could make her believe. She had a strength of spirit that would honor any Nechtanite community, a strength that could get her through worse than this—but how could he make her believe that? His hands cupped her face, and he brushed a kiss across her trembling lips. *Believe, Sibna.*

The shaking subsided, but still her eyes hungered for reassurance. More? Shipner hesitated, then kissed her again, more firmly this time. *Believe, Sibna. You will survive.*

· Her hand reached out for him, like a blind woman groping for a familiar object in an unfamiliar place, and her fingertips brushed his chest, just brushed him . . .

The simple touch sent shock waves through Shipner, and he knew he was lost. *Damn the wretched fire in her soul,* he thought as he gathered her in his arms and locked his mouth on hers. *She's vain and she's spoiled, and I should hold her in contempt; but she has more courage and more character than any ten men on this planet . . . or any other . . .*

They made love most urgently, the violence and loss of Tookh's death fueling their need for each other; and when they had done, Shipner wrapped the blanket around them both and they slept. Sometime during the night, a dream wakened Marta, and she cried out. Shipner soothed her with a gentleness she hadn't thought him capable of; and when she was calmer he

made love to her again. Then they both slept till Dakura's soft voice called Shipner to his turn at watch.

The ship was a fast one, as sailing vessels went;
Retneyabo admired her trim lines and clapped his oldest
son on the shoulder. "Quite a sight, eh, Efkahl?"

Efkahl grinned back at his father. He was nineteen,
with the tall frame and broad shoulders of his father,
but without the bulk Retneyabo had acquired over the
past fifteen years. "I'll bet she can put more canvas to
the wind than any other vessel in the harbor," the young
man said with enthusiasm. "With a stiff breeze, she's
probably as fast as any steamer. And I know she smells
better."

Their gear was already aboard, but Retneyabo had
stalled his own boarding until the last minute. There
were things to be done in Jinka, too, and if he was to
be absent for a time . . .

Efkahl glanced at the signal flags on the harbormas-
ter's tower. "The tide's about to turn, Father. Time for
us to get on board."

Retneyabo was glad he'd decided to bring Efkahl
along on the trip to Mimma. Not only would he be helpful in carrying out the business there, but he was good
company, as well. He was intelligent and witty and—if
he could keep his mind off girls long enough—quite sensible. It would take the sting out of a voyage Retneyabo
was not looking forward to.

Father and son started down the pier together; but as
they neared the ship, a voice hailed from the shore.

"My most worthy Kukhoosh Retneyabo."

Retneyabo slowed, stopped, and turned carefully
around. "Why, Mazh Tabla!" he exclaimed in surprise.
"What are you doing here?"

Tabla approached them with a carefully fixed smile.
"I might ask you the same question," he replied.

"Why, I am going to the Western Coast," Retneyabo
told him. "As you know, I have recently made some . . .
trade arrangements . . . with friends of yours. My invest-

ment lies in the west, and I need to go to Mimma to settle some shipping contracts regarding it."

"Come walk with me a moment," Tabla invited, taking the kukhoosh's shoulder and drawing him away from his son and his bodyguard. "It has come to my attention that you have already sent a ship to investigate your investment there."

"That was our agreement, wasn't it?" Retneyabo asked in feigned surprise. "One ship per year, you said."

"You have not said how you intend to introduce your goods into the economy," Tabla said softly. "I am interested to hear your plans."

"Now?"

"Yes, now," Tabla said firmly. "I'm sure your ship's captain will wait . . . for so important a passenger as yourself."

"No doubt," Retneyabo murmured. "Very well, then." He waved back at Efkahl. "Let us find a place where we can speak privately, and I will lay all your fears to rest."

Efkahl returned his father's wave, then sprinted up the gangplank onto the deck of the waiting ship.

CHAPTER 19

Marta gazed down the fearsome drop at the surging sea far below and changed her mind.

"We're not moving the camp," she said suddenly.

Shipner stopped in the act of tying up a bundle of supplies and turned to glare at her. "What?!"

"Leave things packed as much as possible, so we will be ready for a hasty departure, but we're not going today," she insisted. "Not unless Grendel shows up here, in this meadow."

The tattooed man advanced upon her, eyes hard. Were those the same eyes that had searched the depths of her soul last night? "If that beast shows up here, we may not have time to go over the side!" he growled.

"We must have guards in the daytime as well as the night," Marta said doggedly. "Guards ready to set fire to our trench—surely that will confuse it long enough to let us escape. We don't need to get all the way to the bottom, you know, to be safe from it; we only need to get over the side. We'll hang Tookh's ladder over the side, it will always be ready for us." The ladder was only fifty meters long, but it was enough for that purpose.

Shipner continued to glare at her; then his lips twitched in a sneer. "Are you afraid to go down the ropes, Sibna?" he mocked.

Marta was terrified of rappelling down the cliff face, or even of using Tookh's ladder. But she glared right back at the surly Nechtanite. "Once we are down there, we have lost control of our situation," she said. "If our aqueduct breaks, we are without water—"

"And I will climb back up and fix it!" he barked.

"—and we are without a ready source of firewood. Firewood is most important, Sab Shipner. Our beacon is lost; remember how hard it was to see this place the first time? How will our ship's captain find us again without a beacon? I'll tell you how. We'll make a smoke beacon. We start now, burning green wood, and we burn it day and night until we are found. We can only do that from up here."

For a long moment he continued to loom menacingly over her, but finally he straightened up and turned back to Dakura and Habbel. "She has a point," he said. "Habbel! You come with me to cut some green wood. Dakura, stand ready at that ditch with a torch. It's unlikely the beast will come this way, but we take no more chances."

Marta exhaled, surprised to find she had been holding her breath. She was still in control, she could still face down Shipner if need be and retain her authority as leader of the expedition. And she *was* right.

She had awakened the first time that day to the sound of morning prayer, but although she willed herself a dozen times to get up and join the others, her muscles refused to comply. Instead she stayed wrapped in her blankets, murmuring the prayers until she drifted back into sleep.

The second time she'd awakened it was to the sound of the camp being struck. This time the muscles in her arms and legs responded to her insistence that they move, though they ached abysmally. *From clinging to that tree,* she thought. *From tension. From terror.* Tears sprang to her eyes, but she forced them back and struggled to her feet.

With legs still weak and shaky, she stumbled to the fire and devoured what was left of the stewed meat. As she ate, she tried to sort through what had happened the day before. Parts of it seemed hazy, other parts too real. She stared at her hands and knew they had taken a human life, but she couldn't imagine how they had done that. How had that idea come to her? How had she been able to act on it? Had it been—

The right thing. Yes, it had been the right thing. It was the kind of thing she would have expected from Soln Shipner, would have hated him for doing, even though she knew it was right. In her heart Marta knew that Tookh, safe now in the Everlasting Presence of the Most High, blessed her for what she had done. But she could not bless herself. How had she become this creature, this woman who had taken a human life?

Suddenly Marta knew that it was not Tookh whom Soln Shipner had been training as a warrior: it was herself. Badgering her, mocking her, pushing her each time she wavered, each time she blundered out of her depth and tried to retreat. A dozen times he could have stepped in and taken control, but instead of doing so, he forced her to do it. Behind every insult, behind every cruel barb was a challenge: be better than that. Be better than the others. Be better than you have been before.

So, weak and shaken as she was, she had dared to face him down now over moving the camp. *You told me to be a leader, Soln Shipner, and then you made me be one. So this is what you get.*

What didn't quite fit into this startling revelation was last night.

For a brief time this morning, Marta had entertained the idea that she'd dreamed it. When she'd finally stumbled out of her tent this morning, never by word or look had Shipner acknowledged the intimate contact they'd shared. But as Marta went back over the events in her mind, she knew it had happened. How? Why? Had he suddenly fallen victim to her beauty and charm? Not likely. Not considering the state she'd been in last night. Had his previous contempt for her physical attributes been a pretense, one which broke apart under the intense emotion of Tookh's death? That was an appealing notion, but it would be egotistical on Marta's part to believe it.

No, she was fairly sure that Shipner had come into her tent in the same role he'd been playing for some time, that of the veteran warrior helping a younger one over the hurdles. He'd come, not because he desired her, but because once *he* had been a young warrior who felt the pain of that awful decision, that awful choice which claimed the life of another human being. He'd come to tell her that the unbearable could be borne, that there was light at the end of the tunnel.

So what happened after that? Had he decided she needed comfort of a more intimate nature? Had her abject misery moved him to take her out of pity, even though he felt no real attraction for her?

Pity?

Pity?!

The notion positively incensed Marta. Men had always thrown themselves at her feet, slaves to their desire for her. It was she who pitied them—occasionally—not the other way around. She used men's desire to manipulate them, sometimes to dismantle one—like Fadnar—and infrequently to build them up, like Tookh. She used it consciously, she used it cleverly, and she enjoyed every minute. Even with her husband, for whom she had the greatest respect and who was, she knew, nobody's slave, she used her sensuality to incite and inflame, because it made her feel powerful to see the response she could evoke.

How dare Shipner think she needed sexual intimacy for consolation? In point of fact, she had, but she would never have let Dakura touch her, or Habbel. She had shared herself with Shipner because he was Shipner, and because she *wanted* to—

Now, what a frightening thought *that* was. But it was true, and Marta knew it. She admired—if not his teaching style—his resourcefulness, his skills, and his fortitude in adverse conditions. She was taken with the inquisitive nature of his mind, his dedication to science and his hunger for Knowledge. Even his bizarrely painted body, at first so repulsive to her, now fascinated her as an enigma, a tale of courage and accomplishment written in a language she did not understand. It had been that way for some time, and only now could she admit it.

What bothered Marta most about last night was the

fear that it would not be repeated, that tonight she
would have to sleep alone.

For a short time Marta stood watching the men at
their wood-chopping labor; but she quickly grew restless,
needing to do something useful. She began to sort
through their supplies and realized that they ought to
have some things waiting on the beach below, in case a
precipitous departure forced them to abandon the remainder. Some barrels of water, some smoked meat, a
tent, blankets . . . By late afternoon, three tidy bundles
had been lowered over the cliffside and waited, out of
reach of the tide.

It helped restore Marta's faith in her own leadership
skills to have that done; but looking at the depleted
camp and the two remaining tents, her mind drifted
again. When she wanted to send a tent down to the
beach, Shipner had volunteered his—a logical choice
since he had the fewest personal belongings. But where
did he intend to sleep? With her? Or in with the other
two men? There was certainly enough room with Habbel
and Dakura, and this was hardly a time to be conscious
of status.

The Nechtanite had taken himself off to the farside of
the enclosure with his notes and his flatscreen, and there
he sat, hard at work on his research. Marta wanted to
wander over and ask him about the tent, but she was
too proud. No, it was better to wait and let him bring it
up. If he wanted to share her tent, let him ask.

He did not ask, of course, and when night finally fell
and Marta went off to her tent, it was alone and with
an ache in her chest. Well, so be it. If he was going to
pretend it had never happened, she would, too. She
would just lie here and think of scathing insults she could
sling at him tomorrow, until it made her calm and peace-
ful enough to sleep.

Your face could curdle milk. That was good. Too mild,
though. Marta tugged the blanket up over herself angrily. *If a tree-creeper bit you, the creeper would die.* Better, but not up to her usual invective. *Your kind cleans*

the stable with a fork and spoon. Now, that was much better. *Your mother must have fornicated with a zebra—*

The tent flap snapped open and Shipner entered with his flatscreen, research notes, and other personal items in a crate. Marta started up and sat watching as he stowed them in a corner of the tent, then went back out and came in with a blanket and sleeping mat. These he proceeded to roll out on the ground beside hers.

Marta resolved not to speak until he did, but the resolution evaporated quickly. "Are you moving in?" she asked as he tucked the foot of the blanket tidily under the sleeping mat.

"I must sleep somewhere," he pointed out, "and there's more room in this tent than the other."

Marta ground her teeth and waited. He might have asked her permission, at least. Shipner sat down on the mat and dusted off the bottoms of his bare feet with his hands.

"And is there a reason you set your mat so near to mine?" she asked, determined to make him reveal his intentions.

"Warmth," he replied without looking at her.

"Oh." Of course. How practical. Not that she was expecting any profession of unquenchable desire, but he might at least *acknowledge* that a man sleeping in a woman's tent usually implied that they were sharing more than body heat. "I hope you don't think that because of what happened last night—"

"Last night was an accident," he interrupted.

"An accident!" Marta exploded, coming to her feet in her fury. "An accident? Once might be an accident, but twice in one night is—"

"An accident," he repeated firmly. Marta clenched and unclenched her fists in mute rage. How dare he deny his desire for her! How dare he—

Then, so quickly she could never afterward say quite how he did it, Shipner knocked her off her feet, bore her back onto her sleeping mat, and pinned her there. Angry as she was, Marta felt a sudden surge of desire wash through her at the weight of his body on hers, the scent of his musk in her nostrils.

"Tonight," he announced, "is on purpose."

They came together in a volcanic passion, mouths hot, fingers clutching. It was a different kind of passion than they had shared the night before, and in many ways more familiar to Marta. There was less need in it and more want. He *wanted* her; he *desired* her. And a Nechtanite, he'd said, would only mate with someone who was his equal—

Suddenly she broke away from a kiss so hungry it threatened to steal sanity, pushing hard on his shoulders to hold him off. "Wait, wait!," she panted. "Your knife."

Shipner drew back in surprise, staring down at her.

"Give me your knife," she demanded breathlessly. "You said . . . a Nechtanite warrior always gives his woman a knife to hold . . . to show he does not force her . . ." *Am I your equal or not, Soln Shipner?*

A twitch of a smile tugged at the corners of Shipner's mouth; then he forced it away and solemnly drew his wicked-looking blade from its sheath. With a deliberate hand he thrust it into the ground near her head. "Can you reach it there?" he asked.

Marta lifted a hand to touch its hilt. It was slightly damp from the sweat on his palm. Strange custom. Why did it excite her so?

Then her hands flew around his neck and yanked his mouth back down to hers, hungry and demanding. This was not a time for philosophical questions.

"And Marta was sad," Hassan told his sympathetic listeners, "that the All-Powerful had taken the boy Tookh from her, and she wept for his loss. But she took consolation that he stood in the Everlasting Presence of the Most High, where all Knowledge and all Beauty are granted to the Faithful."

Hassan's voice grew thick momentarily, and he did not dare look at Ari. It had not been a year since Ari's elder sister Pennera had been killed in a shuttle accident. The words of assurance from the old tale were oddly comfort-

*ing now. It was good to think of Pennera having all
Knowledge and Beauty forever; it was good to know that
even the most faithful of the Children like Marta endured
such losses.*

*Hassan sipped water from his canteen and continued.
"But when the Most High inflicts hardship upon his Children, he does not leave them desolate . . ."*

In most of his daylight activities, Shipner gave little
sign of any change in their relationship. He still goaded
Marta, still dropped insults with a deft hand, still pursued his research with hardly a glance to spare for her.
Marta rather preferred it that way. She, too, had work
to do. Shipner's detachment gave her time to study the
habits and needs of her animal specimens, so they might
continue to flourish in captivity, and to record on paper
some of the many things she had seen and learned here.

In two things, though, his behavior was different than
before. One was that, somewhere along the line, he'd
begun calling her Sibna instead of Princess. Marta didn't
know exactly when that had happened, but when she
realized it she felt a certain thrill. Even in the privacy
of their tent, even when he mocked her, he called her
Sibna. Whatever else might happen from here on out,
Marta knew she had his respect.

The other was that he became openly protective any
time she wanted to venture outside the stockade.
There had been no sight or sound of Grendel since the
attack on Tookh at the lake, yet Shipner insisted on
accompanying her anytime she wanted to cut green
wood or ferns in the near forest, or even gather bugs
from the meadow to feed a small insectivore they had
caught in a trap. Marta didn't mind this protectiveness,
however. His presence was reassuring, even as her fears
dwindled and her curiosity once more took hold.

Three weeks after Tookh's death, the three of them
were cutting green wood for their fire, much further into
this part of the forest than they had been before. Having
harvested most of the ferns, saplings and low branches
in the near forest, they were now pressing further into

the woods to get the moisture-rich fuel they needed to keep their fire smoky.

Shipner stood guard while Dakura and Marta did the cutting. They had loaded enough for several days' supply onto a travois, and Dakura was lashing it down when something in the undergrowth caught Marta's eye. She wandered over to investigate it and found two dried, straight stalks similar to the canes they had seen in the interior. It was the straightness of them which had drawn her attention, where the rest of the undergrowth was a twisting snarl. Marta bent to examine the stalks, which were gray and split. They were *exactly* like the canes downriver. What were they doing here, so far from the stream?

Then she realized that one tangle of dried vines wasn't just snagged on the canes—it was woven. The construction was old and brittle from exposure, with large sections broken away, but to Marta it looked like a pack of some kind, with the two canes for uprights and the vines woven basketlike to them.

"Sab Shipner," she called softly, "what do you make of this?"

"Dakura—keep guard," Shipner instructed, handing off the energy rifle before he strolled to where Marta stood. He examined the thing carefully, first with his eyes, then by prodding a few of the vines with his blunt fingers and tugging gently at a cane. "Several seasons old, at the least," he said. "Or several years old, perhaps. I don't know how quickly this kind of plant decays."

"This is a traveler's pack," Marta said pointedly, watching his face to see how he would react.

Shipner poked at it again, but idly now, which meant his brain was racing at high speed. "Some of those Innantans who disappeared here," he suggested.

"No Innantan would make a pack this tall," she told him, for even broken, the canes were still more than a meter and a half long.

Shipner scowled. "There are tall Innantans," he reminded her. "Your husband, for instance."

"This is not a style of weaving used anywhere in Innanta," she insisted. "Even children know how to weave better than this."

"Perhaps it was someone who did not know how to weave until he had to," Shipner countered with a note of impatience in his voice. But his expression did not look convincing, or convinced.

"I want to look around a little," she said, her eyes still on his face. She had long since stopped thinking about the tattoos, and now she could see traces of emotion there. In this case, he struggled with himself: her safety, versus his own curiosity.

"Dakura," he called back, "stay close to us. We want to explore a little."

They poked carefully through the undergrowth for several meters in all directions, but they found nothing more unusual than a tree trunk with unexplained gouges in it. The wounds were old and scabbed over, and there was no way of knowing what kind of animal or event had caused them. All the same, Marta had Shipner boost her up into the tree and she checked the lower branches, hoping to find some other evidence of the packmaker's passage. Alas, there were no convenient artifacts, no letters carved in the wood or tufts of hair caught on a twig.

They took the woven thing back to camp with them, where Shipner took it immediately to his research area across the compound. There he began a most intense scrutiny of the construct, leaving the others to deal with unloading the firewood. Marta let him play with it until evening; then she went and squatted beside him in the gathering dusk, peering down once more at the crude weaving.

"You know," she said casually, "the creature I saw in the interior, the one with the necklace, I'd say it was at least two meters tall. Tall enough to wear such a pack."

Shipner touched the canes, which extended above and below the woven portion by forty to fifty centimeters. After a long moment he asked, "Did it have a tail?"

Marta struggled to remember. "I couldn t tell," she said finally. "It was facing toward me, with its back to the woods." She looked up into his face. "Does that matter?"

"No," he admitted. "Just—construction like this could accommodate a tail, with the canes extending down here to balance the weight over the rump, while the pack rode up higher."

Marta looked out over the ocean for a time, not minding the silence between them, letting her thoughts drift. Innanta was so close out there, and yet so distant from this place. A different world, really, a different culture . . . After a while she turned around and sat looking back at the woods, cloaked now in darkness. Did yet another world, another culture, lie beyond this fortress of trees? Or within it? Might there be something—someone—watching them even now?

"I will come back to this place, Soln Shipner," she told him quietly. "I want to go home, to rest and eat and be free of my cares for a time, but I will come back here. No command by a human being, no matter how holy, will stop me."

He said simply, "Sibna, I never doubted it."

Three days later a ship appeared on the horizon, and Marta shrieked with joy as it approached. It was the same one which had brought them hither more than four months ago. They released a number of animals Shipner had been keeping for his research and lowered the rest over the side of the cliff in their cages, a precious cargo to be taken back to Innanta to prove the existence of multiple complex life-forms on Dhrusil-matkhashi. "We shall have to have a new school at the College," Marta crowed to Shipner. "The School of Complex Zoological Life-forms at the College of Indigenous Life."

"Too cumbersome," Shipner opined. "School of Quasi-saurian Studies would be simpler."

The term reminded her of Robinson, and Marta wondered if he had made it onto that freighter with his research notes and his specimens. Oddly, she found she did not care much. Her need for vengeance had waned as her affair with Shipner washed away the sting of Robinson's betrayal. With the appearance of the ship on the horizon and the prospect of a speedy return to Jinka, that need faded almost entirely.

Habbel volunteered to rappel down first, to help guide the bundles of goods as the others lowered them away. But in spite of Shipner's careful instruction, Habbel landed wrong on the third bounce, smacking his foot up against the granite and breaking an ankle. Shipner climbed down Tookh's ladder and loaded the injured man on his back; then he took over the rope and rappelled down the rest of the way. The ship had sent a small boat ashore, and its crew loaded the goods while the Nechtanite climbed back up the cliff, for he needed to coach the other two down.

There were only two ropes and two rappelling harnesses, however, and the sun was arcing westward, threatening an early darkness in the shadow of the cliff. So after only a brief rest, Shipner took Marta on his back while Dakura wore the other harness, and together they rappelled their way downward.

It was both terrifying and exhilarating for Marta, dropping through the air, landing with a thud and springing back out into empty space again, dropping, bouncing, dropping, while Shipner belayed the line under his thigh. "Will you teach me to do this, another time?" she asked as they sailed through the air.

Shipner laughed. "Just remember, to rappel down, you must first climb up!"

Marta grinned and hugged herself close to him, irrationally happy in his laughter which was, for once, neither derisive nor condescending. Of course, he would teach her. He would teach her many things.

When at last they were gratefully installed on the ship with their cargo, the captain explained that she had been at sea when Hagiath got a frantic message from Kukhoosh Retneyabo to retrieve his research party. The agent had sent another boat, but the captain and crew didn't really know what they were looking for; after two weeks they returned empty-handed. By then this captain was back in port, and she felt sure she could find the place even without the radio beacon to guide her. All the same, she had been glad to see the column of smoke which marked the expedition's encampment on the cliffs.

That night the adventurers told their tales to an astonished crew, as they sailed by moonlight for Mimma. Marta saw in their eyes, though, that these veterans of the sea and its tall tales doubted the existence of monsters large enough to eat a man. It brought tears stinging to her eyes, and she wondered what they would think if they knew it was she that killed Tookh, and not Grendel. When the weary travelers were finally allowed to settle down for sleep in the darkened hold, Marta clung tightly to Shipner and wept into his shoulder for so many things lost: Tookh's loyalty, her faith in Robinson, her own innocence. Surprisingly, Shipner offered no comment on this burst of emotion, but only held her close and was blessedly silent.

It was with great delight the next afternoon that Marta spotted Retneyabo's elder son Efkahl waiting on the pier in Mimma. "Efkahl! Efkahl!" she cried joyously. "What are you doing here? Tell me what's been going on! Is your father with you?"

Efkahl, who had spent most of his life in the role of younger brother to Marta, caught her in a bear hug and whirled her around. "Much has been happening which I must tell you," he agreed. "Father wanted to come, but at the last minute he was . . . detained."

Marta didn't like the sound of that. "Detained?"

"We'll have to put our two stories together to make sense of it, I think," he said cautiously. "But it can wait. Are you all right?"

"I'm fine," she assured him. "And Sab Shipner is fine, but Robinson abandoned us, and Lekish; and then Mahanna was killed and Tookh—"

But Efkahl was beckoning the captain to join them, and he said to Marta, "Not here. I need to get you and your expedition transferred to another vessel as quickly as possible. Rumors will fly the moment this crew comes ashore, and we must be well away by then."

Marta didn't like the sound of that, either. But before

evening they were once more at sea. By lamplight in
Efkahl's cabin, the five of them were able at last to piece
together the events of Robinson's betrayal, his flight
offworld, and Paun's ensuing imprisonment. Marta
learned for the first time of the perfidy of certain mazhel
in keeping the wealth of Dhrusil-matkhashi a secret.
"But they are holy ones," she objected thinly. "How
could they perpetuate an untruth?"

Shipner snorted but said nothing.

"My father says their motives were . . . altruistic, in
the beginning," explained Efkahl, but it was clear from
his careful tone that he did not altogether share this
sentiment. "They did not want to see the Faithful suborned by an easy life, grown fat and lazy through abundance. But it was they who were suborned." Efkahl
grimaced. "My father is . . . charitable in his assessment,
as befits a man of his high character."

"And where is he now?" Marta asked worriedly. "Do
you think those—I will not call them mazhel, they are
unworthy of the term. Do you think those men have
swept him out of sight, as they did Paun?"

Efkahl laughed, if a bit hollowly. "My father is not
easily swept where he does not wish to go. His instructions to me were, if the mazhel detained him, I was to
carry out his mission to Mimma and return with you and
your cargo to our estate. He will meet us there, if he
is able. If not . . ." Efkahl shrugged vaguely. "I have
other instructions."

Marta did not bother to ask what the instructions
were; she knew she would not be told. He was so much
like his father, was Efkahl: the same warm, genial exterior, the same iron core. Shipner was right. Courage
meant doing what needed to be done, even if you hated
it; and both Retneyabo and his son had that quality in
abundance.

As they departed Efkahl's cabin, Marta caught Shipner's hand. "Come share my cabin tonight," she whispered.
"We are still several days' journey from my husband."

In one of those tender gestures that still surprised her,
Shipner carried her hand to his lips, and then cupped its

palm to his tattooed cheek. "I think not, Sibna," he said
softly. "That young man in there is your husband's Presence; it is best if we respect it as though it were the
kukhoosh himself." Then he let go of her and padded
away to his own cabin, and that was that.

They sailed along the southern coast but out of sight
of land; Efkahl apparently feared interception and was
giving no casual observers a chance to report their position. They had a bad moment when a steamer appeared
to port, also bound eastward and capable of overtaking
the sailing vessel. But their captain turned them further
out to sea, and the steamer did not follow.

Shipner, who had passed most of the outbound voyage
on deck, drinking in the sea and the wind, spent most
of the return voyage secluded in his cabin with his research. He read and sketched and analyzed and com-
piled and wrote and sketched some more. Once he
brought his flatscreen up on deck and set it up, presumably downloading something from the communications
satellite orbiting the planet. Marta had wished more than
once that the footprint of that satellite reached as far as
Dhrusil-matkhashi—then they might have used Shipner's
flatscreen to call for help. But the satellite signal was
sketchy even on the Western Coast, so Dhrusil-
matkhashi was out of the question.

For the most part, Shipner continued to behave
toward Marta as he did toward everyone else: he was
still insulting, contemptuous, and argumentative. But
now and then he would slip into his professorial mode,
and they would discuss their findings on the continent,
or speculate on the evolution of life there. They had left
the woven pack behind, for Shipner insisted it would
acquire undue significance if brought to Innanta. But he
had sketched it thoroughly before leaving it, and Marta
often saw him puzzling over the sketches.

On the day they were due to reach port, though, he
approached her with a notebook full of very different
sketches. "Look at these," he directed.

Marta looked at a set of half a dozen heads and two

or three bipedal bodies. The bodies were definitely quasi-saurian, but with proportions and in postures unlike traditional theropods. One had a short neck and correspondingly short tail, giving it a more upright posture. Another had a slender, graceful body, long hind legs, and short arms with flexible, clawed digits, but no elbow joints. The heads were always large in relation to the bodies.

It was the faces, however, that caught Marta's eye.

Shipner had combined features in a variety of ways: large, round eyes in an oval face with a high brow and tiny earflaps; smaller eyes and low brow with flaring nostrils in a protruding muzzle; tilted eyes over a ridged nose with hooded nostrils and ears that were mere openings on the sides of the head. Some sketches were profile, but most were frontal views. One showed small fangs, half of them sported a modest crest, but all had front-facing eyes and a large cranium.

"Weaving would require biocular vision," Shipner said by way of comment. "And opposable digits, though three would work as well as five. Claws maybe, maybe not, but length of the arms would logically increase, because if you're using your hands to do things, a longer arm gives you a better survival chance. And a larger brain-to-body ratio would be required for higher functioning, certainly—therefore a larger brain case than we have seen."

Marta shuffled from one sketch to another and back again. "These are . . . quasi-saurians?" she asked numbly.

"They are what quasi-saurians might evolve into, if they were on a path to sentience," Shipner explained. "Possibly. Just speculation, of course—I would really need to study the fossil record and determine what mutations have been successful, which traits are associated with higher functioning." He reached to take the sketches back from Marta. "Dreaming on paper, you might say."

But Marta snatched the notebook back out of his reach and continued staring at the drawings, first one face, then another, then the bodies. Finally she chose two out of the pack. "Large eyes like this one," she told

Shipner, "and a crest more like this other. The rest I couldn't tell you, it was too far away. Neither of the bodies is right." She flipped back to the full-body sketches. "The neck was longer than this one, but shorter than that. The general tone of the body is right here, very willowy and graceful, but even with a shorter neck it wouldn't be quite right. Less serpentine, I think. But I didn't see it for that long."

Shipner reached for the notebook again, and this time she let him have it. "We don't know that what you saw was intelligent," he reminded her.

Marta snorted. "It probably wonders if *we're* intelligent," she countered, then glanced at Shipner. "Especially you."

Shipner broke into a pleased grin, as though she had just paid him the highest of compliments. "Ah, but at first look, Sibna, I am the most likely to be intelligent," he replied, gesturing broadly at his looping braids. "What witless beast can adorn itself in such a magnificent style?"

Kukhoosh Serai, Mazh Kummel, and Mazh Tabla were waiting in a dimly lit office near the port, in the back of a warehouse belonging to Serai. Elkniar was not there, of course. Elkniar pleaded ill health, but in fact he was suffering an attack of conscience not unlike the one Nrin had suffered two decades ago when he bowed out of the arrangement. The blind old mazh would keep silent, for he knew the disastrous consequences if it should leak out that the Holy Ones had misled the Faithful about the riches of Dhrusil-matkhashi. Elkniar would not do that to Innanta, to the Children of the Second Revelation who struggled so diligently to know and do the will of the Most High.

Neither, it seemed, would Retneyabo. Upon learning of Paun's dealings, the trio wondered at first if the grasping merchant had conspired with his sister to import more than they'd agreed from the western continent. That would have been an easy treachery to deal with. When it became clear, however, that she had acted in one-upsmanship, planning to reveal the secret of Dhrusil-matkhashi for her own personal glory, they began to wonder if Retneyabo wouldn't do the same. Had he bargained falsely with them? Instead of quietly selling the goods he reaped across the sea, would he expose them? When Tabla had caught him at the docks last month, ready to board a fast ship out of town, they truly did not know.

But Retneyabo had reassured them by assisting in their effort to learn where Paun had stashed the creatures and the recordings the Unbeliever had brought her. Retneyabo's resources for such an investigation were, after all, more extensive than those of a holy man, or even of a kukhoosh like Serai, who concentrated on keeping a low profile. When the items had been located last week, Retneyabo himself had provided the barge on which they were loaded, sent out to sea, and scuttled. So much for Paun's plans.

Tonight would provide the final proof. Tonight Retneyabo's own ship arrived, and its cargo, too, would be quietly disposed of. After all, the research expedition had been launched before Retneyabo had struck his deal with them for a share of the profits, and there had been no way to call it back. He had done what he could in sending his son to intercept the returning scientists and their data, hurrying them here to Jinka before they could reveal what they had found. Retneyabo lost a substantial investment in divesting himself of the expedition; but it was nothing compared to what he would gain in the years ahead. And tonight they would bring him a little extra compensation for his trouble.

A knock at the door made Kummel jump, and Tabla frowned. Kummel did not have the disposition it required to bear such pressures as these. Retneyabo was going to be a better business partner, that was clear. Tabla privately wished Kummel would withdraw as it seemed Elkniar was about to do, and leave himself to manage a few kukhooshel in the arrangement. Kukhooshel didn't suffer these attacks of philosophical doubt.

"The ship is coming in now," came a quiet voice.

Tabla sighed and rose from his cushioned chair. "Bring the two women," he instructed Serai, who opened the door to an adjoining room and beckoned to two robed figures inside. The women joined them, and all five filed out of the offices and down the deserted street to the wharves, flanked by several of Serai's men.

The ship was just gliding into its dock as they arrived on the pier. Tabla half expected to hear bellows and snorts from below, a cargo of live beasts from the great river valley of Dhrusil-matkhashi, but all was silent save for the shouts of the sailors and the creaking of wood and rope. Retneyabo's son Efkahl appeared at the gunwale, and a gangplank was lowered for the guests to board. Serai's guards waited, two on the pier and a third at the head of the gangplank.

Efkahl escorted them to the bow of the ship, where Retneyabo awaited them, then stood off some twenty paces to make sure none of the crew came within hearing of the group. "Good evening, Mazh Tabla, Mazh Kummel," Retneyabo greeted them. "And Serai, my colleague. As I promised, I have brought you the fruits of my research expedition to Dhrusil-matkhashi."

"We see nothing and want to see nothing," Tabla snapped. "Let us sign the contract and be gone. It is not wise to be seen skulking about like this."

Retneyabo laughed his hearty laugh. "You worry too much, Mazh Tabla," he chided. "There is no one about the harbor at this hour—certainly no one who would be believed if he claimed to have seen strange creatures on a boat from Dhrusil-matkhashi."

"Here is the girl," Tabla persisted, refusing to waste time. "I attest to the fact that she is Elkniar's granddaughter, and her mother is here with the contract. I trust you have pen and ink for signing."

"I do," Retneyabo said easily. "But let me see her first. You understand, of course," he continued, "that I am not unsatisfied with your original offer, which was permission to take one boatload of goods per year from the wealth of Dhrusil-matkhashi, and the possibility of bringing in occasional manufactured goods from offworld; but—" He paused as the girl pulled back her hood and was prodded forward into the moonlight by her mother. She was thirteen, the perfect age for a sib-batnai; Retneyabo took her chin in his hand to study her face. "Ah, lovely," he sighed. "Not the fireball my Marta was, to be sure, but I am a man of varied tastes. As I was saying, I found your original offer quite generous," he told Tabla, "but if I am to lose Marta now, it seems only fair I should be compensated, don't you agree?"

Tabla blinked. "Lose Marta?" he asked. "No one has asked you to give up your sib-hinan, Retneyabo." The marriage contract was just to bind them all a little closer together.

The kukhoosh feigned great surprise. "Serai, didn't you tell him?"

Kukhoosh Serai turned pale in the moonlight. "They are holy ones," he whispered. "It was unnecessary to advise them of such unpleasant details."

"What is this?" Kummel demanded. "What unpleasant details?"

Retneyabo smiled benignly. "If you knew my sib-hinan," he explained, "you would know she is not one to be quiet about having discovered Dhrusil-matkhashi to be a rich land full of green and growing things, fertile for grazing and farming. There is only one way to silence her."

"No!" Kummel croaked harshly, and Tabla echoed him.

"No. We will take her away for you," Tabla said resolutely. "Spin what tale you want, but we will not be party to the taking of a human life."

"What would you do with her?" Retneyabo asked gently. "Lock her up, as you have my sister, and say that she is deranged? I doubt that excuse will work twice. Rumors will spread which you cannot afford to have abroad. Take her off to work on one of the islands where you smelt the iron ore from Dhrusil-matkhashi? You underestimate her resourcefulness badly; she is not likely to remain silent or secluded. No, Serai has suggested the only real solution. He suggested I accuse her of breaking her marriage contract by fornication with the Unbeliever within my own house. The law allows me to execute them both for that."

"No!" Tabla barked in agitation. "No! I will not be party to this. False testimony and murder—no! It is too much. It cannot be condoned." He felt the sea breeze cold on his sweating forehead. Murder! What was Serai thinking?

"How so?" Retneyabo mocked. "You stand back and allow our schools to teach that Dhrusil-matkhashi is un-inhabitable, when you know that is false. How is your silence in allowing that falsehood different from this? If one child dies for lack of an operation, when the metal for surgical tools lies buried in Dhrusil-matkhashi, is that not the same as murder?"

Kummel joined the protest. "No, Retneyabo, no! We are bringing the iron ore in, gradually, as much as we can without disrupting the economy. How many would die if we allowed economic chaos? We do not murder people by withholding the knowledge of the Land Beyond our Gates. We protect them. We protect the Faithful, not only from economic chaos, but from the corruption that riches would bring. This is the will of the Most High. But to take the life of your sib-hinan to ensure her silence—that would be a sin, a great sin, and we cannot be party to it."

Retneyabo looked at Mazh Kummel, and the mazh was surprised to see tears in the kukhoosh's eyes. "Thank you for that," he said huskily. "I truly did not know how blind you had become, or to what lengths you would go."

Tabla's hackles rose in alarm. "What? What's this? Do you presume to test us? What are you up to, Retneyabo?"

The kukhoosh nodded to his son; Efkahl came forward and bent down to grasp a handle cut into the deck. He lifted it, revealing a hatch to the lower deck. "I presume nothing, honored ones," Retneyabo said softly. "But I wished to consult with other holy ones, as our law permits, to see if they agreed with your assessment. In order to do that, I needed credible witnesses to the truth." Faces began to appear below, pale, astonished faces looking upward in the moonlight. "So I invited the Council of Kukhooshel to accompany me here tonight, from my estate up the coast. It is time to lay this matter before all the mazhel, to see if their wisdom is the same as yours."

CHAPTER 20

"And so they were brought back from Dhrusil-matkhashi," Hassan concluded. "But before departing that shore, Marta spoke both a blessing and a curse; and these were her words:

"'Blessed be this Land Beyond our Gates,

"'And all the creatures who dwell therein.

"'And blessed be those who walked it before us,

"'The Cousins, the Builders of the Leaf Houses,

"'For it is to them that the Most High has given this green place,

"'And all the fruits therein.

"'But woe to the Unbeliever

"'The faithless one,

"'Who left us to die in this place.

"'Let the flesh wither from his bones,

"'And let him be cut off forever

"'From the Children of the Most High.'"

Cecil Robinson leaned back in his comfortable chair and frowned at the official notification. It had arrived electronically only last week, a year and three months after he'd left Dray's Planet, and this printed copy had come over from Mail Services today. It stated that he was under death sentence from the mazhel of Innanta; and while it posed no real threat to him here on Melius, it disturbed him. Two of Marta's expedition had died on Dhrusil-matkhashi after he and Lekish fled, and the mazhel were blaming him for those deaths. Damn it! It wasn't he who smashed the beacon! Did they know that?

What disturbed him most, though, was that the notice of death sentence didn't say which two people had died.

With a heavy sigh, he started to toss the plastic sheet in the direction of his recycle shoot, but then he stopped. He had no tangible remembrance of Marta: no photo, no lock of hair, not even a scrap of paper. The notice was something, anyway: a bizarre souvenir for the most bizarre affair of his life. He laid it aside to file somewhere. Later.

Now he turned his attention to the day's e-mail, full of much gladder tidings. There was a request from the Ashdod Foundation for his personal information, for they were preparing a portfolio on each candidate for this year's Ashdod Prize. There were messages from colleagues at six major universities, a request from *Galaxy Today* for an interview, and invitations to deliver keynote addresses at three interstellar conferences. At the very bottom of the list was a message from his dean. Robinson smirked a little and punched it up.

"Cecil, dear boy!" Clarisse Hahn's hologram cooed patronizingly. Before his trip to Dray's, the woman hardly knew his name, gazing coldly past him at faculty meetings; now she called him regularly, batted her crinkled eyes, and called him by hackneyed pet names. "I've just had the most exciting news!" the hologram carried on. "The Interplanetary Foundation for Life Sciences is negotiating with the Innantan government to send a research expedition to Dray's Planet, and they're waving around absolutely enormous figures for grant money! I'm pulling together a proposal right now, requesting a spaceship laboratory and ever so much more. We can get an obscene salary for you, and fund a dozen graduate assistants and—oh, but call me back when you get in, we'll go over the details. If we land this one, the University will be kissing our feet for ten generations!"

Robinson's smirk faded and he glanced again at the official notification from Innanta. He wondered what Dean Hahn would say when he told her that he couldn't return to Dray's; that in fact, putting his name anywhere on the proposal would probably cause the whole project to be blackballed by the Innantan government. Another sigh escaped him as he leaned his elbows on his desk and rubbed his tired eyes.

Well. Water under the bridge. Robinson straightened up again and opened his calendar to see how many of the speaking engagements he could fit into his schedule. The dates for the Ashdod Awards Ceremony were already blocked out, so he wouldn't inadvertently schedule a conflict. The prize was his, he knew it. Soln Shipner's treatise on indigenous Drayan species had just been released yesterday, and it only served to corroborate Robinson's paper. The victory was clearly Robinson's.

With an effort, Robinson levered himself to his feet and walked painfully over to the coffeepot. The leg braces were invisible beneath his trouser legs, and a vast improvement from the stretcher on which they'd had to carry him off that damned privateer. Nowadays he could sit and stand with no problem, walk short distances with the braces, and work for six or seven hours before his back started to ache abysmally. The doctors assured him that after another eighteen months of physical therapy, he'd come back to almost 90 percent of his previous muscle strength. As long as he worked at the grueling exercises daily.

Robinson opened his bottle of painkillers and popped two, swallowing them down with coffee. Yes, as long as he kept up his therapy, four months from now he might even be able to walk the hundred meters from his office to the teleconference center to personally accept his Ashdod Prize . . .

Marta stared at the preserved body of the dinka-chak in its glass exhibit case in the College of Indigenous Life. "You started it all," she told the little creature softly. "You and your three-bone hip joint and your lizardlike qualities, you're the one who sent us scurrying to find a paleontologist, or something near, scurrying to the Western Desert where we heard tales of Dhrusil-matkhashi. Because we couldn't explain you, we found a bountiful land beyond our gates, but darkness in our own hearts."

And it has changed me, she thought. *Because of my exposure to these Unbelievers and the Land Beyond the Gates, I have changed. I am not the lighthearted girl who toyed with men and played at being a wilderness guide. I have a purpose now. I have a mission.*

More than a year had passed since Marta's return from Dhrusil-matkhashi, and when the winter rains broke, she would set out once again for the new continent with a larger expedition, better equipped, and by the route those clandestine traders had used for decades to access the mouth of the great river. This time they would have geologists, zoologists, botanists, cartographers, and a host of other scientists truly to explore the new land and its varied life-forms. They would also have the blessing of the mazhel, and the backing of the entire University of Innanta.

The mazhel had been aghast to learn of the corruption and deceit in their midst. But rather than simply casting out the guilty ones and leaving behind a gaping wound, they declared a full month of atonement for all mazhel, regardless of whether they knew of the deception or not. For if the Evil One could corrupt two or three such holy ones, who was above iniquity? The mazhel publicly confessed the sin of silence which had been maintained, and collectively begged forgiveness of the Faithful.

The Children of the Second Revelation were stunned to find that those they had trusted so implicitly had proven false. They beat their breasts and wailed to the Most High, for if holy ones could be false, what hope was there for ordinary people such as they? The *scorokhel,* who led worship in the assemblies, called the entire nation to join in the month of atonement, fasting and prayer which the mazhel observed, and this they did while commerce and industry ground to a halt.

During this time, the scorokhel preached to the Faithful, not only on the failings of all humankind to serve the Most High in perfection, but also on the lessons to be learned from this scandal: be ever watchful for Evil, not only beyond the gates of Innanta, but in its very heart. To believe that Knowledge makes anyone, even a

mazh, above temptation, is to open the door to sin. As
the Holy Ones did not hesitate to repent and make
atonement, let no man, woman or child fear to confess
sin, repent, and make restitution. By this means, and this
means only, will we keep ourselves from contamination.

The Faithful heard, and at the close of the month of
atonement, they returned to their work a little humbler,
a little wiser, but cleansed of anger and reproach. They
gave thanks to the All-Merciful that he had given them
leaders who were wise enough to know when they had
erred, and to confess rather than conceal their sin. Life
for the common person got quickly back to normal.

But for those who made policy—the mazhel and, by
virtue of their influence, the kukhooshel—things changed
radically. While the Holy Ones debated whether or not
to withhold knowledge of Dhrusil-matkhashi's life-forms
from other worlds, the opening of a new continent for
exploitation brought ceaseless bickering among the merchants as to who should have the right to mine its riches
and profit from its land. Marta had gone flying to Retneyabo in protest, fearing the land would be despoiled
haphazardly as it had been on other worlds, where
profiteers fought and gouged to seize what they could of
this treasure.

The kukhoosh, of course, was three steps ahead of
her. In the Council of Kukhooshel he proposed, fought
for, and won a moratorium on taking advantage of any
more of the resources until an orderly plan could be
drawn up and agreed upon. Then he pushed through
another proposal that the plan not be drawn up until the
continent could be adequately explored, mapped, and
evaluated, its resources determined, its hazards addressed,
and—here he cited the data Marta supplied him about
disastrous consequences on other worlds—the needs and
requirements of its existing ecosystem understood.

Because they were there, Marta was sure: intelligent,
sentient creatures; and Dhrusil-matkhashi belonged to
them.

All these proposals and resolutions, of course, were
strictly unofficial, as were all the dealings of the Council

of Kukhooshel. But not even Paun—more vociferous and bitter than ever since her captivity—would dare break faith with her colleagues. Especially not after the mazhel blessed the efforts of the Council and called them "well-advised."

The newly chastened Holy Ones also announced, after a time, that they would not forbid exporting information about Dhrusil-matkhashi to other worlds. Such silence was an impediment to Knowledge, and it created reprehensible situations such as Robinson's betrayal of his research party, which had caused the deaths of two people. Thus, when Robinson's landmark paper on quasi-saurian life-forms inevitably passed through the Portal, the Innantans had already reconciled themselves to the information's release.

They had been immediately deluged with requests from research institutions who wanted to explore the new continent. This could not be allowed, of course, but such institutions were promised full reports from Innanta's own research teams. To make sure this promise could be fulfilled promptly, and avoid unwanted attempts by Unbelievers to do it for them, the mazhel asked the University of Innanta to form a new college: the College of Quasi-saurian Studies. It was for them that Marta was leading a scientific expedition to the continent's interior in the spring.

Someone entered the exhibit hall behind Marta now, and she glanced up to see Retneyabo approaching, flanked as usual by his bodyguard. She stirred from her reverie and smiled with pleasure to see him. "Good afternoon, patron. I was just thinking that we will need a much bigger exhibit hall soon."

Retneyabo laughed his hearty laugh. "I agree, my sharp-eyed hawk, but that is now up to the provost and the Board of Regents. They have made the College of Quasi-saurian Studies an interdisciplinary project, so that many kukhooshel may share in the glory of its patronage—and the expense."

Marta came to stand in front of him, reveling as always in the impressive bulk of him towering over her own tiny frame. Whatever else happened in her tumultuous life, he would always be her patron, her support, the foundation from which she could leap to grand adventures. It was a thing she would never cast away, not even for Soln Shipner.

Shipner. Arrogant, presumptuous, maddening man! It had been strange, indeed, working so close to him in the months following their return but parting from him at the close of each day to go to her student apartment alone. The worst part was, it didn't seem to affect him in the least! There was not one shred of sorrow or regret in his eyes when she left him, no sighs or lingering looks or whispered wishes. It seemed he had been content to enjoy her for a time in Dhrusil-matkhashi, but that he was just as content to stay celibate in Jinka.

Once Marta had bemoaned the way her travel companions sulked and sniped about being cut off when they returned from their journeys, but what she would give to hear just one anguished remark from Soln Shipner! No matter how she hinted or goaded, however, he either ignored her openings or squashed them indecorously. "Don't imagine that you are the only non-Nechtanite I have favored with my seed—and most of them were more attractive," he'd say bluntly. "And *all* of them were taller." He liked harping on her diminutive stature.

And Martyrs forbid if she tried to flirt with him! Any sloe-eyed look, any sensuous, slinking movement of shoulders or hips, and he became positively venomous. "Don't bat your eyes at me, Princess, you cheapen yourself and offend my cultural proclivities. If you want to throw yourself at a man, choose someone younger and duller who thinks helpless little midgets are appealing. Like Cecil Robinson, for instance."

Needless to say, she'd given up trying to flirt with him after one or two attempts. Bringing up Robinson's name still sent a shaft through her. Faithless son of a motherless—

"How go the preparations for your next expedition?" Retneyabo asked now, breaking into her dark thoughts.

"Oh, very well!" she exclaimed enthusiastically. "I

submitted my budget to the College of Quasi-saurian Studies this morning. The dean gasped and went pale, but he forced a smile and thanked me politely, so I think they'll approve it." She grinned unabashedly. "The quest for Knowledge is never cheap."

"And your personnel?" the kukhoosh asked.

The grin faded, to be replaced by a pout. "I still haven't got a chief zoologist, if that's what you mean," she told him, turning back to the dinka-chak display. A plague of boils on Soln Shipner! How was she supposed to do this without him?

Six months after their return, as the winter rains dried and a glorious spring spread across the coastal region of Innanta, Shipner had dropped out of sight. Marta knew he couldn't have gotten off-planet, for the mazhel had not yet lifted their restriction, and besides, he had agreed to write and present a full report on their findings as part of his obligation to Retneyabo. Shipner was fanatical about fulfilling his obligations to a patron. But his faculty apartment was cleared of what little constituted his personal belongings, and a terse message to Yatzahl said only that he needed to work uninterrupted on his paper.

It didn't take Marta long to track him down—he was back in that squalid little room near the bazaar—but it took her two months to give in and knock on his door. For one thing, she was angry that he would disappear like that without telling her. Hadn't she been helping him with his report? Was her help unwanted? Fine. It wasn't *she* who started all those discussions with, "Do you suppose the tree-creepers hibernate in cold weather?" and such questions.

For another thing, she didn't have a particular reason to see him; she just wanted to. But she wasn't about to let him know that. Finally she couldn't stand it any longer, though, and on the pretext of needing his advice to plan a return expedition to Dhrusil-matkhashi, she knocked on his door and was bade to enter.

"Oh, it's you, Sibna," Shipner said pleasantly, looking up as she entered.

Marta should have known from this amiable greeting that she ought to duck, but she was too busy explaining her presence. "I want to plan another expedition to Dhrusil-matkhashi, and I need your advice."

"I've been studying your Innantan marriage customs," Shipner went on, as though he hadn't heard her at all, sliding a fresh disk into his flatscreen and calling up a file. "Nechtanites don't marry, you know, and I have always found such customs intriguing—filled with unspoken and unrealistic expectations. But your Innantan customs are different from most I've encountered: everything spelled out neatly in a contract, contracts that allow multiple spouses, contracts with termination dates. Very reasonable."

"I have always thought so," Marta answered cautiously, wondering where he was going with all this. If anywhere. He was prone to ramble on about things which sparked his curiosity, posing questions, wondering out loud.

"I've completed my report on Dhrusil-matkhashi," he told her, "and when I present it to your husband, I'll ask him to arrange for my return to Valla." Marta's heart sank. Going away! How could he go away? They hadn't found the home of the dinka-chaks yet, let alone looked for the packmaker. "However, since there is not much space traffic in this area," he continued, "it may take some time to make appropriate connections. I thought for the brief period I remain here, I might consider one of these lesser marriage contracts."

Marta's jaw dropped.

"As long as it terminated before I left," he elaborated, "I don't consider it to be at odds with Nechtanite teaching. It's the commitment we eschew, you see, both to exclusivity and to a lifelong relationship—not practical for improving the gene pool. Plus we need a larger community to raise the children instead of a two-parent unit, since few Nechtanites live to my ripe old age. But since the purpose of this contract would be purely recreational, and for a brief and specific time, I don't see any harm in it." He was scrolling through information, seek-

ing something. "Ah, here it is. A sib-nurah, you call it.
I think I may take a sib-nurah."

Marta swallowed hard. She ought to rejoice for
Shipner, that he had seen that celibacy was not good for
him, and she ought to offer to help him find a good
temporary wife. That's what she ought to do. But somehow she couldn't get her tongue loose from the roof of
her mouth, and the words wouldn't come out.

"What do you think?" Shipner asked amiably, looking
up at her from his position on the floor.

"It seems . . . sensible," Marta managed. She moist-
ened her lips and swallowed again. "A man should not
be alone," she added righteously.

"Does one need an intermediary to draw up a contract?" he inquired.

Marta took a deep breath and forced her jaw to work.
"If you go to the wife market in the bazaar, the women
will know how it's done."

"Or did you want the position?"

Marta stared at him, shocked into silence for a full
minute. Then she exploded. "Me!" she squawked. "I am
no poor, ignorant woman to sell myself as a sib-nurah!
Only women with no better prospects take contracts as
a sib-nurah. Me! I am the wife of Kukhoosh Retneyabo!
If and when I decide to surrender my status as his sib-
hinan, it will be for a marriage between equals—not to
debase myself as a subservient wife to an ugly, ill-
tempered egotist like you!"

"Well, I won't have you as a *sib-zhakil*," he announced,
"no matter how much you beg me." A sib-zhakil was a
partner-wife; the sib-zhakil and the sab-zhakil were of
equal status.

"*Beg* you!"

"It's no use," he insisted. "You've gone and burned
out your reproductive system so you can't have any
more children. What use has a Nechtanite for a woman
who can't nurture his seed? The only thing you're good
for is a toy."

"A *toy*?" she shrieked. "*A TOY!*"

She went for him with both hands, and fast as his

reflexes were, Shipner couldn't stop her before she'd gotten hold of one of his twining braids. "Go spread your seed among the donkeys!" she hissed as she yanked on it, bringing Shipner up onto his knees in an effort to escape her pull. "No, even they are too good for you. Go spread it among the chickens! *That* would be a mating between equals!" Then she released him and stormed out, muttering imprecations against the Unbeliever, his afflicted ancestors, and his unfortunate descendants.

She was halfway home before it dawned on her that Soln Shipner was probably laughing at her and her predictable temper.

But if he'd wanted to keep her away, he'd succeeded masterfully. The sun would sail backwards through the sky before she went to visit him again. Shortly after that incident he'd presented his finished report to Retneyabo, and a month thereafter he'd given it at a symposium at the University. Marta tried to stay away, but she finally slipped into the back of the auditorium to listen. He was brilliant, of course: articulate, thorough, insightful, confident. As a direct result of his presentation, the dean of the newly formed College of Quasi-saurian Studies had approached her about leading the return expedition. "Sab Shipner recommended you. I asked him first," the man confessed, "but apparently he will leave us now and return to his homeworld."

"Good riddance," Marta grumbled under her breath. It had to be under her breath, because the thought of him leaving made her chest so tight she could hardly speak. That night she cried herself to sleep wondering if this betrayal wasn't worse than Robinson's.

Over the next several months Marta threw herself into planning the expedition, but she found it impossible to get the Nechtanite out of her mind. They would all have died without his expertise, his caution. No one on Dray's Planet had the survival skills Shipner had, and few could approach him in the field of zoology. Those who could had no field experience. Where could she get a zoologist of his caliber for her team?

"I don't suppose we could bring in another Unbeliever, could we?" she asked Retneyabo now. "Someone with a lot of field experience?"

Retneyabo frowned and stroked his beard. Scholars were falling all over themselves to come, of course, but the mazhel were still leery. They spoke seriously of broadening Innanta's limited commerce with Unbelievers—the thing Retneyabo had labored so long and so hard to achieve for his planet—and he didn't want to jeopardize that by asking for too much. "I think it would be a mistake at this point," he said carefully, "to bring in another Unbeliever. Robinson left a bad taste in people's mouth, fleeing against their wishes, and Shipner, in his manner, can be . . ."

Marta sighed and leaned her forehead against the dinka-chak's glass case. "Shipner's an ass," she said simply. How right Robinson had been about that.

Retneyabo watched his sib-hinan with well-concealed amusement. What a surprise Soln Shipner had been for her, a man she could not manipulate, could not dazzle, could not—in his more stubborn moods—even budge. It confounded her beyond mere distraction and into bewilderment. It was good for his little falcon, Retneyabo thought, to have crossed paths with an eagle.

The kukhoosh himself had grown to like Shipner, although some days that took more effort than others. Brilliant, insightful, dedicated, the Nechtanite could be devastatingly blunt or infuriatingly devious, sometimes both at the same time. He possessed not only Knowledge, but Wisdom—a rare quality, in Retneyabo's view. Shipner was not a man to be used, but he could be relied on, once one knew what the linchpins of his ethics were. Those linchpins were still a little hazy to the kukhoosh, but he was learning. Perhaps that was what he liked most about Shipner: the warrior-scholar was a complex and interesting man.

For nearly a year after the expedition's return, Shipner had worked single-mindedly on organizing the information about Dhrusil-matkhashi and preparing a detailed report for the kukhoosh, presenting many facts

and making a strong case for the need for further research. What impressed Retneyabo as much as its content, however, was its timing: Shipner had finished it
exactly twenty-four hours after the mazhel decided not
to forbid sending information about the continent off-
planet.

The kukhoosh had been truly startled, though, when
the Nechtanite requested passage back to Valla. "What!"
Retneyabo cried in disappointment. "You, too, Shipner?
I had hoped that your dedication to Knowledge would
lead you to stay and join us in exploring this new world."

"I have an obligation," Shipner said stubbornly. "All
Nechtanites are called upon to teach the young, and to
defend our position within the community so long as we
are able to do so. My—" He hesitated uncharacteristi-
cally, then continued in a more reflective tone. "My
heart, I'm afraid, is here, locked in the discovery of
Dhrusil-matkhashi; but my duty is on Valla."

As he studied the painted man, Retneyabo thought
privately that it was not only Dhrusil-matkhashi which
had locked Shipner's heart. But he sighed heavily and
said, "Shipner, I owe you much for keeping my sib-hinan
alive in that wild place. It would be ungrateful of me
not to pursue that which you desire. So be it."

In time Retneyabo had been successful, and he was
really quite pleased with his own craftiness in the affair.
But as he looked now at his lovely sib-hinan, the delight
of his heart, he wondered if he had done it for Shipner's
benefit or his own. Marta had changed on that last adventure. She was still fiery as a bolt of lightning and
energetic as a new foal, but much of the playfulness had
gone out of her. Robinson's betrayal had shaken that
supreme confidence of hers—not that it didn't need a
little shaking, and she would probably live longer for the
element of caution it had injected into her style. And he
knew the truth about Tookh's death and understood that
had been a watershed in Marta's life. But there was
more to it than that. In the experience of being out of
her element, stranded in a different kind of wilderness,

she had grown to trust Shipner. Perhaps more than trust him, Retneyabo judged.

"Have you checked outside the University?" he asked Marta now. "There are lots of zoologists who work outside the academic arena, you know. Maybe someone from Mimma or Tehzal Tezzar."

Marta sighed. "I've made inquiries in every major city, had announcements posted in the bazaars—no luck."

"Hm. Well, there is one possibility," he told her. "I've just come from a visit with the Dean of Quasi-saurian Studies, and he's hired an assistant dean who's a zoologist with good field experience. Why don't you interview the man? I've given him Robinson's old office here, since the new college has no building yet."

Marta looked at the kukhoosh curiously. Then her eyes widened. Then she ran for the stairs.

Shipner was unpacking his crate of belongings into a desk when Marta burst in through the open door. He looked up and put on his best annoyed look. "Graduate students are the same everywhere," he growled. "They never knock."

"I thought you'd gone," Marta blurted.

"Your clever husband has outfoxed me," Shipner grumbled. "It seems I am still stuck here." After stalling him off for months, Retneyabo had finally sent for the Nechtanite two weeks ago and announced rather sheepishly that the mazhel would not consent to his departure from Dray's Planet.

"Why not?" Shipner demanded, hands clenching reflexively on the arms of the chair in which he was sitting. He had to get off this world before it sucked him in completely.

Retneyabo stroked his beard and admitted, "Because I told them we need you here, to help explore Dhrusil-matkhashi."

"You did *what*!" Shipner thundered, rising half out of the chair. "You gave me your word you would get me off this planet!"

"Ah, ah, ah," Retneyabo contradicted, wagging a

pudgy finger at him. "I said I would do what I could to
grant your desire. Your heart, you said, was in Dhrusil-
matkhashi; only your duty lay on Valla. I have made it
impossible for you to fulfill that duty, and so now you
may have what your heart truly desires."

Shipner collapsed back into the chair and dropped his
head into his hands, invoking the names of half a dozen
gods neither he nor the kukhoosh believed in. He'd
wrestled with his decision for more than a year, wanting
it both ways. He had withdrawn from Marta, knowing
she was a large part of his desire to stay, and struck
savagely at her pride to keep her at a distance when she
came around trying to hook him back in. But Retneyabo, the master manipulator, had reached out in pur-
ported friendship and deftly snatched the choice away
from him. After a moment Shipner lifted his head, and
said wearily, "You two deserve each other."

"Which two?" Retneyabo asked innocently. "Marta
and I? Oh, Shipner, Marta is a thing unto herself," he
chuckled fondly. "I have taken such delight in cultivating
her talents, guiding my little falcon, watching her grow
into an uncommon woman. My little predator, I call
her." He locked Shipner's eyes deliberately. "It's nice
to find a man who appreciates my efforts," he said pointedly. "As I appreciate his."

Shipner regarded the kukhoosh carefully, reading the
full import of his statement, and knew that, fat and un-
painted though Retneyabo was, this man was his equal.
"For coming from such a backward society," he observed finally, "you are a very progressive man."

Retneyabo had only beamed beneficently at him, un-
offended, a subtle blend of guile and charity.

Now here was the other half of that strange duo in his
office, the two of them roping him ever more securely to
this world. "Well, if you are going to be here for a
while," Marta said with forced nonchalance, "would you
be interested in coming to Dhrusil-matkhashi with me
in the spring?"

Shipner stopped his unpacking and ran a cool, appraising eye over her. "Would I be in charge of the expedition?"

"*I* will be in charge," Marta said dangerously, fire glinting in her eye. Then her tone softened somewhat. "But as you know, I can be reasonable to work with."

Shipner snorted and tossed a bundle of disks into the desk drawer. "Oh, reasonable, yes," he grumbled. "You'll push us for two weeks on foot into the interior and then expect an old man like me to make love to you twice a night."

Marta eyed him carefully. "If you do it right the first time, I won't make you do it twice," she offered.

"And I've changed my mind about offering you any kind of marriage contract," he persisted, sitting in his chair and setting up his flatscreen at one side of the desk. "Nechtanites don't marry, and you'll have to accept that."

Marta swaggered up to the desk, put her hands on it, and leaned across. "I don't want to marry you or anyone else," she said flatly. "The minute I do, Retneyabo is no longer obliged to pay for my schooling and all my other adventures. I'd be a fool to make a marriage contract with anyone."

Shipner looked up into her face for a long moment. Marta could almost see the flashes of light as his synapses fired in rapid succession. "What are you taking to bring down Grendel?" he asked.

"Neurotoxin. Projectile weapon. I'm having six of them made already."

"And our camp defenses?"

"We go up the big river, as that villain Serai's men did, and the ship itself will serve as our base camp. But we won't hide in it, I won't have that. We've got to get out and walk the land, that's all there is to it."

"How many people in the party?"

"Twenty-six, including a certified medtech."

"I want the right to name three Sabiss days when we travel in spite of your laws."

"When hell freezes over!" Marta exploded, jerking upright. "No Unbeliever decides when we must or must not break Sabiss!"

A slow smile spread across Shipner's tattooed face. "When do we leave?" he asked.

Marta's rage faded quickly into a grin. "When the weather breaks," she told him. "We'll explore the river valley first; the mineral deposits there are of immediate interest, and I have to keep my multiple patrons happy. We'll go far enough north to see if we can't find where the dinka-chaks came from—word is there's a geyser field and sulfurous hot springs up there. But then I want to go back to that meadow where I saw the herbivore with a vine knotted around its neck. They must hunt there, whoever made the fire and roasted that haunch by the stream. Maybe they even keep some domesticated animals."

"You may be disappointed," Shipner warned. "You may find they are humans—renegades or castaways. Apparently ships have been going up that river for fifty years."

"Yes, and you first said the dinka-chak was from off-planet," Marta scoffed. "If it were not a sin to gamble, Soln Shipner, I would make you a little wager on this."

Shipner chuckled softly. "Only a fool would wager against you, Sibna."

Heart singing, Marta turned and sauntered out of Shipner's office. Now that that was settled, there were a thousand things to do: supplies to order, laborers to hire, equipment to locate—Dakura would come with them again, she was sure, when he heard Shipner had signed on. Habbel probably would not, but there would be others—men who had sailed to Dhrusil-matkhashi before, mining ore for Mazh Elkniar and the others. They all lived on one of the southwestern islands with their families—they wouldn't be hard to locate. But they must all understand that this was not a treasure hunt, it was a scientific expedition. Keeping the peace was going to be a mighty task, for even the scientists would each have their own personal agendas. Yes, leading this group was going to be, as the Unbelievers liked to say, no picnic.

But I can do it, she thought confidently. *With Shipner*

to back me up, I can do it. We will make a good team, he and I. If we don't kill each other.

Laughing, she skipped down the stairs to where Retneyabo waited.

"Did Marta ever go back?" Ari demanded when he saw that his father intended to stop for the evening.

Hassan laughed. "Of course, she went back," he assured the boy. "She and the Unbeliever made many more trips across the waters to visit the Land Beyond the Gates, to show us the way there; but those are stories for another time."

Ari was struggling against sleep. "That must be why our great cities are on the West Coast now, and not the east," he deduced. "Because we do so much trading with Dhrusil-matkhashi."

"Indeed," his father agreed. "Were it not for Marta, the metals in our equipment and the fuels in our machines would be expensive beyond believing. There would not be enough food to feed all the people who live on our planet, only a few spaceships would come and go between here and the rest of the galaxy, and you would never have met your friend Mohat."

"But did they ever encounter Grendel again?" Ari wanted to know.

"Another time," Hassan repeated firmly. "That story is for another time. You must go to bed now. Look, Mohat is asleep already."

Indeed, Mohat had curled up in his mother's lap and was sound asleep, large eyes closed, his breath whistling softly through the tubes of his crest, and his elegant tail curled comfortably over his protruding mouth and nose. That mouth and its tongue could never shape the sounds that humans made, though he could hear and understand them; and his hands with their three flexible, opposable digits twitched in his sleep, the muted conversation of dreams.

His mother, the Drayan ambassador to Innanta, nodded politely to Hassan and patted Ari fondly on the shoulder, being careful not to tear his fragile skin with her claws. *It was good of them to bring her on this strange adventure through the scorching desert, a pilgrimage for them into Innanta's past and a revelation for her into the hearts and minds of these strange creatures. Someday, when they could understand her gesture-speech better, she would share with them her own people's story of Marta and Shipner coming to Dhrusil-matkhashi. It wasn't quite the same as their version, she knew, but it showed a respect for the intrepid explorers, and she felt these particular humans would understand.*

With that thought, she gathered up her son in her arms and carried him off to her tent.